Pou Mary

SPIRITS
OF THE HEART

CLAIRE GEM

Claire Gem

Erato Publishing
Massachusetts, USA
www.EratoPublishing.com

Dedication

I dedicate this book, as I do all my writing accomplishments, to my husband, Clark. He tolerates my endless hours at the keyboard, listens to me spin tales over dinner and on long drives, and is, quite frankly, the reason I can write such intensely emotional romance. He taught me, over thirty-eight years ago, the meaning of . . .

-Happily Ever After-

One

Just another ordinary, spring day, Miller Stanford thought.

I get up, I work out with Rip at the gym. I do whatever menial crap has to be done before my three-p.m. shift begins. Then I shower off the grime, don my officer blues, and head up to the Psych Center for another long, mostly boring night of security patrol.

But today, Miller knew, was different. Everything was different. Angie was gone. Whisked out of his life almost as quickly as she'd charged in three years ago. On to her new job, her new life, off to Tampa where her sister and mother lived. A whole long way away from Middletown, New York.

Otherwise, it wouldn't be *him* fetching groceries.

As he retrieved his wallet from inside the cookie jar on the counter, along with the mile-long list he'd scribbled on the back of the discarded envelope from the electric bill, Miller had to wonder why he didn't *feel* anything. No sadness, no sense of loss from the abandonment by the woman he'd been living with.

More than halfway supporting. Screwing, when she'd been in a generous mood.

Truth be told, Angie hadn't been feeling generous in quite a few weeks now. Maybe months.

Where had his head been? Had he been that distracted, that removed from the reality of everyday life, he hadn't even noticed his girlfriend had flown the coop—mentally *and* emotionally—way before she'd up and left him?

Miller stepped out onto his front porch. As he turned to lock the door, his gaze snagged on the procession of vehicles lining up at the curb in front of his house. Well, not only his house, but all along the short stretch of ornate, black iron fence outlining the old cemetery next door. At the head of the line was a long, black hearse.

A funeral? To bury somebody in this old place? How is that even possible?

To Miller's knowledge, the State-owned cemetery had reached capacity over thirty years ago. Somebody had been maintaining the grounds, even though many of the headstones were tilted, some of their inscriptions only barely legible. But an open plot?

No, couldn't be. They must be in the wrong place.

His sneakered foot hadn't even made it to the first riser off the porch when it hit him. Miller closed his eyes and dropped his head back, sucking in a breath that whooshed out on a curse.

Ken must have passed. Finally. The poor old coot had been hanging on now for months, on oxygen, with daily visits from an in-home aide. His ninety-fifth birthday had come and gone. Miller's next-door neighbor, Kenneth Rupert, would have to have been the last one left with a reservation in the State Hospital's cemetery next door. His wife, Margot, had succumbed to influenza while an inpatient at the Psych center back in the 70s—one of the last years they interred a body in that small graveyard. Ken had told Miller, during one of his brief encounters with the old man, that he'd paid the extra two-hundred dollars to reserve a spot for himself beside his wife.

Man, I really have been shipwrecked in my own world. How could I not know that Ken had passed?

Snatching his ball cap off his head and swearing again under his breath, Miller's gaze swept down over his attire: an oversized Yankees jersey, athletic shorts, and Nikes. Well, it would just have to do. He couldn't *not* join the small group of mourners as they bid old Kenneth Rupert their final farewells at his graveside.

The service was brief but somber—hell, what funeral isn't? Miller kept to the outer perimeter of the dozen or so mourners who listened as a priest recited the twenty-third Psalm and sprinkled holy water over the casket. An unlikely group, to be sure. There were several who looked to be about as old as Ken himself had been, aided by canes, or with a younger companion clutching their arm to keep them upright until the ceremony ended. There were two middle-aged women in scrubs, one of whom Miller recognized as the home health aide who'd been visiting Ken daily.

Only one lady was dressed completely in black, standing nearest to the casket, with a young man close beside her, gripping her elbow. When the priest completed his departing words and turned to leave, the woman tossed a cluster of long-stemmed, frond-edged, pastel flowers onto the casket. Then her shoulders hunched as she succumbed to her tears and grief. Her companion's arm went up and around to support her.

Could that be Jenna? Ken's granddaughter?

Miller had met her only once, when she had visited her grandfather about six months back. Jenna—he never did know her last name—was about his own mother's age. When she and Miller had stepped out of their vehicles at the exact same time that day, with barely twenty feet separating their driveways, he had felt obliged to walk over and introduce himself. Ask how Ken was doing.

When she turned away from the gravesite, Miller saw that it was, in fact, Ken's granddaughter. Her female companion—a complete stranger to him—eyed him warily. Miller stood motionless, at a loss as to what to do or say, clutching his ball cap to his chest.

Jenna glanced up and forced a teary smile.

"Miller. It was nice of you to come."

Miller's gaze again swept his entirely inappropriate attire and he mustered an embarrassed smile.

"I'm so sorry, Jenna. I didn't know Ken had passed."

She patted his arm as they both turned to exit the small cemetery. "It's not like it was a surprise. Just the kind of thing you never want to admit will really happen. Until it does. At least he's next to Grandma now. Finally."

Miller cleared his throat and stared down at his sneakers. "I'd forgotten he had a plot here," he said.

Jenna paused and smiled up at him. "Yup. He'll go down in history as the last person to be buried in the West Main State Cemetery."

Miller glanced back toward the small, peaceful corner, where not more than thirty or forty headstones dotted the space. Huge old oaks heavily shaded the half-acre lot, keeping the grass from ever developing beyond baby soft and pale green.

"Excuse my curiosity, ma'am, but if Mrs. Rupert was the last patient—before Ken, that is—to be buried in this State plot...well, that was in the late eighties. The asylum didn't officially close their doors until some years later. Where were they burying the patients since then?" He paused, then continued quickly. "I mean, the ones who didn't have family to claim them."

Jenna's lips pressed into a tight line, and furrows appeared between her straggly eyebrows. "You've got a very good question there, Miller. The same one a lot of granddaughters and grandsons are trying to get answers to, right now. There's quite a row going on in the court system, from what I hear. Grandpop told me about it, just a few months back."

Miller blinked, certain he'd just opened the lid to a Pandora-style box he'd probably better have left closed and locked. But the way the woman was looking at him, it would have been rude not to ask for an explanation. "What do you mean, a row?" he asked tentatively.

Jenna stopped walking and turned to face Miller, dropping her head back to scrutinize his face with narrowed eyes, unabashed by his overwhelming physical presence. He towered over the small woman by a foot, yet her tone was decidedly belligerent. "From what I hear, you should be the one better able to answer that question than anybody. You work for 'em, don't you?"

Miller felt a zing of panic stab his chest. He shifted nervously from one foot to the other, staring intently down at the dirty hat he was twisting between his fingers.

"Why do you think working for the State would make me any better informed than anybody else?" he asked. "Back then, I wasn't even a glimmer in my father's eye. Hell, even *he* was barely out of

4

high school. The only reason I know anything at all about this cemetery is from what Ken told me."

He heard the older woman sigh, and felt her warm fingers again on his wrist. "I'm sorry, Miller. This has nothing to do with you, I'm sure. It's just, well, there are a lot of secrets hiding out on those old grounds. A lot of history nobody seems to want to talk about. Most of it, I'm sure we're probably better not knowing. But it would be nice, for the kin of the people who died up there, while they were patients, to have closure. For them to know where they could go to visit their relations' last known place here on Earth. Pay their respects. Say a prayer."

She paused and glanced back toward the gravesite, where the diggers were patiently waiting until all the mourners were gone until they lowered the casket into the gaping black hole in the ground. Turning back toward him, she riveted him with desperate intensity in her pale, watery eyes. She sighed. "To be able to bring a ribbon-wrapped bunch of gladiolas to leave on their graves," she whispered.

As Miller made his way back toward his house, he tried to ignore the fetid tinge of sadness that had permeated his gut. He hadn't been to a funeral since . . .well, in quite a few years. But even then, he hadn't felt the cramp of grief in his chest he felt now. And hell, he'd hardly known Ken Rupert. Guilt fueled his bad feelings.

He should have made more time, paid more attention. Ken Rupert had been his next-door-neighbor, for Pete's sake. Ever since he bought this house and moved in three years ago. There was no denying it: Miller should definitely had made more time in his day, in his life, to pay attention to the living. Instead of grieving the dead. Or, the just-as-good-as dead.

Miller glanced at his watch. Damn. The hour he'd had to run to the store was nearly gone now. Sighing, he trudged back up his porch steps. He'd take his shower and maybe stretch out on the couch for a half-hour before he had to leave for work.

But as he stepped into the tub and reached for his bar of soap, Miller found only a slimy, slender green splinter. He swore and stepped out. Padding out into his hallway—nude—he left a trail of dripping water on the hardwood floor. He didn't give a shit. Slinging open the pantry door, he grumbled as he rummaged through five haphazardly folded towels, four extra rolls of toilet paper, and three half-empty bottles of tile cleaner.

Where the hell was the soap?

Another stark reality hit him. "That spiteful bitch," he snarled, his voice echoing in the hallway. He simply couldn't believe it. Not only had Angie run out on him without any notice, but she took his last, new bar of Irish Spring with her.

Laura Horton's bad feeling began the minute she pulled up in front of Angie's puke green, two-story house and parked at the curb.

Not Angie's house, she reminded herself. Angie's *boyfriend's* house. Although they'd been pretty tight in high school, she and Ang had kept in touch mostly via telephone and email these past few years that Laura had been in grad school. Once, a few years ago, they'd gotten together for their five-year reunion, when Laura had come home to visit her ailing dad.

That was the first time she'd seen the compact craftsman bungalow—after dark—and she hadn't realized it was such an ugly color. She hadn't met *the boyfriend*, Miller Stanford, whom Angie either claimed to love with all her heart, or wanted to eviscerate with a Phillips head screwdriver, depending on the day. Nor had Laura noticed then that the house snugged up tight on one side to an ancient-looking graveyard. The only thing separating the two properties was a narrow strip of grass and a dilapidated, iron fence.

A shiver ran across her shoulder blades as she sat in her car, studying her new surroundings. Her new *home*.

Holy crap.

Chillier up here. Where'd I pack that hoodie?

She turned to dig around in one of the boxes squashed into the back of her tiny car, quickly realizing it was pointless. Nearly everything she owned in the world—besides a few pieces of battered, old furniture—filled the back seat, and passenger side, of her thrifty Kia. When she'd run out of room for boxes, she'd resorted to folding softer items, like her sweaters and sweats, into new plastic trash bags. Stuff crammed every nook and crevice in the car, leaving just enough space beneath the headliner for her to see out through the rearview mirror.

There was no way in hell she was locating her hoodie in Mt. Clothesmore.

Rubbing her hands up and down her arms, she climbed out and sprinted up the steps to the front door. She hadn't been able to reach Angie by phone since she'd left Boone, North Carolina the day before, but that wasn't too unusual. Her friend was a bit flighty, and prone to misplace her phone, her charger, or both. Angie had been juggling courses at the community college with a full-time night job, tending bar at the pub just down the street, for the past two years. Laura couldn't blame her for acting a bit squirrelly at times.

She reminded herself how nice it was of Ang and Miller to rent her their spare room. When Laura landed the job in Middletown, her initial exhilaration had been tempered by a glaring question: where the hell was she going to live? There was no way she could move into her father's tiny condo with his new wife, Deirdre. And securing an apartment on her own was out of the question, at least not until after her first few paychecks hit the bank.

Laura squared her shoulders, which were quaking slightly in the cool spring breeze, tipped up her chin, and rang the doorbell.

Twice. She shifted her sneakered feet against the creaky porch boards, folding her arms against the chill. After another long moment with no answer, she rang the bell a third time, holding down the ancient button a full ten seconds this time. She could hear the electronic buzz through the peeling front door, but no other sounds at all.

Angie *had* to be here—she knew Laura was coming. It was Friday, but Angie's last term of college ended last week, and it was nearly two o'clock in the afternoon. There was only one vehicle parked in the short driveway, a late-model Ford pickup. But Laura wasn't sure what it was Angie was driving these days.

Then, she heard the booming, thumping sound. Footsteps? Deliberate, heavy, booming steps. Did Bigfoot live here too?

A dull click, then the tinkle of chain skittering on the inside of the wood. The door burst open. But it wasn't Angie standing on the threshold.

Two

Laura didn't have time to suppress the involuntary gasp that escaped from her open mouth.

The man was huge, not only tall but massive, with a broad, muscular chest, one lightly furred with golden hair. His bulbous biceps were cut, sculpted like a Greek statue. And he wasn't wearing much more than Michelango's David, with only a steel grey towel snugged around narrow hips to match the steely glint in his blue-grey eyes.

She blinked and swallowed, stumbling back a step. "Is Angie here?" she asked in a small voice.

The giant snorted and crossed his arms over his chest. "Who's askin'?"

For a moment, Laura was speechless. She slid her sunglasses off the top of her head and folded them carefully, staring at them, her brain scrambling for what to do or say next. When she glanced back up, the big guy was scowling down at her like a bulldog whose meal she'd just interrupted.

"I'm Laura Horton. You must be . . .Miller?" she asked. She hated that her voice squeaked and cracked. "I've been trying to call Angie since yesterday, but—"

"You're that friend of hers from South Carolina, right?" he asked. "What the hell are you doing all the way up here in New York? What'd she do—forget something and send you back for it?"

"*North* Carolina," she corrected him, reflexively. Then, increasingly puzzled, she tipped her head. "And, no. I mean, wha—what are you talking about?"

"Angie's gone," he barked, so loud Laura jumped and stumbled back another step.

It didn't faze this guy in the least. He continued at the same higher-than-necessary volume. "So if you've come for a visit, you're a day too late. Your friend doesn't live here anymore. There are a couple of decent motels on the other side of town. As you can see, you've caught me at a bad time." He motioned with one beefy hand down his body, then stepped back and started to swing the door shut in her face.

Panic clutched Laura's chest and she rushed forward, laying a hand on the door. "You don't understand. Didn't Angie talk to you about this? She said I could stay here. She said it was okay with you."

It was at that moment that a box truck with the words ACME MOVING rumbled into the driveway behind the pickup, farting and wheezing as the driver cut the ancient engine. Laura's gaze shifted toward the truck, then back at Miller. "See? My stuff's here," she said through a nervous chuckle.

"Your stuff? Like, you think you're moving in here?" Miller boomed, throwing the door open wide and stepping out onto the porch in bare feet.

Laura fixed her eyes on the big man towering beside her, biting her lip. He was shaking his head, slowly, his expression undergoing a metamorphosis she wasn't quite sure she could read. His angry scowl faded, quickly, as though he'd just remembered something. Then he covered his face with both hands. A moment later, when he dropped them to his sides, his eyes were soft, his sigh resigned.

"I guess Angie did talk to me about this, a few weeks ago. But I figured once she left, it was all off. That you wouldn't show up."

"I didn't know she was leaving," Laura squeaked, her stomach suddenly feeling sour. "Or I probably wouldn't have."

Two guys climbed out of the van and were standing beside it, hands on hips. "Where we unloading, lady?" one called. "We're on a pretty tight schedule this afternoon."

Laura studied Miller's face, pressing her lips into a line. "Unfortunately, it appears, at the moment, I don't have a choice."

Miller closed his eyes and blew out a breath. "Come on. I'll show you where the spare bedroom is."

She followed him down a narrow corridor covered on one side with yellowed, cabbage rose wallpaper, and chipped, green-painted plaster on the other. The hardwood floor was scuffed and scarred. A tarnished brass, lantern-style light fixture hung from chains overhead, casting a pale, sickly light.

As she followed him, Laura's mind raced. What had happened between last weekend and today to cause Angie to move out? And without even the courtesy of giving her a heads up? She was too afraid to ask.

Halfway down the hall, Laura screeched to a halt before she splashed into a puddle of water—one the giant had easily stepped over.

"Uh, I think you might have a leak here," she said, pointing to the floor.

Miller snorted but didn't turn around. "My life's sprung a leak. *Your friend* was the first thing to go down the drain."

Hmm. Really pissed. Maybe better to just step around the puddle and go from there.

He stopped at the end of the short hallway that ended abruptly, a doorway to the left and a set of steep stairs to the right.

"Here it is," he said. "It's not very big, but it looks like *your friend*," he added air quotes around the words, "at least cleaned it up for you. She had all kinds of useless shit stored in here." He swept one hand across the moderately sized space, empty except for an oval, braided rug hovering in the center of the battered hardwood floor.

Laura slipped past him and looked around. The room wasn't much more than ten or twelve feet square, with a single window. At least that would leave enough wall space for her furniture. She hoped. Her room in the condo she'd shared with her roommate in Boone was twice this big. She chewed on one thumbnail and moved to the window.

It faced the graveyard. Of course. Afternoon sunlight slanted through the tall pines dotting the cemetery, casting moving shadows on the headstones. She hunched her shoulders and twisted her neck.

"Where did Angie go?" she asked.

She jumped when he barked out a laugh. "So, you really didn't know? Our big-haired bird flew south," he said, no small amount of facetious irritation lacing his words. "Had her a job lined up and everything. Her sister lives in Tampa, right?"

Laura nodded and turned to face him. "But why did she leave? Without telling either of us?"

His eyes narrowed as he tipped up his chin. "I was hoping," he said, his tone icy, "that *you* could tell *me* that."

Miller clomped up the stairs as the movers called from the front door.

"Where's this stuff goin', lady?"

The room shrank very fast as they carried in Laura's bed, bureau, and desk. When they went back for the last item—her grandmother's trunk—she glanced around frantically, realizing there was no way the antique steamer would fit. She met them at the door and pointed to an empty space near the foot of the stairs.

"Just leave it there for now," she said. "I don't know where Mr. Stanford will want me to put it just yet."

She handed over the envelope with the four-hundred dollars she'd withdrawn from her now-closed savings account in Boone, and the men tipped their dusty ball caps as they whisked out.

Ouch. That was all the money she had left, besides the three-hundred her dad had sent her to help with the move. She'd spent a good chunk of that on gas—even though the Kia was pretty fuel-efficient—and had drifted into Middletown on fumes with less than a hundred bucks to her name.

Laura paused in the doorway of her new room as a fresh wave of panic and desperation washed over her. What had she done? She'd tried, for one of the first times in her life, to strike out boldly on her own, without depending on anybody else for help. Well, aside from the small loan from her father. If dear old Dad had his way, she'd be sleeping on the futon in the *meditation room* of his and Deirdre's condo. Beneath the weird, psychedelic lithographs covering the walls, surrounded by a dozen candles of every shape and size imaginable, all paying homage to the giant Buddha statue in the corner.

She shivered at the thought. It wasn't the Buddha. It was the idea of sharing a dwelling—as well as her father—with her new stepmother. Laura knew it was childish and twisted, but she couldn't help feeling that her father had abandoned her once he married Dierdre.

And now she'd been abandoned again, by a friend she had trusted. Thought she knew pretty well. Guess she'd miscalculated where it was safe to place her trust. Again.

Flopping down on her grandmother's trunk, Laura dropped her face into her hands and moaned.

"Grandma, help me out here. I don't understand where I'm going wrong," she whined.

"Angie didn't mention you were bringing your grandmother with you."

Laura squeaked and lurched to her feet. Spinning around, she found Miller standing at the head of the narrow staircase, glaring down at her. From this perspective, he looked even bigger than he really was. No longer wearing a towel—thank God—he now sported a crisply pressed, navy blue uniform. A nightstick hung from his wide leather belt.

She swallowed, wincing as the prickly ball of anxiety slid all the way down. That's right. Angie had told her Miller was a security officer on the grounds of what used to be Middletown Psychiatric Center. Although the asylum had been closed for years, the state grounds still operated several services in the various buildings, including a homeless shelter. As well as the Alcoholic Rehab Center where Laura would start work, just two days from now.

Miller started down the stairs, nodding toward the trunk. "You keep your dead grandma in that thing? That's weird." There wasn't one iota of humor in his tone. "That can't stay there, you know."

"That's not even funny," she snapped, wrapping her arms around herself. "It won't fit in my room. Is there someplace else I can—"

"Find a place," he shot back, brushing past her. He reached up and snatched an officer's cap off the coat tree by the front door. "There's an extra key underneath the cookie jar in the kitchen," he called over his shoulder as he slammed the door behind him.

Laura sighed and checked her watch. Nearly three o'clock already. She'd better start carrying in all of those boxes and bags out of her car or she'd be unpacking until midnight.

It took her seven trips up and down the porch steps to empty her car. By the time she was through, she was sweaty and exhausted. Her mattress had disappeared underneath Mt. Clothesmore. The double closet had looked fairly spacious until she started arranging her fourteen pairs of shoes, including three pairs of boots, along the floor.

What the holy hell had she gotten herself into? Well, if nothing else, it was close to work. And this job, her first in the field since graduating with her Masters in Substance Abuse, sounded like exactly what she'd been hoping for. Since Miller's house sat right on the perimeter of the state grounds, she could walk to work if she wanted.

Or if her ancient car decided to give up the ghost one unhappy morning.

Still, this whole transition would have been so much easier with a friend, somebody familiar—namely Angie—by her side. That, evidently, wasn't going to happen. Hell, the girl wouldn't even answer her calls. Snatching up her phone, she dialed Angie's number again, but it went straight to voicemail.

Yup, she's avoiding me all right.

Laura started mining away on the mountain of clothes bags, a god-awful job made even harder in such a cramped space. About halfway through, she wandered into the kitchen and rummaged in the cabinets until she found a glass, filling it from the tap. She downed half of the water, then leaned back on the counter and held the cool surface to her temple. Her head ached, and she was so tired, she felt faint.

That's when she remembered she hadn't eaten anything since the corn muffin in the hotel lobby that morning.

I'll make a food run in a little bit. There's got to be something here to hold me over, she thought.

Laura pulled open the steel refrigerator and squinted into the bright, bare space. The top shelf was empty except for a carton of orange juice, which, upon inspection, revealed an expiration date three months past. She wrinkled her nose as she slid it back onto the shelf. There were several white Styrofoam take-out boxes she was afraid to open. Both vegetable bins were crammed full with beer bottles. Miller Light.

So. Angie hadn't exaggerated about Miller's favorite namesake, had she? Groaning, she closed the door and searched the counter for the cookie jar, where he'd said the key was hidden. She found it behind several empty beer cartons, patiently awaiting the return of their refundable bottles.

Hello Kitty? This big, hulking brute of a man has a Hello Kitty cookie jar?

An *empty* Hello Kitty cookie jar, but as promised, a house key was taped to the bottom. As she fingered the yellowed tape loose from the ceramic, she couldn't help but notice the inscription, a child's scrawl in marker, along the bottom rim.

To my big brother, Mills. Happy Birthday. Love, Molls.

She heard her phone ringing from down the hallway, and dashed to catch the call. Finally, hopefully, Angie would explain what the hell had happened.

But it wasn't Angie. A picture of her Dad flashed on the screen of her iPhone as she picked it up.

"Hey, Daddy. I'm here."

"Good! I was worried about you, sweetheart. Getting settled in okay? How's Angie doing?"

Her father's voice boomed into her ear, bringing a wave of unexpected tears to her eyes. How was it that even though she'd grown up and moved out over ten years ago, just the sound of her daddy's voice made her feel like a little girl again?

"Um, I haven't seen her yet," she hedged. No need to spring that surprise just yet. Heavens knew, he might insist she move into their tiny condo. She shuddered. "But yeah, I'm unpacking now. The room's a little small." Her voice sounded squeaky and pitiful, even to her own ears.

"How about dinner, honey? Deirdre and I can pick you up in, say, twenty minutes? We'll go for Mexican. Your favorite, right?"

Laura winced at the sound of her stepmother's name. Not her favorite person in the world, but there was no denying one fact: Deirdre now held the official title of Mrs. Norman Horton. Stepmother. So if Laura wanted to see her dad, Deirdre was part of the package.

She closed her eyes and drew in a breath. She really shouldn't. She should finish unpacking, take a long, hot shower, and bury her face in her pillow. But her head was pounding and she knew if she didn't eat something, she'd have one of her fainting spells again.

That was the last thing she needed. For Miller to come home from work and find her passed out on the kitchen floor.

"Okay. That sounds really good. But give me a half-hour. I'm all grimy from carrying in boxes."

Laura dug through the haphazard pile on her bed until she located her cosmetic bag, clean underwear, and a stretchy tank dress, then padded down the hall to the bathroom. Her reflection scared even *her*—her carefully blown-straight blonde hair had started spiraling around her face from warmth and sweat. Her eyes were spidered with red veins, and there was a black smudge of who-knew-what slashed across one cheekbone.

Yes, a shower was definitely in order.

She turned on the spray as hot as she could stand it and stepped in. Ah, now that's glorious. But when she turned to scoop the soap out of its cradle, she frowned.

How the hell am I going to get clean with this tiny splinter?

As he entered the lobby of the security office, Miller grabbed his badge and swore, watching the digital numbers click over to one minute past three just as he swiped it. Not that being one minute late was a big deal. But in order for him to even be considered for any kind of promotion, his record had to be stellar. Ten minutes early, not one minute late. Every. Single. Day.

It was all that little twit's fault, showing up on his doorstep looking lost and pathetic. What was her name? Oh yeah, Laura.

She sure did smell good, though. And what a rack.

He shook his head and raked a hand through his still-damp hair.

"Time for a haircut, Stanford," his chief called from his desk without looking up. "You know the rules. Can't cover your collar. You're getting close there, buddy."

"Will do, Sarge," he replied. He turned and approached the desk of Patricia, the secretary, reaching for the sign-out log for his weapon. She smiled up at him and batted her eyelashes.

"Too bad you can't let that sunny mop grow, Miller," she crooned. "You'd look real hot with a ponytail." She raised one eyebrow and winked.

Miller pressed his lips into a flat line and made no reply. Patricia Gonzalez was twenty-four with very pretty golden eyes, but probably outweighed him. Plus, her boyfriend was Rip Allen, his buddy and workout partner, a town firefighter who made even Miller feel like a dwarf. Rip was Jamaican born, six-foot six, and weighed two sixty-five without an ounce of fat on him.

"Thanks, Pat," he said curtly as she handed him his pistol, trying to ignore the drag of her long, manicured fingernails across his palm as she did. Followed by her heavily mascara'd wink.

With the desert his sex life had been with Angie over the last couple of months, he had no control over the twitch in the crotch of his pants.

Hell. Why does Pat always do this? Does she want to get me fired? Killed?

"You're on the northwest loop tonight, Stanford," his chief said, standing in the doorway of his office. "You get enrolled for those courses yet?"

Miller felt a surge of panic clutch in his chest for a split-second. Had his boss seen him at After Shocks the other night—again? No.

Couldn't be. Wouldn't matter if he did. He'd only had two beers before heading home, on foot, the half a block to his house on West Main.

Then he realized Sergeant McMahon was talking about the *college* courses they'd discussed.

Yeah, that must be what he means.

Miller nodded. "Yes, sir. My first class is next week. I start with Statistics."

The sergeant smiled and returned his nod approvingly. He was a stocky, balding man whose sixty-fifth birthday was less than eighteen months away. McMahon had taken Miller under his wing when he started with the security division for the State Facility Grounds five years ago. Sarge had planted the seed in Miller's head that when his retirement came up, Miller should go for the position.

But Miller was about twenty credits shy of earning his Bachelor's degree, and an Associate's wouldn't get him in. He needed the sheepskin, or the State Board wouldn't even consider his application.

"If you need any help with any of those courses, you know where to find me," Sarge said.

Miller secured his weapon in his holster, checked the safety, and snugged his cap on his head, nodding to Patricia on his way out.

The late April day had turned balmy, way warmer than it usually was this time of year. Miller tugged at the collar of his shirt as he stepped into the cruiser and flipped on the air conditioning. Awfully early in the season to be needing that.

But he knew as the sun sank below the trees, the air would cool down fast. Middletown wasn't exactly upstate New York, but was far enough north of the city to have a country feel. It had been a small town when he was growing up, but now some of Manhattan was moving up the state. The crime rate had doubled over the past twenty-five years. And even after the State Hospital closed its psychiatric center in the 90s, the grounds were still state-owned and maintained.

The old nursing school was gone, but a mental health clinic operated in the building during daytime hours. There was an alcoholic rehab unit too. Miller knew more than he needed to know about that particular facility, one whose services his alcoholic father had managed to avoid until the bitter end.

Too fucking bad.

A homeless shelter opened in one of the refurbished buildings about ten years ago. Most of Miller's calls on his evening shift involved herding some wayward vagabond toward the shelter. More and more of that lately, though Miller was perplexed to discover that many of those he encountered, especially around the ruins of Talcott Hall, never made it to the shelter.

The ponderous thing was, he wasn't quite sure where they ended up. He directed them, sometimes even followed them in his cruiser partway to the facility. But when he checked in with the shelter's admitting team the next day, the staff looked at him as if he'd lost his mind.

No new check-ins last night, they said.

So where did they go? Miller hadn't seen them again during his entire shift.

They'd simply disappeared.

Three

Thirty minutes was simply not enough time to get ready for dinner with Dad and Deirdre, especially when Laura didn't know where any of her stuff was. She couldn't find the sandals she wanted to wear, and ended up settling for silly-looking rhinestone flip-flops her mother had bought her as a joke. Her hair dryer had done a complete disappearing act, but it would take an extra twenty minutes to dry and straighten her hair anyway. She'd just have to go natural tonight.

When she heard the car horn beep, she stabbed herself in the eye with the mascara wand.

"Dammit!" she snapped, clutching a towel to her eye as she flung open the door and waved, calling, "Be there in a minute!"

Her father waited for her on the sidewalk, his hands in his pockets, staring off into the neighbors' yard—the *dead* neighbors—wearing a scowl. But his face brightened when he saw her coming down the porch steps.

"How's my girl?" he asked, wrapping her in a bear hug.

Norman Horton, or Manny, as most everyone called him, was a handsome man who just turned sixty, with a full head of grey hair and a generous smile. He'd been Middletown's police chief for over twenty-five years. Laura didn't realize how much she'd missed him until she buried her face in his neck and breathed in his familiar dad smell.

"Hey, Daddy. Thanks for taking me out. I've been so busy today I forgot all about eating." She pushed back and studied his face. "How are you feeling? You look good."

"As good as an old man has a right to feel," he replied. He squeezed her waist and steered her toward the car.

Oh, yeah. We wouldn't want to keep Mrs. Horton waiting.

Deirdre Horton sat in the passenger seat of the Cadillac SRS with her eyes glued to her iPhone screen, thumbs flying. As Manny opened the door for Laura, she dropped the phone in her lap and spun around in her seat.

"Laura! How *are* you?"

Her stepmother was in full-blown cheerleader mode today, singing out her greeting with more enthusiasm than could possibly be genuine. Deirdre and Manny had been married less than two years, tying the knot only two months after Manny had been discharged from the hospital. He'd suffered a near-miss heart attack. Deirdre had been his nurse.

Laura pushed her lips into a smile. "I'm good, Deirdre. Good to see you again."

Not.

As her father slid behind the wheel, Deirdre urged, "Come on, Norman, I'm starving. I'll bet Laura is, too. Moving is hell. Isn't that right, Laura?" Her stepmother beamed her a toothy smile rimmed with pale pink, frosted lipstick.

Didn't that trend die in the late 90s? There goes the appetite.

"So El Bandido is still there, huh? Thank God some things don't change," Laura said, unable to tamp down her facetious tone. Her father flashed her a warning glance in the rearview, and she thought, *Okay, I'd better behave.*

The restaurant had been her favorite since she was just a kid, mostly then, she supposed, because of the colorful interior, with larger than life wall paintings and stained glass windows. Tonight, since they were closing in on Cinco de Mayo, the owners had ramped it up a notch. Fluttering banners crisscrossed the dining room, their foil letters throwing sparks of light over everything as they shimmered under the ceiling fans.

"I'm making a pit stop first," Deirdre said, leaning over to smack a loud kiss on Manny's cheek as they were shown to their table.

Once they were seated, Laura took a deep breath and sighed. Just being in a familiar place made her feel better, even if her "homecoming" had gotten off to a rocky start. A very rocky start.

Her mind wandered back to Angie. As though her father was reading her thoughts, he asked, "So how's Angela doing? I haven't seen her in such a long time, I doubt I'd recognize her."

Laura waited until Deirdre had disappeared down the hall to the restrooms, then unfolded the bright red napkin and spread it across her lap. She lifted her shoulders up and twisted them, then answered without lifting her gaze from the table. "Actually, Dad, Angie moved out. When I knocked on the door this morning, it was Miller who answered."

Dressed in nothing but a towel, but she didn't figure she needed to mention that.

"Whoa, whoa, what do you mean she moved out? So, you're moving in with this Miller character? Where the hell is Angie?" The quick anger in her father's tone made Laura cringe. The last thing she wanted to do was stress Dad's heart again.

Fidgeting in her seat, she said, "Miller said she got a job in Tampa, where her sister lives. She packed up and left yesterday morning." She met her father's gaze. "I didn't know anything about it."

Manny shook his head and glared at her. "I don't like this, Laura. Sounds a little suspicious to me."

Like this was her fault, and she was doing something shameful and embarrassing. For a brief moment, she was seventeen again, flashing back to the morning after her senior prom, when she'd stayed out all night and got caught sneaking in at dawn. Daddy had *not* been happy. But back then, it *had* been her fault. Her bad judgment call.

Sudden concern for her father escalated her guilt even further. Manny had suffered a major heart attack just a few years ago, and

Laura didn't want to be responsible for causing him another one. She laid a hand on his arm.

"It's okay, Daddy. I'm a big girl. I can take of myself."

At that moment Deirdre whisked up to the table and into the booth next to her dad. She looked at Laura, then Manny. "What? What'd I miss?"

Manny cleared his throat and folded his arms across his chest. "Laura tells me that instead of rooming with her best friend, she'll be sharing that house with the ex-boyfriend. I'm not happy about this, Laura."

Deirdre leaned forward on her elbows. "You mean they broke up? Where's Angie?" she whispered, her eyes wide and glassy.

The woman does so love gossip.

"She headed South to live with her sister," Laura said. "I'm more than a little pissed at her, actually. She won't even answer my calls." She fished her phone out of her purse. "In fact, I'm going to try to call her again, right now."

She was shocked when Angie answered on the third ring.

"Where the hell are you? And what happened?" Laura snapped, cupping her free hand over her other ear as she slid out of the booth. "I'll be right back, guys. I can't hear a thing in here."

Once outside, Laura hissed into the phone. "You've left me in a really bad spot here, Ang."

She heard her friend sigh. "It's a long story, Laura, and I'm really sorry I put you in this position. But this job offer came up suddenly, and I just had to jump on it. Miller and I have been history for a while anyway. I guess you knew that."

Angie sounded casual and relaxed. Like this was no big deal and it was Laura who was acting out, and making it one.

"No, I didn't know, or I would never have even considered moving in. Why didn't you call me? At least give me some kind of warning?" she asked.

"I drove down, straight through, and there were places in South Carolina and Georgia where I had no cell service at all. Then the damn thing died, and my charger got lost in all the stuff I had crammed into the car. I'm sorry. I know this must have been a real shock." Angie hesitated. "But Miller's okay. He's cool with you staying there, and he's not really a bad guy. He just drinks too much. Sometimes."

When Laura returned to the table, her father and Deirdre were munching on tortilla chips and salsa, and there were three margaritas on the table.

Three.

"Hey, sorry. I guess all is well. Angie got an unexpected job offer and her sister had a place for her to stay." She shrugged. "I guess until I get my first few paychecks in the bank, my roommate will be Miller Stanford."

Her father looked as though he'd been sucking on the limes they used to make the drinks. "I think it would be better if you come stay with us. We have the futon in the extra room—"

"No, honey," Deirdre snipped, "I mean, don't you remember? My sister might be coming down to stay for a few weeks. Did you forget?" She'd clutched Manny's arm with a vise-grip and though her voice dripped sweetness, her glare rivaled a blow torch.

Manny's shoulders slumped. "We can pay for your sister to stay at the Holiday Inn," he offered. But the resignation in his voice told Laura he knew he'd been overruled.

Not that she would have even considered staying with them. And seeing how her father had changed, how the fight had gone completely out of him since his illness, made Laura's chest ache. He'd always been her hero. Her big strong protector. Now, between his heart attack and this overbearing woman, he'd been reduced to a doormat.

Just like Laura. A flash of panic made her feel as though she'd been pushed out of an airplane without a parachute. She reached forward and lifted the giant margarita glass with two hands.

"I'll be just fine for a few months, right where I'm at," she began, trying hard to sound more convinced than she felt. "I'll start looking around for an apartment as soon as I get settled in my job."

"That's right. Let's celebrate," Deidre said, lifting her glass. "To your coming home. A new job, and a new life."

Laura hesitated, meeting her father's tired gaze as they clinked glasses. "Yeah. New life," she echoed.

Her tolerance for alcohol had not increased, which she figured out by the time her glass was half-empty. Plus, she was dog-ass tired, which didn't help. By the time the fiesta-ware plates were delivered with their dinners, Laura found herself actually laughing at some of Deirdre's stories.

"So, we've both realized your father will never be a contender for the surfboard championship," Deirdre finished, grinning over at Manny.

"And I've got the bruises to prove it," he added.

The tamales were every bit as good as Laura remembered, but by the time she'd gotten halfway through her second one, she felt as though her mascara was made with lead. She pushed back from the table and tried to hide a yawn behind her napkin.

"I'm sorry, but I'm exhausted. I'm ready anytime you guys are."

Her father walked her to the door as Laura dug furiously around in her purse for the loose key she'd taken from underneath the cookie jar. The house was dark.

"I guess Miller's not here. I was hoping to meet him." Her father's tone was cold, clipped.

Laura shook her head. "He works till eleven, I think. Angie said he usually came to the bar where she was working when he got off." Her fingers closed around the metal shape in the inside pocket of her purse. "Aha!" she said, holding it high.

"I'll walk you in. At least until you get some lights on." Her father looked over toward the graveyard, eerie in the twilight. "I'm not getting a good feeling about this situation, Laura. Are you sure you wouldn't rather stay with us until you get on your feet? I can make some arrangements for Deirdre's sister—"

"No," Laura snapped, then hiccupped as she brought her fingers to her mouth. "I mean, no thank you, Dad. I think it would be. . . awkward, at best." She tipped her head back toward his car. She continued in a hushed voice. "It would be as bad as when I was living with Mom, and she announced that Violetta was moving in."

Her father scrubbed a hand down over his face. "That must have been . . . uncomfortable."

Laura fumbled with the lock for another few seconds before it finally clicked. Feeling inside the door, she found the switches, and light flooded not only the hallway but the porch where they stood. "There. I'm good now, Daddy. Thanks again for dinner." She hugged him around his middle.

"It's good to have you home, baby," he said into her hair. "See you soon. If you need anything—anything at all—you know my cell number."

Once the door was closed and locked behind her, exhaustion and three-quarters of an excellent margarita caught up with Laura. She yawned so big her jawbone clicked, and she hiccupped again. Then she started to giggle.

"It's easy to see how somebody could get hooked on this stuff," she said aloud, then headed down the hallway to brush her teeth.

One glance into her room reminded her that sleeping in her own bed was not going to happen for at least a couple of hours. Although she'd managed to find her sheets, there wasn't even enough floor space to get all the other boxes off the bed so she could make it up. She groaned.

Wonder how comfy the couch is?

She changed quickly into her favorite sleep attire—a silky tank and gym shorts—grabbed her pillow and her grandmother's hand-stitched quilt, and headed to the living room.

Miller figured he'd better bypass After Shocks tonight, since he was sure there would be lots of questions from Angie's coworkers about her sudden disappearance. Questions that he wasn't quite sure how to answer. He had plenty of beer in the fridge, anyway. He completely forgot about his new roommate until he turned the corner onto West Main and saw the lights on.

Damn. Hope she's a sound sleeper. I'm watching the wrestling match I recorded whether the noise bothers her or not.

He hung his cap on the tree in the hall, kicked off his shoes, and headed to the kitchen to snatch a beer out of the fridge. When he snapped on the table lamp next to the couch, his heart leapt into his throat and he sloshed beer all over the front of his uniform.

There was a woman sleeping on his sofa. Quite soundly, as she hadn't budged when the light came on. But this was not the same little blonde he'd bantered with earlier today. This one looked like she'd stepped out of one of those faerie magazines, only without the wings.

Hell, maybe she had wings. He couldn't tell, since she was wrapped up like a burrito in a patchwork quilt. Her hair, no longer silky straight, fell in ringlets around her face. Bright pink patches glowed on her cheeks, exactly matching the polish on her naked toes peeking out from under the blanket.

What the hell was she doing on his couch? He'd somehow gotten swindled into renting her a room, not the whole damn house.

But she was so freaking cute, lying there clutching the quilt around her, sound asleep with her mouth slightly open. He wanted to unwrap that multicolored tortilla and see what she had on underneath. Maybe nothing. Bet that rack looks awesome in the raw. Her perfect, bow-shaped mouth was pouty, with a plump lower lip that made him want to run his tongue over it.

Hell, it *has* been a long time since I got laid. I'm thinking like a horny teenager.

The moment shattered when her lids fluttered open and she let out a shriek, scaring him so badly he yelped and staggered back a step.

"What the hell are you doing there?" he barked.

She had wiggled up into the corner of the leather couch in a tight ball and was clutching the quilt up to her chin. Her eyes were as round and wild as a frightened kitten's.

"What does it look like I'm doing?" she squeaked. "I'm sleeping. My bed's still covered with boxes."

Miller closed his eyes and shook his head.

This was so *not* a good idea. Thanks, Angie. Thanks a whole hell of a lot.

He took a long pull on his beer and reached for the remote. "Well, I hope you like wrestling, 'cause that's what's playing in here tonight." He dropped down into the recliner and turned on the TV, keeping his eyes trained on the screen.

Maybe if I ignore her, she'll disappear. Her and that lick-able mouth of hers.

Try as he might, he couldn't help watching her from the corner of his eye. For a long moment, she sat perfectly still, but then very slowly touched one pink-polished toe to the floor. Once both feet were on the hardwood, she rose gradually, like a wary cat, readjusting the quilt tighter around her. One foot at a time, she side-stepped toward the doorway, stopping when she got to the television.

She had to pass in front of the screen to get to the door.

"Excuse me," she said. "Sorry." In a flurry of bouncing little steps, she scurried across his line of vision.

Miller suppressed a chuckle. When she reached the door, he called, "You don't have to be afraid of me, you know. I'm a security officer. I protect people. I don't hurt them."

She froze with her back to him. "You don't?" she asked in a very small voice.

This poked him in the gut. Why the hell was she scared? What had that bitch friend of hers told her about him?

As if on cue, the wrestler on the screen snarled like a psycho gorilla, and the boom from his opponent hitting the mat made her jump, and flee.

Echoing down the hallway, he heard her door bang shut, and the lock click.

Laura's heart was slamming a staccato tempo, and as exhausted as she had been, now, she was wide awake. She flung off her Grandma's quilt and paced back and forth in the small empty strip next to her bed, the only open floor space in the entire room. How was she going to deal with this? With Angie here, sure, she would have adjusted, but now . . .

Then she realized the single window in the room had no shade, no curtain, no blinds. And she was pacing, half naked, right in front of it. Sucking in a gasp, she snapped off the overhead light.

The pounding of her pulse was so loud in her ears, she was afraid Miller might hear it down the hall. Re-wrapping herself in the quilt, she crept to the window and peered out.

A full moon—of course—hung over the tops of the trees lining the boundary of the old graveyard. It illuminated the landscape just enough to reveal the curved upper edges of the dozen or more gravestones, glowing silvery, as if they were gathering in the moon's rays and radiating them back out again. She shivered, suddenly feeling very exposed, very vulnerable, and very alone.

Laura turned and snatched at the boxes closest to one edge of the bed, heaving them over to stack them on the floor. If she could just clear a space big enough, no wider than the couch, she could bury her face in her pillow and make believe this was all a very, very bad dream.

She did just that, and stretched up tight along the edge of the mattress with boxes snugged securely along her back. Sleep had almost claimed her when she heard the tapping.

At first, she wondered if it was Miller tapping at her door.

Fat chance, buddy. There's no way I'm unlocking it for you.

But after the second, and then the third set of taps, Laura sat up and listened.

Tap, tap, tap.

No, this wasn't coming from the door. This sound was distinctly one of something solid striking glass. The only glass in the room was . . .

A pathetic whimper escaped her as she spun over and huddled against the boxes, covering her head with the quilt.

I need your protection now, Grandma. If ever you could come to my aid, please let it be now.

The sound continued, regular and in rhythmic bursts, punctuated by what sounded like something scratching at the wooden window frame. Taking deep breaths to keep the panic at bay, Laura struggled to name a logical source for the sounds.

Tree branches. And wind. There had to be a tree close enough to the house, near her window, with branches that needed trimming.

They were swaying in the wind and scraping against the glass and the frame. Yeah, that's it. Makes perfect sense.

She'd have to talk to Miller about trimming back the branches tomorrow.

Shivering, though not at all cold, Laura lay scrunched with her cheek smashed up against a cardboard box. The tapping sound subsided, gradually, like thunder from a rapidly moving storm fading into the distance. It could have been minutes, or hours. She wasn't sure. But eventually, an exhausted, fitful sleep swallowed her thoughts and dragged her under.

Here came Saturday morning—barreling into Laura's new world, though she had no basis from which to judge its normalcy.

What was that high-pitched, mechanical whining? An airplane engine? A space ship? No. It was a vacuum cleaner. One that approached at a rapid pace down the hallway and was now banging against the lower edge of her door.

Shit on a hoagie roll.

She sprang up from her sliver of open mattress, stalked to the door, and yanked it open.

"What the holy hell," she shrieked over the din, "are you doing?"

The operator of the hell-bent cleaning machine was clad only in a pair of cutoff jeans and a wife beater tee shirt. Steely muscles traced an enticing pattern down his arms, enhanced by a gleam of dewy sweat.

Ooh, Mama.

His hair was wild around his face, as though he hadn't even looked in a mirror since he rolled out of bed. Hair a golden, surfer-blond color that *must* have come out of a bottle.

An Avengers hero in off-duty dress.

Those oddly hued, blue-grey eyes met hers the instant she flung open the door. His raised eyebrows and appreciative scan down her body quickly reminded Laura that her sleep attire wasn't exactly prudent.

Miller snapped off the cleaning monster and grinned. "Good morning, Sunshine." He leaned one elbow on the handle of the giant vacuum and kicked one foot over the other. "Meet Big Bertha. We have a standing date, every Saturday morning."

Laura immediately felt the color rise into her cheeks, trying hard to ignore the heat simmering somewhat lower.

She tipped up her chin and snipped, "So, it's okay if you disturb my sleep, but not okay if I interrupt your Friday night wrestling match?"

Miller balanced the handle of the vacuum against the wall and crossed his arms, never taking his eyes off hers. One side of his mouth curved up. Laura couldn't help but notice how a day's growth of stubble outlined those lips rather enticingly.

Amber stubble, like it belonged to a freaking lion.

"I'm so very sorry, new tenant. But nobody asked you to take up residence on my living room sofa last night, now, did they?"

Talk about deflating her sails. He was absolutely right. About everything. She was the intruder, thanks to run-out-on-your-best-friend Angie. Yeah. She was def at a disadvantage here.

Okay. Regroup. Rethink your tactics.

She crossed her arms over her skimpily-covered chest and looked down at his feet. Big freaking feet. With surprisingly well tended toenails . . .

"Well? Can I go back to my weekend cleaning duties? Are you going to continue to bitch about it, or offer to help me?"

"I didn't realize housework was part of the rental agreement," she muttered.

"Your good friend never bothered to discuss the details of the rental agreement with me at all," he shot back. "Just how much did you say you were paying?"

Laura swallowed, trying to concentrate on his feet and not squirm. "She said I could pay her weekly, once my paychecks start coming in." She glanced up just in time to see his grin fade and one eyebrow lift.

"And that will be when?" His tone had lowered almost to a growl. "You know, Angie didn't contribute much to the expenses here, but I kind of depended on what she did throw in. And that disappeared out of the budget—without notice."

Goosebumps were rising along Laura's arms and a chill skittered down her back. "Let me get some clothes on and I'll be right out."

His gaze swept her appreciatively, one corner of his mouth twitching. Little-boy mischief twinkled in his eyes. "I don't know. You might be in a better position to negotiate dressed just the way you are."

She slammed the door in his face.

Miller switched back on the vacuum and finished the hallway, cursing under his breath as he tried to clean around the huge, ancient trunk taking up the corner at the foot of the stairs. He tried to nudge it to one side, but the damned thing must have weighed over a hundred pounds.

Maybe she did have her grandmother in there. Her dead, *fat* grandmother.

He was in the kitchen pouring himself a cup of coffee when his new tenant appeared in the doorway wearing baggy, pink plaid pajama pants and a tee shirt that came nearly to her knees. There was a sleep crease on one of those rosy cheeks, and her hair tumbled down to her shoulders in a golden cascade of spirals.

"Good morning," he said. "Coffee?"

She nodded, causing the ringlets around her face to bounce.

"What the hell happened to your hair?" he asked through a chuckle.

Her eyes narrowed over the rim of her cup. "I couldn't find my blow dryer last night." She sipped, then wrinkled her nose.

"Sorry, no creamer. I take it straight up, and Angie didn't drink the stuff."

"You really didn't know she was leaving?" she asked in such a quiet voice he barely heard her.

"Nope. Kinda knew she and I were over, at least for the past few months." He turned to stare out the kitchen window. "I figured maybe she'd found somebody else and was afraid to tell me."

"I had no idea she was leaving. Obviously, or I wouldn't be standing here right now."

Turning, he studied her face. She looked vulnerable, and a little lost. At first, he was sure she'd known all about her friend's plans. Now, he tended to believe she was telling the truth.

Just what he didn't need in his life right now, or anytime soon. Another woman in need of his care and protection. He already had enough, between his mother and his sister. And he was just barely managing to fulfill his role in taking care of them. But the last thing Miller was willing to do was to fail Mom and Mollie, like his asswipe of a father did.

He cleared his throat. "So where's the job? You taking over her spot at After Shocks?"

She snorted and shook her head. "Hardly. That would be just about the opposite of what I do."

"What the hell does that mean?"

Setting her cup on the counter, she planted both hands on her hips and met his gaze straight on. "I'm a mental health counselor. My specialty is addiction. I'll be working over at the State Alcoholic Treatment Center."

Miller's stomach went as sour as the orange juice he'd dumped down the sink minutes ago. He dropped his head back, closed his eyes, and muttered, "Fan-fucking-tastic."

Four

When the doorbell chimed, both he and Laura jumped. The moment between them had been so intense, so emotionally charged, a fly landing on the counter might have set either of them off. Miller glanced at the wall clock over the stove and grumbled, "Seriously?"

"Look, I'll just get out of your way," Laura said. "Okay if I jump in the shower? I'm guessing the one downstairs is the only one?" she asked as she spun out into the hall.

Yeah, the only *working* one, he thought. There was another bathroom upstairs, but he'd torn the thing apart last summer with every intention of having it redone by now.

That hadn't happened. Yet.

"For now, yeah," he muttered. He heard her bedroom door slam as he made his way to the front door.

The last thing he needed right now was Mama on the front steps. But this week, the gods were punishing him. But he had to wonder—for what?

"Miller, baby." His mother was wearing her most pathetic countenance when he opened the door. She reached for him as though she hadn't seen him in a decade. In reality, it had been barely three days.

Crimony, she should have gone to Hollywood, he thought as he bent to hug her. We'd both be rich by now.

His mother was average in just about every way—average height, average build, average figure, with dull, greying brown hair and duller brown eyes. Even her name was plain—Jane. Over the last ten years she'd aged so fast, Miller swore he could see the grey hairs multiplying before his eyes. She'd never been a particularly strong woman, but now, she qualified as verifiably frail.

"Come on in, Mom. How are you? How's work going?"

She shrugged.

His mother had been working the midnight shift at the Colonial diner for about three years now. He knew she worked her ass off—what waitress doesn't? Yet still, she was always broke.

She followed him into the kitchen and he poured her a cup of his clean-the-chrome-off-your-bumper coffee, knowing she'd have pretty much the same reaction as . . . what was her name? Oh yeah, Laura.

"So where's Angie? Still sleeping I'll bet. That girl works some godawful late hours." His mother took a sip and her face screwed into a clown's scowl. "My God, did you make this two weeks ago?"

Miller figured there was no time like the present to lay his cards on the table. "Angie moved out, Mom. Two days ago. She landed a job in Tampa, packed her stuff in her little shit-box of a car, and took off."

His mother's eyebrows rose, but her look of shock wasn't very convincing. "Well, that was sudden." Her eyes narrowed. "What really happened, Miller? What? Did she catch you screwing around on her?"

The anger in his chest hadn't even had a chance to flare when a golden-haired faerie interrupted them, appearing around the corner from the hallway. Miller blinked. She was wearing the same thing as *he* had been when they first met—and only that. A steel grey, terry cloth towel.

His mother's reaction, not unusual for her, was a bit more dramatic. She actually staggered back a step and slammed her coffee cup on the counter. Black liquid sloshed over the rim.

"Miller, is there any soap other than what's in the shower?" Laura asked, oblivious to the shock waves she was sending out into the room.

He wagged his head back and forth. "Nope. Angie took my last bar of Irish Spring with her," he said stupidly.

"Huh. Okay." Laura glanced at his mother, pulling the giant towel more snugly around her. "Ma'am," she said curtly, giving her a quick nod before she spun on one bare, pink-manicured foot and into the hall. "I'm headed to the grocery store in a bit, Miller. Make a list of whatever you need," she called over her shoulder.

"I'll leave it on the counter. With money. I picked up an extra shift tonight, so I'll be gone before—"

But the slamming of the bathroom door interrupted him. He couldn't be sure if she'd heard him or not.

His mother turned toward him with a malignant glare, one eyebrow arched. "Uh huh. Should have figured," she hissed.

Miller leaned back against the counter and drained the last half of his coffee. "Laura," he began, wiping his mouth on his forearm, "is my new roommate."

"Well you certainly didn't waste any time in an empty bed, did you?" Jane snapped. "I'll bet you haven't even changed the sheets." She started shaking her head, turning for the door. She paused, gesturing toward the empty beer carton on the counter. "You really are just like your father," she muttered with disgust.

Bam. There it was again. The same old verdict, the same old sentence. For a crime he didn't commit.

Jane was halfway to the door when she stopped, as though she'd suddenly remembered the reason for her visit after all. When she turned back toward him, the bitterness in her expression was gone. Poof. Just like magic.

What a fabulous actress she would have made.

She heaved an exaggerated sigh. "It's your life, your business. None of mine," she mumbled. "Miller, I stopped by because I need a favor." Again, her voice dripped warm honey.

Yup. Figured as much.

Miller closed his eyes. "How much do you need this time, Jane?"

After his father's sudden death the year Miller graduated high school, Jane had managed to keep her financial state liquid, or at least, semi-liquid, until Miller bought his own place and moved out. There was a large insurance policy on Dad—part of his benefits as nighttime security officer at the Rockland Psychiatric Center. Since Dad had inherited his parents' older, raised ranch in the next town over, there never had been the worry of a mortgage to pay.

Jane didn't get *all* of that insurance money. Still, Miller just couldn't understand why, about once a month or so, she made the thirty-minute drive to his house—in the old Chrysler she'd had forever, guzzling gas like Pepsi through a straw—instead of just calling him up and asking him to make a transfer.

Guess that face-to-face pathetic factor worked better on him than he cared to admit.

"Your last trip to Monticello didn't go so well, did it?" he muttered, trying not to look at her. She was his mother, after all. He hated to make her grovel. And he was glad, in a way, that she still got out and did stuff with other people. Participated in some group social activity to keep her mind and emotional state on an even keel.

But those monthly bus trips to the casino were sometimes more expensive than Caribbean cruises.

He heard her clear her throat, and he looked up. Hugging herself, she was gazing out the window. Toward the graveyard.

"I get lonely sometimes, Miller."

Zing.

"It wasn't so bad when you still lived home, but . . ."

Double zing.

Miller blew out a breath and reached inside the cookie jar tucked in the corner of the counter for his wallet.

"Will a hundred last you until the next insurance check comes in?"

She nodded. "I'm sorry, son."

And she did sound genuinely remorseful, which twanged at his heartstrings even more. He wanted to wrap his arms around her and tell her it would all be okay. But he knew it would be a lie. It wouldn't be alright. Couldn't be, ever again.

"Have you been up to Brightstar lately?" she asked in a timorous voice.

The final, killing blow.

Miller shook his head and peeled not two, but three fifties out, then dropped his wallet back into the cookie jar, settling the lid on gently. He let his fingers trail down over its brightly painted surface as though it were a treasured pet.

"It's hard, Mom. She doesn't know me. Doesn't even realize I'm there."

His mother nodded, but didn't say another word.

Miller didn't normally work Saturday nights, but one of his comrades was on vacation, and he'd consented to pull the shift as a favor to Sarge. Besides, there never had been any reason for him to keep his weekend nights free anyway—Angie had tended bar both Friday and Saturdays at After Shocks. What else was he going to do? Sit home alone and watch Ghost Adventures? That's all he needed . . .

Something else to stir up his already over-active imagination when it came to things that go bump in the night. Not the best programming to entertain a nighttime security officer who works on what used to be an asylum for the insane. The building where they'd housed those *hopeless ones*—the ones with little chance of discharge into normal society, ever—still stood. Talcott Hall. Like a rotting tombstone on the southwest side of the campus.

With cages, like for human-sized canaries. Appended to the outside of the building were actual, metal-wire enclosures, presumably providing a place for some fresh air activities for the patients who couldn't be trusted the run of the grounds.

Human cages. The very concept made Miller's stomach twist.

Every time he drove past the hundred-year-old brick building, with its gracefully arched but mostly busted out windows, and its rusted wire enclosures, a shiver ran up his spine like a weakened bolt of ice-cold electricity.

He'd heard they even used *that* particular force of nature—electricity—to tame the uncooperative ones here. Electro-shock therapy. Along with what they called hydrotherapy, long soaks in hot and cold water.

Homeopathic psychiatric medicine. Managing their disease in a "humane fashion." Yeah, right.

This particular evening shift began like any other, with Miller swiping in and signing out his weapon. Except today he'd been on time. A few minutes early, actually. He'd made it a point to get out of the house well before his new roommate returned from her grocery run. The last thing he needed right now was more face time with a woman whose very scent made his blood pressure spike.

He'd known better than to ask her to pick up beer. A mental health counselor, specializing in addiction? Living under his roof? What were the odds? He knew she'd probably already noticed the vegetable bins both stacked with his beer supply, and would be watching him with scrutiny.

But, he reminded himself, his beer supply would probably last him a week, maybe two. Unlike his father, he didn't live to drink. He looked forward to a beer or two after work a few times a week. But most nights, he just went home and crashed. Especially now, with Angie no longer working at the bar just up the street. He had no reason to stop in there for a cold one after work either.

Still, he knew, the propensity for alcoholism was a genetic trait. And a little voice inside his head constantly reminded him that he could, if he wasn't careful, end up just like his father.

The early part of his shift was damnably dull. This weekend the rest of the town apparently had more exciting things to do than vandalize the grounds of an old mental asylum. It wasn't the wayward teenagers that bothered him the most, anyway. Those he could handle—the ones who peed their pants when all he did was show them his baton.

It was the mysterious clan who he found lurking around Talcott Hall who made him uneasy. They appeared often, after full dark, wandering aimlessly. Not every night. But regularly, and often enough to where Miller had started blaming the sightings on his imagination, or exhaustion as his shift was getting ready to end.

He'd assumed they were homeless, but every time he tried to herd them toward the shelter, they never seemed to make it there.

On more than one occasion, he'd considered calling for backup. But after ten o'clock at night, there wasn't much backup to be had. Roger Duvall had the route opposite his, patrolling the other side of the campus. The last thing he wanted to do was ask for Roger's help. They'd been fierce rivals ever since they were hired—both on the same day. Roger was older and settled, with a family and a bachelor's degree. And he probably had his eyes on the same promotion Miller did.

Any show of weakness, or uncertainty, could be his undoing. Roger would most certainly blow the incident up in a way that made Miller look incompetent, or worse yet, crazy.

Because to be perfectly honest, Miller wasn't sure if these people he saw were really *real*. He'd seen them all through the winter months, when snow blanketed the campus and the wind howling through the broken windows was so cold, his lips froze trying to talk to them.

They didn't have warm clothing—any of them. And yet they didn't seem bothered by the weather. Two of them—a man of about forty, and a young girl—just seemed . . . lost. Which made Miller's heart ache so badly for them he would offer his help. When they wandered off, ignoring his efforts, he just turned away, his skin prickling as he headed back to the cruiser. By the time he'd climbed in and looked for them in the glow of his headlights, they were gone.

Tonight, it wasn't cold. The late spring breeze was pleasantly cool, and the sky was stippled with stars. The nearly-full moon cast an eerie glow over the overgrown shrubs flanking the boundary of the massive brick building. Miller considered bypassing Talcott Hall this time around. After all, it was ten-thirty, and in another twenty minutes he could head back to the station, turn in his weapon, and clock out.

But something pulled at him, like a car wreck you really want to drive past without looking, but can't help yourself. Nobody, logically, could even get close to this condemned old building without desperation or ill intent. After part of the second-floor hallway collapsed last year, the State erected a chain-link fence all the way around the place. Miller had to actually get out and unlock a padlock on the gate to do a walk-around.

Sometimes, though, a drunk bunch of teenagers got it in their heads to ghost-hunt, and scaled the fence. He'd find them poking around inside with a flashlight, or sometimes with nothing more than a cigarette lighter. One spark could set the whole building ablaze, trapping them inside. Or they could fall through yet another weakened spot in the floor.

That's all he needed on his record. A four-alarm fire, or some kid ending up fried to a crisp, maimed and in a wheelchair, or worse—all because Miller didn't take the time to stop and take a good look around.

And tonight was Saturday night. He'd caught a bunch of mischievous teens more than once on a bored weekend. On those occasions, he didn't hesitate for a moment before radioing in for backup.

Miller killed the engine a few dozen yards before the gate and doused his headlights. He knew damn well if any pranksters saw or heard him coming, they'd shut off their own lights and hunker down until he gave up and went away. It took a minute for his eyes to adjust to the blackness.

The moon was bright and hung above and to the right of the three-story building, backlighting it into a hulking silhouette. Talcott Hall was huge, covering nearly half a city block. At one time, not so long ago, it had been home—a permanent one—to a hundred or more patients. People who'd fallen victim to any one of the multitude of conditions whose symptoms once defined them as insane.

It took a few moments before he spotted them—the orbs of light. They hovered like globs of oil on the surface of still water, just over the tops of the brush around the corner of the building. He'd seen them before. Tonight, there were more than just two.

Blinking, Miller rubbed his eyes with the backs of his hands. There were eight, maybe ten. And their movement didn't jive with

41

reflections from street lamps, or passing cars on West Main Street a half mile away.

They came together, then drifted apart. Like playful, glowing fireflies, they danced in a pattern Miller couldn't quite confirm as repetitive. Their movement seemed intentional. As if they had minds of their own.

His heart rate kicked up, and he felt at his belt for his gun. Not that it would help him, not in this situation. Flickers of light—real light—could mean real danger, from real people. Young, stupid people not always in complete control of their faculties. High on drugs or booze or lust—who knew?

But in his gut, Miller knew these orbs had nothing to do with vagrant teenagers.

Swallowing hard, he snugged his cap down over his head and opened the car door in the dark, having disabled the interior lights so if these were real intruders, they wouldn't see him. Silently, slowly, he rested the door against the jamb without latching it. With one hand on his weapon, the other on his club, he approached the perimeter.

Miller wove his fingers into the cold, metal mesh of the fence and watched, wondering if he was losing his mind. Rumors, plenty of them, had surrounded Talcott Hall ever since he was a kid. He'd been ten years old or so when the State finally closed the facility down and transferred the worst patients to Rockland Psych Center. Since then, the huge building had stood empty, ravaged by vandals and time, crumbling a little more every year.

Most of his friends truly believed the spirits of those who'd died at Talcott Hall had never left. Some of the stories they told him about their midnight excursions into the empty asylum had given him nightmares. He'd never been much interested in poking around in an old building, more out of good sense than fear.

Miller had known, by the time he started high school, that he wanted to be a security officer. Like his father. And even a juvenile misdemeanor could block his entry into the force.

The balls of light continued their dance, undisturbed. Miller watched in wonder as the orbs pulsed in intensity, first brighter, then paling to almost nonexistence. There *was* a pattern to this, he realized. When the balls came close to one another, they glowed brighter, thrumming in an accelerated rhythm. They never seemed to touch, repelling each other like identically charged magnets. But as they drifted apart, their glow faded.

Except for two. Breaking off from the group, the pair rose higher and higher, floating like untethered helium balloons, until they reached the third-floor windows. They hovered there, oscillating in their own tightly inscribed orbits. Sometimes they drew so near, they almost blended into one, glowing brighter as they did.

When the radio on his belt squawked, his knees nearly buckled out from under him and he came really close to pissing his pants.

"Stanford, this is Duval. You copy?"

Fucking Duval. If he didn't know better, Miller would swear the older cop had done this on purpose. He snatched the walkie-talkie off his belt.

"Yeah, I'm here. Headed in. You?" he barked.

"Waiting for you at the station. Parker's already here to take over."

"I copy."

Miller swiped a hand down over his face as he fumbled, struggling with the other to snap the radio back onto his belt. His hands were shaking, and he swore softly as he climbed into the cruiser. Casting one last glance toward the corner of the building, he shook his head. His damned imagination had gotten the best of him. Again.

The strange balls of light were gone. Had probably never been there at all.

Five

Laura had no idea what she was getting herself into by volunteering to make a grocery run.

When she came into the kitchen a half-hour later, Miller (and that woman, whoever she was) were both gone. His mother, maybe? Anyway, a legal-sized envelope lay in the center of the table with a list penciled in such small letters, Laura had to squint to read it. A very *long* list. With two fifty-dollar bills slipped inside.

Hopefully Miller will be home by the time I get back, she thought. She cringed at the idea of having to carry in and put away all this stuff—his *and* hers—by herself. Especially when she had no freaking idea where he kept anything.

Ah, she'd been away from her alma mater for too long. Laura had forgotten the joys of a trip to Shop-Well, especially on a Saturday. Cursing the crowds, the persistent leftward drift of her cart, and the not-quite-two-carts-wide aisles, the ordeal took her almost two hours in all. She pulled into the driveway with twelve bags wedged into the back of her car at a little past two-thirty.

It wasn't until she realized the front door was closed and locked that Miller had already left for work. Early. He had mentioned something about that, hadn't he?

Damn.

By her fifth trip in, she was winded, sweaty, and in a very foul mood. The day was warm, and even with the windows open, the house felt like a sauna. That's when she remembered the ice cream, the last thing on Miller's list.

Swearing, she dug frantically through the cloth green shopping bags he'd left on the table next to the note. Which one was it in? You'd think the checkout packer would have put all the cold stuff together, right? At this very moment, she knew the two quarts of Ben and Jerry's—Miller's Spectacular Speculoos and her Boom Chocolatta—were liquifying, melting into a disgusting, inedible sludge.

By the time she found the two cylinders, their contents had done just that. With her nose wrinkled, she tossed both drippy containers into the trash, muttering words that usually didn't pass through her lips. At least the plastic-lined bags had kept the sticky stuff from oozing out into the back of her car. When she finished cleaning up the mess and putting away the other perishables, she made a second trip to Shop-Well. Just for ice cream.

Which is what she ate for dinner. Almost an entire quart of Boom Chocolatta.

It wasn't until hours later, and well after dark, that she realized the window in her bedroom was still naked. Still facing the creepy old graveyard. A shiver skittered across her shoulders as she draped a towel up over the black rectangle. Why hadn't she remembered to stop by Walmart or Target and pick up a mini-blind or something?

She was already in bed when she heard Miller come in the door. Damn, she realized, she'd also forgotten to mention to him the tree branches scraping against her window. Gotta have that discussion tomorrow.

Her Sunday wasn't much better, but she realized that putting up with Miller as a roommate was probably not going to present much of a problem. He was rarely home. At least, that's how it seemed so far. She climbed out of bed around eight to find he'd already gone.

Where would he be going so early on a Sunday morning? Church? No way. Angie never mentioned anything about Miller being the religious type. Wherever he'd gone, he still hadn't returned at one o'clock when she climbed into her Kia, dressed in the outfit it had taken her two hours to decide on. Today, of all days, she had to look her best.

Manny and Deirdre were hosting a homecoming barbecue in her honor. Whoop-dee-do. A friendly get-together with Deirdre as ringmaster was the last thing Laura felt like doing today. But there was no way of getting out of it.

Six years since graduating high school was a long time. Would she even recognize her old friends? Although she usually didn't bother with much makeup, she grabbed her kit out of her room and started applying just a little. She scrutinized her image in the flecked, sixties-vintage mirror in Miller's bathroom. Had she changed that much? A few pounds heavier, perhaps. Hell, not perhaps. More like an honest five, to be exact.

Maybe a good thing there wasn't a full-length mirror on the back of the door.

She'd finally decided on a floaty sundress in peach gauze that covered those extra pounds quite nicely. As she drove across town to their condo on Deer Run, she'd convinced herself it might be nice to catch up with the kids who grew up in the same neighborhood, and had gone to school with her. Even though Angie ran out on her, maybe she could reconnect with some of her other old friends. Make this transition, this already rocky *new start* to her life, just a little bit easier.

Although Laura thought she'd left in plenty of time, when she got to her Dad's condo, it seemed she was the last to arrive. She had to park the Kia a block away, grateful for its diminutive dimensions. Not bothering to ring the bell, she skirted the side yard of their end unit and followed the clamor she could hear from halfway down the street. She found the backyard already crowded with people—people, she soon discovered, who were even worse than perfect strangers.

Deirdre greeted her with the same over-enthusiastic welcome she'd expected, immediately wrapping her in a bear hug. Laura smiled weakly over her stepmother's shoulder at her Dad, who'd already perched himself in a shady spot under the umbrella on the patio. He managed a half-hearted wave, not bothering to try to unearth himself from behind the occupants crowding the table and standing nearby.

Her father was one of the least social people she knew. Laura could feel his discomfort as sharply as if it were a splinter buried under her own skin. After all, she was just like him.

Deirdre led her around by the elbow, re-introducing her to people she may not have otherwise recognized.

Sandra Tusinski, one of her and Angie's best buds in their senior year, was now Mrs. Peter Watson. Sandi seemed permanently attached to the arm of her heart-stoppingly gorgeous husband, a Johnny Depp clone in Ralph Lauren casual. Sandi sported a baby bump.

Patti McGregor, who grew up next door, was the executive vice-president of the Orange County Trust Bank. She was flashing around a rock so hideously large it looked like it came out of a gum ball machine. And Greg Madison, football star and Laura's high school crush, was now happily married to the beautiful and terminally stuck-up Trena Baker. Trena was holding the chubby hand of a toddler—a mini-me of his father, with the same sandy blond hair and pool-water blue eyes.

It seemed all the people she graduated with had used some kind of time machine, fast-forwarding their lives to settled and successful. And they all seemed sickeningly happy. Yet here she was, not even working yet and facing a brand-new job. Still single, essentially broke and homeless. She didn't even have a boyfriend. Hadn't since her last year of undergrad.

How had this happened? What crucial life memo had she missed?

It all came down to trust. Laura had abandonment issues. She knew that, a plain and simple case she'd self-diagnosed in her first semester of Child Psych. And pulling into town to discover that Angie, her assumed very good friend, had run out on her too didn't do anything to boost her sense of social security.

About halfway through the torturous afternoon, Laura had had enough of the small-talk chit-chat with people who she may have known years ago, but now whose lives and interests were completely different from hers. And having Deirdre flutter around her like a fussing mother hen—*stepmother*-hen—had the artery in her temple ready to pop. Overwhelmed, Laura really wanted—no, *needed*—a few minutes alone.

Her dad's backyard wasn't big but did boast a shade garden tucked into the patch of woods near one corner. Laura knew there was a stone bench hiding among the trees. Casually, she refilled her Solo cup with lemonade and wandered off in that direction.

But sadly, not unnoticed. Patti MacGregor sauntered down the path just a minute or two behind her and joined her on the bench.

"It's so good to see you again, Laura. You're looking fabulous," she said with a wink. "So, did you hear? Grant and Taylor got engaged on Valentine's Day this year."

Ouch. The one name she really hadn't wanted to hear, ever again. Grant Stafford. Her senior prom date. The guy who attracted girls like flies to garbage. The guy who'd taken her virginity, on prom night, and then never even called her for a second date.

Laura shook her head. "I didn't think he'd ever get married." She tried, really hard, to keep the hurt out of her voice, but apparently failed.

Patti laid a hand on her arm and winced. "I'm sorry. I guess that wasn't the best bit of gossip I should have shared with you." She cleared her throat. "I hear you landed a job with the State. That's fantastic. Can't ask for a more stable career than that." Patti's bright red lips curled into a smile that didn't quite scream *sincere.*

Laura sipped her lemonade and studied her fingernails. "Yeah, I was lucky, I guess. They don't take on too many new graduates. Without already being licensed, anyway."

"So what is it you do? Work with addicts, right?" The smile morphed into a grimace.

"Mental Health Counselor. I did my thesis on alcoholism. But yeah, I'll be working with people suffering from all kinds of addiction." She met Patti's cynical gaze, and watched as she slowly shook her head.

"Why? What drew you to the field?" Patti slid a glance toward the crowd in the backyard. "Your dad doesn't have a problem, does he?"

Laura chuckled. "Why do people always assume that an addiction counselor has a family history of substance abuse? No, absolutely not. My dad could take the stuff or leave it. Mom's the same. I actually started out majoring in Sociology, but when I realized the level of need for addiction counselors, I felt a calling."

Patti blew out a breath. "I just can't imagine. I don't know how you do it."

"I like to feel like I'm helping people. Making a difference. I think it's going to be rewarding work."

Laura hoped it would be. Challenging, if nothing else. Nobody had to tell her the recovery rate of addicts was dismally low.

Patti raised one thinly plucked eyebrow. "I suppose. I give you credit, though. I'd be scared to death just having to work on that campus." She leaned closer, casting a glance around. "I've heard some of those old buildings are haunted," she whispered.

Laura blinked. Funny, she'd not even thought of that when she applied for the job. But she remembered now, how when she was just a kid, how some of the older boys in the neighborhood considered the asylum grounds the perfect place for a Saturday night ghost hunt.

She scoffed. "The only hauntings I believe in are the ones that live inside people's heads. And those are the kind of ghosts that can ruin lives."

An hour later—one that seemed to last at least five years—Laura finally caught a moment alone with her dad. She'd followed him into the house. He was probably on his way to the bathroom, but she didn't care. She'd had enough of this jaunt down memory lane, and was getting ready to leave.

"Hey, Daddy?" she called after him as he headed down the hallway.

Manny paused and turned, then smiled and opened his arms. "Are you enjoying yourself, sweetheart? Deirdre thought you'd like reconnecting with all your old friends."

Laura stepped into her father's embrace and kissed his cheek. "It was very thoughtful of her, Dad. But I'm going to be heading out now. I start work tomorrow, and I still have some unpacking to do. Besides, I'm exhausted."

Her father patted her back and spoke softly against her ear. "Are you sure you're okay with your living situation? I'll be honest, the whole thing makes me a little nervous. I can help you find—"

"No, Daddy. I'm fine, really. I'm a big girl now. I can take care of myself." Still, Laura had to fight hard to keep the tears stinging the backs of her eyes from springing to the surface. She felt so unsettled. All these changes. Did she really believe what she'd said? *Could* she take care of herself?

Manny pushed her back at arm's length and studied her face, sighing. "Yes, you certainly have grown into a fine young woman. I'm very proud of you, Laura. But I think, you and me, we're more alike than either of us would like to admit."

Laura lifted her shoulders. "In some ways. But you're so strong—the chief of police, for God's sakes. You're one of the most confident men I know."

Her father pressed his lips into a thin line, then slowly started shaking his head. "Only on the outside, Laura. I do what I have to do, and yes, I'm good at it. But inside, in here," he struck his chest with his fist, "I'm just a sentimental old softie. Not that it's a bad thing. I'm just saying. Go out there and make a life for yourself. Have confidence in what you're trained to do, and do it well. But remember, it's okay to stay soft inside. Makes you a more compassionate human being." He leaned forward and kissed her forehead. "Hopefully, someday, you'll find someone who'll be the yin to your yang. Who understands the person you show the world, but still loves the real you inside."

With the next blink, Laura could no longer prevent the tears from spilling over. This was the first time her father had spoken to her like this. Maybe, she thought, she'd never been mature enough before to understand his message.

"Now," he said, "I'm sorry, but this old man has got to pee. Good luck tomorrow, Laura. And don't forget to say goodbye to Deirdre before you go."

As the bathroom door clicked shut, Laura folded her arms across her chest. Turning, she watched through the patio doors as Deirdre chatted animatedly with all these people—people her stepmother really didn't know. People she'd invited here for Laura.

Suddenly, instead of the jealous contempt she'd felt for the woman up until now, she saw Deirdre in a new light. Maybe she wasn't the domineering badger Laura had thought her to be.

Maybe she was just exactly what her father needed. The yin to his yang. Sighing, she said a silent prayer—*please let me find someone who will love me, the real me, for better or worse.*

When Laura got home around eight, Miller was parked on the sofa in front of a Yankee's game, the coffee table sporting several empty beer bottles. He was stretched out with his eyes closed, apparently asleep, one heavily-muscled arm thrown over his head. She hesitated in the doorway, studying him.

He really was a gorgeous man. Asleep, his facial features looked softer, and his long lashes fanned above strong cheekbones seemed such a disconcerting contrast. His expression was innocent, boyish, but his body was all man. Big man. Big, handsome man.

Scanning the three bottles on the table, Laura wondered if Miller really did have an alcohol addiction. Angie had often alluded to Miller's *problem*. But how much of what Angie told her could she really believe? Hell, she'd certainly pulled a bait and switch on *her* at the last minute. And then there was the way she'd always referred to Miller as her meal ticket.

Meal ticket. It had struck her as odd, especially right after Angie moved into Miller's house. By then, they'd been seeing each other for over a year, and at times Angie really sounded like she was in love. Had she been? Would you really refer to a man you cared about as a meal ticket?

Laura had sunk so deep inside her own head that she didn't realize Miller was awake until he spoke, and her heart leapt in her chest.

"Need something?" he growled, his voice rough with sleep.

51

She shook her head and backed away, but then remembered the noises outside her window. "Oh, yeah. I do. Miller, there's a tree branch or something right up close to the house. It scrapes against my window at night."

His eyebrows rose, and he stared at her for a moment. Then he sat up and yawned, stretching his sculpted arms over his head. The hem of his sleeveless tee shirt drew up, revealing a patch of golden hair just above the waistband of his shorts.

Oh, my.

Laura gulped and her heart rate kicked up a notch. It had been a very long time since she'd been with a man. Or seen one in any state of undress. But this was not the time for her silly, shameless body to remind her of the fact.

Honestly, girl, get a grip.

Miller obviously took note of her reaction, because he broke into a grin and asked, "Like the scenery?"

She crossed her arms over her chest and dropped her gaze. "When you get time, if you could trim back those branches—"

"There's no tree on that side of the house," he said as he stood and stretched again, growling deep in his throat. Then he padded barefoot toward her.

On those big, neatly groomed feet. His hair was wet, and he was clean shaven. On his day off. He obviously took good care of himself.

"Come on. I'll show you," he continued, motioning for her to follow him out the door.

It was dusk, but there was still plenty of light as Laura followed Miller down the length of the porch. He leaned out over the railing and pointed down the side of the house.

"See? No tree."

Laura placed both hands on the peeling, painted rail and leaned around him. The graveyard, from this vantage point, and in the fading light, reminded her of an old Alfred Hitchcock movie set. The strip of land between the rusted iron fence and the side of Miller's house couldn't have been more than ten feet wide. And although there were huge, ancient oak trees scattered among the tilted stones on the other side of it, none stood even close to the fence.

His strip of lawn was neatly mowed, and there were no trees. There weren't any shrubs flanking the house. She could see the narrow basement window lying close to the ground, set into a fieldstone foundation.

Laura felt goosebumps rise along her arms, even though the air was still warm. She rubbed them and looked up at Miller, who was standing close beside her. So close she could feel the heat of his body. And the heat rising up her neck.

"I don't understand," she said quietly. "There was something scratching the glass the first night I was here. I thought, with the wind that kicked up that night, it had to be a branch."

He was gazing at her with such earnest concern in those eyes that looked blue at first glance. But this close, Laura noticed the silver flecks that made reminded her of a wild animal's. A young wolf. She hoped he couldn't hear her heart slamming against her ribs at a suddenly quicker pace.

"No tree. Are you sure you weren't just dreaming? You were exhausted that night," he went on. His lips, full and soft, curved up on one side. "You were passed out cold on the couch when I got home from work. Remember?"

Laura heard the blood rushing in her ears and looked down. She realized he had moved toward her, sliding forward ever so slightly on those bare, beautiful feet. Now she not only could feel his body heat, but she could smell him. Shampoo and Irish Spring. Clean and pungent, almost minty. Leaning one arm on the railing, he'd lowered his head so their faces were only inches apart.

That's when the yeasty smell of the beer hit her, and her shoulders drooped.

She ducked around him and headed for the door, still rubbing her arms. "Maybe I was just overtired. I'd had a rough day."

"And I certainly didn't make it any easier on you." His voice was low and rumbling. "Did I?"

She stopped without turning. "It's okay. I understand. Me showing up must have been a bit of a shock, close on the heels of Angie walking out."

53

"True, but I acted like a real asshole. Sorry about that." The low purr of his voice sent shock waves down Laura's spine. He actually *did* sound sorry.

She twisted her shoulders in a small shrug. "I was a little . . .apprehensive. Angie told me you have a really bad temper."

The words had no sooner left her lips when her brain finally caught up.

Why did I tell him that?

She squeezed her eyes shut and waited for the explosion she feared might follow.

But there was none. She heard the floor boards creak, and then his hands heavy on her shoulders. Warm and solid. It felt good. Reassuring.

"I can't deny that." His voice was low and gentle. "But I've learned to control it. In my line of work, you have to. Look, I'm sorry I gave you such a hard time."

Laura felt the prick of tears behind her eyes. She did so want to trust him. To trust *anyone*.

The moment stretched out until he finally said, "Hey, I did notice there wasn't any covering on your window. I'm off tomorrow. I'll go pick up a shade or something and put it up for you."

Laura's heart did a little tumble. No way did this sound like the selfish asshole Angie described. This man sounded considerate. Almost . . .sensitive.

"I would appreciate that," she said. "Now, I'm turning in. First big day on the job tomorrow." She stepped out from under the weight of his big hands. The loss of their warmth almost stung.

It took a long time for Laura to fall asleep that night, but it wasn't because of noises outside her window. Those hadn't repeated since the first night she'd arrived, which she found odd in itself. Had it been her imagination? Had she been dreaming?

The brief conversation with Miller kept going around and around in her head. Could Angie have been a liar? Was she just making up stories about Miller to justify the real reason she'd stayed with him until the day she got her degree?

She fell asleep with the tangy scent of Irish Spring filling her head.

Laura didn't wake to her alarm clock, but to a crack of thunder that shook the entire house. She sat bolt upright and clutched the quilt to her chin. Although she couldn't see through the towel across her window, she could hear the sheets of rain hitting it like someone had turned a hose on the glass.

Wonderful. No matter how carefully she blew out her little-girl spiral curls today, they would spring back to life before she even got to the clinic. Today was her first big day on the job. She wanted to look sophisticated, mature, a woman who knew what she was doing. Not like Hermione's big sister.

She was due in at eight o'clock, even though her normal shift would be ten to six once orientation was done. Her digital alarm clock on the nightstand told her it was 6:45. Might as well get going.

A half-hour later, she'd just turned off the blow dryer when she heard the annoying beep-beep-beep of her alarm. Oops. She'd forgotten to turn it off.

And Miller was still asleep upstairs. At least, he had been.

Another rumble shook the house, but this one wasn't thunder.

"What the fuck!" Miller's voice boomed from the stairwell, and then she heard him barrel down the stairs. A bang, then another tirade. "Shit! Shit, shit, shit!"

Timidly, she ducked her head out into the hallway. He was at the base of the stairs, hopping around on one foot and holding the toes of the other in both hands. He was wearing . . . oh my. Nothing but a very fitted pair of red, Jockey briefs. And he was all muscle and golden hair, everywhere.

"Sorry," she called, hurrying down the hallway and creeping past him to shut off the alarm clock. When she peeked around the doorjamb, he was sitting on the bottom step, still clutching his toes and muttering.

"You need to find a place for this blasted thing," he barked, kicking it with his heel. "It's a damned fire hazard where it is."

"Hey," she snapped, stalking out into the hallway until she stood right over him. "That *blasted thing* happens to have a lot of sentimental value to me. So, treat it with some respect." She dropped to one knee to examine the ornately carved border along the bottom of the trunk. "At least it looks like you didn't do any damage to it."

"Seriously? *Seriously?* My toenail is split in two, I'm bleeding on the floor, and all you care about is that blasted box?"

Laura looked up, horrified to see there was, in fact, blood seeping through the fingers he had wrapped around his toes. "Oh my God, I'm so sorry. Let me get something . . ."

She dashed into the kitchen and grabbed the roll of paper towels off the counter, stopping to rip off several and run them under the cold tap. But by the time she retraced her steps he had hobbled out into the hallway, where he was leaning against the wall. With burly arms crossed, he stared at her.

"Here, let me clean that up for you," she said, again dropping to one knee in front of him.

Which put her right at eye level with a most enticing bulge in his cranberry-red briefs.

Laura swallowed hard, and forced her eyes to their task. His big toe was covered in blood, and a small pool was already forming on the hardwood.

"Why don't you sit down so I can clean the blood off and see how bad it is."

When he didn't move, she raised her gaze to his. He was watching her with a mischievous twinkle in those silvery eyes.

"I don't know. I kind of like this vantage point better."

Laura felt the color rising up her neck. She scrambled to her feet and ducked into the bathroom. "Well I don't. If you want me to clean up your toe, you'll have to come in here."

But wedged inside his tiny bathroom with him was almost worse. He sat on the closed commode with his foot propped on the edge of the tub while she dabbed at his toe with the damp towels. She could feel his eyes on her as she worked, and she started to sweat.

"Where'd your pretty curls go?" he asked, amused. "What do you do, iron them out every morning?"

"Blow dryer and a round brush," she said. She pressed a little harder on the bloody toenail, and he hissed through his teeth.

"Sorry," she muttered. "Do you have a first-aid kit? The nail isn't split, but you did shave off some skin on one side."

He pointed to the medicine cabinet over the sink. "Band-Aids and ointment in there."

After retrieving the supplies, Laura turned and caught him with his eyes hovering in the vicinity of her backside, which was sheathed in a fitted black skirt. She scowled.

"Can't hurt too bad or you wouldn't have your head in the gutter," she snapped.

He met her gaze with a chastened expression. When he spoke, his voice was gentle. "You look real nice, Laura. I hope you do great today. You nervous?"

The sincerity of his tone made her throat tighten. She was such a sucker for empathy, any show of concern for her. But she'd learned that most of the time, it wasn't for real. When it came from her father, perhaps. But she was second on that totem pole now, and Deirdre always made sure she knew it. The affection from her new stepmother had always come off as phony.

At least, it had up until now. The reunion Deirdre had planned, and Laura's conversation with her dad yesterday had been churning inside her head all night. Maybe Deirdre's affection wasn't as false as Laura had believed.

She nodded, afraid her voice would break if she tried to speak. Her fingers started to shake as she unwrapped a Band-Aid, and she fumbled with the cap from the ointment.

"Here. Let me." Miller lifted the tube from her hand and unscrewed the cap. She held the bandage in her open palm while slowly, methodically, he squeezed glob of medicine onto the pad.

Carefully avoiding eye contact, she kept her eyes on the Band-Aid. She blew out a nervous breath, then fastened it gently around his toe.

As she started to rise to her feet, she felt his heavy hand on her shoulder again.

"Hey," he said softly. "Look at me."

She kept her eyes down on the things in her hands, the box of bandages and the tube of Neosporin. "I've got to get going, Miller. This rain is going to slow me down, and I've got to be there by eight."

He chucked her gently under the chin until she looked up at him. "Thank you. And good luck today. I mean it."

The knot in her throat tightened to searing pain.

If I cry now, I'll have to do my makeup all over.

"Thanks," she sputtered and climbed to her feet, handing the supplies to him so she could straighten her skirt. "See ya."

Just as she pulled up the hood of her raincoat inside the front door, she heard him call from the bathroom.

"And don't worry about Grandma, Laura. She can stay right where she is. I'll learn to be more careful around her."

Laura arrived for her first day on the job with smeared mascara and rapidly spiraling hair.

The Middletown Crisis Center was modern, the brick building a more recent construction than most of the others on the campus. The lobby was all glass and chrome, and the space had a clean, almost sterile quality, right down to the highly polished, marble floors. As the door swung closed behind her, a blast of air-conditioning hit Laura's damp hair and sent a chill across her shoulders.

She yanked on her skirt, took a deep breath, and strode with purpose toward the black enameled reception counter. The young man standing next to it looked up, but didn't smile.

"Good Morning. I'm Laura Horton. I'm supposed to meet with Kayla Riley this morning."

He was an odd-looking fellow. His crisp white dress shirt was a size too large, and Laura couldn't help wondering if he'd borrowed it from his daddy. Small, dark eyes scrutinized her through thick-lenses framed in heavy black plastic. The glasses were huge on his boyish face under a cap of ebony curls.

"Mrs. Riley is expecting you, Ms. Horton. Down that hallway," he pointed. "Hers is the third door on the right." His high-pitched voice was nasal and annoying.

"Thank you," Laura said. As she whisked around the reception desk her right breast nearly collided with the guy's small hand, which he had unexpectedly extended into her path.

"Let me introduce myself. I'm Jonathan Rivers. I expect you and I will be working quite closely together. In fact," he grinned, revealing a row of yellow teeth that looked too small for his mouth, "we'll be sharing the same office."

His fingers were limp and clammy, and all Laura could think was, *how much worse is my life going to get?*

Six

Laura's first day of work sucked so bad, she wished her old roommate, Abby, hadn't given up the apartment in Boone. She'd have packed all her stuff and taken off as soon as she got back to Miller's that night. Well, maybe not without first making arrangements for her grandmother's trunk and her other furniture, but still. That was her knee-jerk reflex to her first horrible, demeaning, infuriating day at Orange County Mental Health Services.

For one, Kayla Riley was not the sweet, easy-to-work-with senior counselor she had seemed during their numerous telephone and Skype interview sessions. The minute Laura entered her office, she could smell it—the scent of a dominant woman who had marked her territory. The entire room reeked of some hideous, albeit probably insanely expensive, designer perfume. It was as if everything, from the outdated geometric-patterned carpet to the matching polyester drapes, had been splashed with the stuff.

The closer to her desk Laura got, the more obvious it became that the woman bathed in it as well.

Ms. Riley was careful to correct Laura when she addressed her as *Kayla*, as she had during the interviews. The woman couldn't be more than ten years older than Laura, but somehow, had managed to achieve the title of senior manager in just the few short weeks since Laura had accepted the job. And there was no denying one glaring fact: the promotion had gone straight to the woman's head.

Riley wore her dark brown hair like a helmet, molded around her skull to her chin, and complete with visor—a razor-sharp line of bangs. The suit she was wearing was so stiffly starched, Laura felt certain it would maintain its shape without the aid of a hanger. She was sure if she looked closely enough, she might even find the price tag dangling from under the armpit.

Riley obviously hadn't gotten used to dressing this way yet, either. She sat straight and stiff in her chair, the starched lapel of her blouse digging into the loose flesh of her neck. Every few minutes, the woman twisted her head and tugged at the collar with two French manicured fingertips.

"Ms. Horton, such a pleasure to finally meet you in person." Riley had shaken Laura's hand, robotically, and then resumed her seat behind the desk. "Please, sit down. Your move went well, I trust?"

No. Actually, my best friend abandoned me, leaving me to fend for myself with her monstrously large, ill-tempered ex-boyfriend. And I have a graveyard outside my window. But other than that—

"Yes, fine. It all went perfectly fine," Laura lied. Then she forced a smile. "I'm really looking forward to getting started."

Riley regarded her from under an arched eyebrow for a long moment, as though she either didn't believe her, or had forgotten what she was supposed to say next.

"Yes, um, well, we're glad you're here too," she chirped. "Our patient load increases on a daily basis, and we need all the trained troops we can get to fill those trenches."

Trenches, huh? Laura was guessing Riley hadn't begun referring to the front lines as such until the day she'd risen above them.

"What sort of patients will I be dealing with to start?" Laura asked, crossing her legs and wrapping her hands around her knee. To keep them from shaking.

Riley coughed, grabbed a tissue out of the stainless-steel canister on her desk, and muttered, "Excuse me." At which point she proceeded to hack into the scrap of paper, and then, to Laura's horror, loudly blew her nose.

Laura winced and swallowed.

"Excuse me. Sorry. These spring allergies," Riley mumbled. The nasty wad of tissue disappeared under her desk and she snatched out two more from the canister. "Well, to start out with, Ms. Horton, you won't be seeing patients." Her tone had gone from sweet and friendly to crisp and businesslike.

Laura sat back in her chair and raised her chin. The job description had clearly stated; *Applicants should be prepared to deal with ongoing clinical cases.*

"But I thought—"

"Yes, well, since you accepted this position, there has been an institutional reorganization." Riley paused, tipped back her head, and narrowed her eyes. Carefully folding her hands on the desk, she continued. "Budget cuts. New fiscal year coming. I'm sure you understand. You are lucky, Ms. Horton—very lucky—I convinced my superiors not to eliminate your position entirely."

Laura's heart dropped a notch lower in her chest, but she honestly wasn't sure it could go any lower.

"Wh-what does that mean? What will I be doing?"

She was shown into a dingy, poorly-lit office halfway down the hallway opposite the lobby. When Laura passed the reception desk, she shrank away, gun-shy after the near-miss boob encounter with the Jonathan creep when she came in. He was no longer manning that post. But as Riley pushed open the door to the musty smelling, cramped space, her heart dropped the final notch.

The room, barely bigger than a closet, housed two '70s vintage, dark wood veneer computer desks, complete with lopsided pull-out keyboard drawers. At one of them sat the small and eerily creepy Jonathan Rivers, tapping away frantically on the keys. The other was piled with a tower of haphazardly-stuffed manila folders that threatened avalanche at any minute.

"You and Mr. Rivers will be working together. I trust you've met? I asked Jonathan to watch the reception desk today, since Sadie was out sick." Riley's voice was overly modulated and sickeningly sweet. A la Deirdre.

Laura nodded as her stomach try to turn itself inside out.

"Jonathan will be happy to get you acclimated. Get you up to speed on the software."

The odd little man twisted in his seat and grinned up at Laura, flashing his uniquely horrible set of teeth. "At your service." His squeal mimicked that of an overexcited child. Which was bad enough. But when he rubbed his hands together and scanned her body with his magnified, watery eyes, Laura feared she might faint.

Treatment records. Her new job would be analyzing treatment records, matching dates for accuracy, and reading and/or listening to recorded therapy sessions to summarize and transcribe into patient records. Laura would be little more than a data-entry clerk, trapped in this claustrophobic space for her entire eight-hour shift. No patient contact, and not the remotest chance of directly influencing a single, troubled soul.

In a nearly windowless space, with barely inches separating her thigh from brushing against that of . . . it. *Jonath-It.*

Her hope of job fulfillment, of using her hard-earned knowledge and skills to make a difference in someone's life, washed away with the torrential rain outside the window and ran off into the gutters.

By midday, Laura's claustrophobia had kicked in full-bore. She'd figured out the software quickly, thank heavens, because having that creepy nerd hanging over her shoulder had her breaking out in hives. At lunchtime, she rose and asked her office-mate where the employee lounge was.

"I'd be happy to show you there," he said, a note of nauseating hope in his tone.

"No. No, that's fine. I'm not really hungry anyway. How about the rest rooms?"

She couldn't believe Bitch Riley hadn't even shown her the basic conveniences.

Laura pushed coins into the snack machines in the lounge to secure a granola bar and a cup of rancid, instant coffee. Even worse than Miller's. Her stomach churning even more afterward, she returned to her office. Maybe she'd be lucky and get a few minutes alone before Jonath-It returned from lunch.

She got five before he crept back in through the doorway so quietly she didn't even hear him until he flopped down in his chair, startling the bejesus out of her. Creepy *and* stealthy. A very scary combination indeed.

The room's single, small window offered a view with little hope of solace. Directly across the road stood a massive, three-story brick edifice stretching as far off to the left and right as Laura could see. Most of its windows were shattered, but they were all crisscrossed with a heavy, iron grid. Enclosed wire cages hung off the building like barred patios. Chain link fence encircled the entire monstrosity. Laura wondered if the fence had been erected to keep intruders out, or something else *in*.

Her new office-mate caught her studying the magnificently hideous view.

"That's Talcott Hall." His chuckle sounded more like a chipmunk than a human. "I mean, it *used* to be Talcott Hall."

Laura forced her gaze down toward the weird little man and asked, "What was it used for?"

The chipmunk giggle again. Then, rubbing his hands together, he whispered, "All-timers."

Laura raised an eyebrow and cocked her head. "An Alzheimer's facility?"

Jonathan shook his head so vehemently Laura swore she heard his jowls flapping.

"All. Timers," he hissed. "The *hopeless* ones. The ones who never got out."

She blinked, scrutinizing the massive brick structure, one slowly but steadily being consumed by vines growing up along its edifice and crawling in between the bars on the windows.

"Is there anything left in there? I mean, why is it still standing?" she asked.

Jonathan shrugged, then his eyes narrowed into conspiratorial slits. "I believe," he said, leaning closer toward her, and causing her to shrink back a little further, "there are records in the basement," he added quickly with a dismissive wave of his small hand. "But you didn't hear that from me."

"What kind of records?" she prodded.

He turned away from her so suddenly she thought she might have spit on him by accident. His shoulders rose nearly to his ears, then dropped slowly.

"Don't really know a thing about that," he said in an even monotone. "Don't know much about that place at all."

By the time Laura plodded up the front steps to Miller's house, she had little left in the way of energy, hope, even sanity. How could her life have gone down the crapper so fast and in only a few days? She'd loved her chosen career, excelled in her classes, and up until today, had been rarin' to go and filled with enthusiasm. Ready to begin on the next bright chapter of her life.

Now she felt like a helium balloon a month after its birth—still filled with air, but not the buoyant kind.

His rare Monday off did not turn out to be day of leisure for Miller. After his rude awakening, and then whacking his toe on that monstrous trunk in his hallway, he was wide awake. He tried to go back to sleep. The grey day and the rain pounding on the roof made for perfect sleeping weather. But thoughts of his new roommate kept floating back into his brain.

She was as different from Angie as a woman could get. How on earth had those two been such good friends? Opposites attract and all that, but all he could see was how timid and vulnerable Laura was, and he knew damn well how aggressive Angie could be. She probably took advantage of Laura the same way she had of him. What a shocking realization it must have been for Laura to show up, after an eight-hundred-mile trek, with everything she owned following in an Acme Moving truck, to discover her friend had run out on her.

Angie didn't just abandon Miller. She abandoned Laura too, and he wasn't quite sure why that should bother him as much as it did.

There was no denying one obvious fact: he was attracted to Laura. She was small and soft, with gently rounded curves in all the right places. Her hair, when she didn't torture it with styling tools, hung in delicate spirals around her face. And those eyes . . .big and round and such a vivid shade of blue.

But there was sadness in those eyes, and from more than just recent events, he felt certain. Miller had a suspicion Laura had been hurt, badly, sometime in her past. That's what made her so jumpy and panicky. Like a frightened bird, trapped and uncertain what to do next.

He couldn't help wanting to wrap his arms around her and protect her, take all the fear and uncertainty away. Smell her talcum powder scent. Feel her warm softness against him . . .

Shit. After trying to go back to sleep for nearly an hour, he climbed out of bed with a painful hard-on and stepped into an ice-cold shower.

An hour later, he returned home with a McDonald's bag in one hand and one from Home Depot in the other. That one held a blackout window shade. He grabbed his tool box from out of his truck on his way in the door.

What a freaking fiasco. The damn thing didn't fit inside the window frame, even though he'd measured it to within a sixteenth of an inch before he left. It was just about a sixteenth of an inch too wide. He had to drive back to Home Depot and have them shave off the offending section. Every trip he made from his house to the truck, from the truck into the store and back again, he got increasingly soaked from the relentless rain. Even though he'd started this project before ten a.m., it was now almost two o'clock, and there was still no shade on Laura's window.

That's when he remembered that today was also his first day of school. Online classes to finish his bachelor's degree.

He was so wet that his sneakers squished when he came in the door the last time. Slipping them off, he noticed the toe of his sock was soaked with blood. When he peeled it off, the band aid came with it, and yes, he was bleeding again. Damn it all to hell.

With a paper towel wrapped around his foot so he didn't drip blood all through the house, he climbed the stairs to change. He brought his laptop back downstairs with him, so he could start looking at his course material while he ate something—he was starving again, the two McDonald's breakfast sandwiches gone hours ago.

He made himself a monstrous sandwich, popped open a beer, and booted up his laptop.

Oh, my. This is going to be more challenging than I'd anticipated.

To start, Miller was not the most tech savvy guy on the planet. He could use an iPhone, pick up his email, and order pizza online—what more did he need? Besides, he knew how to clean, lock, load, and shoot a gun. That had to be a more useful skill than muckin' around on a keyboard for hours on end.

His weaponry training at the police academy wasn't going to help him with this course, however. It took him almost an hour to figure out how to log into the classroom page, find the lessons, and then finally open the first one. A bold script announcement in the course introduction clearly stated that classroom participation would count for twenty-five percent of the grade.

Classroom participation? How the hell does one participate in a virtual classroom? There were no time constraints, other than having each lesson completed by a designated day. How do you know when somebody else is online, in the "classroom" so you could *participate* with them?

He was growling at the screen and on his second beer when he heard the key turn in the lock and the front door open.

Holy shit. Was it that late already?

Miller waited in silence, listening to Laura's raincoat crackle as she hung it on the coat tree. He heard something hit the floor with a thud—her purse? shoes? Too small to be a body . . .followed by a slow shuffling on the hardwood before she appeared in the doorway. Her clothes looked like she'd slept in them, and her hair was wild, standing out from her head in a jumble of zig-zags. There was a black smudge on the side of her face.

He thought she was going to walk right on by. He didn't want to startle her, so Miller didn't make a sound. But she stopped in the doorway and turned to face him, blinking in the light.

Then, she promptly burst into tears.

Miller had no idea how to deal with this. Angie had not been a crier. When Angie had a bad day, she threw breakables. That's why he was down to two full-size dinner plates and only three or four drinking glasses. There was no question that his former strategy for dealing with a depressed woman—ducking—didn't apply here.

Slowly, he lowered the lid to his laptop (that was pretty much instinct, since Angie had taken out one laptop on him last year with a pie plate), and rose to his feet.

"What happened, Laura? Are you okay?" The words came out, but then he held his breath. Because he didn't dare say anything to Angie when she was like this. It was like setting a match to dynamite. He wasn't a stupid man. He'd learned that by the third shattered dish.

But Laura just stood there, her frail shoulders quaking and tears streaming, her face screwed up into a painful mask of misery. His heart clutched in his chest. Miller did not know how to comfort a woman in this fragile mental state.

He hadn't known how to comfort his mother all those years ago, and he hadn't learned a damn thing about the process since.

She breathed in on a sob as she scanned the table between them. "What are you doing?"

Okay, so, not the answer to his question, but he'd go with it. What choice did he have?

"Homework. My class started today," he said, very slowly, as though he were talking to a child. "Laura, what happened to you?"

But her eyes continued to scan the room, the table, him. Besides the two empty beer bottles on the table, there was a cardboard case of Miller Light on the counter, and a messy cutting board from the sandwich he'd made. He hadn't done anything but pull on a wrinkled tee shirt and shorts after getting drenched today.

Suddenly aware he looked like a lazy, sloppy, lush, he winced.

Laura's face twisted into an angry glare, and his stomach soured.

Shit and damn. Here it comes.

"You're drunk," she hissed. "*That's* what happened to *you*."

68

He blinked and swallowed. "Uh, no, I'm not drunk. But that's not the question here." The one step he took to skirt the table and approach her was all it took. She bolted. Down the hall and into her room, the door slamming so hard, the picture hanging in the hallway came tumbling down. The sound of splintering glass on the hardwood made Miller drop back his head and swear. He knew all too well what had crashed to the ground and shattered into a billion little pieces, just like the dream it had represented all those years ago.

"Fuck."

He was stooping with a dustpan and broom in the hallway when Laura's bedroom door flew open and she stepped out, wearing nothing but a pink silk tank-top and teensy little shorts.

Lord in heaven.

She started out into the hallway. Barefoot.

"Don't," he stood quickly and held out a hand. "There's broken glass everywhere."

"I have to pee," she sobbed. Disappearing into her room for a moment, she returned wearing a pair of sparkly flip-flops. She stomped past him and into the bathroom, glass crunching under her feet, and slammed that door too.

Miller sighed and returned to his task. He heard the toilet flush and the shower go on. Good. *At least I'll have time to clean this all up before she attacks again.*

A good, long time. She takes some pretty long showers, he thought. *Hope she's not in there cutting her wrists or something.*

That's when he glanced down at the Home Depot bag still sitting on the floor under the coat tree.

Shit. I never got the shade put up.

Hustling, he finished sweeping up the glass and laid the shattered frame on the kitchen counter. Maybe he'd have enough time to mount the shade before she came out.

He did not. He was screwing in the second bracket when he heard the clap-clap of her flip-flops coming his way. Glancing over his shoulder, he said, "I forgot all about putting this up until now. Had a little problem with the measurements."

But taking his eyes off his work had not been prudent. The screwdriver slipped and plunged into the pad of his middle finger. "Fuck," he muttered, sticking the bleeding digit into his mouth.

Turning, he saw her leaning against the doorjamb with her arms crossed. Her lips were firmly pressed into a line. But when their eyes met, the corner of her mouth twitched.

"You're pretty clumsy. Aren't you?" she asked.

God, she looked cute. And hot as holy hell. She was still wearing that delicious looking tank and shorts, the silky fabric now clinging to the curve of her slightly damp breasts. He was so glad to see the tears were gone, and the amused twinkle lighting up those luminous eyes.

"I'm a big guy. Sometimes we are. Can't wrap our heads around navigation of a ship this big." He smiled back at her, and then let his eyes trail down the length of her body. When his gaze slithered back up to meet hers, he expected to see the mad face again. When he didn't, he felt his man parts twitch.

Whoa, better stay focused here.

He turned back to his work, and finished attaching the second bracket without incident. Retrieving the shade off the end of her bed, he snapped it into place and slowly drew it down.

"There," he said. "Fixed."

"I'm sorry I broke your picture frame," she said in a small voice. "I had a really bad day."

"Sounds that way. Want to talk about it?"

She hesitated for a moment, long enough to where he thought she would say yes. But she didn't. She shook her head, her damp curls bouncing around her face. "I'll let you get back to your email. Or whatever you were doing. Thanks for hanging the shade."

Miller snorted as he gathered up his tools and the empty Home Depot bag. "I wish it was email. That would be easy." He turned to face her then and looked deep into her eyes. "Sure you're okay? You don't want to sit and talk about your day?"

She held his gaze for a long time, and he saw something there—some emotion he couldn't quite put a name too. At least, his brain couldn't. But his southern regions began reacting in their usual less-than-subtle salute.

Dammit, Miller, you're a brainless animal.

Thank God for the Home Depot bag, which he positioned strategically to hide his rapidly tenting gym shorts.

The moment stretched out, and here, in this room, her talcum powder scent was everywhere. It wasn't just coming off her body, but oozed up from the bedclothes or her pillow. Drawing in a deep breath to gain control, therefore, only made matters worse.

And hell, she'd only moved in a few days ago.

Finally, she said, "Maybe. Just for a few minutes. If you're sure—"

"Let me just stash these tools back into my truck and I'll meet you in the living room in five."

The rain had stopped, and the air felt clean and cooler than it had in days. Thankfully, almost chilly. Miller took his time replacing the screwdriver and hammer into his toolbox, carefully in their designated spot. He sucked in deep breaths of the night air. He had to gain control before he sat side by side with her on his couch.

Why am I reacting to her this way? God, I must be hornier than I thought.

Okay, so it had been a while—a long while—since he'd had sex with Angie. Hell, it had probably been months. And the last few times they had been together, he could tell her head wasn't there in the bed with him. Afterward, his body may have been sated, but he'd known something was missing. Gone, if it ever existed between them at all.

He gazed over toward the graveyard, where water dripping off the still-drenched trees made a pattering sound on the stones. Such a dismal, lonely place. He'd felt that way inside for quite a while. And even in the early days, with Angie, there was a part of him that continued to feel empty, hollowed out and aching like the socket of an extracted tooth.

That place, he knew, would always be there. The bliss of a relationship with a woman, the heady new girlfriend high, and some really great sex might distract him for a little while. But it never took away the hole in his heart that throbbed, constantly. He missed his baby sister. Which was sad because in reality, she was still alive. Just not all of her.

Slamming the tailgate, he made his way back into the house, where he found Laura curled up on the end of his sofa. She was wrapped in the same quilt as the first night, when he'd found her sleeping. The night she opened up those big, blue eyes and stared at him as though he was the big, bad wolf.

He paused, really wanting to snatch another beer out of the fridge before going in. But he thought better of it. Laura, no matter how sweet and defenseless she might seem, was a mental health counselor for the State of New York. Specializing in alcoholic behavioral disorders.

Miller worked for the State too, as a licensed, gun-carrying security officer. If she decided to raise any question about his drinking with Sarge, it would hold way more weight than a report from a bitter ex-girlfriend. Not that Angie had ever threatened him, but she'd also depended on him financially the whole time they lived together. He doubted she'd cut off her own blood supply. But he did worry a bit about an anonymous phone tip coming in from a Tampa exchange once she'd flown the coop for her sister's house.

Because after she left, what did she have to lose?

With Laura, it was different. With her credentials, and living under the same roof as him, she would be taken seriously. If that happened, Miller would lose his license to carry, and thus his job, permanently. And there would be no way he could keep up the monthly maintenance fees for his baby sister's private room at the Brightstar Nursing Facility.

Seven

So, she'd had a bad day. And what did Laura do? She'd acted out like a spoiled child. Hysterical tears and slamming doors. Knocking . . .something . . .off the wall and causing a glass explosion in the hallway. Surprisingly, Miller had put up with it, not erupted at her in fury. She was lucky he hadn't told her to pack her shit and leave.

Wrapped in her grandmother's quilt, she made her way to the living room. It was empty. Had he changed his mind? Then she heard the tailgate slam in the driveway. Ah. He was still putting his tools away.

Miller's living room had a cozy feel, even though the suede upholstery, heavy wooden side tables, and oversized flat screen marked it clearly as a man-cave. There were little touches, here and there, that jarred the image. The fluted shades on the lamps in a delicate shade of butterscotch. A framed, antique-looking print of yellow and white gladiolas on one wall. The chocolate brown valances over the window—plain, if not for the scalloped edges sporting ivory fringe.

Angie must have been have had a hand in this, she thought. No man she'd ever known would opt for fringed window treatments or flower prints. Hell, he probably didn't even know what kind of flowers they were. Yet Miller didn't seem to be the kind of man who'd allow a woman to frilly up his place.

Another conundrum, she thought. Miller Stanford was surely a puzzle.

The homey touches caused a cramp in Laura's chest, which she guessed could be called homesickness. But for where? She hadn't had a real home in a long time. Not since those few summers with Grandma. The memory brought with them a fresh wave of tears.

She'd been thirteen when her parents had sat her down at the kitchen table of their modest bi-level on Vincent Drive, both wearing serious expressions that made her stomach cramp. Was one of them sick? Cancer, maybe? God, she hoped not. Had Daddy lost his job? He was the chief of police, and very popular in Middletown. How could *that* possibly have happened? But the news, when it came, was worse, at least to her just-barely-a-teenager's mind.

Mom and Dad were getting a divorce.

Separating, permanently. Laura would get to see both of them still, as much as she wanted, they'd said. But for the foreseeable future, they'd both thought it best that she lived most of the time with Daddy.

Why? Laura remembered thinking. I'm a girl—why wouldn't I live with Mom? Where was *she* going? And most importantly, why were she and Dad not going to live together anymore?

That was the day her entire life split into two factions, divided onto two planes—neither one at ground level. Just like their house on Vincent Drive.

It was nearing the end of her last year in Twin Towers Middle School, so the future seemed scary enough for Laura, even without this drastic announcement. Next year she'd be starting at Middletown High, and although most of her classmates would be moving up with her, it would still be different. Different building, different crowd. One where she'd be one of the youngest in the school, and no longer one of the oldest.

And now, this.

She'd spent that summer with her grandmother, Charlotte, her mom's mother, in the tiny cottage where she lived in Bloomingburg, a town or two away. Grandma Charlotte dedicated the remainder of that surreal summer to gently explaining to Laura why her parents' marriage had fallen apart. Even though, Laura got the distinct feeling, Grandma didn't understand the reasons any better than she did.

Truth was, Laura had felt abandoned by her mother, though at the time she couldn't understand why. At barely thirteen, she was convinced it must have been her fault. Something Laura had done wrong. Failed at. And no matter how hard her father tried to make up for the lack of female influence in her high school years, Laura was always left feeling just a little less than the young woman she'd hoped to be.

Then, just a few years ago, when she almost lost Daddy to that massive heart attack, the relief of his recovery had been tainted with the news that he was getting remarried. He was in love again, with Deirdre. Silly, childish, yes. She freely admitted that. But she still could not help but feel he was abandoning her. Moving on with his life, when she still—even at twenty-six years old—didn't quite feel confident in her own skin.

Laura swiped at her eyes with the quilt when she heard the front door open and shut. Miller came around the corner slowly, silently, like one would approach an animal they didn't want to spook. She could feel his eyes on her.

He sat down, not on the couch next to her, but on the recliner tucked off down one end. Then he leaned his elbows on his knees, and in a deep, rumbling tone that made her chest ache, said, "So tell me what happened today."

A sob escaped without her permission, but she was so tired. And so disheartened.

"Is your boss an asshole?" Miller prodded.

She shook her head, and swallowed hard. "Not an asshole," she sputtered, struggling for control as she turned to meet his gaze. "A pompous bitch."

Miller closed his eyes and huffed. "That can be worse. Do you have to work very closely with her?"

Again, she shook her head, another wave of tears welling. "No. I'm working closely, and sharing an office with, a guy who looks like he was spawned in Middle Earth." She sniffed and blotted her eyes with the edge of the quilt. "One who got kicked out, because he was too weird to stay."

One side of Miller's lips quirked, but then his eyebrows drew together as his gaze slid off to one side. When it flashed back to hers, his smile was gone. "Don't tell me they have you working with Jonathan."

Laura bobbed her head and hiccupped. "Jonath-It."

When Miller's head fell back and he burst into raucous laughter, she felt her skin prickle. Wiggling a little taller in her seat, she thrust her chin out and snipped, "It's not funny. Not the least bit funny."

His laughter faded slowly and he shook his head. "I'm sorry, Laura, but I've known Jonathan ever since he started working at the clinic. He's the one I have to check in with for five o'clock rounds. I always wondered where he was from," he paused, one edge of that perfect mouth curving up, "but you nailed it. Middle Earth. Exactly." He laughed again, a friendly sound that washed over her like a warm wave. "And to think I was worried about the crazy patients you'd be dealing with."

Worried. Now why on earth would he be worried about anything that had to do with her?

Despite her despair, her exhaustion, and her tattered pride, Laura felt a giggle forming like bubbles from seltzer in her chest. Her lips twitched, and she struggled to maintain her serious demeanor. But the sound of his laughter, and to hear he'd been worried about her . . .

The two of them sat there laughing until tears were streaming down Laura's face, but not sad ones now. Finally, Miller rose and held his hand out to her. "Come on, Galadriel. Let me fix you something to eat."

A half-hour later, Laura sat at Miller's kitchen table gingerly sipping on a bowl of Campbell's chicken soup—with stars—while she watched him squint and swear at his laptop screen.

"So, what are you trying to do, anyway? Balance the checkbook?" she asked. She picked up the piece of cinnamon raisin toast he'd made for her and nibbled on the sweet crust.

Now here's a man who knows how to do comfort food.

For a long moment, he didn't answer. She considered just leaving him to whatever it was that was causing his facial features to contort and dance in a way she found completely adorable. When he finally did look up and say, "Huh?" she'd almost forgotten what she'd asked.

She chuckled, nearly choking on a mouthful of soup. "I asked if you were balancing the checkbook."

Miller snorted, then shot her a glance over the top of the screen. "Hardly. Haven't even wanted to attempt that since Angie ran out." As if suddenly reminded, he fixed her with a quizzical glare. "What kind of deal did she work out with you, anyway? I mean, my checks come from the same place yours will. And that would be only twice a month. Your first one, probably not until you've been there a whole month."

The instant clenching of her gut doused her hunger immediately, and she laid her spoon down on the napkin beside the bowl. Keeping her gaze fixed on the tiny stars floating in the broth, she murmured, "I know. Angie told me not to worry about it, just to catch up when I got paid." She looked up. "But I don't expect you to honor that. I can ask my father for a loan—"

"No. No, that's not necessary. I don't think there's another bus trip to Monticello until next month this time."

Now it was her turn to tip her head with a "Huh?"

But he shook his and muttered, "Never mind." His lips flattened and he closed his eyes, resting his forehead on his hand. He was struggling with something. But it was none of her business.

The moment stretched out and she finally asked softly, "Can I help you with whatever you *are* trying to do?"

He opened his eyes and grabbed her gaze. "I'm trying to find a fucking classroom in this little flat, metal box," he said, clutching the sides of his laptop as if he'd like to crush it like a beer can.

She tilted her head. "What do you mean?"

"I'm taking an online class. Would you mind giving me the Cliff-Notes version on how to find the damned *classroom*?" he asked, sounding as though every word caused him pain to utter.

Ah. The man doesn't like to admit defeat. Or God forbid, ask for help.

She rose and came around to stand at his shoulder, and that's when his scent hit her. Not cologne, or shampoo, or Irish Spring. Or shaving cream or aftershave, she realized. Today, it was obvious he hadn't shaved, as a wheat-colored stubble covered his jaw.

No, it was the scent of the man, rising off his warm skin and enveloping her senses. Wild, feral, a little musky. And what it did to the muscles in her middle—and lower—hit Laura by surprise.

His hair looked like he'd let it dry straight out of the shower, since it stuck out over his ears and one unruly hank hung over his brow. At the nape, the ends were curling into a perfectly formed flip. His Yankees jersey hung loosely over his massive chest, but didn't disguise the bulbous forearms that made her think of Popeye. A cute, very sexy Popeye.

She cleared her throat and leaned in, trying to ignore the herd of butterflies that had just erupted in her stomach.

"Here," she pointed to the top right corner of the screen, "is your nav bar."

"My *what*?" he croaked.

She stifled a chuckle. "Navigation bar. See these tabs along here? If you click on them, each one takes you to a different screen." She pointed to the tab marked *Chat*. "I think your classroom discussions would probably be posted in here."

"So how the hell was I supposed to know that? I'm taking a class, not looking for buddies to chat with."

As he turned his head toward her to speak, she could smell the beer on his breath and noticed the two bottles sitting on the other side of his laptop. But he didn't seem drunk, not even tipsy. As big a guy as he was, it probably took a lot before you could tell he'd been drinking.

Down, Counselor Horton. She mentally slapped at the judgmental voice in her head.

"Want one? Got plenty," he said, his tone casual, dipping his head toward the beer.

She studied his face before answering, seeing no defensiveness there. "No, thanks," she replied, shaking her head. Then she quickly continued, nodding towards the computer screen. "Chat rooms. That's how these classes work, most of them. The instructor forms a place where people taking the class can post comments, or questions. Or have discussions." She smiled into his eyes, those pewter ones that held her gaze so intently. Her heart rate kicked up. Taking a step back, she said, "Click on it." Then she swallowed.

The demand sounded so . . .*evocative.*

He held her gaze for another long moment, one in which she could swear the temperature in the room spiked about twenty degrees. His mouth quirked up on one side as he turned back to his laptop and clicked on the tab as she'd asked. Another window opened revealing a list—a *long* list—of messages.

"Holy shit. Guess I'm a little behind on the *classroom participation.*" He laced the last two words with wry sarcasm.

Smiling, Laura laid a hand on his shoulder. It was broad and hard, and the feel of his muscles under her fingertips shot electricity through her. Taking a deep breath, she struggled to focus.

"I'm sure it's not as bad as it looks," she said. "Just scroll through and read a few posts, and respond to the ones you feel like you know something about. Show the instructor you're actively participating, and that you're reading the lectures." She paused, raising an eyebrow. "At least, that you're skimming them."

Laura watched him click and read for a few moments before passing around between Miller's chair and the kitchen counter, where she caught sight of the broken photo frame. The jagged glass fragments clung pitifully to the inner edges of what appeared to be a somewhat aged team photo. She bit her lip.

"I'm sorry about your picture. I'll get you a new frame," she said, lifting the image to study it. A group picture of a football team. High school, maybe? She easily picked out Miller, the tallest, broadest one standing at one end of the rear lineup, his helmet tucked under one arm. "Is this you?" she asked, pointing.

He glanced over and cleared his throat, hesitating a beat too long before answering. "Yeah, that's me. High school football. We made the championship playoffs. They took that picture when we qualified." His voice was strangely flat and thick. Not buoyant with pride, as she might have expected. There was an undercurrent to his tone. Almost . . .what? Remorse?

"Cool," she said, not really knowing what else to say. Afraid to ask for more. She looked over and found he'd turned away from her, hunched even closer to his laptop screen. This was obviously a topic he didn't want to talk about.

Laura returned to her seat and tried another spoonful of the soup. But the comfort food wasn't as enticing as it had been a few minutes earlier. She stirred the bowl and watched the stars swirl and spin wildly to the surface before disappearing again.

We have a lot in common right now, she said silently to the tiny stars. Swirling aimlessly, with no control over where we're headed. In an endless sea of golden broth. In, for sure, over our heads.

After a moment, Miller glanced up, his eyes traveling from the bowl to her face and back. He nodded toward her soup. "Now, don't stop eating. You're gonna need every ounce of strength you can muster to ward off the romantic advances of old Jon . . .what did you call him?" he asked through a chuckle.

"Jonath-It," she spat, bristling. "Now my appetite is completely gone. Thank you very much."

"Oh, come on. Lighten up. It'll get better. I'll bet in no time you'll be the Hobbit's boss-lady." He winked and tipped his chin toward her soup. "Eat."

Laura started to push away from the table, but Miller caught hold of her wrist. A hot thrill rippled up her arm and across her shoulder blades. His hand was calloused and huge. But warm, and very, very gentle. He held her as though she were a piece of fine bone china that he was afraid he'd splinter. She raised her eyes to his face.

"Why do you care?" she murmured, tilting her head.

He held her gaze intently, and again, she saw that . . .something. Some emotion swimming in his eyes, but she couldn't quite name it. It surprised her. It made her chest tighten, and her cheeks feel flushed.

And it scared her to death.

"I don't know." He said the words so softly, she almost didn't hear him, his head shaking slightly side to side. Looking down, he turned her hand over so her wrist was exposed, then started moving his thumb in small circles ever so gently on the sensitive spot over her pulse. "You're so fair. So . . .delicate. I can't help wanting to protect—"

She shuddered, and his movement abruptly ceased.

"I'm sorry. Are you cold?" Miller released her wrist and stood. He moved to the window, lowering the sash where an ever-strengthening breeze billowed the curtains on the threat of another evening storm.

This was so not the picture of the man Angie had painted. No insensitive, selfish monster. Instead, a kind, considerate—if not a little goofy—guy. But in a charming way.

When he turned back around and caught her staring at him, he rounded the table's edge and grasped her shoulders, lifting her to her feet. Dumbly, she let him. Partly from shock, another part from the fact that these last few days had taken every ounce of fight out of her she'd ever had.

If she'd ever had any at all.

She gazed up into his eyes, glowing silver and boring into hers, as though he were speaking to her without words. A chill slithered up her spine as he leaned closer, their faces only inches apart. His scent enveloped her, and her knees went weak.

In that moment, if he had kissed her, she wouldn't have stopped him. It's what she wanted right then, and badly. *Needed.* For him to hold her in those big, strong arms and rock her, murmuring into her hair while she buried her face into his strong chest.

But he didn't. Instead, he released her, taking a step back as he grabbed the hem of his own shirt with both hands and slipped it over his head. He turned it right side out, then fitted the neckline over her crown. One at a time, as though she were a helpless child, he slid her arms into the sleeves and pulled the jersey down over her hips.

He didn't even try to cop a feel of her butt.

Standing there before her, bare-chested, broad, and veiled with golden hair, Laura felt suddenly warmer. Perhaps not only from the jersey now hanging over her shoulders.

"There. Fixed." He smiled down at her, and Laura felt all the anguish and disappointment of the day melt like dripping ice cream on a hot summer day. With a soft push, he seated her back into the chair, lifted her spoon, and held it out to her.

"Now, eat. Please."

Laura drew in a shaky breath and blew it out. She looked down at the stars floating in the bowl, then back up at Miller. Finally, she took the spoon out of his hand and said, "If you're still offering, I think I'll take that beer now."

Eight

The next morning, Miller lay with his hands crossed under his head. He stared up at his bedroom ceiling and listened to the incessant whine of Laura's blow dryer echoing up the stairs.

Why does she do that to her beautiful curls? And why in the holy hell should I care?

He was more confused now than he'd ever been in his life. In the past seventy-two hours, he'd gone from breathing-fire mad (when Angie stalked out) to complete shock (to find Laura on his doorstep) to . . .to, what? Something strange was happening here. He was experiencing a drastic shift in the way he reacted to things. What was different now that had been missing before?

Caring.

He'd never felt a sense of loss at losing Angie. When she announced she was leaving, all he felt was rage. How dare she, after he'd practically supported her all the way through her college degree?

No grief. No broken heart. Not even a twinge.

Wow. He'd been so wrapped up in his own world, his own problems and goals and set-in-stone routine he hadn't even noticed his feelings for Angie had evaporated like early morning mist. He wondered how long it had been that way. Figured it was probably why she had turned into a class-A bitch over the last few months. And then went job-hunting—far, far away from him.

Heartless, selfish bastard. She'd called him that as she stalked down the steps with the last box of her shit pressed up against her huge cushion of boobage. That had stung a bit. Not losing access to the rack, but the *heartless* comment.

Miller knew, at times, he could be selfish. But heartless? That struck a bit closer to home. He sure must be, though. Because other than worrying about who was going to run errands and help pay the electric bill, he hadn't yet felt one moment of anguish since Angie screeched away in her crappy little car.

In fact, the first thing he'd done was go back into the kitchen to make sure she'd stocked the fridge with beer like he'd asked her to. Then he'd snatched one out, popped off the cap and slammed the metal disc into the trash can with the force of a bullet.

And now here he was, lying in bed, asking himself why he wanted so badly to go down and talk to Laura before she left for work. Another woman. And one he'd known only a few days.

What was happening to him? Was he becoming a complete soft-ass pussy? Was the protective shield he'd erected around his heart crumbling? Maybe he was just horny as hell.

So, he forced himself to lie there, listening to her travel up and down the hall from the bathroom to the kitchen in her flip-flops.

Clap-clap-clap.

Then back from the kitchen to her room.

Clap-clap-clap.

A few minutes later he heard her bedroom door latch shut. Shortly after that, the click of heels on hardwood. Then the jingle of something metal . . .her keys.

He bolted upright. She was leaving.

Miller nearly fell over his own feet running down the stairs to catch her before she left, to say goodbye and wish her a better day. But as he reached the last step, he heard the front door *thunk*. Standing at the end of the hallway in his underwear and bare feet, he listened. The deadbolt clicked, and he felt his heart sink. And also, like a complete idiot.

Miller sighed and climbed back up to his room, flopping down on the bed. He didn't have to be at work until three, but he had to get a haircut before punching in today, for sure. And he hadn't worked out in three days—better get his ass down to the gym. He glanced at the clock. He figured he'd have time to run by the barber and still make it to the gym before nine, when Rip usually got there.

When he got down to the kitchen and saw his laptop still sitting on the table, he groaned. Got homework to do too. And *class participation.*

Shit on dry rye.

By noon he was back home, showered and shaved and ready to tackle his online class. Or so he thought.

How did technology get so far ahead of me?

Miller spent the first hour clicking aimlessly around on his classroom site, trying to catch up. He finally found the lecture, all fourteen pages of it. Single-spaced. Before he got a third of the way through, his eyes were crossing and he had fallen into a repetitive fit of yawns.

God, this stuff's as dull as dry oatmeal. How am I ever going to get through this course?

But when his iPhone dinged to indicate a message, he got a brisk reminder from his calendar.

Brightstar payment: due on April 29th

A stinging reminder. That's why he had to get through these courses, and get his degree. That's why, no matter how boring or painful the time spent, he really had no choice. He'd made up his mind, years ago, that his sister was going to have the best care possible for the rest of her life. Even though it hadn't been his failing that stole her life away from her.

On Miller's eighteenth birthday, in his senior year of high school, was when it happened. The event that changed everything.

Middletown High's football team had made the regionals, and he was their star quarterback. The first game took place in Albany, two hours from Middletown, and his sister Mollie begged him— *begged him*—to pick her up early from middle school and drive her there. He did that sometimes, for home games. To the funny looks from his coach, and the incessant teasing of his teammates. But she was his only sibling, his baby sister, and she idolized him.

And oh, how he adored her.

But this day, the first game of the playoffs, Coach warned him, reminding him of the strict rule—he *had* to ride with the team on the bus.

He'd also informed Miller that talent scouts would be there, particularly one Coach personally knew, from Notre Dame. Miller could well earn his complete college education, maybe even get picked up by a pro team, if he just kept his head where it needed to be. On the game.

"Please, Mills, *please*. I'll bring my pom-poms and cheer for you from the stands. You know I'm your good luck charm." Mollie bounced up and down beside him that morning, her hands fisted in the hem of his tee shirt as he combed his hair. He watched her in the mirror, her tumble of curls bouncing around her face like chocolate brown Slinkees. His heart clutched.

"I can't this time, Molls. I just can't. It's against the rules. Coach said so. But Dad's bringing you. And you can bring your pom-poms and sit right at the top of the bleachers. I'll be able to see you through the whole game."

He wasn't sure if her little-girl pout and the sheen of tears in her eyes signified pre-teen drama or real disappointment. Mollie had just turned ten years old.

Ten minutes before kick-off, warm-ups were over. Still, his father and sister had not arrived. Miller found it hard to concentrate on the conversations around him, people he'd been introduced to. The rep from Notre Dame, Dennis Wayland, was a tall, broad man in a suit that might have fit him ten years ago. Now his open jacket gapped around a decidedly extended gut. Miller guessed it would take a team of Budweiser horses to get the buttons to match up with the holes.

Hell, it was probably Budweisers that caused the gap in the first place.

Just before kick-off, Wayland shook his hand and complimented him on his talent. Miller thanked him and shrugged, but couldn't come up with anything else to say that might convince the scout his heart was enthusiastically set on a professional football career.

Miller was distracted, consumed with a bad feeling stirring in the pit of his stomach. His gaze strayed continually back to the stands. He scanned the top row of bleachers, again and again, looking for Mollie's Middie-Blue and white pom-poms. The ones he'd bought for her birthday last month.

Dad had given him his word. He would leave work a little early, swing by and pick up Mollie, and be there in plenty of time.

Coach Bronson pulled him aside.

"What the hell are you looking for? Didn't your latest lay make it today?"

Miller had a hard time controlling his temper then. A bolus of fury bubbled up in his throat, mixing with the worry and nerves. His fist clenched and itched for impact. But he swallowed the sour ball of bile, remembering that no matter how bad he was feeling, he had to maintain respect for his coach.

"My father is bringing my little sister," he growled through gritted teeth. "They're not here yet. I'm worried something's happened to them."

Bronson's eyes narrowed and turned flinty. "Wipe those girly-ass emotions off your face and get your head out of your ass. They probably hit traffic or something. Don't you realize it's your future on the line here, boy? You brushed Dennis Wayland off like a fly, and don't think he took that too lightly. He came to see you play. *You*," he hissed, poking a finger into Miller's chest.

By halftime, Miller had resigned himself to the fact that dear old Dad had let him down. Again. Both of them. He *and* Mollie. He'd probably forgotten all about his promise. Stopped at the pub on the way home to down a few, and was home right now, sprawled on the couch in a drunken stupor. While Mollie cried into her pillow up in her room.

If only.

Miller blew the game, missing several critical passes he shouldn't have, and fumbled three times in the second half. Every time the ball skittered out of his grip, he looked down at his hands, convinced they belonged to somebody else. Like his brain wasn't communicating with them. As though his mind was already preparing him for something traumatic. Pre-shock. Or something.

The more mistakes he made, the more Coach Bronson railed him.

The rep from Notre Dame left before they'd even started the final quarter. Middletown High's team, the one that hadn't lost a game the entire season, got walloped, 37-22. Miller blew the chance of a lifetime, a fact the coach kept shouting at him over and over in the locker room after the game.

When he saw the uniformed officers waiting outside the gym, the bitterness in Miller's heart turned to panic, and then ominous dread when they started toward him. That's when he spotted his mother in the back seat of the cruiser, sobbing violently into a handkerchief.

He never picked up a football again.

Miller punched in three minutes before three, signed out his weapon, and ignored the doe eyes Patricia gave him.

"Aw, you went and had it all cut off," she moaned, scrutinizing his haircut.

"Is that why Rip shaves his head?" he barked. "So you can't bug him about his hair?"

She slid him a sly smile. "I get to do more with Rip than just look at him, Stanford. With you, it's all about the eye candy."

Miller rolled his eyes and headed for the cruiser.

The day was overcast, warm, and humid. Sarge told him to be sure to check out the rear perimeter of the fence surrounding Talcott Hall, as the afternoon patrol reported a break in the fence.

A break in a chain link fence? Around an abandoned old building? What kind of bored, destructive crazies do we have in this town?

But he'd nodded and tipped his hat to Sarge before heading down to Talcott Hall.

It was the oldest, and one of the biggest, buildings on the site. At one time, it had housed the most violent, the most disturbed of the patients. But the huge brick structure had been vacant since the late nineties.

Why the State didn't just rip the sucker down, Miller couldn't be sure. He suspected it had something to do with the cost of disposing of asbestos and lead. The State was probably just waiting until it collapsed on its own, when the cost of removal would be covered by disaster funds.

As he pulled up Bolles Ave. along the front of the building, he couldn't help but cast a glance toward the Crisis Center, right across the street. He wondered how Laura was holding out today. That Jonathan character was creepy as hell, but he wasn't dangerous. Miller was sure it was just the ick factor that had Laura all freaked out last night. And Jonathan certainly ranked high on the ick scale.

Speaking of things disgusting, the sight of the fence encircling the building made his lip curl. The chain link acted as a wind filter for all the litter people tossed out of their windows as they drove down Monhagen Ave. The bright red and white logos of Wendy's, McDonalds, and Burger King clung to the north side of the fence like cheap, ill-planned billboard advertising. Miller slowly followed the road to where it ended, and pulled the cruiser up onto the grass. He'd have to walk from here on around.

A job best done in daylight. Otherwise, he rationalized, how could he see where the fence had been breached? He climbed out of the cruiser and rested one hand on his baton and the other on his gun.

The weeds on the backside were overgrown, almost chest-high in places. The ten or twelve-foot wide ledge of solid ground beyond the fence fell off into a marshy stream, so he was careful to hug the line. But after yesterday's rain, his boots sunk in the soft earth, in places almost to the ankle. When he felt water seeping in around the laces, he swore.

He'd gotten about halfway down the length of the stretch—no small distance, at least a hundred feet—when he spotted it.

The lower edge of the chain link was twisted and ruined. Damn, somebody must have wanted in pretty bad. It would have taken a sizable pair of bolt cutters to clip the metal ties holding the fence to the post and rail. It would have also taken a very strong man, or three, to wrench that steel mesh up and off to one side, like a medieval curtain. And secure it with a big hook suspended from a length of heavy-duty steel chain.

Holy shit. What the hell *is* that?

Calling for backup, Miller's heart rate kicked up a notch. There'd been incidents of kids climbing over the top of the fence. But nobody had ever done this kind of damage to the formidable perimeter security before.

Thank God it was still daylight. He and Duvall would have to perform a search.

They began in the large, front room on the first floor, where they found the homeless guy curled up in a corner. He was illuminated by a patch of sunlight eking its way through the web of vines that clung to what was left of the window. Miller felt a chill ripple his shoulders.

The room was creepy enough in its own right. Spray-painted graffiti covered the peeling, puke-green plaster walls. Overturned chairs and tables littered the floor, along with an old sofa with the stuffing spilling out of it.

And along the back wall of the giant room, lined up like foreboding sentries, were three crude plywood boxes. With padded satin linings. Coffins.

The man was old—very old—with a long, straggly grey beard and a matching pallor that made Miller wonder, when they first spotted him, if he was dead. Weapons drawn, he and Duvall approached slowly. Miller hugged the wall opposite the one with the coffins, never taking his eyes off the man. His partner flanked him a few steps to his left, sweeping the area with his eyes and his gun. Every nerve in Miller's body jittered as though he'd stuck his finger in an electric socket. He could barely hear over the pounding of blood in his ears.

The ancient man wore tatters. A faded denim jacket with one shoulder seam torn open covered what looked like a filthy tee shirt and equally dirty jeans. They were five sizes too big for him, and hung in loose folds over a body that couldn't comprise much more than skin covering bone. Miller didn't know which emotion to side with—the repulsion, or the pity he was feeling simultaneously.

"Hey. Hey there. Old man," he barked.

No movement.

The pallid skin stretched over the man's cheekbones was nearly white and looked papery thin. Miller couldn't tell if it was from a coating of dust, or the effects, perhaps, of post-mortem blanching. Parched, cracked lips framed a mouth hanging open, revealing a swollen, turtle-like tongue, round and dry. Miller halted and strained to see if he could see the man's chest moving. Under his baggy clothes, it was impossible to tell.

"Old man. Hey. You don't belong in here," Miller said again, nearly shouting this time. Still, no reaction.

As he drew closer, a flicker of movement caused Miller to flinch and tighten his grip on his weapon. But it wasn't coming from the old man. Just above the grizzled, old head, a tiny, industrious spider was busy fashioning a web. A gossamer thread stretched from the brick wall behind to the strands of frizzy, white hair fanning out around the too-still, too-pale face. Miller's stomach turned over on itself.

Shit. We got a stiff.

Over his shoulder, Miller said, "Call for EMS. And the coroner. I think we're too late." When he got close enough to reach out with one booted foot, Miller nudged the body's torso.

When the man's eyes flew open and he howled, Miller stumbled back, his heart pounding deafeningly between his ears.

"Fuck!" he heard Duvall's shocked reaction, then the message he barked into the radio. "Porter? You copy? Get that ambulance here. Stat."

Nine

An hour later, Miller stood beside Roger Duvall along the backside of the chain link border surrounding Talcott Hall. They watched as one of the maintenance crew wielded an enormous bolt cutter.

"Is that a meat hook or what?" Duvall muttered, chewing on one end of a reed he'd plucked as he'd followed Miller into the brush.

"Haven't the foggiest," Miller replied. "I've never seen anything like it. But I know one thing. That pitiful old guy they just hauled off in the ambulance couldn't possibly have done this. I'll bet he couldn't even lift that thing."

The maintenance guy, Roy, was so ancient Miller had to wonder why he was still on the job. But his hands, their bumpy gnarls distorting the blue surface of the Nitrile gloves he wore, wielded the tool expertly. As short as he was, he had to lift it almost to eye level in order to cut the chain securing the hook apparatus to the fence. With a grunt, he heaved the handles of the tool together and the chain snapped. The strange-looking object fell to the grass with a heavy thump.

"It took more than one man—and strong ones at that—to lift the chain link up this high," Roy said, then coughed and spit into the weeds as he knelt to examine the hook. "What I'd like to know is . . .why?"

Good question, Miller thought. This was no random act of vandalism, and had taken some real effort. What kind of statement had the crazy bastards been trying to make?

"What the hell is that thing?" Duvall asked.

"This here's a prosthesis," Roy said.

Miller blinked and glanced over at Duvall, who didn't even try to hide his smirk.

"A what?" they asked in unison.

"The guys who lost a hand in the war," he hesitated, glancing over his shoulder, "one of them wars, anyway. Well, this is what they fitted them with. So they could still pick things up." Roy straightened and lifted the hook, examining it.

Miller leaned closer as he snapped on the pair of gloves he had tucked in his belt. The steel tongs of the hook emerged from a tan, plastic tube of sorts, about as big around as a man's forearm. A leather harness was attached to the plastic with rivets, and there were several straps dangling from it. Narrowing his eyes, he tried to imagine how one might attach this to the stump of an amputated limb, and grimaced.

"Looks antique. How old do you think it is?" Miller asked.

"Well, it's two-prong, and they've been around for over a hundred years. But by the looks of this leather, I'd say this one can't be more than twenty, thirty years old, maybe."

"So, Vietnam era?" Duvall asked, holding open the rim of the evidence bag. Miller slid the contraption inside.

Roy nodded. "Yup, probably. What it's doing out here, holding up a chain link fence, I have no idea." He turned toward them. "You guys find anything inside?"

"Just the homeless guy. We thought we had a stiff on our hands. But he was still breathing. Poor bastard," Miller muttered, shaking his head. "There was no way he could have done this." He lifted a hand toward the fence.

Roy squinted up at him. "This here *his* prosthesis?"

Miller hesitated a minute, unsure of what Roy was asking. Then he said, "No. He had both his hands. But he wasn't in any condition to answer too many questions when we found him." He tilted his head and studied Roy. "So, how come you know so much about artificial body parts? How'd you know what that thing even was?"

Roy coughed again and pulled a filthy handkerchief out of his back pocket to wipe his mouth. He pressed his lips into a grim line as he handed the hook apparatus to Miller. "My older brother served in 'Nam. Came back with a stump in place of his right hand." Roy looked down, shaking his head. "He never was the same," he added, his voice tinged with sadness.

"I'm sorry," Miller said, realizing as soon as the words left his lips what a lame, overused sentiment it was.

"Me too," Roy snapped back. "I was only fifteen when he came home that way. I had nightmares for years. But my brother's over it now. Yes, indeedy. Ain't bothering him one bit anymore."

Miller glanced over at his partner in the ominous silence that followed, but Duvall just shrugged and lifted an eyebrow.

Roy cleared his throat and went on. "Six months later, we found him hanging from the rafters in our basement." He lifted his watery blue gaze to Miller's. "Not three feet away, he'd nailed the leather straps of his hook—his *prosthesis*—to one of the support posts. Hung it there like a fucking trophy."

That night shift was one of the longest Miller could remember. Roy's story, and the image of the hook-for-a-hand, kept spinning around in his head in a sickening cyclone. Duvall punched out early, around ten, leaving Miller to patrol the entire campus on his own. He wasn't sure if the change of scenery was a blessing or a curse, since he was so damned jittery. Wound tighter than a transformer coil, he was cocked and ready to jump at anyone and anything who appeared in the glare of his headlights.

Not a good way to be when you're carrying a loaded gun, along with a club that could bash somebody's brains to a pulp in a fit of panic.

So when the little girl appeared from around the rear corner of the fence surrounding Talcott Hall, Miller stomped on the brakes so hard he left three feet of rubber.

Although the weeds were tall along the side of the enclosure, the child appeared to almost drift through them, without causing the grasses to so much as sway. Miller froze and swallowed as she drew nearer, traveling way faster than somebody her size should be able. Especially without running, which she wasn't.

He'd seen her three or four times before, and had even spoken to her once. Unlike many of the homeless who showed up seeking shelter, she wasn't dressed in rags. Tonight, her bright pink top glowed in the beam from his headlights. Almost pulsated. And although he couldn't see anyone else, she was speaking, animatedly. Apparently to herself.

He threw the car in park and climbed out slowly, half afraid he'd scare her off. More afraid she'd disappear into the misty night air, leaving him wondering—again—if he'd imagined the whole damned episode.

It wasn't until he'd stood and closed the door behind him that he saw her companion. The man was stooped and round-shouldered, hobbling along through the weeds with a bad limp. Almost dragging one leg behind him. His hair was classic homeless street bum, long and grey and stringy. His eyes, when he raised them, were sharp and clear blue, piercing the space between them with such intensity it made Miller's heart rate kick up to a gallop.

The instant his gaze met Miller's, the old man stopped, immediately silencing his young companion with a raised arm across the front of her chest.

Part of an arm. His right arm ended in a blunt, misshapen bulb about six inches above where a wrist would have been.

Miller sucked in a gasp and staggered backward a step, instinctively clutching the butt of his pistol.

Holy shit. *This is the guy who breached the fence.*

It took only a few seconds before Miller regained his composure and stepped forward. This man was guilty of trespassing, and destroying state property. Time to do his job.

"Stop right there," he barked. "Sir, I need to ask you some questions."

Neither responded, and for a moment, Miller wondered if they might both turn and run. The last thing he wanted to do was to start a pursue-and-apprehend by himself, in the dark, in the tall grass growing out of muck so thick it could suck your shoes off. Great night for fucking Duvall to cop out early, he thought bitterly, trying to tamp down his nerves with anger.

But the pair didn't flee, didn't move or say a thing. He took another step toward them, saying, "Come out here in the open and keep your hands within view."

All *three* hands. Christ.

As Miller spoke, their images began to flicker. Both figures wavered in the light beam ahead of him, as objects do through heat rising off pavement. Confused, Miller blinked and freed one hand to scrub his face, squinting to clear his vision. He squeezed his eyes shut and swiped his forearm across them, but when he opened them, the man was gone.

Miller hadn't heard a sound, no footsteps or grasses rustling. The man had simply disappeared.

Damn, he may look like an old bum, but that sucker sure could move quick, he thought.

The little girl looked around her, seeming as startled as Miller was that she was suddenly standing alone. Then her face crumpled and she sank to the grass. Covering her face with both hands, she started sobbing uncontrollably—agonized, heartbreaking sobs that tore at Miller's heart.

A heart that was pounding in his ears now, so loud he was surprised he heard her cries at all. But they echoed in the silence, in the darkness, resonating with pain Miller felt more than heard. As though the sounds were coming from inside his own head.

Hands shaking, he reached for his radio, then swore. Duvall was gone. There was nobody else out here. At least not until the next officer showed up at eleven to relieve him.

Miller stepped forward slowly, expecting at any moment the girl to do the same disappearing act as her companion. But she did not. When he was within an arm's reach away, he crouched down so he was at eye level with the child, whose face was still hidden behind trembling, little girl hands. With fingernails painted a brilliant pink that matched her blouse.

"Hey, hey," he murmured, reaching out toward her. But oddly, even though he was sure he'd gotten close enough to touch her, he couldn't reach. It was as though his arm just wasn't long enough.

A cold chill washed over him. This was getting too freaking weird.

"Hey. Little girl. Let me help you," he tried again, and she finally lowered her hands. She was younger than he'd first thought— ten, maybe. Tears streaked her reddened cheeks, glistening in the beam of his headlights. Her pale, golden hair was baby fine and wispy, but tousled and disheveled. As though it hadn't seen a brush in good long time.

She met his gaze with eyes like the man's, clear and blue and strangely luminescent. The sadness Miller saw behind them made his chest ache.

"Where did your friend go, sweetheart? The man who came out with you. Where did he go?"

She stared at him with lips quivering before her face crumpled again. "I don't know. I don't know where Daddy is. I've been looking and looking for him. Every time I think I've found him, he goes away."

Miller swallowed. Yeah, that's one way to describe the mysterious vanishing act.

He drew in a breath and tried again. "What's your name, sweetie? Was that your daddy with you?"

Head bobbing, the tears flowed freely now, and she wouldn't take her eyes off Miller's face. He felt a lump growing in his own throat, as though she was somehow transferring her pain to him. His hands, clasped in front of him, began to shake.

When she spoke again, her voice took on an echoed quality, as though she were receding into an empty culvert. "I'm Greta. And I'm looking for my daddy. He used to live here. But I keep coming back to find him, and nobody knows where he is." She dropped her chin to her chest and ground her knuckles against her eyes.

"Greta," he repeated, a stab of pity piercing his gut. So freaking pathetic. A forlorn little girl . . .his own memories rose up like foul-smelling steam. Swallowing hard, he pressed on. "Greta, honey, what's your last name?"

When she looked up, Miller gasped. Behind her, against the fence, a bright red McDonald's French fry box clung to the base of the chain link. *Directly* behind her, yet he could see it clearly. That's when he realized he could see . . .*right . . .through her.*

Shock seized in his chest, causing his breath to hitch. He staggered to his feet and took a shaky step backward.

I must be imagining this.

When the child spoke again, her voice echoed, as though from within tiled walls.

"Sanderson," she said. "My name is Greta. Greta Sanderson. Can you help me? Can you help find my daddy?" Her voice was fading now, along with her image. Just before she disappeared entirely, her last words cut through Miller's chest like a searing, hot bullet.

"I'm lost. I don't know where to go. I need my daddy."

Ten

"So, you're back in Middletown. Your alma mater. Welcome home."

Sadie Keller was one of Laura's new coworkers, and her exaggerated screech of enthusiasm made Laura wince. They were sitting in the break room a few minutes past noon, and Laura had just finished consuming what had become her customary lunch from the vending machine—a granola bar and bitter coffee.

"Yeah, I'm back," she muttered. "But somehow I don't feel like I've come home."

A hefty woman in her early forties, Laura guessed, Sadie's heritage was definitely Mediterranean. Italian, or Spanish. Her jet-black hair cascaded in a violent sheath of ripples past her shoulders, and her ample bust and hips made her the ideal olive-skinned Venus. Her lipstick appeared to have a mind of its own, though, encroaching well beyond the perimeter of her already generous lips.

Sadie worked the front desk, and also acted as the liaison for the Spanish-speaking patients they dealt with. That percentage, Laura learned quickly, was a large one.

"Are you a native?" Laura began, then immediately added, "from Middletown?"

Sadie shook her head, her hair accentuating the movement in dramatic waves. "Nope. Grew up in Jersey," she said, turning to dig around in her slouchy leather purse. "Moved here when I hooked up with Frankie."

She retrieved a pack of Marlboros from her bag, along with an Easter-egg purple lighter. Holding them up apologetically, she said, "My one big vice. Headin' outside for a bit. Wanna join me?"

Laura followed her outside to one of the metal patio tables set behind the building. A graveled area shaded by towering oaks, the patio held a half-dozen tables, a place for the treatment center's temporary occupants to relax or take their meals. Sometimes, Sadie told her, they held counseling sessions out here, when the weather was nice.

Too bad the spot's view was so depressing: the decrepit Talcott Hall, with its massive brick towers and shattered windows. Softened only by the lacy encroachment of vines that covered the chain link fence, as well as the sides of the brick edifice, the building stood ominously close. Right across the street.

As Sadie lit up and puffed, Laura gaze wandered in that direction. "That place is really creepy," she said absently, more to herself than her companion.

But Sadie shot back, "Teelll me! You don't have a freaking clue. You're lucky we don't have to work after dark. Most of the year, anyway." She blew out a stream of smoke that hung in the humid air around her head like a low-slung cloud.

Laura turned toward her and asked, "Why do you say that? Anything weird happen there?"

Sadie bobbed her head, her hair bouncing. "Whoo-whee. Yup." She took another puff and blew the smoke off to the side, then ducked her head low and whispered, "My boyfriend and me, Frankie? Well, one night he picked me up kinda late. It was after the time change and all. It was full dark." She sucked deep on her cigarette, and her dark eyes rounded like a cartoon character's.

When she paused, smoke drifting out of her nose like a Chinese dragon, Laura prompted her. "So? What happened?"

"Well, it wasn't so much what I saw, but what I *felt*," she said, hunching her shoulders up around her ears. She squeezed her eyes shut and shook her head. "There's some bad energy over there, I'll tell you. Bad energy."

"What do you mean?" Laura pressed. "Did you see something? Hear noises? What?"

Sadie drew in a deep breath and blew it out, dropping her cigarette into the damp grass and grounding it out with a red patent-leather clad toe. She shook her head again, but wouldn't meet Laura's gaze.

"I'm telling you, you just need to steer clear of the place after dark. It's when the crazies come out."

"But I thought the last patients were transferred out of that building over twenty years ago," Laura said. "To Rockland, right?"

Sadie fixed her with a serious stare. "Nuh-huh. I'm talking about the ones who never left." She stood then and headed back toward the door, a more than obvious signal to Laura that Sadie wouldn't be sharing anything more.

Laura's curiosity was piqued. When she got off at five o'clock, she decided to take a walk around the perimeter of Talcott Hall. The early evening sun was still quite warm, and she realized within a few minutes that her linen suit and three-inch pumps were not the best attire for an afternoon stroll. But she'd go as far as the intersection, she thought, slinging her jacket over one arm. To the same corner where one of the gates in the chain link was located.

Her shoes swung from her hand at her side, and she soon discovered the pavement was also way too hot for bare feet. The mowed grass poked at her sensitive soles, and after yesterday's rain, was quite squishy in spots. She grimaced and swore when she stepped in one particularly marshy place and a squashed cigarette butt surfaced to catch between her toes.

Yuck.

She'd only gotten about halfway down the length of fence when she heard a car coming up behind her. And then stop.

Turning, Laura saw it was a cruiser.

Great. Now I'll get arrested for wandering around where I shouldn't be.

When the engine died and the car's door opened, she was both relieved and embarrassed to see Miller step out.

"And where the hell do you think you're going, little lady?" he asked, one eyebrow arched and a smile playing around the edges of his lips.

Laura stopped and crossed her arms, jutting her chin. "Are there rules about where I can and can't take a walk around here?" she asked.

Miller's eyes scanned her body, catching on the shoes dangling at her elbow, then on down to her bare feet, now nearly immersed in soggy grass.

"I'd be careful about going barefoot around here. There's broken glass," he paused, pointing toward the ruined building beyond the fence, the one with nary a window left intact, "virtually everywhere."

Laura sniffed and raised her chin. "Not the smartest move I've made recently," she mumbled before meeting his gaze with narrowed eyes, "but I've made quite a few questionable moves in the past week or so, haven't I?"

Miller leaned back against the fender. "There was no way you could know you were heading into the situation Angie left you in."

Heaving a huge sigh and thinking, *No kidding*, Laura twisted her shoulders. She turned and pointed toward Talcott Hall.

"Any way of getting in there to take a look around?" she asked.

Miller hooked a thumb in his gun belt and paused a beat before answering. "Technically, it's off limits to the public. Too dangerous."

Laura sighed and turned to stare at the building. "I sure would like to get a closer look than this fence allows."

She heard his heavy boots clump around the front of the car toward her. When he spoke again, he was so close behind her his breath blew hot on her neck.

"I might be persuaded to give you a tour. Sometime. When Sarge isn't around, anyway."

His voice was low and rumbling, and a hot thrill zinged down her spine causing a veil of damp sweat to coat her skin. She took a step forward, away from him, but when she did, her bare heel slid on the wet grass, down toward the ditch filled with nasty-looking brown water. She flailed both arms in an effort to regain her balance, bopping herself on the side of her head with the heel of one shoe in the process.

"Hey, watch it there," he barked, grabbing her upper arm.

If he hadn't, she'd be on her ass in the muddy grass. Embarrassed, her cheekbone smarting from the smack from her shoe, she stumbled back against his chest, laughing.

"I am such a klutz," she shrieked as she turned to face him.

And there they were, pressed up against one another in broad daylight. In public.

Miller cleared his throat and stepped back, but didn't let go of her arm. "You okay now? Let me give you a ride back to your car," he said, his voice thick. He glanced from side to side over his shoulder. "I'm not really supposed to have any physical contact unless I'm in danger," he added, locking his gaze on hers. "Am I?"

She blinked up at him. He was so much taller—and *bigger*—than she was, and it made her feel small and insignificant, yet safe and protected, all at the same time. Her mind spun out of control, along with her heart rate. The searing rays of the late afternoon sun illuminated his eyes so brilliantly they glowed like silvered glass.

Laura swallowed and looked away, absently rubbing her throbbing cheekbone. "No," she murmured. "Why on earth would you be in trouble?"

Once she was settled into the cruiser beside him, Miller didn't start the engine right away.

"What did Angie tell you about me, Laura?" he asked. "Besides that I was a *heartless, selfish bastard*."

She looked at him for a long moment, then shook her head. "She never said that to me," she began, looking away out of the window. "She just said you drank too much. Sometimes." Glancing quickly back toward him, she added, "And it could make you mean."

Miller tried to control the flare of anger he felt bubble up into his throat. Seriously? Yeah, he liked a couple of beers during the game. After a rough night at work. When he came home from visiting his sister at Brightstar—"

"She never said you hit her or anything," Laura added.

A lion roared inside Miller's head. "Did Angie bother to tell you about the times she launched herself on me like a hellcat on fire?" he asked. Keeping the rage out of his tone was a real effort, but the last thing he wanted to do now was to give this woman any reason to believe anything her friend had told her was true.

Part of him was like, *why do I care?* Another part of him screamed, *She's got to believe me.*

Flickers of memory made his stomach twist. Him, just a boy, his sister sitting in a highchair. His father bellowing at his mother. The sharp crack as his father backhanded Mom, and then her sobs. His baby sister screaming, panicked.

He'd been only ten years old. There was absolutely nothing he could do to make it stop.

Dragging his thoughts back into the moment, he found himself gazing at Laura's profile as she stared out the window, obviously avoiding eye contact. Her hair, which he was sure had been ironed stick straight when she left for work this morning, was inching up in joyous ringlets, teasing the curve of her cheek in a way that made him *want*.

Want to reach forward and tangle his fingers in those curls, to feel their silky softness against his skin. Tuck them behind an ear he was sure was as perfect as a pink shell. Bet she smelled heavenly, too. He took deep breaths in and out, trying to stay focused in the present. Trying to remember what the hell he'd just asked her.

A moment too long wore on. "Well?" he prompted. A safe word, one that wouldn't give away his temporary mental leave from the conversation.

She wagged her head from side to side, making those delectable curls sway and bounce. It caused his heart to leap in a most unexpected way. When she turned to face him, her eyes were shiny with unshed tears.

"I'm not sure what to believe, or who," she said, her voice cracking on the last word. "I trusted Angie, and she abandoned me. I trusted my dad, and he . . .he replaced me." Her next words came out choked on a sob. "My mother was my best friend. My female role model. And then she came out of the closet. Introduced me to her new wife. I'm not really sure sometimes who I am. Who I'm supposed to be. How can I believe or trust in anybody else?"

Tears streaked down her face as she squeezed her eyes shut, and Miller's heart clenched. He reached forward to lay his hand on her arm.

"I know I'm a big guy, Laura, but I would never, ever hurt a woman. Hell, I'd never hurt anyone unless they represented a threat to me, or to somebody else." He waited a beat, watching the tears stream down her face in dusky rivulets.

This woman had been abused. Maybe not in a physical way, but in a way that scarred her too deep to see on the outside.

"It sounds like you've had your share of disappointments in life. With people you trusted. I totally get that. I've got a few scars of my own," he said softly.

She opened her eyes then and met his in a penetrating gaze that made his heart ache.

"Not that you have any reason to trust me, Laura. But I'm telling you, you can. I am what I appear to be. A simple man. With simple goals in life."

She searched his eyes and for a moment, he was engulfed with an overwhelming desire to pull her into his arms and hold her. Bury his face in her rapidly spiraling hair. Kiss her pouty lips until they curved up into a smile.

But he was on duty, dammit. If Duvall drove by and caught him here, with her, in his cruiser, like this, there would be hell to pay.

He drew back, reaching forward to trace a finger down her cheek, carving one tear off her soft skin with his thumb. Their eyes remained locked.

"I think Sarge is off this weekend," he said. "And Duvall too. If you want to take a look around Talcott Hall after work on Friday, I'll meet you here at five."

But Friday didn't come soon enough for Laura. She was too curious, too bored, too much in need of a distraction from her present situation.

From the situation at work. From her dubious living arrangement with Miller. From her entire freaking life, for God's sakes.

The following afternoon, Laura left work and pulled into Miller's driveway at nine minutes past five. By six o'clock she'd changed into shorts, a tee shirt, and running shoes. She called in an order to After Shocks down the street (which, she discovered with a quick online search, boasted the best burgers on the west end of town), and ordered a burger plate to be ready for a seven o'clock pickup. Should be plenty of time, she thought, to take a quick jog up onto the campus and around the perimeter of old Talcott Hall.

She was winded and sweaty by the time she'd crested the slow rise leading toward the old abandoned building. The day started out seasonally warm but breezy. A breeze that died just about the time she started heading up the hill. She knew that at any moment, Miller's cruiser could track her down and hinder her progress.

But another online search proved that the old State hospital grounds always had, and still were, open to the public. Nothing prevented anyone from wandering anywhere on the campus. Except, of course, the places now locked behind chain link fence. Laura had no intention of scaling any secured perimeters. She just wanted a closer look . . .

The night before, the history of Talcott Hall had kept her glued to her computer screen until after midnight. Sadie's description, "the craziest of the crazies," had ignited a curiosity Laura couldn't squelch. She loved mysteries, and exploring the unexplained. She also had an intense interest in the history of mental illness treatment, since her career hinged on understanding the many facets—both positive and negative—of treatments utilized in the development of the field.

And her starving mind was having a hard time concentrating on her new job, subsisting solely on perusal of old medical histories day after day. This was so *not* what she'd expected.

Eventually, she knew, she'd get her chance with the patients. Licensing requirements stated that half of her three thousand hours of clinical training would be case management. But she'd expected the division to be more balanced—maybe one week on records duty, the following on patient contact. Riley had made it sound, pretty clearly, that Laura would be on case management duty indefinitely.

Or at least, for the next fifteen hundred hours. Almost thirty-eight weeks.

Sigh.

All the while she was struggling to keep her attention on her boring, uninspiring work, she endured the sickening, snuffling sounds of her office mate, Jonath-it. He struggled with allergies, or sinusitis, or some unidentifiable condition Laura didn't even want to know about. She could swear she'd even heard him fart once, at which time she made a quick exit to "retrieve more files."

What she'd learned about Talcott's history had nauseated her enough. Apparently, at the turn of the 19th century, an entire new regime of mental health care came about due to the influence of a doctor by the same name. He believed in the "humane" treatment of mental illness, though such methods at that time included hydrotherapy and electric shock treatment.

Hydrotherapy sounded soothing, until one realized that it may include fairly scalding the patient in high water temperatures for many hours at a time, essentially draining all the fight out of them. And if that didn't work, there was always the option to wire them up and zap them. Or go poking around in their brains with instruments not much more sophisticated than a knitting needle.

Lobotomies, she'd learned in Psych History, were still performed up until the mid-1950s, though none of record at this facility.

What Laura found most disturbing in her research were the diagnoses for the patients residing at the State center: many were admitted for diabetes, alcoholism, and shell shock.

Diabetes? Seriously? Yet there was a time when the slurring of words, tremors, fainting spells and seizures of diabetics were looked upon as a form of mental illness. Ignorance was clearly the cause of this misdiagnosis.

Alcoholism? Today it's known to be a behavioral disorder, not truly mental illness.

Shell shock. Now it's called Post Traumatic Stress Disorder. PTSD. Yes, it's real. And it affects hundreds of thousands of those who have been exposed to situations worse than the human mind is equipped to deal with. This, she knew, was one of the few admitting diagnoses from those days that truly qualified as mental disorders.

As she made her way along the largely unattended shoulder of the road, nearing the locked gate, Laura heard what she thought, at first, was the whine of the breeze. She paused, listening. Intermittent blasts of cooler air gusted against her damp skin. She spied the purple horizon in the east. A roll of distant thunder followed two quick blinks of lightning flashing from within the darkened mass.

But the sound wasn't the wind, or the thunder either. No, this had a pattern. She stopped at the gate and listened. Then, she heard it again. A sob, then plaintive though indecipherable words. High-pitched and hysterical, it sounded like a little girl.

Approaching the fence, she laced her fingers through the mesh and leaned her sweaty forehead against the cool metal.

"Lady, have you seen my daddy?"

Laura gasped and wheeled around, slapping her hand to her chest and careening back against the fence. The voice had been as sharp and clear as if a child was standing right behind her.

In reality, the words sounded as though they'd come from inside her own head. But there was no one there.

Frantically, Laura scanned the area, her head whipping from side to side. But aside from a car turning out from a side street two blocks down, she saw no one. Nothing.

Her heart was drumming so loud now she couldn't hear, and when the next clap of thunder shook the ground, she squeaked in surprise. Had she imagined a voice and words in the wind whining through the fence?

She glanced back toward the rapidly approaching storm clouds. They were rolling in the sky, like an organizing tornado in a weather disaster movie. Cinder-grey and varying hues of purple tumbled over on themselves, as if the storm was crawling straight toward her with ominous speed. As if it were alive.

Her pulse whined in her ears, and she rubbed her arms to ward off a sudden chill she wasn't sure was coming from the inside or out. Heart slamming against her ribs, she took off at a jog back down the street toward home. But her heartbeat was already too fast, and quickly, she found herself out of breath. She tried to keep going, but when she began to shiver and sparkles littered her vision, she knew she was risking a faint.

She'd put about a hundred yards between her and the fence around Talcott Hall when she was forced to stop and rest. Squatting, she dropped her head between her knees and clasped her hands behind her neck.

Breathe deep. Long and slow. In and out.

The first fat drops of rain began spattering the pavement around
her, sending tiny bursts of steam up into the air. Gooseflesh rose as they began their assault on her arms and the back of her neck.

The beep of a car horn sent her nearly tumbling off into the ditch on the side of the road. Jumping up, she spun around and saw Miller's cruiser parked within feet of her. How the hell had he crept up on her like that?

His door swung open and in seconds, he was standing next to her, one hand gripping her elbow.

"Hey, are you okay?"

Eleven

"You scared the hell out of me! Again!" Laura snapped, yanking her arm free and staggering backward.

But her tirade was punctuated by a blinding flash of lightning that sent her falling straight back into Miller's arms. It was close, the electricity palpable in the air, raising the hair along her arms with the charge.

"You're gonna get us both fucking killed," Miller growled, bustling her toward the passenger door. He yanked it open and pushed her in without ceremony, slamming the door and hurrying around to reclaim his seat behind the wheel.

"What the hell are you doing out here?" he barked. His angry shout startled her already frazzled nerves, and she squeezed her eyes shut.

She was such a loser. Never in the right place at the right time. Always in somebody's way, messing up somebody's plans. The unwanted fifth wheel that threw the entire cart off balance.

Unbalanced. She'd learned the definition of the term, never once thinking it might apply to herself. Until this moment.

Were her own emotional problems the reason her interest had always been drawn to the mentally unstable? Is that why she'd been so determined to become an expert in the field? Some sick, sixth sense kind of self-diagnosis?

The large, warm hand on her knee caused her eyes to flutter open, and she met Miller's gaze. He didn't look mad. Just really . . .concerned.

"I'm—I'm sorry," she stuttered. "I was just taking a walk . . . a little jog. Around the campus. The storm blew in so fast—"

"It did that," Miller replied, his voice suddenly soft. He studied her with a creased brow. His jaw was set, and rain trickled off the one lock of tawny hair stuck to his temple. Drops ran along his jawline, as if his hair were crying. "Never seen one blow in this quick. Is that what has you so scared? You look kind of . . .pale."

She shook her head and drew in a shuddering breath, realizing she was actually panting. "I thought I heard something. Somebody. Up there by the fence. It spooked me."

Miller hadn't removed his big hand from her leg, but somehow, she welcomed its warmth. Its strength.

He sucked in a breath, his eyes widening. "What did you hear?"

"A kid. I thought I heard a little girl crying, and talking, like, really fast. Panicked even. Somewhere over near that old building." She paused and shook her head, pinching the bridge of her nose between her fingers. "But that's impossible, isn't it? The place is locked up. There's a fence all around it. What would some kid be doing in a creepy old place like that?"

When she opened her eyes, Miller had tipped his head slightly, and one of his eyebrows arched. "We did find a breach in the fence recently. On the backside. Are you sure you didn't see anyone?"

She shook her head. "No. But as I was standing there, searching in the weeds beyond the fence, I heard her again, loud. Clear. This time, from behind me." *Or from inside my own head.* She shuddered. "But when I spun around, nobody was there—"

"What did she say?" Miller asked.

Laura's throat closed up and she swallowed down the painful knot of more threatened tears. "She asked if I'd help her find her daddy. I swear, Miller, it sounded like she was speaking directly into my ear."

Miller closed his eyes, his head falling back against the seat.

"What? Why are you doing that?" A flash of indignation flared in Laura's chest. "You think I'm crazy, don't you? Just another hysterical, irrational woman." She spat the words, repeating a phrase she'd heard Angie use when quoting one of her arguments with Miller.

His eyes flew open. "No," he said, his voice sharp with conviction. "No, not at all."

She blinked, trying to read his expression. But she didn't know him well enough to decipher the grim set of his lips, the slow oscillation of his head. Was he just humoring her? Pacifying her?

"What, then?" she rasped.

"I've seen her." His words were almost a whisper, and ran through Laura like a jolt of electricity.

A long moment stretched out before she asked, "What do you mean, you've *seen* her?" She heard the quiver in her voice, and wondered if he had as well.

Miller cleared his throat and sat up straight in his seat, turning to look out his side window. He crossed his arms over his chest. Laura's skin felt chilled on the spot where his hand had been.

Rain was hammering down on the roof and hood of the cruiser now with almost deafening clamor. Laura couldn't see anything. It was as though the storm had swallowed the car and whisked them into some weird suspension of time and space. Another flash of light cut through the wall of water, almost simultaneously as another boom vibrated the entire car. A shudder rippled across her shoulders, and she hugged herself.

"There's a little girl who hangs around here. She always asks me to help her find her father. But whenever I try to lead her down to the homeless shelter, so I can get her some help . . ." He trailed off.

"But I didn't see anyone," Laura said.

"Even if you had," he said, keeping his gaze trained toward the rivulets streaming down his side window, "if you'd blinked or turned around fast, she'd probably have disappeared."

A half-hour later Laura sat across from Miller in a booth at After Shocks. The foam box holding the to-go burger she'd ordered earlier was open on the table before her. Miller's roast beef sandwich and fries had just been delivered, set next to his already half-empty glass of Coke.

"Who do you think she is?" Laura asked.

Miller shook his head. "No idea, except that her name is Greta. Sanderson, I think she said. At first I thought she'd wandered away from the homeless shelter over on Seward. But I checked at the desk, and nobody was missing a child."

"Isn't there a safe house on the grounds too? For abused kids?" she asked.

Miller nodded. "Yup. And that place's locked down tight to protect the kids lucky enough to find their way there. I doubt they'd even tell *me* if one of their kids had wandered off."

Laura plopped her chin onto her hand, thinking. "But if our little girl had gone to the safe house to get away from her parents, why would she be looking for her father?"

Miller shrugged. "Dunno. What's really weird is that most times I see her, it's at night. What little kid would be wandering around that creepy old building in the middle of the night?"

"But today it was daylight," Laura said.

"Yes, but there was a storm blowing in. I've seen her just before huge storms too. Like, she materializes out of the energy in the air." He drained his glass of soda before fixing her with an eerie stare. "And she's not always alone. Last night, there was a man with her. An older guy, missing one hand."

Laura winced. "My coworker, Sadie, she says some weird stuff happens over there. But she wouldn't go into detail." A shiver skittered across her shoulder blades. "Do you believe in ghosts, Miller?"

He stopped chewing and held her gaze for a long moment, but didn't give her an answer. He glanced at his watch. "I only get a half-hour," he said in way of apology before taking a monstrous bite out of his uncut sandwich, one that reduced its volume by a third.

Laura stared down at her burger and heaved a sigh.

"What's the matter? Did I just scare the appetite outta you?" he asked around a mouthful. "You don't eat much to begin with, from what I can tell." His quirky smile warmed her, prompting an unbidden grin.

"That's what my roommate always said," she said.

Miller cocked his head to one side. "Roommate? Boyfriend?"

Laura wrestled the burger between both hands and lifted it, leaning over the plate. She shook her head, then took a bite. "Nope," she said, chewing. "Abby was definitely not a boy-type. Just a roommate. I still had three years left for my degree, and I was living with my mother. But when Mom's new wife moved in, I just couldn't stay. That's when I moved in with Abby."

He grunted, turning his focus to his meal. As she ate, Laura studied the man sitting across from her. He'd had a haircut, because those golden curls no longer flipped up along his collar. The overstuffed sandwich looked miniature in his big hands, and he attacked it as though he hadn't eaten in a week. The subdued glow from the low-slung light pendant over their booth played patterns along the strong, straight cut of his jaw as he chewed.

What exactly, she wondered, had been Angie's problem with him? Aside from that first morning she'd arrived, Miller had been nothing but nice to her.

Laura blinked back into the moment when Miller asked, "So, no boyfriend then? I find that hard to believe, as cute as you are." One eyebrow raised, he was tipping his head and studying her with a barely suppressed smile.

Dropping her gaze to the golden-brown burger bun, Laura shook her head. "No boyfriend. Not since my first year of grad school, anyway."

"Huh. No time? Or are you . . ." He trailed off and shook his head. "Never mind. I can definitely see how college could extinguish a social life. That online course is kicking my ass already." He lifted his drink and drained it. No straws for this macho man. "And that was just from trying to find my way around the," he plunked down the glass and made air quotes, "*virtual classroom.*"

Laura couldn't hold back her grin. "It can be a little tricky."

"Hey," he said, leveling his gaze on hers. "I really do appreciate your helping me get oriented the other night."

There was something about the tone of his voice that sparked a warm glow in the middle of Laura's chest. Sitting there with his still-damp hair tousled every which way, her heretofore image of *scary, macho man in a uniform* faltered, revealing a softer, more vulnerable side. Taken back, and more than a little surprised, she didn't think her response through clearly before she heard herself saying, "No problem, Miller. I'd be happy to help you anytime. And no. I'm not like my mother. I'm not gay."

He did a quick eye roll before looking away. Sliding out of the booth, he muttered, "Well, alrighty then."

By the time they exited the front doors of After Shocks, the rain had ceased, and although there was steam rising off the pavement, the air had cooled considerably.

"I take it you can get home safely from here?" Miller asked. He fixed her with that quirky grin that melted something deep inside her.

She nodded. "Got it. As long as I can get past the cemetery, I'll be good."

"Shit," Miller muttered, a scowl twisting his features. "Get in. I'll drive you to the damned front door."

He pulled into his driveway and threw it directly into reverse, again glancing at his watch. "If you don't want to get me fired, you need to get out of the truck."

Laura waited until he raised his gaze to meet hers. "Hey. Thank you," she said softly. "I've been kind of . . .lost lately. But unlike our elusive little girl at Talcott Hall, I probably won't be disappearing anytime real soon."

His eyes on hers caused a warm rush to rise into her cheeks. He had the most incredible eyes, and right now, she felt as though she could almost read what he was thinking.

Ooh. Maybe better not try to do that.

"That would be A-okay with me," he murmured, patting her knee, maybe a little too briskly. "Now get out. I'm late."

Laura lay awake a long time that night, listening to the rain pounding down on the roof. The storm had resumed with a fury, and although the thunder and lightning had ceased, it had been raining for the past several hours, and hard. Gusts of wind blasted walls of water against her window in intermittent bursts. Yet even though she was alone in this strange house, she felt more secure than she had in weeks.

Her encounter with the baffling Miller Stanford this evening had somehow opened up a place in the vault protecting her feeble and fragile confidence.

She left the hall light on, and her door open a crack. That way, she not only had a nightlight of sorts until Miller got home from work, but she also knew when he *was* home. He always flicked off the light when he got to the top of the stairs.

With her grandmother's quilt pulled up to her chin, her gaze strayed over toward the new window shade. That was so sweet of him, she thought. To install that shade for her just days after she'd arrived, unannounced, and not properly invited.

The man had her completely perplexed. His entire persona, never mind Angie's description—*hulking, insensitive brute*—just didn't fit the softer side she was catching glimpses of every day she got to know him better.

And yes, the store of Miller Light bottles in the vegetable bins did dwindle by two or three bottles every few days. But so far, Laura hadn't seen anything to indicate alcohol abuse. Nothing about Miller's personality fit the diagnosis of a behavior disorder.

She was just drifting off into a warm, fuzzy sleep when she heard the key in the front door. It thudded closed, and then the deadbolt click.

In her mind, she imagined him, pulling off his rain slicker and hanging it next to his cap. Now he was bending to untie the heavy black work boots—the ends of his laces made a tiny tapping sound as they danced against the wood floor. Now he was slipping them off onto the mat under the tree. The heavy thump-thump of his feet traveled down the hallway into the bathroom, and the door clicked quietly shut. The sound of the shower spray echoed in the hallway.

After about ten minutes, the door creaked open again, and she heard him head back toward the kitchen. Time for his near-nightly ritual. Any moment she'd hear the screech of the heavily loaded, plastic vegetable bin.

Then, silence. He'd stopped. Why? She sat up in bed, suddenly uneasy.

After a brief moment, his footsteps resumed, returning in her direction. He'd apparently decided against those couple of beers tonight. But when his steps didn't end at the foot of the stairwell, she slid down under the quilt and held her breath.

Her door sighed as it swung open every so slowly, allowing the light from the hallway to crawl silently across the floor and up onto the foot of her bed. She lay perfectly still, although she winced when she realized her bra and panties were on full display, strewn across the back of her desk chair.

A few seconds passed, and the door swung closed, almost but not quite clicking shut. As Miller climbed the stairs, the third step sounded its characteristic squeak. Seconds later, the hall light went out.

So. He had come to check on her. Make sure she was home and safe. A warm flush started in the middle of her chest and radiated outward until her whole body melted into blissful relaxation.

Laura sighed. No, definitely not the man her friend had described to her. She needed to find out more about that whole situation as soon as possible. Tomorrow. Tomorrow she'd call Angie and find out exactly what her friend's deal with Miller Stanford had been.

Miller thought about firing up the laptop he'd left on his kitchen table. But hell, it was almost midnight. Not tonight. He was dog-tired, bone-weary, and sweaty-icky-miserable under his clothes after wearing his slicker for the latter part of the evening shift. Plus, his mind was rapidly drifting out of his control, like an loose feather on a strong gust of wind.

Laura. No doubt of her name now. It was singed into his brain like a hot-iron brand after tonight. She'd looked so helpless, so vulnerable huddled there on the side of road where he found her. He could still almost smell the fresh, earthy scent of her hair when she'd fallen against him after that first crack of lightning. Like fresh cut grass. On steroids.

Damn. He couldn't deny it. She was attractive, enticing. Smelled like the first day of spring. Seemed in needing of protection. That was his calling, right? His duty? His mission in life? It was only natural he would feel the urge to protect her.

No. Absolutely not. The last thing he needed now was another helpless female depending on him.

But as he climbed into bed and turned out the bedside lamp, another, more disturbing thought sprung into his brain. Laura had obviously been pretty shaken up after making contact with the same little girl that had haunted him these past several months. He'd almost convinced himself he'd dreamed up the elusive sprite. Now, somebody else had seen her. Or heard her, at least. Now, there was proof.

There was a little girl—Greta—wandering about in the vicinity of Talcott Hall, lost and alone, searching for her father. The mangled breach of the chain link fence, the homeless man they'd rescued from the bowels of the monstrous old building—he knew he hadn't dreamed those up. But this child. And the eerie, maimed bum with her—he'd hoped he'd imagined them both.

Now, there was no doubt. He had to find out who the child was, where and how she eked out her survival, and how he could help her.

Miller fell into a dreamless, exhausted sleep. Then, bam. The ringing of his cellphone jolted him full awake. His digital clock read seven a.m. He rolled over and snatched it off his nightstand, squinting at the caller ID through blurred vision.

Mom

Shit. What now?

"Hello?" His voice came out like he'd been sucking on gravel for the past seven hours. Hell, he might have been. Did he snore? He didn't know. Angie'd never complained about—"

"Son, we've got trouble. It's your sister. She's come down with . . .something. They don't know what, but the antibiotics aren't working. They called me about an hour ago. Said they were transferring her to Rockland. She's in . . ." His mother's voice broke, followed by a long pause. "She's in intensive care, Miller."

"Fuck," Miller muttered, swiping a hand down over his face as he pushed up to a sitting position. "Sorry, Mom. I was dead asleep. Are you going? Can I pick you up?"

"I'm already halfway there. I gotta get off this phone or I'm gonna get pulled over. See you there."

His mother never had embraced the advanced technology of hands-free, and in New York State, it was a misdemeanor if a driver got caught talking on a cellphone. Muttering curses, he clambered to his feet and grabbed a clean pair of briefs out of his top drawer. He was headed for the downstairs shower—the only place where there *was* an operable shower—when the whirring noise commenced.

Laura's godforsaken blow dryer.

He stepped into a pair of athletic shorts and was pulling a Yankee's tee shirt over his head when he made it to the bottom step. The turbine engine abruptly ceased. Just as he passed the bathroom, the door swung open and Laura squeaked in surprise.

"Oh. You're up early," she said, nervously pulling down the sides of her short, black skirt and fiddling with the waistband.

He grunted, pausing only for a second before continuing on toward the kitchen. "I gotta run to Rockland."

The next six hours, for Miller, came straight out of a hellish nightmare. He met his mother in the ICU waiting room, a tiny, closet-like space. The walls were covered with bright, flowered wallpaper that threatened to cause his eyes to explode out of their sockets. Six orange, plastic chairs ringed the perimeter. His mother sat in one of them, sobbing into a handkerchief.

"What's going on, Mom? How is she?" He had a hard time getting the words out, it seemed, around a sudden ball of something thick and sharp binding the base of his throat.

His mother stood, falling against him. Simultaneously, Miller closed his arms around her shoulders, and his eyes against what he was sure would be a killing blow.

News he didn't want to hear, yet knew he couldn't avoid. News he'd been fearing, hanging like an invisible guillotine over his life, for the past twelve years.

After a few moments of uncontrollable sobbing, his mother pushed back and gazed up into his eyes.

"She's stable, they're telling me. But it's terrifying, Miller. She's hooked up to all these machines. Flashing lights and beeping sounds. And there's a tube," she paused, choking on another sob, "a big, plastic tube in her mouth. A breathing tube."

Miller's mother was right. His chest clenched in horror as he stood at the foot of the hospital bed. His baby sister looked more like a robot from a futuristic sci-fi movie than a brain-damaged, twenty-two-year-old young woman.

All the tubes and tape and monitors flashing and beeping weren't the scariest part. The most terrifying was the inch-wide, clear plastic tube snaking into the corner of her mouth, held secure by a swatch of white bandage tape. And the sound of the respirator, hissing and clicking and hissing again as it forced breath in and out of Mollie's ravaged lungs.

The doctor walked in. After a cursory, mumbled introduction and vapid handshake, Dr. Whoever said the words with as much emotion as one would say *pass the salt.*

"Your sister has pneumonia." His dark eyes met Miller's, expressionless. His exotic accent was tinged with the melodic lilt and metallic twang of India. "She's stable as of right now, but she's not responding to the medications as rapidly as we'd hoped."

Miller's mom crushed her hankie to her mouth and turned to stare out the window, where brilliant sunlight streamed in as though everything in the world was okey-dokey, A-okay. Dr. Whatever-his-name-was stood straight and stiff, clutching a metal-clad chart to his chest like a white-coated robot.

"How did this happen?" Miller barked. "She lives under very controlled conditions. I mean, it's not like she goes running around in her bare feet in the rain on a chilly night."

The doctor held up his hand and closed his eyes, nodding. "I know this might be a hard concept for you to assimilate, Mr. Stanford."

Are you trying to make me feel like a fucking imbecile? *Assimilate?* Seriously?

"But your sister," he continued, "because of her egregiously impaired state, doesn't get much physical exercise. Even with all the physical therapy she's provided. This allows the bacteria already in her lungs to settle, fester . . ."

Fester. Now that's a cheery description.

The doctor went on. "Pneumonia often doesn't make its presence known until it's gained a rather strong foothold—"

"So, cut to the chase, Doc. What are Mollie's chances of surviving this thing?" Miller tried to keep the irritation and impatience out of his voice. The panicked look his mother flashed up at him told him he hadn't been successful, and that perhaps his volume and tone had been a little over the top.

Which was confirmed by the subtle move by the doctor—one small step backward, his dark eyes blinking rapidly.

"At this point," the doctor replied, ". . .at this point, Mollie's chances of recovering completely from this infection are no better than 50/50. I'm sorry. But I'm an honest man, and quite frankly, I don't want to impart false hope." His voice was now softened by something Miller found not only distasteful, but terrifying. *Pity.*

The drive back to Middletown was one of the most depressing journeys Miller had ever taken. Twenty minutes out, and one glance at the numbers on his dash clock told him he'd barely have enough time to change into his uniform in order to punch in on time.

Double jeopardy. He couldn't afford to lose this job. Not only would he lose his house and livelihood, but he'd no longer be able to afford to pay to keep Mollie at Brightstar Nursing Facility.

If she survived.

Shit. Maybe it really didn't matter anymore. What quality of life did she have anyway? And his wishing for her to recover, survive, in the same godawful condition, was no better than a desperate child coveting a broken, hideously maimed doll.

As he swung his truck off the exit onto Rte. 211, Miller slammed the steering wheel so hard with the flat of his palm he nearly swerved off the ramp.

"Damn you, Dad. Damn you to hell for doing this to her. To Mom. To our family. You and your blasted boozing it up every single, fucking day until you couldn't walk a straight line or speak a sentence without slurring. And then getting behind the wheel of a car." Miller swallowed against the lump of bile rising in his throat, and narrowed his eyes, willing the powerful wave of emotion away. "I hope you're fucking burning in hell," he growled.

Miller's sister, Mollie, nearly died in the crash that day on the way to see him play a stupid, high school football game. His father, drunk on his ass, had picked her up after downing two or five too many beers at the pub on his way home from work. Then they'd set out on their two-hour long trek to Albany for the playoff game.

They never made it.

His father had paid the ultimate price. Sadly, Miller hadn't shed a single tear at the man's funeral. Because the whole time, his sister was lying in a hospital bed fighting for her life.

He would never forget going with his mom to view the totaled Chrysler in the police tow lot. To look at the car, you'd swear nobody could possibly have survived. The sedan looked as though an angry giant had crushed it in fit of fury. Not one piece of glass remained intact, the force of impact spidering every window into a sickening mosaic. His father's blood splattered the steering wheel, now twisted off at an angle by the rescue team's efforts. That was hard enough to see.

But the killing blow was finding Mollie's cheerleader pom-poms in the car.

They found one crammed into the narrow space between the shattered windshield and buckled dashboard. The other lay splayed on the floor behind the front seat. As Miller reached in through the window and lifted it away from the mat, the blue and white paper shredded and tore away from the handle. He felt his heart follow suit.

The paper strands were stuck to the rug with crusted, dried blood.

Twelve

Another Friday finally arrived, and Laura felt as though she'd worked three months instead of only three weeks. Her brain was numb. She'd analyzed and entered data from close to two hundred patient charts this week alone. Although her mind was swimming with tidbits from each report, the monotony of the tasks had left her feeling as though her brain had been soaking in straight vodka.

She'd learned that at any given time, the West Wing of the Center housed from ten to thirty-five temporary residents, most of them having been "sentenced" to a thirty or sixty-day stint after a DUI, or domestic violence charge. After their discharge, all the notes from caregiver records, along with some actual recordings of counseling interviews, had to be organized and entered into the Center's new database.

Laura was glad to do the audio transcriptions, and only partially because the headphones blocked out the noises her office mate continually emitted. Listening to the voices of these troubled souls, and how the counselor drew out information from them, each in their own unique styles, fascinated Laura. It's what she'd been trained to do. The thrill from some breakthrough, a carefully scripted line of questioning that led a patient to a self-realization of the root of their addiction, sometimes brought her to tears.

Which only elevated her frustration to a new level. How long did Riley expect her to stay sequestered from the patients? How long before she'd be allowed to gain the real experience, the front-line exposure, she so desperately craved?

Laura wasn't sure if it was that frustration, aggravation, or exhaustion that pushed her to the breaking point. But at four-thirty that Friday afternoon, she'd reached it.

This was ridiculous. It had been three weeks. She had to get out of this office, and into the role she'd studied for so diligently for the past six years. It was time to assert herself. Confront Kayla Riley and ask some hard questions. Find out how long she'd be acting as glorified data-entry clerk. Budget cuts be damned.

Riley's office door was open, and it looked as if she was in the process of tidying her desk, preparing to leave for the day. Laura rapped on the jamb, and the woman froze in place, glancing up from under her helmet of dark brown hair. First she narrowed her eyes, then blinked, wearing an expression Laura couldn't read. Indignant? Annoyed?

"Yes?" Riley asked, tipping up her chin. "May I help you?"

Ah. Clueless. She doesn't even remember who I am.

"Ms. Riley, I've been here three weeks. I was wondering how long I'll be assigned to case management."

There. Not a question, a statement. Laura drew in a breath and squared her shoulders.

Riley folded her hands on her desk. "Miss . . .Horton, is that right?"

Yup. Completely clueless.

"Laura Horton. I'm the one with the Master's in Addiction Counseling, remember? Appalachia State? Graduated Magna Cum Laude?"

For a brief instant, Laura saw a flash of . . .something pass across her boss's face. As if she'd called her an obscene word, or bitch-slapped her. But just as quickly, it was gone.

Laura paused, then crossed her arms over her chest and leaned against the doorjamb. "I know you told me there were budget cuts, Ms. Riley. I'm not asking for a raise. I'm asking when I'll be permitted to do the job I was trained for. I know half of my internship is case management, but is that all I'll be doing for the first fifteen-hundred hours?"

Riley's wide-eyed, frozen silence was a bit unnerving. Laura's initial courage was evaporating fast, and for the moment she couldn't believe her own audacity in approaching her new boss this way.

This wasn't like her. At all.

I mean, let's face it. I'm alone, and this is my only chance at gainful employment. In a town where my choices are to either live with my walkaway ex-friend's ex-boyfriend, or in my father's condo in his wife's new age meditation room.

Laura suppressed her shudder at that thought.

But now her heart was pounding so hard she was afraid the buttons on her blouse would vibrate loose.

Riley's lips pressed into a thin line and she dropped her gaze to her clasped hands. "How are you coming with the transcriptions?" she asked.

That jolted Laura, and for a split-second her mind went blank. Transcriptions? Oh, right. The chart analyses.

She cleared her throat. "I've completed just under two-hundred records these past weeks. Enough to get a pretty good idea of how things operate here. The mode of treatment each counselor prefers." She paused, racking her brain for specifics. "For example, I notice that Counselor Wolff takes an aggressive approach with his patients. Whereas Counselor Timmons utilizes a more sympathetic line of questioning."

Riley lifted her gaze and smiled, nodding slightly. "Excellent. So, you *have* been paying attention."

Boosted a tad, Laura stood up straighter. "Yes, ma'am. I'm not sure why you should be surprised." There. Maintain your ground, Laura thought.

"Well, considering the surroundings you've been working in," Riley continued, one side of her lips quirking up, "it must have proven quite a challenge." She motioned with one hand. "Come on in and close the door, Ms. Horton."

Laura lowered herself into the chair across from Riley's desk. Good to sit down, as her knees had started feeling a wee bit spongy.

Her boss' wry smile had thrown her off balance, and Laura wasn't quite sure what would happen next.

"I figured, with you coming straight out of school," Riley began, "you'd have an inaccurate and perhaps somewhat euphoric image of what this job entails. In contrast to what they teach you in graduate school, it's not all warm fuzzies and miraculous breakthroughs," she said, riveting her with a critical gaze.

Laura blinked and tipped up her chin. "I've been through hundreds of hours of clinicals, Ms. Riley. I think I have a pretty good idea of what I could be facing," she said, although her tone was laced with a whiney, desperate note. She couldn't help it. Not after the weeks she'd been through.

Riley's smile was warm and kind, of a flavor Laura hadn't thought she was capable of. "I figured the best way to introduce you to how our counselors operate was by *not* having you work with them." Her eyes were filled with mischief.

Laura dropped back in her chair with a huff. So, this had been a test. Her first weeks of work had been nothing more than a test of her dedication, her patience, and her tolerance.

Riley continued, a glint of humor tainting her words. "By sticking you in with our dear Jonathan, and having you read and listen to our counselors in action, I figured you'd either sink or swim."

In disbelief, Laura lifted her gaze to the ceiling. She wasn't sure if she should be in awe of Riley's wisdom, or just plain pissed off. But Riley must have interpreted the huge sigh that escaped her as awe, because her boss stood and extended her hand.

"You've proven you're a swimmer, Counselor Horton. Welcome to the team."

Twenty minutes later, Laura left Riley's office floating six inches off the ground. She'd been assured that on Monday morning, she'd be working one-on-one with Anne Timmons, the counselor who Riley felt had a more successful approach. It was obvious to Laura that it was also the approach Riley herself gravitated toward.

It was a gorgeous summer afternoon, with not a threatening thunderhead in sight. She left through the center's front entrance without even casting a glance toward Talcott Hall. Her mind was too busy buzzing with the excitement of her victory.

Laura had walked to work that day, and she made her way down Dorothea Dix Drive with a decided bounce in her step. The sun filtered through the trees lining the street, casting dappled shadows. She wanted desperately to share her good news with somebody, but who?

Her dad would ask too many questions. Her mother didn't give a crap—she hardly ever spoke to her mother anymore. It was as though they came from different planets. And she knew Miller would be working.

Miller. There was no denying that her attraction to him was becoming a distraction, to say the least. And she was pretty sure he felt the same way about her. But Angie had been out of his life barely a month, and Laura couldn't help feeling a little guilty for even considering acting on her feelings. Letting herself go a little. Maybe even having a fling with him.

But why the hell should I feel guilty, she rationalized? She's the one who walked out on him, remember? Now's as good a time as any, she thought, to call Angie and find out exactly what her deal with Miller had been. She pulled her cellphone out of her purse and dialed.

She was a little surprised when Angie actually picked up on the third ring.

"Hey Ang. How you doing down in sunny Florida?"

Laura heard room sounds, or wind, maybe, in the background.

"Got you on speakerphone, Laura. I'm driving home from work. How are you, girl?"

"I'm good. But I need to ask you a couple of questions, Ang. Can you talk for a few?"

"Uh-huh." Her friend's voice flattened in tone, as though with reluctance.

"Angie, what exactly happened with you and Miller? I mean, first you tell me he's an asshole, and can get pretty mean when he's drunk, and I'm thinking *why am I even considering moving in with them*? Then you tell me he's okay, just likes his beer too much. Then

I show up and you're gone. Like, *gone*. What the hell, Angie? What happened between you two?"

A long silence left Laura listening to Miley Cyrus on the radio in the background, accompanied by the whoosh of passing cars.

"Angie?"

"Yeah, I'm here." Angie cleared her throat. "Look, Laura, Miller and I have been history for a while now. I mean, we hadn't even . . .you know, done *the deed* in months."

Laura hunched her shoulders. "TMI, Angie. Just tell me what happened. Did you love him? Are you two really done?"

Angie sighed long and loud. "Oookay. So, you know I wanted to finish my degree without having to take out any more loans, right?"

Squeezing her eyes shut for a step or two, Laura forced herself to say nothing more than, "Yeah."

"Well, Miller makes pretty good money. Owns his own house and shit. Didn't mind taking care of the bills while I used most of my measly paycheck and tips from After Shocks for my own stuff. I mean, I pitched in some, but—"

"Don't," Laura snapped, pinching the bridge of her nose between her fingers. "Don't tell me you were just using Miller as a meal ticket. I mean, I've heard you call him that more than once, but seriously, Ang—"

"Not saying it was right, Laura. Not saying I'm proud of it. Miller is a nice guy. He's got some shit going on of his own, stuff I couldn't begin to help him deal with. I think he might have been actually glad I didn't lean on him for more than food and a roof. Besides, he knew I was just riding it out until I got my degree. I mean, like I said, we hadn't slept together in months."

Laura felt her heart go cold in her chest. "Yeah. So, you used him, and then painted him as the big, bad drunk dude."

"I'm sorry if I exaggerated some about Miller, Laura. I really am. But a girl has to do what she has to do, you know? And yeah, I planned it this way. But I'm not a completely heartless bitch. I didn't want Miller to lose the few bucks I contributed, plus be alone all the time. He's got kind of a soft heart, in case you haven't already figured that out. You're kinda takin' my place. You know what I mean, girlfriend?"

By the time Laura hung up the phone, she couldn't decide if it was fury or self-pity bubbling inside her. Again, she'd been betrayed. By a girl she'd called her friend. Girlfriend. Yeah, right.

You are no girlfriend of mine, Angie. You are a selfish, heartless user. And I'm not sure right now whether I should hate your guts, or thank you for disappearing out of both Miller's, and my life.

Oh well. Good to have it all out in the open. She was done trusting and being the follower. Done feeling sorry for herself. Done waiting on other people to do the right thing for her. It was time for Laura Horton to stand on her own two feet and take what she wanted. She'd taken that leap with her new boss, and it was exactly what she'd needed to do.

It felt good. Freeing. Empowering.

Starting today, she was leaving the past behind her. Starting this minute, Laura Horton was moving on, strong and sure, grabbing life by the horns. Not cowering in the shadows, waiting for it to kick her in the ass.

By the time she reached the corner of West Main, she paused to slip off her heels and her suit jacket. The sidewalk would be cool enough here to walk on barefoot, shaded by the towering oaks dotting the graveyard it flanked.

When she got to the edge of Miller's yard, she stopped. His truck was in the driveway, which wasn't too unusual. Sometimes he walked to work, like she did. But as she drew closer she saw the living room window was thrown open, and she could hear the blaring of the TV.

Hmm. Must have had the day off today. Maybe he's working the weekend shift again.

The minute she pushed open the door she knew something wasn't right. The living room was empty, the light from the television flickering over a coffee table littered with empty beer bottles. Another had rolled off onto the floor and lay next to a puddle of spilled beer.

At least, she hoped it was spilled beer. Because the house smelled a little like it's exterior color. Puke green. And Miller was nowhere in sight.

She stepped forward to glance into the kitchen. The laptop was still perched there on the table, open, also flanked by another two, empty bottles. But no Miller.

It was then she heard the sound of retching coming from behind the closed door of the bathroom. Laura closed her eyes and sighed. Okay, here we go. This is more like the man Angie had described to her. Originally.

What a way to bring down her lofty, good mood. And here she'd planned to celebrate tonight. She'd even been considering calling up Dad and asking him to meet her for a glass of wine. Friday nights Deirdre sometimes went out "with the girls." Laura had hoped to score an evening alone with her dad.

Now, what would she be facing here at home? A stinking, filthy drunk? She tiptoed down the hallway in her bare feet, hoping to get past the bathroom and into her room before Miller came out.

No such luck.

She was directly in front of the door when it swung open and she came face to face with—

"Oh, my God. What happened to you?" she asked, lifting her hand to her mouth.

Miller was wearing a stretched-out, white tee shirt spotted down the front with, well, what she was sure was vomit. And . . .jockey briefs? His breath reeked of sour beer, and his hair was sticking out straight from his head as if he'd be struck by lightning. Blood shot eyes met hers, and his were wet.

Well, the act of vomiting often brought folks to tears.

Miller squeezed his eyes shut when he saw her. "I'm sorry, Laura. I made a mess in the bathroom. Gotta get stuff to clean it up." He pushed past her and opened the closet in the hallway, grabbing a bottle of Lysol spray and a new roll of paper towels.

"What happened to you?" she repeated in a small voice. "No work today?"

"I called in sick," he muttered. "Had to go back up to Rockland this morning."

She of course assumed he was talking about Rockland Psychiatric Center, the sister facility to what was once Middletown Psychiatric Hospital.

"For work?" she asked.

He shook his head as he lowered down on his hands and knees in front of the toilet. "Not for work."

She watched him spray and wipe the splattered seat and floor, and was filled with a mixture of confusion, pity and curiosity. This was a side of the man she hadn't seen before. But again, not the mean, angry, demanding drunk Angie had described.

Correction: the man Angie had *conjured*.

But he was, without a doubt, suffering the effects of overindulgence at the moment. Her training acted as an instinct, rising to the surface of her consciousness like some sort of sixth sense. It whispered into her brain: *Something is eating this man from the inside out.*

She waited until he rose to his feet, moaning as he bent to wash his hands and splash water on his face.

"Do you want to talk about it?" she asked again.

He leaned forward heavily with both hands gripping the edges of the vanity. With his head dropped forward, water dripped from his undried face.

When he raised his gaze to meet hers, the anguish she saw in his eyes tore a jagged hole in her heart. This big, strong, dominant man had been brought to his knees by something equally big. Something bad.

"My baby sister." His voice was gruff, thick. "They transferred her from Brightstar to Rockland Hospital Intensive Care. She's in a coma."

Two hours later, the living room was clean and quiet, with a soft, instrumental melody playing on the music channel. Laura had cleared off the coffee table, then re-scoured the bathroom, just in time to dodge out of the way for Miller to rush past her and toss his guts again.

She'd moved into the kitchen, shut down and closed the laptop, rinsed and stashed the beer bottles back in their carton, and wiped down the table. Then she returned to the bathroom and re-scoured it again. When she came out, she found Miller lying on the couch with one arm tossed over his eyes, still wearing the stained tee shirt. But thankfully, he'd at least pulled on shorts over his snug, very revealing briefs.

He lurched when she set the glass of water down on the table with a click, but settled quickly. She knelt beside the couch, and he relaxed back and groaned when she laid a cool, wet cloth over his forehead.

"Now, tell me everything. For heaven's sakes, I didn't even know you had a sister."

"I almost don't. Not anymore." he grumbled, but quickly qualified, "I shouldn't say that. Mollie is still alive. At least she was, as of two o'clock this afternoon."

She blinked at the starkness of his words, but drew in a calming breath and remembered to don her counselor face. Show no surprise, no judgment.

Lifting the glass of water, she said, "Here. Hydrate. It'll make you feel better."

Grunting, he pushed up on his elbows and took the glass, taking two or three swallows before handing it back to her. He slapped both hands over his face.

"Geez, why am I so sick? I'm not exactly a teetotaler." He squinted towards her through his fingers, as though the effort to focus was painful. "Do you think I'm coming down with something?"

Laura shook her head. "Not likely. What time did you start drinking today?"

"I got home about three," he said.

"So, you've consumed over a half-dozen bottles of beer in less than," she paused to glance up at the clock over the mantle, "what, three hours?"

Miller closed his eyes and moaned.

"I'd say you're one step away from alcohol poisoning."

His eyes flew open, then a disbelieving scowl twisted his features. "I'm a pretty big guy, and I drink a beer or two almost every night. How the hell can I—"

"You may drink often. But obviously—thankfully—you usually don't drink enough, in a short enough time period, to send your liver into toxic defense mode. At least, not until today." She paused, then added, "Which is a good thing."

The logical part of Laura's brain had kicked in, overriding her emotions. She was analyzing Miller as though he were one of the drunks she'd interviewed during her clinical sessions. As she did, a sort of shield went up between them, invisible but permeable, like those images of cell membranes she remembered from her early biology courses. A solid barrier, but allowing some things to pass through. But only certain things.

Miller heaved a huge sigh, then hiccupped so loud she jolted, ready to dodge out of the way in case he needed to make a run for the bathroom. But he closed his eyes again, settling that big, burly arm across his face. For a long moment, neither of them said anything. Soon, Laura heard the soft roar of Miller's snoring.

She sat there for a long time, just watching him sleep, wondering about the details of Miller's anguish. He'd said his sister was in Brightstar. That, she remembered, was a long-term nursing facility. Most of their patients were permanent residents. What kind of awful tragedy could have befallen her to put her in a place like that?

Laura wondered if perhaps Miller had been responsible. Maybe that's why he drank so much—an effort to anesthetize the pain of guilt and shame. Maybe he'd had an accident with her in the car. Maybe it had been after a few of those beers he drank every day.

But no, that didn't make sense either. If he had a DUI on his record, he wouldn't have qualified for his weapons permit, or even gotten the job as a security officer. No use conjecturing anyway. The only real way she could understand Miller's behavioral disorder was to find out what baggage he was carrying around in his head.

She hoped, with her education and training in mental health and substance abuse, she could help him.

Laura suddenly realized just how tired she was. It had been a long week, and today she'd ridden a rollercoaster of emotion, from anger and frustration to exhilaration at work, then the stress of dealing with Miller when she got home. And the pinching sensation in her chest was just empathy, right? Surely, her professional armor wouldn't let her feel anything more than that for Miller, who'd turned out to be her first, unofficial patient.

Her eyelids grew heavy and she yawned so big her eyes watered.

I should find something to eat, then hop into the shower. But I just need to lay my head down here on the edge of the couch for a minute or two . . .

When Miller opened his eyes, his head was pounding and his mouth tasted sour. Yet, he was oddly comfortable, even though his couch wasn't exactly a Sleep Number. Glancing down, he discovered that close to his side nestled the golden-haired head of an angel. One small hand lay softly on his middle, and her breathing was slow, regular. She was asleep.

Had he died? Surely not. This would be the farthest thing from his just desserts in the afterlife. Besides, he thought, glancing down over her back, he didn't see any wings.

At least, not visible ones.

Seeing Mollie this morning had pushed him over a jagged edge, one he tried to avoid at all costs. She'd deteriorated, the doctor told him. Her lungs had not only ceased to function on their own, but were now filling with fluid. The social worker had approached he and his mom to discuss end of life plans.

So, what did he do? He'd done just like his father. He bought a case of beer, came home, and proceeded to guzzle half of them. A quick fix to ease the pain in his heart, dull the foreboding of what he feared he'd be facing in the days to come.

By the time Laura came home, his body had already begun its purging of the poisonous onslaught. He should have known better.

Although he liked his couple of beers, he wasn't used to drinking that much all at once, especially on an empty stomach.

Which, he realized, was still empty, as it proceeded to make a loud, gurgling sound.

Laura's head popped up and she blinked, dazed. Then her eyes rounded and she pushed up to sit, staring at him. "Uh-oh. You gonna puke again?"

He chuckled and shook his head. "No, no. I'm just hungry, I guess."

Sleep still fogged those beautiful blue eyes, and her hair had resumed its crazy-curl glory, flattened only slightly on one side from sleep. A fold in his tee shirt had pressed a pink line across one flushed cheek. She looked absolutely delectable.

But, he realized, she didn't smell very good. No, wait, that was him. Well, maybe now, both of them.

As if she'd read his mind, she wrinkled her nose. "One of us smells like barf. Race you to the shower." With that, she popped up and sprinted into the hallway.

Miller's aching head wouldn't allow him to move that fast. He pushed up onto his elbows first, then swung his feet to the floor. His cell phone lay on the table, and he lifted it. No messages or missed calls. Good. No changes yet.

But no good news either.

He yawned and stretched, then pulled his stinky shirt up over his head. After he drained the glass of water Laura had left on the table, he made his way into the hallway. He rapped on the bathroom door, loud enough to be heard over the spray of the shower.

"What? I'll be out in a minute," she called.

"Can I come in and brush my teeth?" he asked. "I promise, I won't peek."

A pause.

"Okay."

Thirteen

He pushed open the door and stepped over her clothes, lying in a heap on the floor. Black skirt, it looked like, a white blouse of some kind. And splayed right across the top, a lacy pink bra.

Down, boy.

Miller took an extra-long time brushing his teeth, rationalizing that his mouth was probably more foul than it had been in a long time. He was just rinsing when the water spray turned off.

"Are you done out there?" she asked.

"I don't know," he growled. "Am I?"

Another pause. "Come on, Miller. Hand me a towel, will you?"

"I'll get you a clean one."

He retrieved one from the hallway closet and returned. "Stick out your hand and I'll give it to you."

"Why don't you just leave it on the vanity and get out of here?"

"Because I don't want to," he shot back playfully.

She growled. "Miller, I'm getting chilled. Come on." The curtain rustled and her small hand appeared, waving around in the air.

He brushed the towel against her fingertips but snatched it away before she could get a hold on it.

She growled again, and he heard her stomp her foot against the bottom of the porcelain tub. "Miller!"

His laughter rumbled up from deep inside, from a place he'd thought didn't exist anymore. She's fun, he thought. Cute and sassy and damn, sexy-fun. Her hand had disappeared behind the curtain, and she was silent, but only for a moment.

"Okay, big guy. You want play hardball? I can play hardball too."

He staggered back a step when the curtain zinged along the metal bar and there she was, standing in front of him, completely nude. Wet from head to toe, her pale skin slick and shiny. One hand rested in a fist on her hip, and she was wearing a cocky grin.

"Or should I say, blue-ball?" she growled.

Miller blinked. Her wet hair clung to her cheeks and over the tops of her shoulders. Water streamed from the pale strands down over round, perfect breasts topped with rosy points standing at full attention. His gaze traveled down over her flat stomach and landed on the golden patch between her thighs.

And yes, even in his distressed state of mind, with a hellacious hangover on the horizon, he pitched a tent in his shorts in less than twenty seconds flat.

Frozen, afraid to move that the beautiful dream would end, he stood with the towel dangling loosely from the end of his fingertips. She reached forward and snatched it out. Her evil grin zinged him clear to his core.

"Touché," she said, grinning devilishly as she proceeded to wrap the towel around herself.

Miller rubbed a hand down over his face and shook his head. "Okay, you got me. And yes, you play blue-ball very well." As he turned to leave, though, he was shocked to hear her clamber out of the tub. Thrilled to feel her hand on his arm.

"Wait."

He turned and she stepped closer. So close he could smell the fresh, minty scent of his own soap. The clean, grassy perfume of her shampoo.

"Kiss me, Miller. Please."

Miller blinked in shock and reeled back a few inches. She must be kidding. Teasing me, again. Surely . . .

Riveting his eyes with hers, round and as clear blue as water in a sparkling pool, she whispered the words again. Miller swallowed hard and felt a rush of heat head south, rendering him momentarily light-headed.

Was he dreaming this? Post-alcoholic delirium?

But when she lifted one hand to cup his jaw, her pupils dilated, creating ever-widening dark, round windows in the blue. He felt as if he could almost see into her mind. And he wanted, badly, to climb inside and join her.

Laura reached up to wrap both hands around the back of his neck, drawing his face down to hers. When she did, the towel came loose and pooled in a damp tumble over his bare feet.

"Kiss me, Miller. Please," she murmured against his mouth.

So, he did. Her lips were soft, moist, and yielding. At first, her touch was tentative, almost timid, her lips brushing across his in feathery swipes that sent heat pooling between his thighs. With her now-naked form there before him, he was sorely tempted, yet unsure if he should bring his hands up to touch her. He left them hanging loosely at his sides, though his fingers curled into fists, struggling for control.

Then she opened up for him, parting her lips and running her tongue along his lower lip. His now, full erection twitched and he sucked in a gasp. But he accepted her invitation.

He had to be dreaming this. Or maybe he really *had* died. Man. So far, the afterlife was showing great promise.

She tasted like mint, and her breath was hot on his face. Their tongues tangled and dipped and teased in a way that made his knees weak. His hands went to her back, sliding up and down the warm, damp smoothness of her skin, but staying well above her waist. She'd taken him by surprise, and he wasn't really sure how much to assume.

Is she testing me? Or does she really want this?

Seconds later, he had his answer. It was she who broke the kiss, and he let his hands fall away as she took a step backward.

"What's this?" he asked, the words coming out guttural and thick. "Is this how you intend to pay your rent?"

She gazed up at him from under heavy lids, a hint of humor playing at their corners as she slowly shook her head.

Only teasing him, he thought as his heart sank. But then, he'd started it with the towel game, hadn't he? Her smile zinged him again, hitting him in that same, mysterious place in his chest.

"I'm just really, freaking happy right now," she whispered.

He nodded dumbly, his brain not working well enough to question her further. All the blood, it seemed, had headed south.

But she went on to explain anyway.

"Something pretty special happened to me today. I quit playing the timid pee-on at work. I stepped up and took control. I confronted Riley. It worked. Thought maybe I needed to take what I want a little more often." She shrugged. "And right then, I wanted a kiss. Now," she said, her fingers trailing down his chest and hooking into the waistband of his shorts, "now, I want more."

Laura's head was spinning with the exhilaration of taking control. Asking for what she wanted. No, *demanding* what she wanted. She'd never been this bold before today. For a moment, standing there before Miller wearing nothing more than what God gave her, a tiny, panicked voice inside her head squeaked: *what the hell are you doing?* But her inhibitions dissipated as quickly as if she'd imbibed in too much alcohol, or was tripping on an illegal drug.

And damn, but it felt *good*.

Guilt would have chained her from making any advances toward Miller if she hadn't spoken with Angie today. She would never, ever had betrayed a woman she thought of as a friend. Not that Angie had done anything to secure that wobbly halo in recent history. Still, Laura was not that kind of girl. She would never betray *anyone*.

Learning today that Angie and Miller had been over—really over—for at least the past several months was freeing. Her bold move with her boss and her job situation today had been incredibly exhilarating. Now her body, her sexuality that had been so long left alone and wanting, stepped up to the forefront. And Laura wasn't about to stop the tide.

Her attraction to Miller had been instant, and explosive, since the moment she first set eyes on him. Standing in his doorway in nothing but a steel-grey towel that first morning, she at first had been intimidated. Even a little afraid, thanks to Angie's misleading innuendos. But her girl-parts wouldn't listen to what her brain kept screaming: this is a big, bad-boy dude who drinks too much.

For a while, she'd believed Angie's stories. But Laura's common sense, and being with Miller for several weeks now—*living* with him—told her she had no reason to disagree with her instincts. Now, in this moment—this incredibly freeing moment—those instincts overrode the tirades of logic.

She lifted up onto her toes and tilted her head to have easier access into Miller's hot mouth. His neck was thick and strong under her fingers, and when he began rubbing his roughened hands up and down her back, she felt the heat coil in her lower belly. Instinctively, she thrust her hips forward against his erection, and his groan served to spike her excitement even higher.

Finally—*finally*—he slid his big hands down to cup her ass, squeezing as he pulled her close.

Hot dampness pooled between her thighs as she ground herself against him, their tongues dipping and darting in what quickly became a beautifully choreographed dance. As if they'd done this before. Lots of times. As natural as breathing. His breath accelerated to hot blasts on her cheek. Suddenly, it felt as though she couldn't get enough air, her heart beating so hard and fast there was ringing in her ears.

She broke the kiss, panting, searching for his eyes. Those silver-flecked, wolf-like eyes had darkened to flint, looking more wild and feral than she could have imagined. He held her gaze with clearly etched intensity, almost desperation. Miller shifted, but not enough to break their body contact, skin to skin from the chest down. The heaving of his furred chest stroked her peaked nipples, and her knees wobbled.

"Are you sure," he asked, his voice deep and gruff, "are you sure you want this? I mean, we hardly know each other, Laura."

He was right, of course. They hadn't had nearly enough time to develop any kind of real relationship. But there had been a spark between them, ever since that first day. Laura was sure it was purely physical, and she knew all too well how acting on those animal impulses could drag her heart down as well.

She'd fallen victim to lust once before. Her first time, on her prom night. The aching, empty realization that the asshole was never even going to call her again still haunted her. She knew what it had been like to be used.

She blinked and held his intense gaze, unafraid and uninhibited. In just the short time she'd known him, she already knew Miller was a good man. A decent man. One with a heart, but one with a big, aching hole in it from the carnage his father wreaked on his family. And then Angie, using him like she did.

Was it fair of Laura to "use" him? No, of course it wasn't. She had to make it clear. She had to be totally honest and open about this.

"Miller Stanford, I don't think I've ever wanted anything so badly in my entire life." Swallowing hard, she added, "But you're right. We don't have much more between us just yet. We're just roommates. I don't want to spoil that." She searched his eyes, seeing a glint of . . .what? Disappointment? Did he think she was going to turn him down after all?

Or maybe he *wanted* more with her. And she just clarified that as of right now, she hadn't considered that possibility. She huffed out a small sigh.

"I'm not usually the kind of girl who . . .you know. Just gives it up so easily. Freely. But dammit, Miller. I've been living encased in some kind of invisible, emotional armor now for so long, and I'm tired of it. I think it's held me back. In my relationships. In my job. In my life. I'm ready to be free. Can you understand that? Can you just make love to me—" she hesitated, then corrected herself. "Can you just have sex with me, knowing that's all it is? Just sex? I don't want to lead you on."

He blinked, and it was then she noticed for the first time how his eyelashes, so long for a guy, were golden, like the hair on his chest. They cast a sharp contrast against the silvery glint of his eyes. His brows drew together and he tipped his head, a pained expression contorting his handsome features.

"I don't use women, Laura. I'm not asking you to spend the rest of your life with me, but I do want you to know—my feelings for you are starting to go beyond just a physical attraction. I feel like we've developed a . . .a connection. I know it's quick. But it's there. Does that scare you?"

She nodded slowly. "I don't know if I'm ready for that, Miller. I don't know if I even know how to have a relationship with a man. I really, really like you. I think you're an honest, honorable, but very sensitive man. I don't want you to think that if we make lov . . .have sex, that I'm committing to anything long term." She blinked. "I don't know if I'm capable of giving you that. But I'm willing to give it some time, and see."

She felt his chest expand as he drew in a deep breath, and then he folded her against him again, wrapping his arms tightly around her. Burying his face in her hair, his breath blew warm on her neck. The heat sent a shiver down through her, though it wasn't from cold.

It had been so long. So very long. And her body was starving—not only for affection, as it always had been. But for satiation that only a man could provide.

Then he rumbled, "I understand. This has all been happening too fast. But I won't expect anything more from you than you're truly capable of giving, Laura. I'll go in with my eyes wide open. You call me sensitive, but I'm a pretty tough guy, too. Thank you for being honest. It's more than I got from Angie, for sure."

Laura cringed, ashamed for what her friend had done. Embarrassed she hadn't known the girl well enough—even though she thought she had—to realize she was capable of such cold-hearted selfishness.

"I'm sorry about what Angie did to you, Miller. I don't ever want you to think I'm the same kind of girl. I'm not. I mean, I have my own issues, for sure. But self-seeking like that?" She hesitated. She was being selfish, right now, anyway. Her body wanted him, with no strings attached. No emotional complications. Not yet. "I know I'm being greedy, wanting you like this. But you're a guy. You'll get as much out of this as I will, won't you?"

He groaned against her neck, and the ache between her thighs intensified.

"I want you, Miller. I want you to take me upstairs to your bed. But if I have to stand on my tippy-toes for another minute, I'm gonna get a Charlie horse."

His rumble of laughter shook her from the inside out. In one smooth movement, he slid his hand down the back of her legs and scooped her up, cradling her as if she were a feather. Laura nuzzled into the crook of his neck and breathed deep.

She felt as though she were flying, floating on a cloud as Miller carried her up the stairs. Her eyes closed, she savored the moment. Branded it into her memory. Cherished every second of this empowering, carefree day until he stopped walking, and she felt herself drifting down onto his bed.

When she opened her eyes, she suddenly realized she'd never seen this part of the house. She'd never even been to the top of the stairs.

Miller's bedroom was large, appearing to take up almost the entire second floor. A king-sized bed with a heavy, leather-upholstered headboard dominated one wall, facing the front of the house where two dormers provided cozy window seats. It must have once been the attic. But the space had been expertly finished, boasting a soaring cathedral ceiling finished in honey-pecan oak boards. An enormous paddle fan spun methodically, high over her head, the movement at first making her feel a little dizzy.

Or was that from the thrill of what she'd just done? She'd *never* done anything like that before in her entire life. Been the aggressor. She'd always been the pursued, never the pursuer. The beta to every man's alpha.

The wimpy, sappy, pee-on beta to every single person in her entire life.

But the heady thrill of her earlier success at work, after taking charge as she'd never dreamed of doing, had given her courage. Plus, getting the real scoop on Angie's status in Miller's life had burst the floodgates open wide. An emancipation making her feel a wee bit cheeky.

Well, maybe more than a little bit.

Guess this was a day for major changes. She heaved a huge sigh as she watched Miller drop his underwear and climb up on the bed next to her, his enormous shaft standing at full attention.

My God, the man was huge. All over.

Might as well embrace the moment.

Miller's head still pounded ferociously, and his stomach continued to feel as it was filled with yesterday's garbage. But as he carried the soft, delicate woman up the stairs to his room, he realized that what women claimed might well be true—a man's sexual instinct overrides everything else. Everything. Depression. A head-banging hangover.

Everything.

Why did they always make that phenomenon sound like a bad thing?

It *was* true. All the blood drained from his head, his heart, and his stomach, pooling right in his groin. And his every ache and worry faded from consciousness. What a magical cure this was.

As he lowered Laura onto his bed, he couldn't help but notice how small she looked in the midst of an acre of king-sized mattress. Angie hadn't been a petite woman—not overweight, but sturdy and sizeable, always claiming more than her share of the sleeping space. He somehow knew that wouldn't be an issue with this slight waif of a woman.

But enough with comparisons. Let's get down to the business at hand.

She was gazing up at him with clear, blue eyes so intent on his, he felt a shiver skitter down his spine. As though she were looking inside his mind.

Yet in truth, what he saw in those eyes couldn't be anything else but . . .trepidation. She had crossed her arms across her chest, and drawn her knees tight together and off to one side. Her body language was saying something completely different from what it had been just a few minutes earlier.

He sat beside her and lifted a golden curl off her forehead, brushing her cheek with his knuckles.

"What's wrong, Laura? You look scared half to death. If you've changed your mind—"

"No," she shot back quickly. "I want you, Miller. My body needs you. But I'm not very experienced at this . . ." Her mouth twisted into an apologetic smile. "I mean, I'm not a virgin or anything. But I've never really been very good at this."

A jab of pity shot Miller straight through the chest. What kind of horny, selfish bastards had this woman been with, anyway? "What would make you say something like that? You're beautiful. Sexy as hell." He gestured to his arousal. "You can see what you do to me."

Laura Horton may well not be a virgin. Physically. But it seemed as though, in this moment, she embodied the definition in every other sense of the word.

Miller had never been with a virgin.

He reached both hands out to frame her face, never taking his eyes off hers. "Tell me, sweetheart. Tell me why you don't think you're very good at this."

Her eyelashes began fluttering frantically and she shifted her gaze away. "I told you—didn't I? About my first time. In high school. Not only did I come away from that experience shell-shocked, but disappointed. It was over in about forty-five seconds. And then the asshole snatched a filthy, obviously well-used towel out of his console and threw it at me. *Don't bleed on my seats*, he warned."

Miller drew back and closed his eyes, willing down the wave of disgust and rage welling up in his chest. "And since then? Didn't you say you had a boyfriend up in Boone?" he murmured in a tight voice.

"Dean wasn't much better. Made fun of me for not knowing how to *properly please* a man. He'd always wanted . . ." she trailed off, bringing her hands up to cover her face. "I don't like doing the oral thing. At least, I've never wanted to. Dean said he couldn't . . .he couldn't get it up for me unless I did that first." She lowered both hands to curl into the comforter. "*For me*. Like he was doing me any kind of big favor. Once he came, it was over. If I wanted anything for myself, it was up to me." She paused and sighed. "Afterward. In the shower," she added in a small voice.

A mixture of pity and anger coiled inside Miller. So, this is why she's so timid. Has no self-confidence. At least, one big, contributing factor. And stepping up at work today may have addressed part of her asserting herself. But now he knew—it would be up to him to lift her up the rest of the way.

"Here," he said, standing and pulling back the duvet. "Climb under so you don't get chilled."

She did as he asked, sighing as she drew the comforter up to her chin. Seemingly relieved she was now covered. Not quite so exposed. So vulnerable.

Miller slid in beside her and drew her into his arms, taking her mouth. He started gently, sweetly, running his tongue teasingly over her bottom lip, but not attempting to explore inside. Then he began weaving a pattern of kisses, pressing them along the line of her jaw to her ear. She shivered when he licked, then nipped her lobe.

"I'm going to show you," he breathed into her ear, "what making love should be like. I know, you prefer to call this just sex. But unless your man is invested in pleasing you, then it isn't even that." He drew back and tipped up her chin so she couldn't avoid his gaze. "If a man isn't committed to making it as good for you as it is for him, then it doesn't even qualify as sex. It's just plain fucking."

She blinked in surprise at his vulgarity, though he'd tried to keep his tone soft. When he felt her stiffen in his arms, he drew her close to him and stroked his fingertips down the smooth, silky skin of her back.

"I'm not asking you to fall in love with me, Laura. But I refuse to just fuck you. I'm going to make love to you, and show you what a wondrous experience it can be—for both of us."

Fourteen

A buzzing sound jarred Miller back into reality just as the first fingers of dawn were creeping through his blinds. He blinked, confused for a moment. It was Saturday, so it couldn't be his alarm clock. He sometimes set it early to meet Rip at the gym before it got too crowded. But as he rolled over to squint at the glowing red number, he thought, hell, that's not right. Six-thirty a.m. He'd never called Kip to set anything up that early.

But it wasn't his alarm. It was his phone. Within seconds he was fully awake and bolted upright, grabbing for the device on his nightstand, but he'd already missed the call.

It was from his mother.

Shit.

He raked one hand through his hair and it all came flooding back like the living nightmare that it was. His sister was in ICU, in a coma, fighting for her life. He swung his feet to the floor and dialed his mother.

"Hey, Mom. What's happening. Mollie. . .?" He was almost afraid to ask the question.

"She's a little better. That's why I called you." His mother's voice sounded lighter than it had in days. "The doctors came in very early this morning, and said they might take out the breathing tube later today. She's started . . ." A pause, a deep breath. "She's started breathing on her own." Her voice was strangled with emotion.

Miller squeezed his eyes shut, and for a minute he couldn't form words around the ball in his own throat. Finally, he swallowed and pushed on. "That's great news, Mom. Thanks for letting me know."

Feeling as though a Mack truck had just backed down off his shoulders, Miller flopped against the pillows. Only then did he allow himself the luxury of revisiting last night's memory—the delicious, decadent exploration of Laura Horton.

A twinge of hurt pinged his heart when he remembered how she'd gathered one of the extra blankets around her as she crept from his bed sometime in the middle of the night. He'd heard the door hinge sigh, then the creak from the third riser on the stairs as she made her way down them. She must have thought he was asleep. But he hadn't tried to stop her.

Why, he wondered, hadn't she wanted to spend the night with him? Sleep beside him? Wake up and start a new day with him in the morning?

He was assuming too much, he knew. After all, they'd known each other barely weeks. They'd shared their bodies, but that was just sex. For right now, she'd made it plain—that's all Laura wanted. He couldn't help but wonder why the notion bothered him.

Still, this was a wonderful morning. Molls was on her way to recovery, at least from this latest threat. The spring sunshine was streaming through his windows and warming everything, from the air around him to the polished oak boards under his bare feet. And there was a new kind of warmth inside of him. He probably had Laura to thank for that. As he stretched and yawned, his stomach sounded a very audible *good morning*.

Miller dressed and made his way to the kitchen. His hunger, along with a kind of light-headed giddiness he *never* got from the drinking, made him want to celebrate with food. A big breakfast.

Pancakes. He'd make pancakes, just like he used to do for Mollie back in the days . . .before.

Laura awoke to the warm, vanilla-scented aroma of something wonderful, mingled with the salty scent of bacon. Just like when she used to stay with Grandma.

Breakfast. How many men had she known in her life that would make her breakfast?

How many men in her life had made her feel the way Miller did last night? Hmm. Best not think about that too long or hard right yet.

She pulled on sweat pants and a big tee shirt, stopping in the bathroom on her way to the kitchen.

"Good morning," she said moments later as she peeked around the corner.

Miller was standing at the stove with his back to her, his broad shoulders stretching his Knicks jersey taught above a pair of blue athletic shorts. His muscular legs, dusted with golden hair, brought flashes of memory back. She knew exactly what it felt like to wind her legs around those hard, massive trunks. Her heart rate kicked up a notch.

He shot her a look over one shoulder, his mouth curving up.

"Hey, Laura. I figured you might be hungry this morning. I know I am." He turned, holding out a plate heaped with bacon draining on paper towels. "Pancakes aren't quite ready. But you can nibble on some bacon while you wait."

A wash of some emotion Laura couldn't put a name to wrapped around her like a fuzzy blanket and squeezed. "That's so nice of you to cook for us, Miller." She wanted to ask, *what are we celebrating?* The incredible sex they'd shared? But she was glad the words never made it out. He flipped one last trio of pancakes on the griddle, and then turned to face her.

"My sister is out of ICU. Looks like she might be out of the woods." His voice got a little thick around the last few words, and Laura's heart clenched.

"I'm so glad, Miller." She helped herself to a cup of his high-octane coffee, diluting it by half from the carton of creamer. "What's wrong with your sister, anyway? Do you mind talking about it?"

His long pause had her wondering if maybe she'd asked the question too soon. But when he faced her again, holding the platters of pancakes and bacon, he met her gaze and said levelly, "Brain damage. Pretty extensive. She was in the car with my drunken father when he hit a dump truck. Head on." His tone was flat, controlled.

Whoa, now that's a pretty hefty burden to be carrying around in one's past. Laura blinked and dropped her gaze to the swirling cream in her coffee. She knew Miller had issues, demons he was fighting. Angie had alluded to as much. But this was more intense than she had imagined.

Yet, he blurted out the story as though he knew it by rote. With far less emotion, in either his tone or his facial expression, than she would have expected. Laura wondered how long ago it had been, how much time he'd had to learn how to talk about it that way. How long it had taken him to build the wall.

She swallowed, struggling to maintain her neutral counselor face. "That's terrible, Miller. I'm so sorry. And your father?" she pressed quietly.

Miller's chin shot up and his tone grew even icier. "He got exactly what he deserved out of the deal. He's been dead ten years, and Mollie has been in Brightstar Nursing Facility ever since." He clicked the platters down the table. "Come on, let's eat. These are my own special recipe, you know. No Aunt Jemima or Bisquick here."

They sat, and truly, Laura was at a loss for words. This information had caught her entirely by surprise. All of her counselor wisdom seemed as though it might still be asleep. Or perhaps she'd left it down the hall in her tiny room.

She was too closely involved—there was the problem. This wasn't a random patient at the Center. This was the man with whom she'd been entangled between the sheets with just hours ago.

As Miller began to eat, Laura was aware of the awkward silence that had fallen between them. Time to change the subject.

"So, I'm pretty happy this morning myself. It was a pretty big breakthrough yesterday at work," she said brightly.

"You started to tell me last night," he said, forking a huge hunk of dripping pancakes into his mouth.

I did. Right after I dropped my towel and kissed you silly.

Feeling the blood rush to her cheeks, she swallowed and bobbed her head. "I confronted my boss, Riley. And guess what? I start seeing patients—in real live counseling sessions—starting on Monday."

"Hey, way to go." Miller lifted his coffee mug in her direction. "Congrats. I guess I gave you a mini-in-service on dealing with drunks last night, didn't I?" he grumbled. "I mean . . .before. When you first got home. I'm sorry about that."

Laura felt that same pinch in her chest of . . .what? Empathy, dammit. She had to quit doing this if she was going to survive dealing with sad, damaged people every day.

"What you do in your own house is none of my business," she said in a small voice. "I just did what I could to make you more comfortable." She raised her eyes to meet his. "Like any decent roommate would have done."

A slow smile crept across his face. "You certainly made me more comfortable." He kept his eyes trained on his plate of food. His eyebrows rose. "Roommates. Yeah. I like the sound of that."

Laura spent the rest of the weekend putting her room in order, trying to make the small space feel at least a little bit more like home. She'd learned from Miller that the washer and dryer were downstairs in the basement, and he'd welcomed her to use them along with the ironing board and iron he left set up down there. Which was fortunate, since many of her clothes had come out of the boxes in a horrendous mass of wrinkles.

That didn't change the fact that the basement was über-creepy. The washer and dryer lined the far wall, snugged up tight to the age and damp-darkened concrete block. But worst of all, the ironing board was set up directly beneath the narrow, high window. The one that faced directly toward the graveyard.

The view was different from this angle, Laura mused as she waited for the iron to heat up. Standing on her tiptoes, she could just barely see the black bars of the iron fence through a brush of lawn that, from down here, mimicked an overgrown hayfield. A sudden chill drew goosebumps along her arms, and she shuddered.

I'm standing, she thought grimly, at about the same level as the dozens of coffins buried under the grass just yards away from here. If I had x-ray vision . . .that creepy thought, along with the cool dampness of the basement, crept into her brain, and she shuddered again.

Best to keep my mind on getting a nice, crisp press on my work shirts, and the sound of the baseball game droning from the living room upstairs. But as she spread out the first sleeve and reached for the spray bottle sitting on the window ledge, she heard, or more *felt*, the thumping of footsteps outside. Running. She glanced up in time to catch sight of a pair of feet dashing past the window. Small feet, clad in pink sneakers.

Laura's heart leapt into her throat before she realized it was probably just one of the neighbor's kids, taking a shortcut through Miller's side yard. Though she hadn't recalled seeing, or hearing, any children in the neighborhood as of yet.

Setting the iron on its stand, she grabbed the basket of clean laundry she'd already folded from the dryer and headed for the stairs. Wouldn't hurt to let Miller know he had a kid running around in his yard.

She ducked out of the stairwell and into her bedroom, setting the basket on her bed. Then she turned to glance through the window, having raised the shade earlier to let the glorious morning sunshine bathe her room in yellow light.

Her front-row view of the graveyard wasn't nearly as scary as it was after dark. Not on an early summer afternoon like this. The stones took on a silver cast when shafts of sunlight flickered through the trees overhead to dance along their weathered surfaces. The scene would have been peaceful, almost beautiful in a melancholy sort of way.

If not for the little girl wandering up and down the rows, stooping at every marker, running her fingers along what remained of the engravings, some weathered to almost illegible.

Wispy blonde hair hung to her shoulders and looked unkempt, as if it hadn't seen a brush or a washing in a while. She wore a bright, pink polo shirt a size too small, and dirty white shorts. Grass stains smeared her knees with green above her used-to-be-white socks and pink sneakers.

The worst part was the expression on her innocent face—she couldn't have been more than nine or ten years old. But her features, twisted with panic as she hurried from one stone to the next, tore at something deep inside Laura's chest.

It reminded her of how she'd felt in those first few days after her mother moved out, and she'd watched her father fall into a silent pit of deep despair. Lost, abandoned.

She reached to unlatch the window. Open it and call to the girl. But before she had the chance, heavy hands gripped her shoulders from behind, and she shrieked, her heart nearly choking her.

Why hadn't she heard *Miller's* footfalls? His stomping on these hardwood floors usually echoed throughout the entire house.

"Hey, hey, it's okay, Laura. I'm sorry. I thought you'd hear me coming," he said, turning her to face him and drawing her into his arms. "What's got you so mesmerized?"

She twisted away, pointing out the window. "It's her, Miller. It's the little girl I've been hearing. She's out there, reading the headstones."

"Where, Hon? I don't see anyone."

It was true. When she turned back toward the window, there was no one wandering among the graves, save for a squirrel sniffing for acorns.

"She was there, Miller. Just two seconds ago, I swear."

He tipped his head and gazed down at her with a raised eyebrow. "There aren't any little kids in this neighborhood I'm aware of. Most of my neighbors are in their eighties. The folks on this street have lived here since the houses were new—"

"Don't make it sound like I'm imagining this," she snapped. "It was *her*. Desperately searching the graveyard. Maybe the same one I heard up there by Talcott Hall. *Our* little girl. The one who needs our help. And I damn well intend to—"

He pulled her back to him and shushed her as she buried her face in his chest. "Help her. I know. We will. We'll get to the bottom of this."

She felt his hand run down over her hair and start rubbing small circles on her back. In a few moments, she'd regained control and tipped her chin up to meet his gaze.

"Who is she, Mills?"

The way he closed his eyes and sucked in a breath, it was as though she'd slapped him. She wasn't sure why. But he recovered in seconds and held her shoulders firmly in both hands, looking deep into her eyes.

"I spoke to her the other night. I told you. She said her name is Greta. And I'm thinking her father may have been one of the patients in Talcott Hall."

It was hard to hear the nickname coming from Laura's lips. Nobody had ever called him that except for Mollie. His Molls.

And he had to admit it, the whole subject of this mysterious little girl had him spooked. Not only did it touch a tender spot in his own heart, making him think of Mollie—the way she was before the horrific day that changed everything. But he also wasn't one to believe in ghosts. Yet some pretty strange stuff had been happening to him lately, even more so since Laura arrived.

If this Greta was homeless, then why hadn't the authorities sheltered her in the home? Or found a foster family for her? How could such a young child be out there, surviving on her own, without anyone knowing or caring?

The alternative explanation sent ice washing down Miller's spine. He didn't believe in ghosts. At least, he never *admitted* to believing in them.

If I deny their existence, they won't exist.

But *what if?* What if Greta was a lost spirit searching for her father . . .her father's spirit? Presumably, they were both dead, right? He could swear he'd seen them together that night. The night after the grotesque, hook prosthesis showed up on the fence.

Was he losing his mind? His imagination was working overtime with all the stress he'd been under lately. Or had Laura's arrival sparked some unexplained phenomenon, stirring up the spirits of two wandering souls?

He knew one thing for sure: Laura was stirring some kind of phenomenon inside him. And he wasn't sure whether he felt good about that, or if it scared him to death. He knew what it was like to care about someone, and then something like what happened to Mollie takes them away. He wasn't sure if he wanted to risk that kind of hurt ever again.

Tomorrow, he thought. Tomorrow at work he'd examine that prosthesis more closely. It was still locked up in the evidence room. Maybe by researching where the damn thing had come from, he could answer some of the questions whirling around in his head.

He went into work a little early on Monday, and after signing in and retrieving his weapon, he asked Patricia for the key to the evidence room.

"Whatcha looking for, Stanford?" she asked absently as her thumbs flew over the keypad of her phone.

"Just checking on something, that's all," he replied. "Sarge here?"

She looked up and shook her head. "Went to the shop for a new tire on one of the cruisers. He should be back any minute."

Miller rounded the corner and unlocked the door to the evidence room, which wasn't really a room at all, merely an oversized closet. It didn't take long for him to locate the hideous apparatus, lying at eye level on the top shelf. He reached for the neoprene gloves in the box hanging on the wall and snapped on a pair.

Not that there were any fingerprint worries—the forensics team had already dusted the thing and been unable to decipher anything of use. No, Miller just didn't want to be touching the thing. It was creepy looking enough, like something Captain Hook wore. It was eerie just knowing those worn leather straps had encircled somebody's arm at one time.

Some poor bastard's *half* an arm.

It was heavier than he remembered from the day they found it. The hard plastic body was supposed to mimic flesh tone, an image thrown off by the shiny surface. It appeared to be complete, with a leather harness for attaching it to the upper arm, and various buckles for adjustment. A metal cable ran along one side, threaded through an eye and connecting the top of the harness to the *hand*, a two-pronged, stainless steel hook. Miller tugged on the cable and the hooks spread apart, enabling the user to grasp objects. When he released the cable, the hook drew together with a soft click. He winced.

Miller wondered how a person would operate the thing, if not by using his other hand. Assuming he had one. He hunched his shoulders up to his ears.

Sarge came around the corner and walked up beside him. He reached forward to finger the leather harness dangling from the prosthesis.

"This," he held the looped end up to his own body, "straps around the man's shoulder, on his good side. By flexing his shoulder front to back, the cable gets shortened, and the claw hook opens." He demonstrated, rolling his shoulder back and then forward again.

Miller raised his eyebrows and blew out a breath. "Pretty clever design. How old do you think this thing is?"

"I did a little research. The inventor was named Dorrance, and he came out with this split hook version around 1912." Sarge pointed to the hinge connecting the metal claw to the plastic body. The letters spelling out *Dorrance USA* were pressed into the circular metal disc. "Pretty revolutionary. The design works so well, some amputees still use them."

"Huh," Miller said, turning the body over in his hand. The underside of the plastic was chipped and ridged. "This one looks like it got used pretty hard." Looking closer, Miller realized that some of what he thought were cracks down near the steel banded "wrist" were actually letters. Three of them—*T E S*—had been carved into the hard plastic. He pointed to them and glanced up at Sarge. "A monogram?"

Sarge shrugged, handing the harness back to him. "Could be. Did we ever get a name on the John Doe you guys found inside Talcott Hall?"

Miller shook his head. "I don't know. But this couldn't have belonged to him, anyway. He had both his arms."

His sergeant tilted his head, his eyebrows lifting. "I do know that amputees who got these things considered them pretty precious merchandise. I can see why they'd chisel their initials into them. Make sure nobody made off with theirs." He paused and met Miller's gaze, then poked a thumb in the direction of Talcott Hall. "Especially if they got themselves locked up in a place like that."

"Wait," Miller said, shaking his head with a chuckle. "I mean, what's the probability that there would be more than one man missing part of his arm in a psychiatric hospital at the same time?"

Sarge didn't smile. "Ever heard of PTSD, Stanford? Just imagine how screwed up in the head a guy could get if he came back from the war not only *shell-shocked*, as they used to call it, but missing a body part too. I'd be willing to bet there were lots of them who became permanent residents up the hill."

Miller heaved a huge breath and blew it out. "Are there records, Sarge? I mean, names of the people who were admitted there? Maybe we could research those initials—"

"Don't go there, Stanford." Sarge barked the words like a direct order, then snatched the prosthesis from Miller's hands and dropped it back onto the shelf with a clunk. He turned on his heel and headed for his office. "Do us both a big favor, and don't even think about going there."

Fifteen

Laura was so excited, anticipating her new role at work, she'd pushed the thoughts of the mysterious little girl she and Miller had seen to the very bottom of her mind. She had enough on her plate now, without heaping on any additional uncertainties. Adding to that, she struggled with the fact that she and Miller had slept together. That certainly complicated her living situation, especially since she couldn't tell, by the way Miller had become so aloof afterward, whether he regretted what they'd shared or not.

Did *she*? Part of her screamed *Yes, you fool. You're not ready for any kind of relationship, especially with someone you barely know.* Another part, deeper inside a heart that was calloused on the outside, but bruised and insecure on the inside, screamed, *This is exactly what your life needs right now.*

So by the end of that next week, Laura had almost forgotten about the mysterious child. She'd chalked up this Greta's existence to stress and an overactive imagination.

Which is why, on Friday afternoon, as she sauntered down the last hundred feet of sidewalk toward Miller's house, she was completely flabbergasted to hear the sound of a child sobbing— coming from off to her left, from the ancient graveyard.

It was early, barely five-thirty, and the sun hadn't even begun its descent behind the wall of pines lining the cemetery. Laura slowed her steps and peered cautiously between the trees, but didn't see anyone. No one at all.

But the sobbing was plaintive, and loud enough to carry to her over the stone wall fence. Her logical brain wondered if this was a child who got lost trying to find the Children's Shelter.

Maybe she's flopped down behind the headstones and that's why I can't see her.

As she turned onto the grassy patch between Miller's house and the black iron fence, Laura continued to scan the plot. From this vantage point, the headstones were lateral, so she could clearly see behind them. Moving from those closest to the street and back toward the woods, she continued to search behind every row until she reached the rear boundary.

Nothing. Then, suddenly, the sobbing ceased. Silence.

"So you hear her too."

Laura shrieked and spun around, slapping a hand to her chest. A woman clutching a large bunch of lavender flowers was standing near to the open place in the iron fence.

"I'm sorry. I didn't mean to startle you," the woman said, brushing a wispy strand of greying, brown hair back from her face. "I was bringing flowers to my Grandpa's grave."

Laura blew out a breath and tried to slow her racing heart. "It's okay. I didn't hear you drive up. I was looking for . . .I thought I heard . . ."

The woman stepped forward and extended her free hand. "I'm Jenna Carlisle. My grandfather, Ken Rupert, he used to live next door. He passed a couple months ago." She lifted the bouquet she held forward, ducking her chin toward the flowers. "Gladiolas, well, they were his favorite. Whenever I see a bunch, I feel like I just have to bring them."

Laura shook the woman's hand. Her grip was strong and confident, and she looked Laura straight in the eye.

"I'm Laura Horton. I'm Miller Stanford's new . . .roommate."

The edge of the woman's mouth twitched. "Yeah, I see that Angie chic moved out. She was quite the piece of work. She was storming up and down the front steps the day after my grandfather died, actually. Loading up her stuff when the funeral home came to retrieve him."

Laura tried to hide her shudder. "I'm so sorry," she said quietly. "How old was he?"

Jenna drew in a deep breath and dropped her gaze to the ground. "He had a good long life, Ken did. Last few years weren't the best, but he was a trooper." Her eyes rose to meet Laura's. "I've been out here a half-dozen times since then. I've heard her too. The child."

A chill washed through Laura as if someone had pushed ice water through her veins. She looked away, chuckling nervously. "So I'm not completely crazy, then."

"No ma'am, you're not crazy. Have you ever seen her?" she asked.

Laura stared at the woman, wondering how much she should reveal. After a moment, she nodded once. "Yes. Yes, I think I have. Do you know who she is? Does she live around here?"

The laugh that barked from Jenna's throat was hoarse and kicked off a fit of coughing that kept her from answering for a minute or two.

"You'd think," she sputtered as it subsided, "that watching what happened to old Ken would keep me from lighting up another smoke. Tough habit to break, though. Just can't seem to manage it."

Feeling awkward and at a loss for anything else to say, Laura glanced down at her watch. As if she had something to do, even though all she was headed into was an empty house with nothing to keep her busy until bedtime.

"Well, it was nice to meet you, Jenna. Again, I'm sorry for your loss." Laura wrapped her arms around herself and started back toward the front of Miller's house.

"She used to come here, you know. With her grandma. Years and years ago. In fact, I used to play with her. We were about the same age, back in the late sixties. She'd come here and her grandma would just lean on the wall and wait for her."

Laura paused and turned back toward the woman. Cocking her head, she asked, "Wait for her. Why? What was she doing? Did she have a relative buried here?"

Jenna's eyes narrowed and she tipped up her chin, studying Laura. "Thought she did. That's what she always said. Told me to keep looking for the name Sanderson. Thomas E. Sanderson. It was her daddy's name."

Laura's heart rate kicked up a notch. Could it be?

"Her name . . .the child's first name? What was it?" she asked.

Jenna shrugged. "Hell if I can remember. I'm lucky I can remember my own kids' names these days. The only reason I remember the last name—at least, her daddy's last name—is because she kept sayin' it, over and over again. While she searched the headstones."

Laura shook her head. "Did you . . .did she ever find the stone?"

Jenna's head began oscillating side to side and she continued to fix Laura with an eerie stare. "Nope. It isn't here. She said her daddy died up there in Talcott Hall, and was buried in the State Cemetery. At the time, this was the only State burial ground there was. But there's no Thomas Sanderson buried here. No Sandersons at all."

When she got to work on Monday morning, Laura couldn't wait to get into the online records system to start researching the name *Sanderson*. There was no way she could be sure—no way she knew for certain that the little girl Jenna used to play with was the same little girl she and Miller had been seeing. At least, the same child's *spirit*. And who knew if they'd even shared the same last name?

In her early perusal of the software program, Laura had noticed a folder labeled *TH_Records*, but at the time, didn't pay it much mind. Now, the folder was her first destination once her computer booted up.

Until a reminder popped up on her screen, declaring *Meeting with new client: ten-fifteen a.m. Prescott Room. Kayla Riley to assist.*

Crap. Okay, so this is exactly what she'd wanted, exactly what she'd been looking forward to since last week in her showdown with her boss. Direct patient contact, face-to-face consultations. But not this morning. She'd so hoped to have a few moments to research the Sanderson name in the Talcott files.

And what did that say? *Riley to assist*?

"Good morning, Ms. Horton. All set for your first session?"

Laura jumped when her boss spoke from the open doorway in an authoritative, and not particularly quiet voice. Breathing deep and smoothing down the front of her skirt, she rose to face her.

"Yes. Yes, I am, Ms. Riley. In fact, I've been looking forward to it all weekend. But I thought I was scheduled to go in with Counselor Timmons?"

She wasn't sure if Riley's wry smile was genuine or taunting, but when she reached forward to hand Laura a manila folder—a mighty thick one—she recognized a challenge.

"Change of plans." Riley glanced at her watch. "You have about ten minutes or so to take a look at the client's records," she said in a clipped tone. "I'll see you in the meeting room in a few."

When she'd disappeared into the hallway, Laura plopped back into her chair and huffed. The folder in her hand was filled with at least fifty sheets of paper or more. Another test, she thought. She's testing me to see how well I can perform on short notice—and with *her* breathing down my neck the whole time.

Miracle of miracles, of all people to come to her rescue seconds later, it was Jonathan. He popped around the edge of the doorway, glancing nervously back over his shoulder before scooting in and closing the door behind him.

As he sat, he leaned forward and spoke in hushed tones. "She's cutting your milk teeth on Jeremiah Budinski. There's no way you can read all that in ten minutes, and she knows it," he said, motioning toward the folder in her lap. "I'll clue you in. Jeremiah is a regular here—in and out every six months or so. Ends up in the drunk tank, usually after beating up his regular squeeze." Jonathan narrowed his eyes. "But he must be pretty good in the sack, because the chick *never* presses charges on him."

A sudden surge of bile rose into the back of Laura's throat, but she swallowed it down and tried to take deep, slow breaths. "So," she began, "what's the approach been so far?"

Jonathan spun around to his computer, which was already booted up and ready, and tapped a rapid staccato on the keys. A document filled the screen and he scrolled down, pointing at the last entry dated less than three months ago. "He's getting worse," he muttered. "And Riley's been the one handling him the past three times he's been in."

Jonathan shook his head and clucked, then spun his chair around and locked gazes with her. "Riley's an enabler. She's been using the *oh, you poor boy what happened to you in your childhood?* routine. Not worrrking!" he sang out, flipping his hands up on both sides of his head.

Laura gulped, again trying to suppress the panic attack she felt coming on hard and heavy. "So, what do you recommend?"

Jonathan pushed his black-rimmed glasses up onto his nose and leaned back in his chair, which emitted an ear-splitting squeak. He crossed his arms.

"Depends, my lady. Do you want to help this poor soul? At the risk of pissing off the high and mighty Queen Riley?"

Oh, boy. Now that was quite a choice, Laura thought. But before she could answer, Jonathan continued.

"I say, go in innocent, curious, and listen—a lot. This creep likes to spill his guts. Then, when he starts making excuses about how he gets his jollies—smacking around his lady—nail him." He made a pistol with his right hand and pointed it at her.

"Nail him?"

"Let him know—it doesn't matter that we are *only* his addiction counselors. Remind him, we can report him. He *will* be held accountable for assault and battery. He needs to know the consequences of his actions. Stop depending on a get-outta-jail-free ticket from us." Obviously satisfied with himself, Jonathan bobbed his head and grinned, flashing his strange, little teeth. Then he added, "Don't be a Timmons. Go more with Wolff's approach. You can't pussy-foot around this kind of abuser."

As Laura made her way down the hall to the meeting room, clutching Budinski's file to her chest, she considered Jonathan's advice. It sounded like Riley had been using the classic addiction counselor's approach: treat the patient as a sole entity, try to make him understand the reasons behind his addiction and his violence. Confrontation, no matter what Jonathan said, wasn't a smart tactic.

But some things she'd learned in her second year of grad school, during family counseling sessions, just might.

The meeting room resembled a small, comfortable parlor or den rather than a treatment space. No desk to divide the counselor from the patient, just three wingback armchairs encircling a low, round table, where a pitcher of water and glasses sat on a tray. Two walls were cloaked with built-in bookshelves, crammed with an assortment of psychology reference books and old issues of periodicals on the subject. The windows in this room covered nearly the entire outside wall, and were lined with homey, paisley-patterned drapes.

She'd been the first to arrive, and as she settled into one of the chairs, she couldn't help but notice the view. The corner of Talcott Hall, it's three, ominous, angled turrets visible in a line down the western side of the building, loomed just across the street. Some small saplings, she noted, had taken root in the tops of two of those turrets. And a large bird, possibly a hawk, coasted in to disappear behind the bricked upper edge. Must have built a nest up there.

Every creature makes the best of a situation, she thought. Establishes a home and goes on living their life, even if it's atop the ruins of what used to be a house of horrors.

The sound of footsteps and Riley's voice brought her back to the moment.

"Right in here, Mr. Budinski. Today I'd like you to meet one of our newest counselors, Laura Horton."

They appeared in the doorway, Riley wearing her usual navy business suit and helmet hair. There was a a short, stocky man beside her. Budinski appeared older than the forty-two Laura had gleaned quickly from his records, nearly bald with liberal grey lacing what hair remained. He wore dusty, Dickies work clothes, his hand fisted in a faded Yankees ball cap at his side.

And *attitude,* written clearly all over his face. She hadn't even met the man, hadn't spoken a word to him, and he already looked pissed off that Laura was breathing.

She stood, stepped forward, and extended a hand. "Mr. Budinski, my pleasure. Counselor Riley tells me you're a frequent visitor here with us. That's unfortunate."

The look of shock Riley shot her didn't ruffle her. She continued smoothly. "Have a seat and let's talk about what we can do to fix that."

Budinski appeared as taken aback as Riley. But he shook her hand and flopped down in one of the chairs. Slapping both his knees, he leaned forward, his watery grey eyes boring straight into Laura's.

"So you're the new girl, huh? You don't look old enough to have graduated high school. How do I know you're even qualified to look at my records?" he asked, his voice gruff and raspy.

"I assure you, Mr. Budinski, my qualifications are as good as Ms. Riley's here." Maybe better, she thought, but wisely bit back the words. She tipped her head toward the other woman who sat stiffly on the edge of her seat, as though she intended to end the session rather quickly. "In going through your file, it's become pretty obvious to me. I believe your problem, your recurring relapses into drink and violence, can't be fixed unless we examine all the contributing factors."

Budinski snorted and scrubbed a hand down his face. "Some more of this dissection of my childhood, huh? Same old shit—"

"No, Mr. Budinski, not more of the same old shit. I'm sure Counselor Riley has done more than enough in helping you to examine your history, your internal reasoning. Your justifications— excuses, if you will—for your failure to break the cycle. I'm thinking it's time to look beyond the individual." Laura continued to speak quickly, as Riley's expression and her raised hand told her she was about to get cut off and shut down. She tapped Budinski's record folder with three fingers. "Your file here indicates your immediate family consists only of yourself and your wife, Sabrina. Is that correct?"

Budinski blinked, then cut his gaze from Laura to Riley and back. "Yeah, but what the hell does she have to do with this?"

"Well for one, she's the victim of your abuse, in almost every instance, from what I've read. She may well have a *lot* to do with your problem. I think before we can go any further to help you understand how to beat your addiction and repetitive backslides, I'd like to invite her in. Speak to both of you, at the same time."

Budinski's brows knitted, then he tipped his head to one side, considering. "Maybe it *would* help for you to see what I'm going through at home. It's not all me, you know."

Riley finally found her tongue and barked, "We are an addiction facility here, Ms. Horton, not family counselors."

Laura turned to face Riley and spoke with crisp conviction. "I'm aware that's been the protocol up until this point, Ms. Riley. But I'd like to suggest we try an alternative approach, since obviously," she hefted the two-pound folder in her boss's direction, "the ongoing treatment isn't working. With, of course, the client's willingness to cooperate."

When she turned her gaze back to Budinski, he was nodding. "Sabrina's comin' in to visit me day after tomorrow. We can set the session up for then, can't we?"

"In my office, Ms. Horton," Riley snipped as soon as the client disappeared around the corner of the hallway.

The echo of her office door slamming hadn't faded before Riley spun around and faced Laura, both elbows drawn back, a look of fury contorting her features.

"How dare you?" she hissed. "How dare you question my tactical approach in treating this patient? You . . ." She stepped into Laura's personal space and poked a fingertip into her chest, "*You* are the newbie here, remember? You don't even have your certification yet."

Laura refused to back away, even though the blast of Riley's sour coffee breath engulfed her senses. Swallowing hard, she crossed her arms over her chest and narrowed her eyes.

"That's true, Ms. Riley. Thank you for pointing that out. But everything I said in there was true, wasn't it? You haven't made any progress with this patient at all. In fact, records show he's gotten worse over the past three months since you took over the case."

Riley staggered back a step, her hand falling to her side. Laura wasn't sure what she saw in the woman's eyes as they flew open wide, her mouth describing a perfect "O." Was that shock? Anger? Or perhaps . . .intimidation?

When Riley spoke again her tone had darkened to a growling whisper. "You couldn't possibly have had time to read through the entire record in the few minutes I gave you. Who helped you? That Jonathan worm?"

Laura felt one of her eyebrows drift up toward her hairline. "Worm, hey? That's not a very nice way to talk about one of your staff, Counselor Riley." She narrowed her eyes and leaned in even closer toward Riley's face. "And no, I hadn't even seen Jonathan yet this morning."

It was a bold-face lie. But Laura, knowing Jonathan had truly come to her rescue, didn't want to throw the dweeb under the bus. Even if he did snort and snuffle and fart just a few feet away from her.

A knock on the door interrupted their showdown, and Laura watched Riley's eyes roll over her shoulder in that direction. "Yes?" she called, nearly puncturing Laura's left eardrum.

"Ms. Riley, the group session is ready to begin in Conference Room A. Jonathan told me you were the facilitator?"

Laura recognized the voice of Anne Timmons, jarring a memory into her brain.

"Be right th—" Riley called, but Laura spoke into her face before the words finished leaving her lips.

"That's right. You promised me I'd be working with Counselor Timmons this morning. What happened to that plan, Ms. Riley? Why the sudden change of protocol?"

Now it was Laura's turn to point a trembling finger in Riley's direction. She was not, however, foolish enough to make contact with the woman's crisply pressed white shirt.

Laura couldn't believe it when Riley backed down. She braced her fingers along the top of her helmet bangs and closed her eyes. "Yes. Yes, well . . .Budinski was readmitted over the weekend. Un-unexpectedly." She was beginning to stammer. "I-I wanted to get a second opinion on the case. An unbiased, impartial second opinion." Riley spun away from Laura and whisked around the edge of her desk, grabbing a handful of tissues from the box on her way.

"Unbiased, impartial. Yep, that would be me," Laura said quietly. "Now you've got my unbiased, impartial second opinion, Counselor Riley. I think you've been coddling this patient. And he's made no progress. In fact, he's backsliding. It's time for a different approach. Before he kills his wife. And we—you and I *and* the State of New York—all become involuntary accomplices to manslaughter."

Riley remained with her back to Laura and loudly honked her nose into the tissues. A prolonged silence preceded a response Laura wasn't sure she believed she'd heard.

"Thank you for that, Counselor Horton. When Sabrina Budinski comes in to visit her husband, we'll set up a family counseling session." She finally turned to face Laura, tipping up her chin and studying her with narrowed eyes. "I, of course, will facilitate," she hissed.

Riding an exhilarated high at her seemingly successful morning, she couldn't wait to document the session in Budinski's file. Her eyes were riveted to her computer screen when her coworker, Sadie appeared, filling her office doorway in a neon geometric-print sheath dress. Laura caught sight of the bright colors in her peripheral vision and jumped.

"Sorry to startle you, Laura. Headed out for a smoke. Come tell me how your first counseling session went," she said, a mischievous smirk making her dark eyes twinkle.

Warm, humid air engulfed Laura as she followed Sadie outside. The noonday sun bathed the entirety of the patio space, all except for one table tucked up close to a massive old oak tree. That's where Sadie headed, pausing at the end of the pavers to slip off her heels before stepping onto the plush carpet of grass.

"Ah, dia glorioso," Sadie hummed as she slid onto the bench. She turned toward Laura and narrowed her eyes. "And I hear you've had a pretty glorious day of your own."

"I have," Laura replied, unable to contain her grin. "Still not sure I won't end up with a pink slip by day's end, though."

Sadie shook her head. "Don't worry about that. Riley hasn't been in that job long enough to make those decisions. Not by herself, anyway." She lit her cigarette and blew smoke off to one side. "So things are looking up for you here, then. Back in your hometown." She smiled.

A flush of heat rose up Laura's neck, remembering just how her new situation had improved since those first days. She kept her eyes trained on the acorns scattered on the grass around her feet and nodded, still smiling. "That it has. In more ways than one."

"Hmm, now that's a loaded comment. What other wonderful things are going on in your life?"

Laura met her gaze briefly before sliding it away toward Talcott Hall. "Well, my roommate situation has improved. I'm getting along with Miller much better now."

She watched as Sadie's perfectly shaped, dark eyebrow lifted and she tipped her head. Then she jumped when the flat of the woman's palm slapped the metal table. "*Miller*. Miller Stanford? Our security guy?"

Laura's cheeks were burning as she quirked a sly smile and nodded.

"Well, I'll be damned. Is that who you're living with? I thought he had a girlfriend. Some barmaid chick. Amy or something?"

"No, her name is Angela. And he did. She was a good friend of mine in high school. She's been living with him for the last three years. But Angie moved out." Laura snorted. "The day before I got here."

"Well, aren't you a lucky girl? Stanford's a hottie. Hear his temper can get hot too, though. Watch your step around him, Laura." Worry tainted Sadie's words.

"Never fear. I can handle myself," Laura began, distracted. The mammoth, brick behemoth called Talcott Hall had drawn her full attention now. Her gaze snapped back to Sadie's face. "Hey, tell me something. Are there any records in our database on Talcott? On their patients, I mean."

Sadie glanced back over her shoulder, blowing smoke in that direction. "There's a file. But I think it's password protected. I got bored one afternoon and tried poking around in there, but I couldn't get the folder to open."

"Who would know how to gain access?" Laura asked. "You think Jonathan might?"

Sadie shrugged. "Possibly. One thing about Jonathan. He might be a weird little twit, but he sure is a whiz when it comes to the computer stuff. If he doesn't have the password, I'll bet there's a way he can find it."

Sixteen

Ever since Laura had stumbled her way into his life, Miller found himself watching the clock on the dash of his cruiser every afternoon just before five o'clock. His main job was to patrol the grounds, if his services weren't required with new admits to the Rehab Center, or transferring patients between buildings. He figured, what harm would it do to do a loop around the Rehab Center around five o'clock?

Maybe he'd catch Laura and have a few minutes to chat with her.

Miller couldn't believe how his life had turned around in just a few short weeks. Before, he was okay. Angie wasn't the love of his life, but he didn't have to spend too much effort on her either. In fact, the most enjoyable times they spent together had been when he'd stopped in at After Shocks for a drink after work, and she'd been tending bar.

Flirtatious conversation with a bowl of popcorn on a waist-high bar between them. Some not-too-bad sex when they got home. Once in a while. When she'd been in a good mood.

That's what their entire relationship had been like, he thought. Consistently inconsistent. Fluffy and insubstantial like popcorn, yet with a very substantial barrier keeping them from getting too close.

But it had worked. For almost three years, anyway. It had filled the empty hole in his life that he wasn't quite sure how to classify. Miller had always thought of himself as a loner. No real close buddies in school—not since the football team, anyway. Once his bright new career in the sport had come screeching to a halt, he'd made a point to avoid his teammates. They hadn't seemed to mind.

Angie and him . . .yeah, it'd been good. While it lasted. But he had to admit, he'd been more angry than hurt when she announced she was leaving.

And then, this Meg Ryan clone shows up on his doorstep, looking every bit as adorable as the actress when Miller first saw her in City of Angels. Not a movie he'd ever have chosen to sit through, but his baby sister begged him to rent it, sit and watch it with her. In his senior year of high school.

Just three months before the accident.

Miller tried to ignore the stab of pain in his chest at the memory as he turned the corner onto Bolles Avenue. He glanced at his dash clock yet again: 5:03. She should be stepping out and starting her block-and-a-half walk home any minute.

Feeling more than a little foolish, Miller pulled over to the side of the road right across from the Rehab Center, threw the car in park, and killed the engine. No real *reason* to do a walk around Talcott Hall's perimeter, but the move would give him an excuse to linger in the area just a few minutes longer. After all, it had been just days ago when they found that poor homeless dude doing his best to die there in the corner of the front room. Miller, as well as his sergeant, was still wondering just how the old guy got in there. And who had gone to such trouble to ruin the chain link fence.

It certainly couldn't have been the homeless man. He barely had the strength to keep breathing. And he still, from what Sarge had told him from the hospital report, wasn't in any condition for questioning.

Miller had encircled three-quarters of the perimeter, keeping a casual eye on the Rehab Center's front doors, when he finally saw her come out. But she wasn't alone. Laura was in an animated discussion with—what the hell? Jonathan?

I thought she hated the guy? Guess she's gotten over her aversion to that nerdy geek.

Miller scrubbed his hands down his face and headed in her direction.

As he drew closer, Jonathan saw him first and halted in mid-sentence. "Hey there, Miller. How ya doing this evening? I was just walking our new counselor out. Have you met Laura Horton?"

Laura's face registered surprise as she turned toward him. And something else. What was that? Color rose into her creamy pale cheeks, and she stammered, "Oh yes, I know Miller, Jonathan."

I guess the hell she does.

Jonathan's gaze flitted nervously back and forth between Miller and Laura. Then he paused and cleared his throat.

"As I was saying, Laura, I think I can probably get that passcode you're looking for. It just might take me a day or two." He winked at her conspiratorially, then patted her shoulder. "I'll see you tomorrow. Have a great evening. You too, Miller."

Jonathan nodded in Miller's direction as he turned on his heel and started off briskly toward the parking lot, his waddling gait reminding Miller of Daffy Duck.

"What passcode?" Miller asked as soon as Jonathan disappeared around the side of the building.

Laura blinked up at him with those huge, baby blues and Miller felt a jolt go straight through him. Now, he was certain, his own cheeks were flushed. All he could think about was how she'd held his gaze with those amazing eyes as he'd crested his last orgasmic wave only a week ago—right behind hers.

"To the Talcott Hall file," she replied. "I want to see if there were any patients by the name of Sanderson admitted there. You know, the little girl we keep seeing? Greta?"

Miller felt a tightening in his chest as alarm bells went off in his brain. Sarge's words echoed there.

Don't go there, Stanford. Do us both a big favor, and don't even think about going there.

"Laura, this is a can of worms you don't want to open. You're talking about official State records, and patient confidentiality. I wouldn't want you to jeopardize your job—"

"I have the authority to research patient records, Miller. Signed off on all of that confidentiality blah-blah-blah as part of my initial hire. I won't be breaking any rules."

He folded his arms and squinted down at her. "None of *your* patients could have ever stepped one foot inside Talcott Hall," he said. "Unless you get many octogenarian alcoholics."

She had tipped her chin up, almost belligerently, and folded her arms over her chest, matching his defiant stance.

Hmm. Got a bit of attitude going for her this evening.

"So, what's got you all fired up?" he asked. "You act like a bullfighter who's just speared the bull."

"Maybe I have," she quipped, her intense blue gaze never leaving his own. "I had a pretty good day today. I mean, a *really* good day."

Miller felt cold fingers of irritation creeping up the back of his neck. "You did, huh? And I don't suppose your coworker—what do you call him? Jonath-It?—had anything to do with that *really good day*?" He didn't even try to keep the cynicism out of his tone.

"As a matter of fact, he did." Laura shifted the strap of her shoulder bag higher and twisted her neck. It might have been to relieve a kink, but to Miller the action looked almost . . .challenging. Like that bull swinging his massive head.

"Do tell," he growled.

"Well, if it hadn't been for Jonathan's cueing me in on my first patient's background this morning, I wouldn't have stood a chance at succeeding. In front of my boss. That's pretty big."

Miller studied her, wondering how she'd transformed from the sweet, delicate bird he'd assumed her to be, to this lady hawk. Before his eyes. "I still don't see what that has to do with snooping around in Talcott Hall records."

"Oh, it doesn't. Totally unrelated," she snapped back. Fisting both hands on her hips, she glared up at him. "Didn't you tell me you wanted to figure out this little girl's story? This Greta? Try to help her?"

"I do, but—"

At that moment, Miller's two-way squawked. "Miller, this is Control. You copy?"

Heaving a sigh, he snatched the device off his hip and responded. "Yeah, I copy."

"We've got a suspicious character stalking around the homeless shelter. The desk staff say they've not seen him before. Can you go over and check it out?"

Shit and damn. But I'm on duty. And this *is* my job.

"I'm on my way," he said, trying to ignore the smirk on Laura's face.

"Guess we'll have to continue this discussion at a later date," she quipped. Then she started off down the sidewalk, calling back over her shoulder, "Later, Stanford."

Miller couldn't be sure why Laura's attitude had irritated him so. Why should he care if she decided to go digging in some old records? Sarge had told *him* not to pursue the matter, not Laura. Miller had no more control over Laura's actions than he did over anyone else in his life. Wasn't *that* the truth?

He shouldn't care, and that was a fact.

But he did. And *that* fact bothered him more than anything she was doing, or trying to do.

And was he even sure he hadn't dreamed up this Greta Sanderson? Oh, yeah, Laura claimed to have seen a little girl wandering around the graveyard next to his house. But hell, it could have been a kid visiting any one of the nearby residents. Miller never really paid much attention to his neighbors—the living ones, anyway. He cringed inwardly remembering how he'd been completely unaware his elderly next-door neighbor had passed until he inadvertently stumbled on the man's burial service.

Plus, it seemed living next door to a graveyard creeped Laura out, and she had a pretty good imagination. Those non-existent branches scratching at her window the first night she'd been there? Yeah, she definitely hadn't gotten used to having dead neighbors. And up until today—just now—he'd really thought Laura was the meek, timid type.

Wait, though. That episode the night after she stood up to her boss? How she came on to him, full-blown and bare-ass naked in his bathroom? There wasn't anything meek and timid about her then. Maybe there was a side to Laura Horton she'd kept well disguised up until now. Maybe she was more like his ex—and her friend—Angie, after all.

Miller twisted his neck and blew out a breath, feeling a little twinge of sadness. He'd liked Laura better when he thought she was the kind of woman who needed taking care of. He knew how to do that.

And felt much more comfortable with a woman who wasn't more alpha than he tried to convince the world he was.

The controller's call to investigate the "prowler" outside the homeless shelter proved to be a man looking for his wife and son. Apparently, the asshat had disappeared two months ago without notice, and came home to find his apartment occupied by a couple he'd never met. His wife and son had been evicted, and—who would guess? Without any income, other than the meager wages Mom made working at the liquor store down on the corner, they hadn't been able to pay the rent. Got evicted. Go figure.

Miller wondered sometimes where people hid their brains other than up their own asses.

The call a few hours later on his dispatch radio came from Duvall, and he sounded . . .weird. Out of breath, under stress. Miller had just finished writing out a ticket to a driver who thought the route through the State grounds would make a quick shortcut home—at warp speed. As Miller returned to the same place he'd spoken with Laura earlier on Bolles Avenue, he saw Duvall's cruiser sitting at an odd angle, right in front of the main locked gates to Talcott Hall. As though he'd swerved and . . .what? Ended up in the ditch?

He parked across the road and got out, searching his field of vision for his partner. The light was fading now, but it was barely seven-thirty. Plenty of daylight left.

Duvall was nowhere to be seen. He snatched up his radio.

"Duvall, you copy? I'm here. Where the hell are you?"

Static scorched his ears for almost fifteen seconds, and Miller was just about to repeat his message when Duvall's voice cut through the white noise.

"I'm here. Geez, got a hell of a start. You up front by the cruiser?" Duvall's voice sounded more strained than Miller had ever heard it. He was the older, more experienced cop. Unflappable. Something big must have flapped his wings tonight.

"Copy that."

"Be there in a few."

Within minutes Miller saw the tall grasses along the side of the fence sway, Duvall's cap coming into view seconds later. He was traveling along the same path he'd seen the little girl—Greta—and the strange amputee dude travel that night, along the perimeter of the chain link.

"What's up?" Miller called, waving a hand to catch his attention.

His partner seemed distracted, repeatedly looking behind him, and then over toward the empty brick building, as he struggled to make his way through the tall brush.

Breaking through onto the paved area, Duvall stopped and yanked off his cap, scratching at his balding scalp.

"Shit, Stanford," he said, then crouched into a squat and scrubbed his hand over his face, "does this kind of weird shit happen all the time over on this side of the campus?"

Duvall was obviously shaken, and Miller convinced him to climb into the passenger side of his own cruiser while they waited for Roy to come in and fire up the tow truck. There was no way they were getting Duvall's cruiser out of that muddy ditch without a winch.

"So what happened? What'd you see?" Miller asked, once Duvall had been sitting silently in his car for two or three minutes. The older man was staring, blankly, toward the abandoned brick building.

Slowly, he met Miller's gaze. He didn't know Duvall very well, only brushed past him now and again at the station, but he could tell the guy was spooked. His naturally pasty complexion had taken on an almost greenish pallor that made Miller a bit uncomfortable.

"You sure you're alright?" he pressed. "You don't look so good."

Duvall sucked in a deep breath before he spoke. "I almost hit a little girl," he said, his voice tight. His eyes were wild, panicked. "In fact, I was sure I had." He rubbed the back of his neck. "A kid, Stanford. She couldn't have been more than eight or nine years old."

Miller could hear the anguish in his partner's voice, and it made his gut twist. He'd never been particularly fond of the man, but he knew Duvall had a family, kids of his own. He could imagine how upsetting this was for him.

"So what happened? If you'd hit her, surely she couldn't have run off—"

"I'm telling you, one minute there was nothing, and the next, there's a blonde sprite in pink standing two feet in front of my bumper. I had no time to react, hit the brakes, nothing. I cut the wheel but I was sure I hit her. No way I could have missed."

A blonde sprite in pink. Miller's head rocked back as he asked, "Did you hear anything?"

Duvall shook his head, then suddenly scrambled with the handle and threw the door open. He leaned out and vomited onto the pavement. Miller grabbed the roll of paper towels he kept under the seat and handed them over.

He gave the man a minute to pull himself together before he said, "If you'd hit somebody, you'd have heard the impact. There'd be evidence on the bumper."

Pulling the door closed, Duvall tore off two towels and wiped his mouth. He balled up the paper and tossed it to the floor, then swiped a hand down his face.

"No impact. No marks on the bumper. No . . .no blood." He stared at Miller with haunted eyes. "I searched the whole area, Stanford. No kid. Not a trace of anything at all."

Seventeen

Miller was staring at his laptop screen with owl eyes when Laura slipped around the corner into the kitchen. It was well past midnight, but she had been tossing and turning since around ten. She just couldn't sleep.

Realizing he hadn't seen her yet and not wanting to startle him, she murmured softly, "Hey, Miller."

He lifted his eyes over the top of the screen and blinked at her. Almost as though it took him a moment to realize who she was. Laura scanned the table but didn't see any beer bottles. He must be really engrossed in his class work.

"Hey, Sunshine," he said, but his tone was flat, almost cold.

This is what she'd been afraid of. Their last exchange outside her building this afternoon—she'd come off too cocky, and she knew it. This was what had been eating at her gut all evening.

Taking charge may have been a good thing at her job. It certainly hadn't seemed to bother Miller, either, the night she all but forced herself on him. But these were brand-new—these confident, independent lady shoes she'd tried on. Laura wasn't sure yet they fit too well.

"I'm sorry about this afternoon. I guess I was riding a little high, after having my first successful patient session and all. I didn't mean to—"

"You don't have to explain anything to me, Laura. You don't owe me anything. I'm just trying to keep my nose clean and follow Sarge's orders. He told me, in no uncertain terms, to steer clear of digging into any old records. That's what I'm doing. What you do is your own business." He pressed two fingers to the bridge of his nose and groaned. "Shit, I'm tired."

Laura took two steps toward him, skirting the table, and laid a hand on his shoulder. "So you're not mad at me?"

He leveled his gaze on her, holding it for a long moment without saying a word. As though he were trying to make up his mind about how to answer. Finally, he grumbled, "Not mad."

Not mad . . .but, what then?

When he turned his attention back to his computer screen, her heart sank. He had closed himself off to her, that was pretty obvious. She cleared her throat and folded her arms, rubbing her hands up and down the goosebumps rising on her bare skin. They weren't just coming from the breeze wafting through the kitchen window.

She tried to engage him in conversation again. "The prowler they called you about. When we were talking. How'd that turn out?"

He grunted, never taking his eyes off the screen. "Just an asshole who'd abandoned his family and came looking for them in the shelter."

Laura stood there another few minutes, waiting beside him. She'd really hoped to convince Miller to take her to bed again tonight. To cuddle and hold her, if nothing else. Like the fast and furious flight of a bottle rocket, her blast of self-confidence seemed to have burned itself out by the time she got home today. And she was feeling more than a little needy of some attention.

But either Miller really was engrossed in his class work, or she had put him off more than she'd feared with her tough-girl attitude today. Her stomach twisted and made a gurgling sound, and she pressed her hand across her middle.

It was only then that he turned to look at her again, this time his eyes sweeping up and down her body. She'd worn one of her more feminine sleep togs, a cami and taps in pale pink satin with lacy edges. And she could tell he noticed her nipples poking against the silky fabric, because his gaze lingered there a bit before lifting to her face again. She felt the heat rise into her cheeks.

"Are you hungry *and* cold?" he asked, one corner of his mouth twitching.

She shook her head, twisting her lips nervously. "Not hungry. A little . . .stressed, is all. Lots has changed in my life in the past few days," she said in a small voice.

He turned toward her then, gripping her upper arms in his two beefy hands. Looking directly into her eyes, he asked, "Are you sorry we slept together, Laura? Is it going to make things weird between us? I mean, I never even suggested anything like that—"

"No. No, I know you didn't. It was all me, Miller. And, as I told you, what I did Friday night was completely out of character for me. I'm not usually so . . .so brazen." She swallowed and turned away, feeling the sting of tears behind her eyes. "Not sure I'm made to be that way."

He was on his feet and folding her into his arms before she had the chance to draw another breath. "As long as you're not sorry it happened. And just so you know, it doesn't have to happen again. Not if you don't want it to. I don't want things to be strained between us, Laura. You're my roommate, remember?" He tipped her chin up and searched her eyes, and she could see the humor in his now, crinkling their corners. "Friends. Roomies, right?"

Laura swallowed the huge ball of tightness in her throat and bobbed her head, unable to say anything, fighting to hold back the tears. Damn it, she wanted to be strong. Independent. Resilient. Why did she always fall apart like this? Did she really not have the capacity to grow a big-girl backbone?

Miller wrapped her in his arms again, stroking her hair as her cheek pressed against his chest. She closed her eyes and sighed. This, she thought, is exactly what I need right now.

This is one confusing woman, was all Miller could think as they stood there in his kitchen. That afternoon outside her workplace, she'd brushed him off like a fly, as if she were irritated by the fact he was breathing. He knew he'd bristled at this . . .obsession she had with digging into the old Talcott Hall records. Maybe he'd come off a little too sharp, too dictatorial. But he didn't want to go against Sarge's orders. And he sure as hell didn't want Laura to jeopardize her job.

She felt good, pressed up against him like she was, all soft and warm with her silky hair under his fingers. And his body betrayed him. He knew she could feel his growing arousal pressing against her, and silently swore. God knew, he didn't want to pressure her, regardless of the fact that their romp the other night had been the most wonderful sex he could ever remember. But it certainly did seem to have complicated their situation.

She wasn't pulling away, though. Of course, she wasn't responding to him poking her in the belly either.

Miller had just become aware of a foul scent blowing in on the breeze when Laura asked, "Do you smell that? Were you cooking something?"

He turned and strode to the window. "No, I wasn't. Maybe somebody started their fire pit."

"At nearly one o'clock in the morning?" Laura asked. She wrinkled her nose. "And it doesn't even smell like wood smoke. It's . . .acrid, almost."

Miller pulled up the window sash higher and leaned on the ledge with crossed arms. The moon was nearly full and super bright—seems like they've had more than their full moons lately—and he could see the haze of smoke hovering in the air over the gravestones next door. A pang of alarm rang in his head.

"This is more than a fire pit," he said darkly. He reached for his phone on the edge of the counter and checked the screen. "Maybe I'd better call the station. Just to be sure the night guy hasn't dozed off while one of our buildings burns to the ground."

He turned as he hit the speed-dial for the station and saw Laura standing there watching him. Arms crossed under those luscious mounds again, she had her shoulders hunched, and he could clearly see the pebbling of goosebumps on her upper arms. She was studying him with an expression that seemed a little sad. Also, tired. The dark crescents under her eyes underscored the look. Miller felt a stab of pity for her.

A two-minute conversation with the overnight operator informed Miller there'd been no alarms called in, and that Randy was on patrol tonight. Did he want him patched through?

"No, not necessary, Tom. Probably just some idiot burning garbage," he said, and hung up.

But something in his gut didn't feel right, and the chokingly pungent smoke continued to intensify as another breeze rustled the curtain.

Kip. Maybe Kip is on at the fire station tonight. For his own peace of mind, he just had to check this out.

"Listen," he said, crossing to Laura and tucking one buoyant curl behind her ear, "I have to go make a lap around the grounds, just to be sure."

She blinked up at him, those big blue eyes shining with some emotion he couldn't identify. Hell, he hardly knew her well enough. And he sure wasn't going to start trying to read anything into that soft, mournful gaze.

Tired. She's got to be exhausted, that's all.

"You go on to bed, get some sleep. Your alarm will be going off in only a few hours, and it's only Monday. You've got a long week ahead of you." He ran his hand up and down her arm. "And you're freaking freezing. Go get snuggled under Grandma's blanket, keep the door locked, and I'll check on you when I get back."

Miller bent his head and thrilled at how she tipped up her chin and closed her eyes, silently begging for his kiss. This was the Laura he *thought* he knew. The one he hoped she really was. Not the bossy bitch he'd caught a glimpse of today.

Her lips were full and warm against his, and he was so tempted to sweep her off her feet and carry her up the stairs to his bed. Let the whole damn town burn down around them while they fanned flames of their own. But he couldn't do that. And even if there hadn't been some mystery fire burning in the area, he probably shouldn't.

It was too soon. What happened between them had happened too fast. Maybe shouldn't have happened at all.

He cupped her cheek as he drew back and searched her eyes. "Will you be okay?"

She nodded, those sexy curls bouncing around her face. Then she turned on her bare heel and padded off down the hallway.

Miller grabbed his jersey off the back of his chair and pulled it over his head. Snugging a ball cap on, he snatched his truck keys and locked the front door behind him. Hitting another speed-dial button on his phone, he called the Middletown Fire Station.

Thank God, Kip answered. He'd recognize that deep, accented baritone voice anywhere.

Obviously, Kip had noticed the caller id. "What the hell you got goin' on, Stanford? Working the overnight?"

"No," Miller said as his truck engine growled to life. "Has anybody called in anything? Got a hellacious shit-ton of smoke hanging over my block."

Kip paused, probably checking multiple call lines and computer monitors. "Nope. Nothing so far."

"Well, I'm headed to check it out. Got a bad feeling in the pit of my stomach. Gonna drive around the grounds, do a quick visual. I won't be able to sleep until I do, anyway," Miller said as he turned onto the campus.

Kip hesitated only a moment. "Look, let me go make sure Wayne's awake, get him up here at the command station. I'll jump in the squad truck and meet you. We can scope it out together. I'll meet you at the security station in . . .say, ten minutes?"

Miller breathed a sigh of relief. He was no fireman, after all. Kip was much better qualified to identify something suspicious than he was, at least when it came to fire. Besides, driving around this campus at night was creepy enough. He hated to admit it, but he was still a little shaken up by Duvall's episode earlier that afternoon.

The poor bastard was certain he'd slammed into a little girl. He'd even gotten down on his belly on the pavement after the tow truck pulled out the cruiser, studying the undercarriage. Duvall seemed convinced he'd find a tiny body wedged under there. But they hadn't found any evidence of him colliding with anything other than the bank of the drainage ditch. And the shelter didn't have anyone show up injured. No bleeding walk-ins at the E.R.

Duvall had been such a mess after it happened, he'd tossed his guts again twice before they'd gotten back to the station. After filing a report, a call in to Sarge, and Duvall got sent home early. And probably wasn't sleeping any better than Miller would be.

Kip pulled in just as Miller was climbing out of his truck.

"How ya doin' man?" Kip growled as Miller climbed into the fire rescue van. "You look, like, weird. What's up?"

Miller yanked on his seat belt and then pulled off his cap. "I don't know. Just got a bad feeling about this smoke, Kip." He raked his fingers through his hair and shook his head. "Smells kind of . . .funky. Don't you think?"

Kip wrinkled his broad nose. "Got that right. Smells sorta like, I dunno, like barbeque. Like somebody's grilling somethin'. Somethin' that stayed out on the counter a little too long."

"And who the hell would be grilling at this time of night? Mighty big fire pit they got too."

Kip drove the squad truck up onto the State grounds proper, and as they reached the top of the hill, they broke through the cloud that seemed to hover over the lower terrain.

"Looks like it's hanging low." Miller shifted in his seat and scanned the grounds in a sweeping motion. "At least from up here we'll be able to see where it's thickest."

Kip pulled up on the street between Talcott Hall and the Alcohol Treatment Center, parked, and killed the lights. Both men climbed out without a word. The damp night air wrapped itself around Miller's bare arms and he swore, realizing he hadn't even taken the time to grab a jacket.

"Lots of humidity in the air tonight," Kip remarked, almost as though he'd read Miller's mind. "That's why the stuff is hanging low, like fog."

They stood there, both men turning in slow circles, squinting in the dim light of the streetlamps that were too far apart on this part of campus. Miller couldn't see any brightness, no glow anywhere that would indicate the source of the smoke. But it was definitely heavier on the west side of the grounds. But what was even over there?

The revelation hit both of them at the same time, and their eyes met.

"Incinerator," Miller said.

Without another word, they both jumped back into the truck and headed toward what used to be the facility's incinerator. Tucked in a small hollow on the far west end of the grounds, the place hadn't been operational in at least twenty years. But local kids, Miller knew, liked to climb in through long-ago broken out windows and hunker down to party. He'd had to chase them off more than once.

But what was there to burn to cause this much smoke? The building was brick, and other than the battered, peeling wooden door that lamely held its place even after all these years, Miller couldn't imagine what there was inside the place to catch fire.

As they bumped down the crumbling, single-lane road leading to the building, Kip's headlight beams lurched and flashed wildly against the noxious fog, which got thicker the lower they drove.

"Shit, man, what the hell *is* that?" Kip barked, pulling the collar of his jacket up to cover his nose and mouth.

And he's a fireman, Miller thought. The putrid smell was burning his eyes and nostrils, and was beginning to make his stomach feel a bit queasy.

Or maybe it was just that greasy cheeseburger he grabbed on his way home from work.

By the time the grade leveled off, Miller could barely see anything. It was like the densest fog he'd ever imagined, so opaque the headlights were all but useless.

"The building's right about here," Miller said after a few minutes, pointing off to the left.

Kip slowed to a stop, and Miller watched as the smoke swirled in sickening waves just inches in front of the bumper.

"Still no flames. No glow . . .nothin'. There any chemicals stored out here? Piles of rags? Maybe they're smoldering. Gettin' ready to self-ignite," Kip suggested.

Miller shook his head. "There's nothing. Nothing but an old brick shell with an antiquated, iron monster of a furnace." He nodded in that direction. "It's over in there. Come on. We better take a look."

They slowly stepped out into night air that seemed to have dropped ten degrees cooler down in this hollow, Miller thought with a shudder. Hunching his shoulders up against the chill, he groped his way around the front of the truck and stood beside Kip, who pulled a heavy, black flashlight out of his belt. One that could double as a weapon. He snatched a smaller replica out of his back pocket and handed it to Miller.

"You think I need to call for backup?" Kip murmured. "A tanker truck. In case there really is something burnin'?"

Adding to the gooseflesh on his arms, the hairs on the back of Miller's neck started prickling, and he rubbed at them anxiously.

"Don't know. But I don't like this, Kip. Not at all. Doesn't make any damn sense."

Pulling his radio from his belt, Kip turned away toward the truck. He heard his friend mumble into the device as Miller moved closer, slowly, to where he was sure the old furnace building stood. Careful to test each footfall before he put weight on it. The ground here, he knew, was rutted and strewn with all sorts of trash—old tire rims, twisted pieces of rusted metal from abandoned farm machinery, a loose brick here and there. He could see them all, in his mind, from previous visits. But with his eyes, he couldn't see anything at all.

If he'd held his arm out in front of his face, it would disappear in the noxious fog. And he had his own shirt neckline pulled up over his nose and mouth now, trying to ward off the smell of something horrible. Acrid, and rotting. And burning. He swallowed hard as bile rose into his throat.

A rare breeze rustled the leaves in the trees surrounding the hollow, and in that brief instant, the smoke cleared enough so Miller could see the building, or what was left of it. The crooked, leaning brick shack with the heavy wood door, painted a bright blue at one time. But now it was peeling and blistered, and splashed in a few places with neon obscenities painted in spray-can graffiti. Courtesy of the local punks.

Miller blinked fast as he caught sight of the gaping hole on the front wall where a window used to be. That's where it was coming from. Smoke—ugly, grey smoke billowed lazily out of the opening. As if something was smoldering just inside.

He approached, but the smoke was so thick, he might as well have been trying to see through mud. Miller cast a nervous glance over his shoulder in Kip's direction. The last thing he felt like doing was going inside the old shack alone.

A moment later, he heard the stomping of Kip's heavy boots, then a crunching noise quickly followed by a muttered curse.

"There's all kinds of shit strewn about here, Kip. Watch your step."

Kip's flashlight beam formed an eerie, glowing circle as he drew nearer, and Miller's mind skipped back to the night he'd seen the orbs floating around Talcott Hall. They looked just like this, he thought. Floating circles of light. A shudder ran down his spine.

"I got the station on standby. See anything, man? Signs of where all this stinky shit's coming from?"

Miller could barely make out the massive form of his friend, even when Kip stood within several feet of him. His throat spasmed as he went to speak, and he coughed, fighting a gag reflex.

"I know, this is something bad. Something nasty burnin'. Come on, we gotta go check it out," Kip said. Then after a pause, he continued. "Maybe we should get back-up from the station?"

Sputtering, Miller snatched a crumpled McDonald's napkin out of the pocket of his shorts and spat into it. "No. No fire. Not yet, anyway."

Miller led the way, pushing on the warped wooden door with both hands, then laying his shoulder to it when he realized it wouldn't give. When it finally broke free, he stumbled over the threshold—a raised two-by-four he hadn't realized was there—and nearly ended up on his ass.

"Fuck!"

"You alright, man?"

He felt Kip's powerful fingers close around his upper arm. Geez, the guy had big hands.

He couldn't see a damn thing, couldn't breathe, and didn't like the odd sensation creeping over him. An overwhelming sense of . . .what? It wasn't fear. It was sadness. Grief.

What the hell?

He shrugged out of Kip's grip. "I'm okay. The incinerator's over that way." Miller waved his flashlight toward where he knew the monstrous, steel contraption sat. Feeling Kip close by his side, he made his way in that direction.

As they drew closer, the smoke began to suddenly dissipate. Rapidly, as if some giant fan was running behind them and blowing the putrid fog away as they approached. By the time they'd taken the ten steps to bring them up to the ancient furnace, Miller could see the hulking incinerator clearly. The smoke still hung in a thick cloud overhead, though there was no sign the firebox had been its source.

The contraption resembled a huge turbine, a steel cylinder four or five feet in diameter, lying on its side. A complicated network of pipes and boxes, presumably electrical connections, covered the thing like a mantle. Almost every inch of its dull, grey surface was also decorated with neon graffiti.

Centered on the end of the cylinder just feet before them, the door was closed, a heavy steel hasp locked down over its edge. Basically square but with an arched upper edge, the shape of the door vaguely reminded Miller of something, but at that moment he couldn't remember what.

Kip strode forward and held his hand a few inches from the metal surface, testing for heat. Then he stepped up close and pressed both palms against it.

"Cold as a tomb," he muttered. "No fire comin' from in here," he said. He boldly grabbed the hasp and wrenched it upward. It squealed and screamed in the silence, and Miller felt another shudder run through him.

"If it's cold, then why are you opening—"

But Kip set his big hands around the handle and yanked with both arms. The thick door squeaked on hinges long unused before swinging open easily. Miller staggered back a step as the putrid odor they'd been smelling in the smoke wafted out into their faces. Kip coughed, gagged, and spat into the dirt beside him. Miller felt his already queasy stomach do another slow somersault.

They flashed their lights over the interior, but there was nothing inside but fluffy, pale ashes.

"Don't know what was going on here, but it's over with now. Done," Kip said. "*Been* done. For a long, long time."

"Garbage. This is where the staff used to burn all the garbage from the wards. But as far as I know, it's been shut down for almost twenty years," Miller said. He scanned the room with his light beam, then aimed it up toward the ceiling. He could see the steel grid of interior beams clearly. The smoke was gone.

"What the hell?" he muttered.

He looked over and watched Kip twist his broad shoulders and draw them up to his shoulders. "Dunno. Some pretty weird shit for sure. Let's get outta here."

Once they'd climbed back into the squad truck and Kip hit the headlights, they could see the mysterious fog had cleared. Even though they'd practically had to cut their way through it just minutes earlier. Disappeared, without a trace.

Kip started shaking his head, his lips pressed tight. "Don't like this place you work much, Stanford. Don't like it one bit." Then he turned to stare at Miller, his eyes bloodshot in the lights from the dashboard. "That sure didn't smell like no garbage burning."

Miller opened his door and spat out at the ground, trying to get rid of the foulness still clinging to his nostrils and mouth. "What the hell was that, Kip? It was worse than burning rubber, like old tires, or tar, or even—"

"I know exactly what that smell is, Stanford. And it's one I don't relish even thinking about." Kip continued to glare at Miller with a look he couldn't ever remember seeing on his friend's face.

Fear.

Kip held his gaze, wide-eyed, his words almost a whisper. "That there was the smell of burning flesh."

Eighteen

Laura crept into her bed and pulled her grandmother's quilt up over her head, but there was no way she would be falling asleep. Her skin was still pebbled with the chill from the night air, drifting in through Miller's kitchen window. Not only was it cool and damp, but laced with something fetid. She shivered again and wiggled her nose, trying to clear the odor from her airway. Burying her face into the folds of the soft, sweet-smelling quilt, she squeaked out a small sigh.

She was feeling so very lonely tonight.

Her entire new start here in her hometown had begun so rocky, so bizarre. Nothing like what she'd expected. Completely the opposite of what she'd hoped for. And the way she'd faced the obstacles, with a new courage, a new brazenness foreign to her—she wasn't at all sure *bold* had been the right thing to do. She also was very unsure she could continue wearing this new emotional armor. It just didn't feel right.

And boy, had it complicated her living situation. At first Miller had been gruff but civil, even cute and funny in a way she thought she might become fond of. But there was more under the macho exterior of Miller Stanford than she'd expected, and more than she might be able to deal with at this point in her life. What had Angie said?

He's got some shit going on of his own, stuff I couldn't begin to help him deal with.

She'd been right—the situation with Miller's sister was heavy stuff. Since Laura had no siblings, she could only imagine how that burden weighed on him, and not just financially. He seemed like a pretty emotional guy, despite his intimidating demeanor. And Laura had sat through enough psychology classes and group sessions to understand the impact on a big brother who stood by and watched as his father destroyed not only his mother's, but his baby sister's life. Memories like that could heap on a sentence of guilt strong enough to last a lifetime.

That guilt, she knew, was not only unfounded and irrational, but could cause all sorts of deep-seated behavior patterns in children of an abused household. Particularly when alcohol was involved. The classic pattern had their progeny going one way or the other—becoming completely anti-alcohol, or falling into the same pattern as the addicted parent. Many times, the damage went deeper, only coming to the surface unexpectedly during times of extreme stress or trauma.

Miller didn't seem to fall neatly into either of those paradigms. Then again, Laura had only known him a few weeks. For all she knew, he could be a ticking time bomb. And now, by sleeping with him, she'd involved herself. Even if it never went beyond a one-night stand.

Yet she couldn't deny the niggling sensation deep in her chest, one insisting she definitely did not want this to end with a one-night stand.

Laura had drifted into a fitful doze when she heard the echo in the hallway about an hour later. Miller's key in the lock, him throwing the deadbolt behind him, his footsteps on the hardwood. Part of her sighed in relief. She didn't like being alone here, at night. Yet another part of her brain tensed and snapped her back into full awareness. Would he come to her? Or simply go on up to bed alone?

She felt like someone had wrapped a cat's cradle around her heart with dental floss, and way too tight. Any move she made, any way this situation with Miller played out, it could end up with some powerful hurt. Laura's biggest fear had always been rejection. She'd managed to get herself in a position where yet another rejection was not only possible, but probable.

Lying quiet and still under the blanket, she heard him coming down the hall. Even if he was a making a deliberate effort to be quiet, for a guy as big as Miller, his heavy footfalls thumped on the wood floors. He paused at the base of the stairs. Then her door, which she had left ajar, swung open ever so slowly. After a moment's pause, it began to drift closed again.

Laura's heart squeezed. She loved how he always peeked in to check on her before turning in for the night. But tonight, a sudden urgency bubbled up inside her and she whispered, "Miller?"

The door paused in its movement, then swung open again. It was so dark, she couldn't see his face—he'd already turned out all the lights. But his silhouette filled the space, and he rumbled, "Why are you still awake?"

Laura shimmied up on her elbows. "The fire. Did you find it? Is everything okay?" As she spoke the dusky scent that had saturated the air earlier wafted across the empty space and reached her nostrils. She could smell it on him. "You smell like smoke," she said.

He chuckled, a deep throaty sound that made Laura's skin tingle. "Yeah, I guess I do. Better go hose myself down before I turn in." She heard, more than saw him lift his shirt up and over his head. "We couldn't find anything. Lots of smoke down by the old incinerator. Stinky smoke. But no sign of any fire."

Laura blinked. "Weird."

"You got that right. I'm gonna hop in the shower. You go on to sleep. It's nearly two a.m. You've got to work in the morning, don't you?"

"Uh-huh," she answered in a small voice.

Ten minutes later, though, Laura was still lying awake when the bathroom light flicked off, blanketing the hallway in darkness once again. Laura started when she heard Miller's voice again on her threshold.

"May I come in?" he asked softly.

"Please."

Her mattress creaked as the big man settled down on the edge, tentatively, careful not to crush any part of her. As the darkness again thinned she could make out his massive outline, but not his face. His voice was low and rumbling when he asked, "What's wrong, Laura? Why can't you sleep?"

She shook her head, although she knew he probably couldn't see it. "I don't know. Just can't settle tonight. I feel all jumbled up inside. Like a pile of blocks set off kilter. Like I might just crumble into a disorganized heap at any minute."

His warm, strong hand cupped her cheek then, and she sighed and turned her face into his palm. His skin was rough and smelled like Irish Spring. She breathed in the clean scent, one she'd come to associate with this man since the day she first met him.

"You're sorry about what happened between us the other night. Aren't you?" It was a statement, not a question.

When she shook her head again, adamantly, she knew he could feel it.

He ran his fingers along her jawline, then tucked her hair behind her ear.

"Don't you worry about anything being . . .expected of you. Not by me. We're two adults, and we gave in to some urges that night. That's all."

Laura was so confused. She wasn't sure if she felt relief or disappointment. Part of her was rapidly becoming fond of this big, clumsy hulk of a man. Another part of her didn't want to put herself—her living situation, or her heart—in jeopardy just now. Hell, she wasn't sure if she even knew how to do a relationship with a man. In truth, she had little experience beyond the prom night disaster, and the geeky college boyfriend who had a thing for blow-jobs—and nothing more.

Miller sat with her only a moment longer before pinching her chin between his fingers. "You go to sleep, now, hear? I'm home, there's nothing on fire anywhere around here, and there's nothing you should be worrying about. Except getting yourself good and grounded in your new job."

The rest of the week flew by for Laura. Alternating counseling sessions with several of her colleagues, she found herself abandoning all thoughts of her personal life underneath the problems of her patients. She came home mentally and emotionally drained every night, and since Miller was gone by the time she got there, she had the house to herself.

This is really perfect, she thought one night as she heated up a can of soup for her dinner. Almost like having a place of my own. It was only after she'd snuggled into bed and turned out the light that the worry demons came out to play.

How long would it take her to save enough money to move out, *really* get her own place? And how badly did she even want that? After her and Miller had done the deed, she had to admit, she couldn't keep her memory from wandering back to that night. He had been so attentive, so gentle and caring. Laura craved that kind of attention more than breath. Yet he hadn't come to wake her once since the night of the mysterious fire. Hadn't gotten up early enough to see her off in the morning.

The truth was pretty plain, although she hated to accept it. To him, it had been a fling. A one-time roll in the hay. There wasn't any other explanation that made sense. With a heavy sigh, Laura scooted down and pulled the quilt up over her head, dreading the blaring of her alarm she knew was only a few hours away.

Friday arrived before Laura believed, and having walked to work, she made her way down the sidewalk toward the house. She'd gotten about halfway there when an odd swishing noise drew her gaze—into the graveyard.

She stopped. Just a bunch of stupid squirrels scampering around in what was left of last fall's rotting leaves. That's what it had to be.

She'd about convinced herself of this logical explanation when she heard the laughter. Giggling. A child's exuberant glee. Laura's heart sped up to warp speed. Searching the area frantically, she could see no one. And the laughter, it seemed, permeated the air around her, seeping into her brain. She laid a hand on her throat, struggling to still the racing pulse pounding there. Quickening her steps, she rushed toward the porch.

Her trembling fingers failed to fit the key into the lock the second, then a third time. When the keys hit the porch floor, she swore out loud. As she stooped to scoop them up, a light tap on her shoulder drew a shocked shriek from her, and she scrambled upright.

Laura's breath died in her throat when a strange warmth closed around her middle. Arms—small ones—seemed to embrace her in a gentle hug. Looking down, she saw nothing there.

In the next second, the sensation was gone, but the sound of running feet and gleeful giggling echoed in her brain. Keeping her eyes glued to the task, Laura fumbled frantically with the key. Finally, the lock clicked open, and she practically fell through the entry.

Throwing the deadbolt, Laura leaned back against the door for a long moment, her blood pounding in her ears. Was she losing her mind? Having a breakdown? Trembling all over, she bit her knuckle as the tears came.

A half-hour later, Laura padded barefoot around the corner into the kitchen.

If I just eat something, brew myself a cup of chamomile tea, I'll feel better.

Opening the fridge, she perused the contents. Several Styrofoam containers littered the shelves, but none of those were hers. She knew Miller often brought food home from After Shocks when he got off work. But she'd bought a bag of veggie mix from the grocery store on her last run. She could stir-fry that, and dump it over some of that boil-in-bag brown rice. A little soy sauce, and—"

"Have a good day?"

Laura screamed and dropped the bag of veggies on the floor, nearly peeing her pants. She wheeled to find Miller standing within two feet behind her, his eyebrows and hands raised. His clothes and hair were rumpled.

"Whoa, whoa, sorry, girl. Thought you'd see my truck in the driveway," he shot defensively. "I was taking a nap."

"What the hell are you doing home? It's Friday, isn't it?" She was shrieking, and her voice hurt even her own ears. Closing her eyes, she huffed, "I'm sorry. No, I didn't see your truck. Besides, you sometimes walk to work anyway. Just like I do."

She felt his big hand close around her upper arm. "I'm really sorry, Laura." But she could hear the amusement in his voice, and sure enough, when she opened her eyes, he was trying hard not to laugh. Heat flooded her face along with anger.

"It's not funny, Stanford. It's creepy enough living here, in this house, next door to a spooky old graveyard. Sometimes I feel like . . .like . . .I'm an extra in an episode of Ghost Adventures." She shook out of his grip, bent to retrieve the veggies, and slammed the fridge. "I'm stir-frying these. With rice. Want some?"

"Where's the beef?" he asked.

"Funny. No beef, caveman. Veggies, brown rice, soy sauce. Want some or not?"

She'd bent to snatch a frying pan and pot out of the cupboard, and was arranging them on the burners when she felt him come up close behind her. One heavy hand landed gently on each of her shoulders.

"What's wrong, kid? Have a bad day? Bad week? Hell, I haven't seen you since, what, Tuesday?" His voice was low and gentle, and Laura felt a lump rising into her throat. This was what always blew through her defenses. The compassion. The caring. Except she'd never been able to figure out when it was real, and when it was male bullshit.

She shook her head vigorously, afraid to say anything for fear it would come out on a sob. Sucking in a painful breath, she managed, "No. Just tired. Long week. I'm fine."

"Hey," Miller said, turning her to face him. She kept her gaze down toward the floor, down toward those huge, perfectly groomed and manicured, size thirteen feet.

God, the man had nice feet.

With a single finger under her chin, he forced her to look up at him. Blinking fast, she silently swore when the action forced a single tear to leak out and start its trek down her cheek. He reached up with his thumb and brushed it away.

The way he was looking at her, those feral, silver-grey eyes filled with such concern, made her squirm. She couldn't hold his gaze. Cutting hers to the side, she said, "So what are you doing home? Off today?" Then she remembered when he'd taken a day because his sister had been so ill. She immediately studied his eyes and asked, "It's not your sister again, is it? She's still doing okay?"

"She's fine. They transferred her back to Brightstar on Wednesday." His smile crinkled the corners of his eyes, and Laura felt her knees go weak. "But thank you for asking."

"So why are you home?"

"I'm picking up tomorrow's shift for Roger. He hasn't been right since that . . .that incident last week. He's going to take his family off for a long weekend. I'm working his Saturday night."

Laura sighed. "Well, I'm sorry for the scene tonight. I was just a little shaken up when I came in, that's all. I had another . . .encounter on the way home."

She felt him stiffen. "What do you mean?"

Nervously, she combed her rapidly spiraling hair away from her face with one hand. She stepped back and turned in a fidgety circle, stammering, "I've got to eat something first. I'm starving. Let me get this stuff going and I'll tell you over dinner."

"Why don't you let me buy you dinner?" he asked, gently sliding the bag of vegetables out of her hand. "Where's your favorite place to eat? And don't say After Shocks."

Forty minutes later Miller found himself sitting in a booth at El Bandido's on the other side of town. He hated Mexican food, but he wasn't about to tell Laura that. She'd obviously had not only a rough week, but another bizarre incident with this strange child-spirit. She reminded him of a piece of brittle, bone china that could shatter any moment—especially with someone as clumsy as him around. No, he'd eat fajitas tonight, and not complain one bit. He'd make believe it was top sirloin someone had cut into sizzling strips.

The waiter took their orders for drinks—a Coke for him, a house margarita for her. She'd at first ordered a soda like he did, but he'd prodded her.

"I know you're a counselor, Counselor. But one margarita isn't going to land you in rehab," he'd muttered, leaning close across the table so he knew the server wouldn't hear him.

The jittery way her eyes were darting around the room, landing everywhere but on his face, told him she needed something to slow her down. Help her settle.

A few minutes and three or four sips into her drink later, Laura clasped her hands on the placemat in front of her. She kept her gaze trained on those hands, obviously avoiding eye contact, just as she'd been doing all evening. Clearing her throat, she began the story of her eerie experience on Miller's doorstep an hour or so earlier.

Miller sat and listened without saying a word, trying not to show any reaction. But he couldn't ignore how his heart leapt in his chest knowing Laura had heard the child—again.

Hell, had *felt* her. Or, at least, thought she had.

But his heart skipped into a stuttered staccato when Laura told him about her encounter with Jenna the week before.

"So wait," Miller said when she'd finished her story. "Jenna says she knew a little girl back when she was just a kid? That she played with her? In the graveyard?"

Laura snorted out a little laugh as she sipped her drink. "Yeah, weird, right? I guess playing in a graveyard isn't something you'd forget about no matter how old you get."

Miller blinked fast and shook his head. "But this doesn't make any sense, Laura. What makes Jenna think this is the same little girl she knew fifty years ago? Or rather, her ghost? It would have to be a ghost. The girl would be as old as Jenna is now."

Using her straw to swirl the ice in her drink, Laura again avoided looked at him as she spoke. "I don't know. She must believe in ghosts too, I guess. She says she's heard her, sobbing, more than once when she's come to pay her respects to her granddad." She lifted her gaze to meet his. "She's never seen her, though."

Miller groaned and swiped a hand down his face. "That still doesn't explain why she thinks the sounds, whatever they are, have anything to do with her childhood friend."

Laura suddenly sat back against the booth and hugged her middle. "The child you saw—what did you say her last name was? I couldn't remember when I was speaking with Jenna, but the name she gave me sounded awfully familiar." Her blue eyes were round and intense on his.

Miller narrowed his eyes. It took him a moment to thumb through the haze of crap that had been floating around in his head these past days to come up with the answer. Then he got it.

"Sanderson. She said her name was Greta Sanderson."

Laura's little gasp made Miller jump. She laid a hand over her mouth as her eyes rounded even bigger, like some character in an Anime film.

"Oh my god," she whispered. "Oh. My. God."

"What?"

The waiter appeared just then, at the exact wrong time to set two steaming plates down before them. And another plate with shredded cheese and vegetables. And another, a round, covered dish keeping their tortillas warm. There was enough food here to feed the entire guest list of the homeless shelter for the week, he thought.

"Can I get you anything—"

"No. No, we're good. Thanks," Miller snapped, ignoring the indignant glare the waiter shot him before spinning on one heel and stomping away.

"So what? What about the kid's name?" he pressed.

Laura hadn't budged. She sat like a statue, still staring at Miller in a frozen trance.

He reached across for her hand, the one that wasn't still covering her mouth. Her fingers felt cool and clammy in his, and he could feel she was trembling.

"Did Jenna tell you the girl's name, Laura? The one she used to play with . . ."

Her head starting wagging from side to side, but she never took her gaze off his face. Miller was almost afraid she was going into shock, by the looks of her. When another thirty seconds had passed and she still hadn't said a word, he squeezed her fingers. Probably a little harder than he meant to.

Because she winced. But then she closed her eyes and said in a hoarse whisper, "Jenna didn't tell me her name. But she did tell me what she was searching for. A headstone. One with her father's name on it."

Laura sat silent for another long moment, and Miller's impatience bubbled up. He shook her hand a little, urging her on. "And that was?"

"Sanderson," she whispered. "Thomas E. Sanderson."

Nineteen

Miller was looking forward to his weekly visit with Mollie. At least he knew she was on the mend. One bright spot in his life had just pulsed a bit brighter.

He drove to Brightstar that sunny, Sunday morning, his mood feeling lighter than it had in months. Years, maybe. He stopped by a roadside stand and picked up a bunch of colorful spring flowers just before hopping on the highway. Bright colors, it seemed, were the only thing Mollie reacted to anymore. The only thing that would make her eyes light up and a hint of a smile brighten her face.

Even if Miller couldn't be sure Molls knew who had brought them for her.

Visiting hours at the facility didn't officially begin on Sundays until eleven. Until the patients had been roused, medicated, fed their breakfasts, and cleaned up. But the nurses at Brightstar knew Miller well, and didn't hesitate when he strode up to the reception desk at a little before nine a.m.

"Mornin', Sarah. How's she doing this morning?" Miller asked.

The nurse, a full-figured woman of about fifty, shifted her attention from her keyboard toward Miller. Her smile accentuated the lines around her eyes and mouth, lines he was sure she earned, each and every day she worked here. The dedication it must take, he thought.

"She's up, had her bath, and I think Norma just finished feeding her breakfast," she replied. Then her face sobered. "Been kind of lethargic after this last stint at the hospital, though, Miller. I think it took a lot out of her." She scooted her chair over from her desk to where she could reach the counter separating them. Patting the back of his hand, she said, "I wouldn't stay too long today. She's been sleeping more and more. I'd like her to get in a nap before your mother gets here."

Miller made his way down the maze of corridors on his familiar path to Mollie's room. Unlike many of the patients at Brightstar, Mollie's was a private room, one he paid a substantial upgrade fee to maintain. But having another person in the room had always seemed to agitate her. He did wonder sometimes, though, if her being alone so much was really better for her. Would more social interaction improve her condition?

The doctors claimed no. They felt quite certain, due to the extent of the damage the accident had done to Mollie's brain, that improvement beyond her present state wasn't probable. In the ten years since her last surgery, Miller had to admit, it seemed they were right.

He turned the last corner and pushed through the heavy, double doors to Mollie's wing. Some of the patients here, those more ambulatory, lined the hallways like wheelchair-bound gargoyles, perched silently outside their doors. A few recognized Miller and beamed bright smiles when he approached, but other than a grunt or a groan, few reacted. Most couldn't speak, and many just sat staring at the wall on the opposite side, oblivious to his passing.

But color drew their attention. A time or two he had to sidestep an outstretched hand, reaching for the bunch of flowers he carried at his side. Those in this ward, he knew, were here to stay. Most had sustained brain injuries so egregious, they would never be able to return to a functioning life outside of a trained nursing environment.

Just like his Molls.

Fighting against the tightening in his throat that seized him every time he came here, Miller arrived at Room 303, where the door was partially open. He heard the television droning a cartoon as he lifted his knuckles to rap lightly on the door. God forbid he walked in when one of the nurses was tending to one of Mollie's more personal needs.

She was alone, lying back against the stack of pillows arranged so her head wouldn't flop awkwardly off at a painful angle. Her mouth was slightly open, and a droplet of milky colored drool snaked down the crease from her lip to her chin. Swearing under his breath, Miller approached as quietly as a man his size could, snatching a tissue off the bedside table. Before touching her, though, he murmured gently, "Mollie? Molls, it's me. Miller."

It only took a moment before her dark eyelashes fluttered. It took several seconds before she managed to bring her eyes into focus, but they were fixed on the vivid, dancing images on the television above the foot of her bed. He reached forward with the tissue then and wiped what remained of her breakfast from her face. Then he lifted his other hand, the one holding the flowers.

The red cellophane wrapped around their base crackled, and that drew her attention. Slowly, she rolled her head in his direction, glancing at his face and blinking. No sign of recognition, just like always. Miller felt his heart crack like an ice cube dropped into warm water.

"Look," he said, his voice thick, "look what I brought you, Molls." He held up the bouquet and her eyes traveled lazily over them, then back to his face. There was a hint of a question in her expression. Or was there? Hell, most of the reactions Miller saw from his sister, he was certain, were just figments of his hopeful imagination.

He pulled up the bedside chair and sat close by her side. He held the bouquet toward her, hoping she would reach out to touch them like the patients in the hall. But her hands remained limp and flaccid on the blanket on either side of her body.

As always, the pain Miller felt whenever he saw his sister like this began to morph into anger, then fury. Hatred for his late father. Anger was the perfect balm to staunch the bleeding of his own agony. And then there was the guilt.

Why hadn't he just picked her up himself that day? Told the coach to stick his rules where the sun didn't shine? Why hadn't his mother called out of work so she could drive Mollie to the game, instead of relying on that rat bastard husband of hers? Why hadn't he done something to stop the momentum of the inevitable? Derail the disaster train he knew his father was on, dragging the whole family with him.

As his vision blurred with tears, he rose, laying the flowers on the bedside table. He rolled it away, far enough from Mollie's bed so she couldn't inadvertently clutch at them, maybe end up with leaves or petals in her mouth. While his back was turned, he heard a small sound behind him.

"Hi."

The word was clear and un-garbled. Miller spun to see his sister had turned toward him even more, her whole body this time, in his direction. At first he thought she was looking at him, but then realized her gaze drifted beyond.

Had she spoken the word, though? Impossible. Mollie hadn't uttered a legible word since the day of the accident.

He took a step back towards her and reached out, laying his hand over hers. "Hi, Molls. Do you see the flowers? I brought you flowers. The nurse . . .maybe we can get your nurse to put them in a vase—"

"Hi."

Miller staggered back a step, his heart leaping into his throat. He'd seen her say it this time, watched her dry, cracked lips form the simple word. Her voice sounded rusty from disuse, but it was the most wonderful sound he'd ever heard in his life. Excitedly, he reached for the call button on the side of the bed and mashed it.

After only a second, the nasal voice of the nurse at the central station crackled through. "I'll be right there."

No need for her to ask what she wanted, Miller thought. If Mollie ever did press the call button, it was by accident.

"She spoke," he chattered into the speaker. "I'm Mollie's brother, and I heard her. Come quick."

Miller slid the bedside table further out of the way, reaching out to lift both of Mollie's hands in his own. They felt cool and limp, and she made no effort to return his grip. Staring into her eyes, Miller searched desperately for some hint of recognition. Some spark of cognizance. Could it be true? Could her brain finally be relinking all those broken connections after all these years?

His heart sank when he realized she still wasn't looking at him. She was staring, more pointedly now, at a spot behind him and to his left.

The flowers? Was she staring at the flowers? Oh, thank God. What a good idea it had been to stop by and pick up those flowers.

But when Miller turned to lift the bouquet off the table, he staggered back and barked in surprise. Standing next to the bedside table, with one hand lying across the top of the flowers, was a little girl.

A blonde little girl, with hair chopped short and ragged to her chin, hair that looked like it hadn't seen a washing in quite a while. She wore a bright pink shirt and dirty white shorts. Her tiny fingernails, those now lying across the red cellophane encasing the bouquet, were painted a matching pink.

Terror and disbelief washed over Miller when he noticed that her fingers looked unnaturally pink, too. Especially when he realized why. He could see the red cellophane right through them.

His heart stopped. His breath died in his throat. And for a moment, he wondered if perhaps this was all just a dream.

"Hi," the little girl said, but she wasn't looking at Miller. She was staring straight at Mollie.

The knock on the door made Miller jump, and he watched in stunned silence as the door swung slowly open.

"Good morning, Miller. Did you say you heard Mollie say something?"

His eyes drifted from the nurse's questioning expression to the little girl with her hand on the flowers and back again. But the nurse didn't seem to acknowledge anyone else in the room.

"She . . .she said hi. Hi. She said it twice. Clear as day. I heard her." His voice shaky and tight, Miller had a hard time getting the words out. Then he lifted a hand toward the little blonde girl and said, "Her. I think it was her Mollie was talking to."

One of the nurse's dark eyebrows lifted as she scanned the room, then creases formed on her forehead. "Talking to . . .who?"

Although Miller could still see her, one hand lying on the bouquet, her form was rapidly fading. Becoming more and more transparent with each moment. Dumbfounded, and entirely uncertain as to whether he'd imagined this whole bizarre episode, he stood frozen to the spot, and silent.

"Miller? Mr. Stanford, are you alright?" the nurse prodded, and stepped forward to lay a hand on his arm.

He blinked once, then once again. The vision of the child was gone.

"Can I get you anything? A glass of water? How about some orange juice?" She turned over her shoulder and called out into the hallway, "Agnes, can you please bring in some orange juice for Mr. Stanford here?"

When Miller's knees folded, he was grateful the chair he'd been sitting on hadn't moved. Turning, he studied his sister's expression. The light had gone out of her eyes. Again, she was staring, unfocused, toward the chattering, animated characters on the television screen. Her mouth was open, and another drizzle of drool was snaking its way toward her chin.

Miller dropped his face into both hands, and did what he seldom allowed himself to do. He broke down and cried. His sobs rumbled from the depths of his soul, a tortured soul that would forever blame himself for not protecting his baby sister from this fate.

The remainder of Laura's weekend was long and lonely, so much so she was actually anxious to get back to work Monday. Miller worked the night shift Saturday, then had been gone by eight o'clock the next morning, before Laura had even crawled out of bed. Sundays, she knew, he went to visit his sister. He hadn't come home until late that afternoon, in a sullen mood. So aside from offering to share her dinner with him, which he refused, they hadn't spoken. She hadn't interrupted his immersion in the Sports Channel all evening.

It was as though, even after their brief encounters with what felt like real intimacy, Miller had again returned to his distant, loner persona. They had digressed into simple roommates. And Laura couldn't help feeling an overwhelming sensation of loss.

When Laura turned the corner into her office bright and early on Monday morning, she was surprised to find Jonathan already at his desk. His shift was staggered from hers, a half-hour later. But the way he spun around and leapt to his feet, it was obvious he'd come in early—and was waiting for her.

"Good morning, Counselor. Good weekend?" he chirped.

Laura still found the strange little geek irritating, but had realized over the past weeks that the man under the nerdy façade actually had a good heart. He'd helped her that first morning when Riley tried to sabotage her first patient session, after all. And since then he had backed off, giving her a chance to settle into her new job without invading her space. Too much, anyway.

But it was Monday morning, and her weekend, in truth, had been a bit lonely.

"Well?"

Laura realized she'd drifted back inside her own head when Jonathan pressed for her answer, standing with both hands lifted beside his head.

"It was okay. A weekend," she answered feebly. "How about yours?"

"I'm soooo glad you asked," he answered, excitement twinkling his watery, grey eyes. "Actually, I've been here all weekend. Working on that little project you asked me to." His face twisted into a grin so gleeful, he looked like a psycho clown.

Laura blinked. "What project?"

"Why the Talcott Hall files, of course. Don't tell me you've lost interest in that can of worms already," he said. "I hope not. Because I did it." His voice lowered to a hissing whisper. "I cracked the key. We're in."

Laura's gaze shifted nervously to the open doorway. She reached behind her to click the door shut before asking, "Jonathan. Couldn't you lose your job for that?"

He waved a hand jerkily in front of his face as though she'd blown smoke at him. "No, no, no. The way I went in, nobody will link me—either of us—to this little caper."

She tilted her head, one eyebrow lifting. "Are you sure?"

"As sure as I can be. Because you see, before I worked on figuring out the passkey for the TC files, I hacked into somebody else's account creds." He pressed his lips flat and nodded.

"Somebody else's account . . .whose?" Laura grabbed the edge of her desk and dropped down into her chair. She had a strange feeling the rest of this news would be more worrying than she could deal with this early on a Monday morning.

But Jonathan was nodding vigorously now, hands clasped in front of him and looking very pleased with himself. "You got it. That was the easy part. It amazes me at how some people pick such simple, stupid passwords. Her dog's name is Freddie, and he was, she boasted to everybody who'd listen to her last year, her very first pet. Freddie01. How much simpler could it get?"

Now it was Laura's turn to shake her head. Holding up one hand to slow down Jonathan's avalanche of words, she asked, "Who, Jonathan? Who has a dog named Freddie?"

"Why, Kayla Riley, of course."

Laura's stomach dropped so hard she thought it might have bounced off the seat of her chair. "You mean to tell me you used Riley's credentials to crack the Talcott Hall records?"

"Brilliant, don't you think?" Jonathan crossed his arms over his bird-like chest. "So, when would you like to start digging through the archives?"

Twenty

Standing behind Jonathan, watching over his shoulder as he logged into the computer in the abandoned lobby, Laura knew she should back away. Not get involved in this any further than she already had. Miller warned her that opening the Talcott record files could be a can of worms that could cost her her job. And even though Jonathan, with his slick method of manipulating his way into the files, assured her they wouldn't get caught, the whole thing left a bad taste in her mouth.

And sent shudders up her spine. Why, a little voice kept whispering in her head, were the Talcott Hall patient records such a secret? She knew all about patient confidentiality laws, but the facility had transferred all their patients out over twenty years ago. Many, she was sure, were probably already dead. And the information she was looking for had nothing to do with a *live* patient, anyway. That thought sent another quake quivering through her.

Most of the staff here in the outpatient wing of the Addiction Center were usually gone before five-thirty. Jonathan asked Laura to hang around after quitting time at five until they could use the computer at the front desk to log in with Riley's credentials and begin searching the files. It would have a time-stamp, true, but Riley didn't punch a time clock—and she never stayed until her designated shift was over at six. Even if someone from further up the command chain investigated the breach, Riley might not be so eager to admit she hadn't even been in the building at the time the records were opened.

"Why is this so important to you, Jonathan? What are *you* looking for in the Talcott files?" Laura asked in a hushed tone that echoed in the tile-and-glass lobby. She knew what she was looking for—evidence of what might have happened to a certain Thomas Sanderson. But it perplexed her how her coworker had jumped on the bandwagon without even knowing why she needed the information.

Jonathan's fingers paused on the keyboard as he glanced back at her over his shoulder with narrowed eyes. "You forget I've worked here a long time, Miss Horton. Since this facility opened, in fact. The mysteries surrounding Talcott Hall have hung over this entire campus like a foul-smelling cloud, ever since they constructed the chain link fence around the place. When families started coming around, asking questions. About ten years ago."

"What kind of questions?"

Jonathan swiveled to face her. "Back in the day, when the place was fully occupied and being treated, the *Seldon H. Talcott way*," he drew air quotes around the words, "the families still wanted nothing to do with their sick kin. Most simply abandoned them here. *The crazies in the family closet.*" He set his lips in a grim line and shook his head. "That was just the beginning, when attitudes toward treatment of mental illness finally started coming out of the dark ages. In fact, Dr. Talcott was one of the first in his field who believed in treating the insane as sick people, and not hopeless genetic anomalies."

Laura sighed. She knew from her undergrad studies of the history of the disease that there was once a time when mentally ill patients were treated like rabid animals, or criminals. Oftentimes their families feared them, and just wanted them gone. So, they dumped them in insane asylums and forgot about them—literally. In most cases, when the patient died, the family wouldn't even want to be involved in the disposition of their remains.

Things began to change just after the turn of the century.But society's attitude toward their "mad" kin, even then, hadn't changed.

"I think that's the saddest part about this whole field," Laura said. "So often, because of ignorance or fear or I'm not sure what, people tend to shun their family members who suffer from any sort of mental impairment."

As she spoke, Laura watched Jonathan's fingers fly over the keyboard as a series of security boxes opened up, asking for usernames and passwords. She cringed as she saw him type kriley86@omh.ny.gov into the username field, followed by the simplistic password he'd figured out. It took three sets of security fields, but then a new screen opened up on the browser—

NYS Office of Mental Health

Official Records of Admissions—Middletown State Homeopathic Hospital

Below the official title, a bulleted list of links loaded, each designating a year. But the list only went back as far as 1996. Laura scowled.

"This may not help. I'm not sure how long ago this patient was here . . .or when he died." She tipped her head, figuring. "A woman I met, near the graveyard next to Miller's house, said she used to play with the man's daughter when she was a kid. She's got to be in her fifties. The girl's father was already dead at that time, which would be at least forty years ago." Sighing, she felt the breath whoosh out of her in disappointment. "This man must have lived, and died here back in the 1970s. We're not going to find what I need from these records."

Jonathan squinted up at her. "They only input the most recent records into the computer. I'm sorry, but when you told me you wanted info, I figured it was recent."

Laura wrapped her arms around herself to ward off the sudden chill that seemed to come from inside her, rather than from the air in the room. "No. The records I need go back farther than that. Quite a bit farther." She laid a hand on Jonathan's shoulder. "I'm sorry to have put you through this, Jonathan. But to be honest, even I didn't know what I was looking for until a few days ago." A shudder ran through her. "I still don't. Not really."

"There are paper records, you know."

Laura's head shot up and she locked gazes with Jonathan. "Where? Were they sent to Rockland Psych Center along with the last patients? When they shut it down?"

Jonathan's head started oscillating slowly from side to side. "I can't be absolutely certain," he began, "but I know before it closed, the records were kept in the basement of Talcott Hall."

Laura blinked in surprise. "The basement? Well, even if they're still there, they're probably completely useless by now. The windows are all broken out, and Miller said he's actually seen homeless people, and mischievous kids, crawling into the basement. And then there's animals. Raccoons, mice, moles, lots of other creatures who just love using paper to build their nests."

But Jonathan's head was still wagging back and forth, though more forcefully now.

"No." He riveted Laura's eyes with knowing intensity. "I know they're still perfectly safe, completely intact."

She folded her arms across her chest and tipped her head. "And just how," she said, narrowing her eyes, "could you be so sure of that?"

Had Jonathan been down there? Had he really worked here long enough to have had access to the building at some time? And why? Besides, he didn't look old enough to have been of working age back in the 1996, when Talcott Hall shut and locked its doors.

Swiping a finger under his nose and sniffing—making Laura cringe—Jonathan shifted his gaze out the front windows of the lobby, where just the eastern corner of the giant brick building was visible.

"I wasn't always a . . ." he paused, clearing his throat. "I didn't always have such an elevated position here at the Psych Center. I started working here in 2005. I'd just turned sixteen, and my uncle got me a summer job working in the maintenance department."

Laura's head shot back. "Oh," she said. So . . .so you have been in that building," she breathed in awe. "My God, Jonathan, what was it like?"

He closed his eyes and pinched the bridge of his nose. "Not pleasant. Not a nice place to be, even for the few minutes, sometimes hours, I had to spend in there."

Laura swallowed. "But you've been in the basement, then." She couldn't keep the hopefulness out of her statement. "Maintenance . . .I mean, what kind of maintenance? Surely there were occasions when—"

"Oh yes, I've been in the basement. Plenty of times. Spent a whole week toting a bunch of records from the Admin building down into the bomb shelter."

"Bomb shelter?" Laura squeaked, quickly remembering late twentieth century was a time of war and uncertainty for her country. She'd learned about them in history class, but wars that weren't fought on American soil didn't hold much significance for a child. And Laura had been born in 1989. She was still a toddler when even the Gulf War was going on.

Jonathan's head dropped to his chest and he stared at some random spot on the floor. He was traveling back, she could tell, to that time in his mind. And she could also tell, by his haunted expression, those memories still creeped him out.

"The shelter . . .it wasn't very big. It always made me wonder who it was really for. I mean, Talcott Hall housed hundreds of patients at one time. There was no way they would all have fit in that tiny space." He swallowed, and when he raised his eyes to hers, there was a sheen in them. "The bomb shelter was for the staff. *Only* the staff. If we'd ever been attacked, bombed, or showered with mustard gas or anthrax, they would have left them all up there to die." His voice had lowered to a strangled whisper.

Laura shuddered. So even the supposed, humane philosophy of the Homeopathic Hospital still had its flaws. Its limitations. Its brutality.

"That's awful, Jonathan. It must have made you feel really bad when you realized that."

He nodded soberly. His shoulders lifted and dropped with a deep sigh. Then he blinked rapidly and returned his gaze to hers.

"But I do know one thing. When they were moving the patients off to Rockland in 2006, they boxed up all the medical records. And being the youngest member of the staff with the least seniority, I was assigned the task of taking them to Talcott Hall. To the basement."

Realization dawned on Laura and she sucked in a breath. "They put them in there? In the bomb shelter?"

"Yes, ma'am," he replied quietly. "It was four, twelve-inch-thick concrete walls with a locked steel door. Three feet under the ground, waterproof. There was no way, any way at all, those papers would have deteriorated. No bugs could have gotten to them either. It was airtight—they actually had a hand-cranked blower in a pipe that came up out of the floor. With this big, filter thing."

"Holy crap," Laura whispered, feeling a chill she hadn't noticed in the room moments earlier. "Scary place, huh?"

"Yes, indeedy." He studied her face thoughtfully. "But that's where they stored those records. The ones from the late 1870s up. Until they started transferring the information into the computer system." He turned back to the monitor and pointed to the screen. "Anything before 1996 will be down there. In that creepy, black hole."

Laura's stomach twisted. She knew it would be almost impossible for her to actually get inside the building. At least, not without Miller's help. She bit her lower lip.

"It's still there, then? Sealed up?"

"As far as I know. We've had people come around, from time to time, looking for their relatives' records. Trying to find out where they're buried. In fact, that's why the chain link fence went up. Not that it would have mattered anyway. The last time I was down there, that vault was padlocked up tight. Nobody will be able to access those records without the key."

The key, Laura thought. One most likely in the possession of Security. She wondered if Miller knew anything about it, where it might be kept. But her shoulders drooped in defeat, because he'd already made himself perfectly clear on that point. There was no way Miller would risk his job by trying to gain access to the Talcott Hall files.

Miller came home that Sunday with the intention to tackle his online class, in which he was falling farther and farther behind. But after an hour of chasing meaningless words around on the screen with his eyes, he gave up. He was too shaken, and had fallen too deeply into his own pit of depression to concentrate. Even when Laura came through the kitchen a time or two, once even offering to share her dinner with him, he'd only been able to manage a grunt in reply.

His pain and grief over Mollie had already destroyed one relationship. He didn't dare even try to share that burden with Laura. Likely, she'd go running the same way Angie did.

The next day, donning his uniform for the Monday night shift seemed even harder when he'd had only one day off. A truly shitty one at that. So, after punching in and retrieving his weapon, Miller was so distracted he nearly fell over the frail old man standing just outside the station door.

Stumbling to the side, he mumbled, "Geez, I'm sorry. Didn't see you there." But when he turned toward his cruiser, the old man called after him.

"Ain't you one of them cops who came and got me outta Talcott Hall?"

Miller froze, his back to the man, as the bottom dropped out of his stomach. Turning slowly, he saw he was being scrutinized with a piercing set of icy blue eyes.

He wouldn't have recognized the old guy anyway, since the last time Miller had seen him—what had it been? Two, three weeks ago?—he'd looked more like a corpse than a living human being. But he had a bit more color in his sunken cheeks now, though he didn't look to be an ounce heavier. The crotch of his baggy jeans hung nearly to his knees.

"Excuse me, sir? Can I help you?" Miller asked cautiously.

The man twisted his shoulders beneath his oversized flannel shirt and shoved gnarled hands into his front pockets. "They tell me two cops came and got me outta ol' Talcott. I don't remember, ya see, because I'd been sleeping there for, oh, I dunno. A couple days, maybe?"

Miller turned and took a step toward the man, drawing his eyebrows together. "How did you even get in there?"

The man coughed and spat on the pavement. "I used to live there. Used to be my home, back in the day. Had me some friends in there, too. Until the State decided some of us were all hunky-dory fine to go back out on the street." He shook his head sadly and stared at the ground. "But that was after my best friend was gone anyways. So, it didn't matter none."

Miller shifted uneasily. "Look, Mister . . ."

"Chaffee. Lawrence Chaffee." He stuck out his hand and Miller reluctantly took it. The skin was like cool paper over raw bone. Miller tempered his grip, fearing he might tear it.

Coughing with nervousness, Miller continued. "Mr. Chaffee, that building is off limits now. You should have figured that out by the eight-foot, chain link barrier." Miller remembered just how the fence had been breached that night, and his stomach did a slow turn.

Chaffee was bobbing his head. "I know, I know. But I had nowhere else to go, ya see. The place where I usually sleep, up there under the railway near the heating plant, well . . ." He paused, his mouth twisting. "Well, some of them younger folk have taken to doing their druggie thing up there. I got scared to sleep there anymore."

Making a mental note to pass that information on to his partner, Duvall, he asked again. "But how did you get in there?"

Miller knew. He knew damn well how Chaffee had gotten in. As easy as ducking through the big gap in the fence held up by that . . .thing. The prosthesis. But he was curious to see what the old man knew about it, if anything.

Chaffee scratched a straggly, grey beard as the corners of his eyes crinkled in amusement. "That's a funny thing now, ya know. Remember I told you I had me a best friend up there at The Hall?"

Miller nodded, adding, "But you said he was gone by the time they discharged you."

"He was. Died about a month before that, of a hellacious flu bug. Got down in his lungs, and, well, he was dead in about three days. We all figured his little girl brought it onto him, ya know. She'd been by to visit him 'bout a week or so before. Rumor had it she got real sick with it too."

Miller's patience with the old man's rambling was growing short. "That's too bad, Mr. Chaffee. But tell me—if your friend was dead before you ever left Talcott Hall, then how'd he help you get back in that night?"

A full grin split the man's beard. "With his right arm. He just hooked that thing to the fence and yanked it up like it weighed nothin'. Nothin' at all."

A cold chill washed over Miller at the man's words, but he set his jaw and said, "You're not making sense, Chaffee. You said the man was dead. And no man I know of could lift a huge hank of chain link with one hand—"

"Oh, he's dead alright. But he ain't never left here. He's waitin'. For me, I guess. Figured I'd be joinin' him that night."

A shudder ran across Miller's shoulders remembering how he, too, had thought Chaffee had already been dead when they found him. But the old man's mind must be half gone, thinking like this. Imagining his dead friend was still alive. *Waiting for him.* Yet something in the back of Miller's mind stirred even more uneasiness in him. *He just hooked that thing to the fence and yanked it up like it weighed nothin'.*

Miller pushed the thought aside, concentrating on the matter at hand.

"Mr. Chaffee, where are you staying now?" he asked.

"Up there at the shelter. They let me in when the hospital put me out go a few days ago. Not sure how long they'll let me stay, but I sure can't fend for myself like I used to. I'll be seventy-five next November. Last ten or so been pretty rough." He got a far-off look in his eyes, then shoved his hands back into his pockets with such force Miller feared he'd push his pants right down off his narrow hips.

"Figure I'll just wait till the next time ol' Tom comes around to help me over," he said with a knowing smile.

Senility, Miller thought sadly. And maybe a little crazy even before that. He had been a patient here, after all. Sadness squeezed in his chest. How sad, to be old, senile, *and* homeless. Guess he had a good reason to depend on imaginary friends. Chaffee might have crawled in through that gap in the fence, and seen the prosthesis holding it up. Then his mind had run off and spun a tale so it made sense to him.

His friend, the one that died before Chaffee got out, probably wore one like it.

"No family, Chaffee?" he asked, already knowing the answer.

He shook his head sadly. "The Missus run off when they locked me up in here, back in '90. Never did have any kids." Lifting his shoulders in a helpless gesture, he regarded Miller with an almost apologetic expression. "Nobody left alive now. Just me."

A pang of pity zinged Miller's chest. "Let me take you on back there now," he said softly, motioning toward his cruiser. "To the shelter. Come on. I'll drive you down."

But Chaffee was shaking his head. "Nope. Thanks a bunch, but it's nice day. I'd just as soon walk." He turned to leave, but then stopped. His cold, blue eyes riveted Miller's. "I almost forgot why I come up here in the first place. To tell you two cops who found me—"

"It's okay," Miller said. "You don't have to thank us. It's our job. Besides, old man," he pointed a finger in Chaffee's direction and narrowed his eyes, "you were trespassing. Just so you know, for next time."

Anger flared in Chaffee's eyes. "Thank you?" he screeched. "Hell, if I was a younger man, I'da come up here to whoop both your butts."

Miller's eyebrow rose and a muscle worked in his jaw, a mixture of surprise and humor filling him. "Oh, really. And why would that be? What'd we do to you? Besides save *your* skinny as . . .butt?"

Chaffee's eyes narrowed. "Looky here, Mr. Officer Man. You do me a favor. Next time you find me driftin' off somewhere, you just leave me be. I got friends waiting for me. I'd just as soon be getting on after 'em, if you don't mind." He turned and began shuffling slowly away. He called over his shoulder, "And you tell them other cops you work with the same thing. If you come across me someplace, just leave me alone. Then you don't have to worry about arresting me for trespassin'."

"That's my job, Mr. Chaffee. To keep people out of places that are off limits to the public. Like Talcott Hall," Miller called after him.

The old man stopped but didn't turn around. His next words were so low Miller almost didn't hear them.

"You can't arrest a dead man now, can you, Officer?"

Miller couldn't get Lawrence Chaffee out of his head the whole night. It was a weird coincidence, how he'd talked about a dead friend who'd "helped him get in." Into Talcott Hall. He remembered the night after, when he'd encountered a little girl—*the* little girl—accompanied by a man with half an arm. There had been no mistaking it. No prosthesis covered the rounded stump just below the elbow.

And how he'd disappeared so fast Miller thought he might have imagined him. And then the girl . . .how she'd faded away.

Like a waking nightmare, the footage of what happened weeks ago popped into Miller's brain. Tearing the prosthesis off the chain-link fence. Standing in front of the evidence closet with Sarge. Finding the three letters carved crudely into the plastic on the underside of the false arm. A monogram.

T. E. S.

And Laurence Chaffee's haunting claim that a friend had gotten him into Talcott that night. A friend who was waiting for him. *Ol' Tom.*

He must be losing his mind. It was the stress, all the big changes happening in his life over the past few weeks. First, Angie walking out, which bothered him more financially than emotionally. Then Laura showing up. A sweet, timid, damsel-in-distress who was turning out to be so *not* timid, he couldn't believe it. And of course, Mollie's illness, and his visit to her last weekend.

Where he thought he saw—again, the little girl. A ghostly little girl.

He probably needed to contact the Employee Assistance program and ask to go talk to someone. Of course, even though the program administrators claimed to be sworn to secrecy about such things, Miller would live in the perpetual fear of Sarge finding out. Especially now, he couldn't jeopardize his job, his income. Things would be tight for a few months, at least until Laura starting filling in the gap Angie left behind.

And oh, how she had filled another gap already. Another strain on Miller's emotions. He found himself very drawn to the woman. But she wasn't as much of a pussy-cat as he'd first thought. And he'd already shown too much of his Achilles Heel to her. His love/hate relationship with drinking. The gaping, open hole in his heart left by his sister's injuries.

In fact, she'd even mentioned his "sensitivity" the other night. This didn't sit well with Miller, making him feel way too vulnerable. His softer side, his weaknesses, were way too much information for a woman to know. It granted her immense power over him. And to a woman who, for all he knew, could manipulate him in the same way as Angie had.

No, Laura wouldn't be like Angie. Laura actually seemed to care about him, his problems. And she was a counselor, wasn't she? True, she specialized in addiction counseling, but Miller couldn't help but wonder if his perceived weakness for alcohol addiction wasn't at the root of all these unsettling feelings, these crazy imaginings.

The ghost sightings.

Laura wouldn't think he was totally nuts about that either. She claimed to have seen this elusive little girl. In fact, she seemed to have made it her mission to find out who she was, what her story was.

Or had been.

At least, in talking to Laura, he wouldn't be risking some whistle-blower spreading the news around that he'd sought counseling. Or would he?

As he sat in his cruiser with a three-quarter moon hanging over the hulking shadow of Talcott Hall, Miller watched the light orbs dancing, and wondered. Surely, there must be a logical explanation for this, as well as all the other crazy shit happening over the past few months. Even if the root was embedded inside his own, tortured mind.

He would just have to risk it. He would sit Laura down, just as soon as he could, and see if she'd be willing to help him sort all this out. After all, Miller never had gone for the counseling everyone urged on him after the accident. After his sister ended up a sad, twisted thing, all those years ago.

Maybe he should have.

They say everything happens for a reason, though Miller had never been able to figure out who "they" were, or how the hell they knew so much about everything. Maybe that's why Laura had come into his life. Maybe it was time to open up and let out the guilt, the hatred, the pain that had been eating him up every day of his life since then.

Checking his watch, he saw he had only twenty minutes left until his shift ended. He would do it. He would open up to Laura about his doubts and fears, and ask for her help as a counselor. Hell, she already knew how screwed up in the head he was anyway. What did he have to lose?

Hoping Laura was still awake by the time he got home, Miller turned the key in the ignition and headed back to the station.

Twenty-One

Laura had turned in early, but couldn't go to sleep. Today had unsettled her, started a war inside her head that had dragged her heart down with it. As curious as she was to find out who the elusive little girl was, and why she kept appearing to her, Laura was also not willing to risk pissing off Miller any more than she probably already had. God, if he found out Jonathan had hacked into the computer records for Talcott, both he and Laura could be in hot water.

Sighing, she checked to be sure she'd set her alarm before turning over and drawing Grandma's quilt over her head.

That's when she heard the front door lock click. Wow, she thought, he's home early. Glancing back at her clock, she saw it was barely after eleven. He must have come straight home.

When she heard his heavy footfalls coming down the hallway, she knew in a moment her unlatched door would swing open. He always checked on her before he turned in, which was so sweet of him. He was an awfully caring, soft-hearted guy.

What she didn't expect was to hear the low rumble of his voice from the doorway.

"Laura? You still awake?"

She shifted toward him, blinking in the light from the hallway as it framed his silhouette.

"I am. Can't seem to shut it off tonight. What's up, Mills?" she answered softly.

Immediately after the nickname left her lips, she squeezed her eyes shut and silently cursed. She knew that's what Mollie had called him. She remembered the flash of pain she saw in his eyes when she'd used it.

He hesitated only a moment. "Can I . . .can I come in?" he asked tentatively.

Laura shimmied up so her back was resting on the headboard, pulling the quilt up to her chin. "Sure, Miller. What's the matter? What's happened?" She couldn't ignore the niggling fear in her chest that maybe his sister had fallen sick again.

Another part, the guilty part, feared he might somehow had gotten wind of her Talcott records breach this morning.

Swinging the door open wide, Miller made his way to the edge of her bed and sat heavily. His expression, even in the dim light filtering in from the hall, was serious, almost grim. "I need to talk to you. I mean, like, in a professional capacity. Would you be willing to do that? Privately?" He sounded cautious, uncertain.

Mollie, Laura thought. Something's happened to his sister—

"I've been having all sorts of weird things happen to me lately. I'm sure it's just stress, but I'm really beginning to think I'm losing my fucking mind." He swiped a hand down his face. "I know it's the middle of the night, but would you mind?"

Laura swung back the covers and reached for the robe she had hanging off the edge of the headboard. "Of course not. Meet me out in the living room in five. I gotta pee first."

When she came down the hall she saw the living room was still dark, but the porch light was on. The front door was ajar. She pushed through the screen and stepped out, the coolness of the plank floor rippling through her.

Miller was standing at the end of the porch facing the graveyard, and he turned when he heard the screen door squeak.

"It's a nice night. Didn't think you'd mind if we talked out here," he said.

"I don't mind," she said, pulling the tie of her robe more snugly around her waist. She crept up beside him and laid her hands on the railing. He had once again directed his gaze out into the dark, toward the cemetery. From this angle, it lay hidden in near blackness. The thick border of pines blocked even the glow of the streetlamp on the corner.

He sighed heavily, turning away from her. "I'm imagining things, Laura. I mean, more so than before. My mind . . .it's running away with me. Some really weird shit."

Laura heard the tension in Miller's voice and felt a pang of pity for him. He hadn't been right since his visit to Brightstar yesterday. Something, she knew, must have brought him down even more than usual.

She laid a hand on his arm. "What kind of stuff, Miller? Are you still seeing those weird orb things you told me about?"

He nodded. "Yeah, almost every night. I still can't figure out what the hell causes them. It's got to be some kind of light refraction, a streetlamp or headlights reflecting off something." He shook his head, his lips tightening into a grim line. "But it's more than that." He turned to face her. "You remember I told you about the night we found the homeless guy in Talcott Hall? The way the fence had been broken free and then chained up with that . . .thing?"

She nodded, remembering how shaken up she'd been when he'd recounted the story.

"Well, the old guy didn't die. He was waiting for me outside the station when I went into work today."

Laura blinked, and paused before cocking her head. "You don't think you were imagining *him*, surely."

"No. He was real enough. But he said some crazy shit when I asked him how he got in that night. About a friend of his who had *yanked the fence up with one arm*." He drew air quotes around the words. "A friend who was waiting for him."

Confused, Laura reached up to thread her fingers into her disheveled curls. "You think there was somebody else in there? That you guys missed when you combed the building?"

Miller shook his head. "No. But the prosthesis. It was carved with some sort of monogram. Initials. They match—"

Then they both heard the sound. Feet, running. But not down the sidewalk in front of Miller's house. Beside it. They both tensed, and turned to lean over the rail, looking toward the back of the house.

Laura gasped and covered her mouth with her hand when she caught sight of a flash of white and pink darting in through the open gate to the graveyard.

"Do you see her? You see her too, right?" Miller whispered.

Tears welled in Laura's eyes as she answered, "Yes, Miller. I see her too. She's the same little girl as I saw running beside the house that day I was in the basement, doing laundry. The same one, wearing the same clothes."

When Miller turned to face her, his wolf-like eyes were wide and wild-looking. "Well maybe I'm not so crazy after all. She was there at Brightstar. On Sunday. With Mollie. She was standing in Mollie's room, right beside her bed. Then, she just faded out of sight."

A chill rippled through Laura. Now he was sounding a little . . .unstable. Imaginings like this, right there while he was visiting his sister, could very well point to a stress-related illness. She shifted her gaze away and laid her hand on her throat. These types of hallucinations sounded like the DTs.

But he hadn't even been drinking much lately. Not since the day—the one when Mollie went into the hospital. And he wasn't in nearly deep enough to have delirium tremors. They were a withdrawal symptom from a deeply addicted alcoholic. One who went cold turkey after long-time, intense abuse. Miller, from what Laura could surmise, didn't even come close to this diagnosis.

He spun suddenly, and Laura stumbled back.

"I've got to get to the bottom of this. There has to be some logical explanation." He stepped around her and headed for the steps.

"Wait," she said. "Let me get some shoes. I'll go with you."

He turned to stare at her in shock. "Okay. Maybe you better." He raked a hand through his hair and looked away. "So I don't imagine more than I really find," he mumbled.

Miller waited for Laura at the bottom of the porch steps, listening, his eyes combing the darkness for any movement. From this perspective, all he could see was a single shaft of the streetlight glaring through the tops of the pines, its bright beam rendering everything else even more invisible in the darkness. Within moments, Laura reappeared, her robe replaced by a light jacket over flannel pajama pants, sockless sneakers on her feet. She had her arms wrapped tightly around herself.

"Here," she said, pulling a tiny, purple flashlight out of her jacket pocket and handing it over. "I keep this in my purse."

Miller took the thing, smirking at how it looked like a doll's toy in his big hand. "I don't think this will help us much." When he saw her frown, he quickly added, "But thanks. It will be enough to keep us from stumbling over a marker."

They crept around the side of the house and made their way slowly toward the opening in the iron fence. Cricket song, as they neared the patch of woods behind the house, was deafening. Laura huddled so close to Miller he had to set each foot down carefully so as not to step on her. He was glad she'd joined him, though. At least he'd have a witness if he did hear or see anything.

When they reached the gate's entrance, they both froze. Laura gazed up at Miller with terrified, rounded eyes.

"Do you hear that? That's what I heard the other day. The day I met Jenna here."

A child's soft sobbing drifted to them above the cricket symphony, rising and falling in volume. A cold chill washed over Miller, and he instinctively slipped his arm around Laura's shoulders.

He heard it too.

"Greta. That's the name the little girl gave me that night outside of Talcott. I'm going to try to call out to her," he said, trying desperately to keep the quiver out of his voice.

His words boomed into the silence. "Greta," he called. "Greta Sanderson."

Even the crickets' song stopped. Complete silence fell around them, so intense that Miller wondered for a moment if he'd gone suddenly deaf.

"Greta Sanderson. We're here to help. If there's some way we can help you, please show yourself."

And I hope to God I don't pass out if you do.

Mere seconds passed before she appeared. He would like to have believed she'd stepped out from behind a stone, but there were none close enough to either side of where she manifested. In the center of the wide path defining the center of the graveyard—the one wide enough to permit a hearse to drive through—she simply *appeared*. Even in the inky blackness, her body seemed to glow, emanating a feeble light that surrounded her like a halo.

Miller knew immediately this was the same child he'd seen that night near Talcott Hall. She was about eight or ten years old, with disheveled, blonde hair chopped raggedly just below her jawline. And even in the near blackness, her white shorts and bright, pink sneakers glowed as though illuminated from within. He heard Laura suck in a gasp and tightened his hold around her.

Thank God, she sees her too.

"Are you Greta?" Miller asked gruffly. "What are you doing here? What is it you want?"

The child drew both fists up to rub her eyes as she sank down into the grass. A sob escaped her that ripped through Miller like a sword to his heart. An echoing, tortured wail, one that resonated around them. Louder than should be coming from a small child, twenty feet away.

Or was it coming from inside his own head? It was difficult to tell.

He felt Laura take a small step forward. "Greta, what are you looking for?" Miller was surprised at her boldness as she said, "We want to help you, Greta. How can we help?"

The little girl lowered her hands to fold tightly beneath her chin. "I'm lost. I don't know where to go. And I can't find my daddy."

The child's voice echoed as though she were standing inside a culvert, the sound pulsating in its intensity, garbled. Miller started to tremble, his stomach turning sour.

When the child suddenly clambered to her feet, Miller's heart leapt in his chest. He could feel Laura trembling now too, and squeezed her shoulder. The tiny flashlight slipped from his grasp and landed on the grass with a soft thump.

Greta took a step toward them, then another. As she drew closer, her image grew less distinct. Almost transparent, wavering like a reflection on water. Her voice, fading quickly in a tremulous echo, was barely legible.

"My daddy died up there." She pointed up the hill, toward the Psych Center Grounds.

Toward Talcott Hall, Miller thought.

"He died while I was sick. Real, real sick. I couldn't go see him, to say goodbye. Now, I can't find him. I can't find my grandma, either. I don't know where I am . . . I am . . . I am."

Like a candle flame sputtering in the rain, Greta's image faltered.

"Please show me where my daddy is," she pleaded. "So he can take me home."

Home . . . Home.

And then, she was gone. Miller staggered backward, dragging Laura with him until their backs collided with the shingles of his house. His breath was coming fast, and his blood whirred in his ears like a high-pitched turbine. Laura turned into him and burrowed her face against his chest. Her shoulders shuddered as if she were crying, and her fingers twisted into the crisp cloth of his shirt.

It took a few minutes before either of them could move, and the song of the crickets again underscored the silence of the night. Miller swallowed, his nausea subsiding some as he stroked his hand down Laura's silky curls. When her shoulders stopped heaving, he looked down and lifted her chin with two fingers.

"So maybe I'm not crazy after all," he said, his voice coming out tight and gruff.

Laura shook her head violently. "If you are, then so am I. But Miller, what are we going to do? She's come to us—the two of us—for help. How can we help her spirit go free?"

His stomach did another nauseating twist as the answer came into his mind, plain and clear. One he didn't want to acknowledge.

But it appeared as though he—neither of them—were being given any choice.

"Her father is obviously not in there," he grumbled, pointing toward the cemetery. "But he's got to be somewhere. We have to find his grave, wherever that might be, and bring Greta to him. Bring father and daughter together. One, last time."

Twenty-Two

Miller guided Laura back inside the house, locked the door behind them, and flicked off the porch light. They stood there, inside the doorway, and he folded her into him, burying his face in her hair. She smelled sweet and clean and . . .well, a little like Irish Spring. Her body was still trembling, though he couldn't tell whether it was the night air or from the bizarre experience they'd just shared.

He was more than a little surprised when she pulled back, looked deep into his eyes, and lifted herself up on her toes so she could reach his mouth. Her lips were soft, tentative as she brushed her mouth across his, her breath hot on his skin. She smelled minty, clean. So damned inviting. He waited, though, letting her make all the moves. He groaned in relief when she covered his mouth with hers and parted his lips with her tongue.

She tasted minty, too. Sweet and hot, he answered her kiss, stroke for stroke, and felt his arousal grow taught in his groin. He pulled her closer, so their bodies pressed together, chin to knees. He knew she could feel his erection pressing hard into her belly, and she answered with a thrust of her hips against him.

Miller was lost. There was no way he could deny this woman, and he knew it. He didn't even want to try.

He combed his fingers into her hair and gripped the back of her head, exploring deeper with his tongue. She moaned and drew one knee up between his legs.

"Make love to me, Miller. Please. I feel a little lost. A little like that child-spirit out there. I need to be held. I want to feel cherished. Wanted," she whispered.

"Oh, I want you, all right. But what scares the hell out of me, Laura, is how I'm starting to need you." He pulled back and gazed into her huge, blue eyes. "*Need* you. And not just like this." He searched her face as he fiddled with one errant, blonde curl and tucked it behind her ear.

He waited, searching her eyes for some sign she understood what he was saying. But there was only open, pure innocence in those eyes. She had no idea what it meant to be loved. He could see that now. And like a pinprick to his heart, he nearly winced when she replied, "I'm yours, Miller. I'll give you whatever you want. To please you. I just want to make you happy."

"Laura, I love you. Are you ready for that? I mean, I've never felt this way about anyone in my life."

She blinked fast as though he'd hit her with something too complex for her to understand. "Why?" she asked in a small voice.

"Because I've never felt so alive since the day you came waltzing into my house. Into my life. At first, like a shy bird. One I soon realized was a well-disguised lady hawk." His mouth curled into a wry smile. "And because you don't think I'm crazy."

He watched as her pale, gold eyebrows grew together, her eyes glistening. "I don't know how to do that, Miller. . .the love thing. I mean, other than family. I don't know if I'm ready for—"

Miller didn't give her the chance to finish saying what he not only didn't want to hear, but didn't believe. His mouth crushed hers with a hunger, a passion he'd never known. She didn't resist, but dove into the pool of desire right alongside him.

He would show her. If she didn't understand his words, then he would show her. Show her what it felt like to be loved.

Unzipping her jacket slowly, he pushed it down over her shoulders and it fell to the floor. All she wore underneath was a silky tank, and he could see her pert nipples poking through the fabric. His cock twitched.

233

But before he could bring his hands up to cup them, she latched her fingers under the waistband of her silly, cartoon-printed sleep pants and slipped them down. She wore nothing underneath.

Miller groaned at the sight of her. She took his hand and led it down to where her golden patch covered her sex. "Touch me, Miller. See how much I want you."

He dropped his head back and moaned as his fingers slipped across her soft folds, already slick with desire. "My god, Laura, you're killing me here."

When he opened his eyes, she was staring up at him, her face inches from his. A glint of humor transforming her expression into that of a mischievous little elf. With both hands, she pushed him back, one step . . .two . . .three. Now his back was against the hallway wall, and her hand was cupping the bulge in his trousers.

"If I'm going to kill you, I want you to enjoy every minute."

Deftly and with more ease than he could believe, she flipped open the button on his uniform pants with one hand. Tugging on the zipper tab, she demanded, "Lose these."

Miller's throat was thick with passion, and his voice came out gruff as he said, "Upstairs, Laura. Let's go upstairs."

But she was shaking her head slowly from side to side, that glint of mischief piquing his excitement even more. "I want you here. Right here. Take me here, Miller."

Miller had never done it up against a wall. Had never realized how mind-blowingly exciting it could be. And with a waif of a woman like Laura, it was effortless. He cupped his hands around her soft, round ass and lifted her, light as a feather. As he did, her legs wrapped around his waist and he spun them, so it was her back was up against the wall.

And Miller lost his mind, along with his heart in his own front hallway that night.

"There's a key. Jonathan told me the records were stored in a bunker, a bomb shelter in the basement of Talcott Hall. But in order to get in there, I'm going to need the key."

It was already four in the morning, and Laura realized there was no sense at this point in actually trying to go to sleep. Hers and Millers frantic lovemaking—first in the hallway, then in his shower, then again on his acre of mattress—hadn't tired either of them out. If anything, it had only served to fuel the fire of their partnership. They had been paired for a purpose, assigned a joint duty, standing out there by the graveyard last night. They both knew it, and Laura wasn't sure if she was the one unhappier about it, or if Miller was.

He was laying on his back, his hands folded behind his head, the sheet barely covering the parts Laura figured, by now, she knew pretty well. Light spilling in from the streetlamp highlighted the golden hair covering his chest, tapering to a narrow line at his navel. Like an arrow, pointing the way to the place Laura knew had given her pleasure beyond any she'd ever experienced. She laid her head on his flat belly and sighed.

Everything happens for a reason. That's what Grammy always said. She and Miller had been brought together by forces outside themselves, charged with a duty that was both scary and treacherous. For both of them, their livelihoods might be at stake. But Laura also knew she couldn't go on ignoring the lost child wandering the graveyard. On the grounds of the abandoned asylum. The one who was begging for their help.

After a few moments of silence, Laura asked, "The key, Miller. Do you know where it's kept? How I can get it?"

His sudden growl made her jump. "You can't go in there by yourself, Laura. The place is a house of cards. It's falling down. The second-floor hallway caved in last winter and almost killed three stupid kids who tried camping out on the ground floor." He sat up and held her shoulders, looking deep into her eyes. "I won't let you go in there alone. Hell, neither one of us should go in there at all. Who knows if we'll find the answers, even in the records?"

Laura's heart leapt hearing the tone in Miller's voice. Like he was actually considering helping her get into the building. She fisted the sheet in her hands.

"Jonathan said all the records prior to 1996 are down in the bomb shelter. Surely, they must include information about what they did with the bodies of the patients who died."

Miller's mouth twisted. "What about this child? Jenna said she used to play with her when they were kids, right? She might well still be alive. Maybe she can tell us something—"

"No, Miller." Laura shook her head adamantly and slipped off the bed, dragging the sheet with her and wrapping it around her nude body like a haphazard toga. "Don't you understand? The child Jenna played with *is* our little girl. Greta." She stood beside the bed, exhaustion and frustration coiling around her insides. "That child is dead. But for some godforsaken reason, she's trapped here. She can't leave—move on. Until she finds out where her father was buried."

Miller stared silently into the darkness for a few moments, then began shaking his head. "It's crazy, Laura. This whole thing is fucking, lunatic-driven crazy. Like the patients who used to live there left some of the cuckoos messing their minds up, and we've both caught the disease."

Laura sighed. Maybe Miller was right. Maybe mental illness, at least of the flavor borne by some of the people at this psychiatric center, had a reasonable, logical cause. Tainted water, maybe? Insidious, toxic fumes? She remembered the night the smoke came, covering the entire campus, along with Miller's house on the perimeter, like a suffocating blanket.

Maybe she was losing her mind too. The thought sent a shiver through her.

"I can't do it, Laura. I can't go any further with this, not without risking my job. Hell, my career." He rolled toward her and reached out his arms. "Please, come back to bed. Let me hold you while you sleep the few hours left before you have to get up for work."

Laura ran her fingers through her tumbled curls, hesitating only a moment before climbing back onto the bed. She nestled into the crook of Miller's shoulder, complete peace consuming her when his heavy arm came around to encircle her.

Just before sleep claimed her, she heard his low rumble in the darkness.

"You're not going in there either. No fucking way. There's got to be another way."

When the late morning sunshine woke Miller, he knew he'd missed her. He must have passed out cold to not even had heard or felt Laura slip out of bed. Had she slept with him the whole night— at least the few hours that were left before her alarm went off? Groaning, he turned to look at the bedside clock. Ten minutes past eleven. Shit, he'd missed his date with Rip at the gym this morning too.

His whole life was coming apart at the seams. Between all the weirdness with this Greta—was he really believing he'd spoken with a ghost last night?—and Mollie's slow deterioration, he had a good excuse for tipping off his rocker. He felt like Laura's appearance in his life, and this . . .thing that had developed between them was the only *thing* keeping him afloat.

And that scared Miller half to death. His feelings for her were taking hold of his heart with such intensity, he feared what was growing between them could be the final hammer blow. If she didn't feel the same way. And as of right now, he had no idea if she did. Or ever could.

An hour later, sitting in front of his laptop with a steaming mug of his high-test coffee beside him, he was swearing under his breath at the class page on the screen when his cellphone buzzed. Snatching it up, his chest seized.

Shit. *Brightstar.*

Laura knew she'd have at least an hour between counseling sessions this morning. Her first task was to find Jenna, and see if she could shed any light on the little girl she used to play with as a child. Greta Sanderson.

Her first group session had just ended and she headed back to her office, unsure of where she would even start in her quest to find out who Jenna was, and how she could contact her. Damn, why hadn't she asked Miller about it last night? Okay, they had gotten a bit distracted.

Oh my, yes. And what a glorious distraction it had been.

I'll call him. He should be up by now, she thought, glancing at the wall clock. Hell, it was well past noon. Her heart squeezed when she saw her discreetly silenced phone was buzzing from inside her purse. *Miller.*

He's thinking of me too. We really must be on the same wavelength. What a special, sweet guy this Miller was.

"Hey, Mills," she murmured into the phone.

She nearly dropped the device when he blasted into her ear, "Don't ever fucking call me that again, Laura. Never . . .fucking . . .again." But his last words broke around a sob.

And Laura's heart broke with them.

"She's gone, Laura. Mollie is gone."

Twenty-Three

After clicking off the phone, Miller hurled it down and it slid across the floor, where it exploded into pieces against the far wall. He needed to hit something . . .break something . . .*hurt* something. His fit of grief was so intense, his rage so blind, so soaked with the pain of loss and fury, he proceeded to trash the only demon left to blame.

Yanking open the fridge, he snatched out the eleven bottles remaining of a twelve-pack he'd bought the day before and smashed them, one at a time, over the stainless-steel divider of the kitchen sink. Beer splattered the backsplash, the countertop, the cabinets. Tiny fragments of glass threw off sparks of light as they scattered across the countertop, catching the sunshine streaming in through the window, oblivious.

That done, he left the sink full of broken, brown glass and stormed to the pantry cabinet.

He rummaged frantically, throwing boxes and cans to the floor in his frenzy until he found the bottle of Appleton Estate he kept for times when Kip stopped over for a quick one. The heavy glass of that bottle, however, proved too thick to shatter against the now dented stainless sink divider. After two desperately fierce attempts, he stormed to the front door, fisting the neck of the bottle as it hung at his side. He stomped across the porch and down the steps to his truck, retrieving his hammer.

Miller bashed the heavy glass under the heavy steel tool, crouched down behind the trash can beside the house. And there he left the ragged shards, lying in a viscous, golden pool of rum. Visible, pungent steam rose from the warmed pavement. Swearing, he clutched his hand to his body as pain shot up his arm.

The neck of the rum bottle hadn't exactly broken off clean.

The fumes and the pain pushed the horror of this godforsaken day to a tumultuous crescendo. His emotions peaked, shattering whatever was left of his macho armor. Nausea overtook him, and he wretched miserably into the can.

When Laura stumbled through the front door twenty minutes later, Miller was hunkered down over the kitchen sink, struggling clumsily to wrap his left hand in a dishtowel. The tan, checkered cloth was rapidly soaking bright red. With his blood.

"What the . . ." Laura froze, her handbag dropping to the floor. For a brief moment, panic seized her chest, her breath catching. She covered her mouth with her hand as a lump formed in the base of her throat. But now was not the time for her to fall apart.

Her training, her patient care persona kicked in. She strode forward, reaching for his hand with authority.

"What happened?" Her tone was calm, even.

She didn't get an answer, but she didn't need one. The pile of broken glass in the sink and strewn across the counter spoke for itself. As did the splatters of blood marking Miller's path across the kitchen. And although she didn't expect the big man to accept her ministrations without a fight, he did.

Unfolding the towel, she suppressed a gasp when she saw the jagged slash across his palm, from thumb to forefinger. It was deep. It was bleeding badly. He needed stitches.

"Hold this," she ordered, squashing the towel into his palm and folding his fingers around it. Miller didn't raise his eyes, just stared dumbly at his hand as if it belonged to someone else.

Shock. He was going into shock.

She squeezed both her small hands around his huge one and shook it vigorously until finally, she broke through his haze. Slowly, he raised his eyes to meet hers.

"Tight. Hold this tight, Miller," she barked. "You're bleeding. Bleeding bad."

He blinked, and his brows knitted as he stared at her. In that instant, the pain she saw in those flinty eyes cut her more deeply than the glass had his skin. But this pain had nothing—absolutely nothing—to do with the wound on his hand. She swallowed, sucked in a breath, and moved forward. On autopilot.

It took only a second for her to rip a strip off the hem of her gauzy skirt, which she then proceeded to use as a makeshift tourniquet to wrap around Miller's wrist.

"It's got to be tight," she growled through gritted teeth. She yanked on the tied ends of the cloth, cinching the binding so hard it bit into Miller's skin. "Or you'll bleed to death before I get you to the E.R."

Through it all, he hadn't said a word. Hadn't fought her, hadn't flinched. Although he'd made eye contact with her, Miller wasn't there. It was clear the man had already shielded himself from the pain. From reality.

A kind of shock, she prayed, he would someday recover from.

Miller moved through the next days in a fog of unprecedented misery. Moments branded his memory in snapshots of horror. One scene his brain still hadn't made sense of—him, flat on his back on a board-hard surface, a scrawny, serious-looking young man wielding a needle and coming at him, aiming for . . .his hand?

Yet he'd had no impetus to rise up in his own defense. A pinch, and then numbness spreading up his arm like frost. Someone pressing a cool cloth to his forehead as he faded in and out, the surface beneath him feeling like a stone slab.

He didn't remember how he got to Brightstar, but he clearly recalled meeting his mother there. Her grief bounced off him, though. His own had already saturated him, and he didn't have an ounce of will left to help bear hers. Numbly, he heard the droning of whatever the social workers were saying, but couldn't make out the words.

His heart hit rock bottom when Miller watched his mother sign papers for them to release Mollie's body to the funeral home. This was it. The end of a horrifying saga that had begun in the parking lot of a high school gymnasium, almost twelve years ago.

It wasn't as though they both hadn't known it was coming. That this story would not have a happy ending. And each had dealt with the grief up until now in their own, twisted ways—yet both in denial. His mother, in her endless treks to mindlessly gamble away every last cent of her—as well as Miller's—money. But for what? For a future she knew she could never win back.

And Miller, on a virtual treadmill, determined to earn enough money to keep Mollie as comfortable as possible. To keep his little sister alive, such as it was. Even though she hadn't even known who he was from that horrible day forward.

He remained stalwart and dry-eyed throughout the funeral home fiasco, where his mother made decisions that were grueling, futile, and meaningless. What would Mollie wear? Seriously? To rot in the ground around her? What kind of flowers should decorate her casket? What background music they would be playing. Like planning a fucking wedding. Except instead of the beginning of a new life, they were choosing the details for an ending.

You don't choose a casket for a wedding.

Through it all, vaguely, Miller remembered Laura being there. Dreamlike, in almost every snapshot. Her firm grip on his elbow. Her fresh, clean scent vying with the artificial, flowery funeral home miasma. Words she murmured as she clung close to his side. Words of encouragement, he guessed. He wasn't sure. He didn't hear them.

At one point, his mother's gut-wrenching sobs broke through, and he reached to hold her as she moaned pitifully against his chest. And that's when something strange happened. Miller felt a chilled calm settle over him. A wall of ice encasing his heart. Locking his own vulnerability away, protecting him from any further pain.

His heart was so splintered, so bloodied and raw, there was no way he was opening himself up for this kind of emotional agony, ever again. Of any kind.

Love hurts. Way too much to take a chance on it, in any way. Ever again.

It had been two weeks since Mollie's funeral, and Miller had yet to say more than three consecutive words to Laura the few times she'd seen him. He'd had bereavement time off, about a week, from what she could figure. But during that time, he'd been home very little. When he was, he was holed up in his room.

One time, his friend Kip had come to see him. Laura had never met the man before, only heard Miller speak of him. The fireman. Kip arrived early one evening while Miller was still off from work. He was a huge man with ebony black skin and kind, pale golden eyes. He introduced himself through the screen door, and asked if he might speak to Miller. Laura sighed.

"You're welcome to try, Kip. I haven't been able to get through to him since the day—"

"I know," Kip replied. "I probably can't do much better. But I've got to give it a go."

As hard as Laura had tried, from the day Mollie had died until now, she just couldn't reach through to Miller. He had erected a wall around himself that nobody—not even his best friend Kip—was getting through.

Life for Laura had stabilized—to a degree. She had fallen into a comfortable rotation between patient sessions and records entry. She and her boss, Kayla Riley, had called a silent truce. Her first paycheck had been deposited in the bank this fine, sunny Friday afternoon. She was anxious to let Miller know she'd have the first installment of her almost-two-months-in-arrears rent ready to give him.

Part of her was grieving for—and with—this man she'd started to have real feelings for. Another part was fearful that whatever they'd begun, whatever connection they'd started to share, might have been shredded and trampled in the wake of Mollie's death.

Since that day, he'd completely locked her out. Two weeks had passed, and although Laura knew that was no way long enough for Miller to move past his sister's death, he showed no signs of letting her in. He treated her, truly, like a roommate. Like someone he barely knew, and had no desire to know any better.

Having lost her grandmother—a woman who'd been the rock in Laura's life—she understood Miller's grief. She knew how it felt to be lost, emotionally abandoned. She'd never been able to let anyone else in either, and it had been nearly five years.

Laura hung on to Grammie's quilts, ones the stalwart old woman had sewn for every one of the milestones in Laura's life. They were her comfort, and her security. She wished now she had something she could share with Miller to offer him some comfort. But she had nothing.

In some strange twist of fate, she and Miller made perfect roommates. And now, Laura felt quite certain they would never be any more than that.

It was very warm for a mid-June afternoon, and Laura was regretting her decision to walk to work earlier that morning. Shoes swinging from her hand, purse slung over the opposite shoulder, she made her way down Dorothy Dix toward West Main, wondering whether this would be a Friday night when Miller was off. His schedule had been so sketchy of late, she never knew when to expect him to be home.

Of course, her quest to solve the mystery behind Greta and her father had been cast to the wayside the day Miller's sister died. This wasn't the time for Laura to be asking Miller any questions. Hell, to be asking anything of him at all. She wasn't really sure if that time would ever come.

Fortunately, it seemed the mysterious appearances of the little girl had dissipated as quickly as morning mist. The last time Laura had seen her was the night before Mollie passed, with Miller. He told Laura he'd seen Greta just a day or so before that. In Mollie's room, at Brightstar. But neither had seen her since then.

Had Greta been coming for Mollie? Coming to guide her from her tortured life to the next step on this ladder of existence? Laura shook her head sadly as she swayed lazily down the sidewalk in front of the cemetery. If so, maybe they had both moved on to the next stage, the next dimension. Or, Laura thought with a shudder, now they might both be lost—trapped in between the worlds of the living and the dead. Just like Greta had been for God knows how long. Would Mollie be searching for her own father's spirit?

The thought caused a twinge of pain in Laura's heart.

Which only added to her disappointment at seeing Miller's driveway empty. He wasn't there. He must be pulling a Friday night shift again.

Laura unlocked the front door and left it open so the cooling evening breeze could make its way through the screen door. After stripping off her stiff work clothes and slipping on a pair of shorts and a tank, she made her way into the kitchen and poured herself a glass of iced tea.

Lemonade, water, iced tea. Those were the only beverages in the house since the day Miller wiped the place clean of every trace of what he saw as the demon who'd taken his sister away. Laura supposed it was easier to blame a *thing* than to blame his father. Or himself, which is what she secretly believed he was still doing. But certainly better than turning to drink to ease his own pain.

No matter what Angie had thought or told Laura about Miller's drinking, she was now quite certain—this man was definitely not an alcoholic.

She stepped out onto the front porch, lazily deciding whether she should make herself a salad, or order something in from After Shocks. She had money now—her very first paycheck. Maybe she'd celebrate and eat out tonight. Turning on her heel, she headed down the hall to grab her purse and a pair of flip-flops. After Shocks was only a half-block down the street.

The bar was sparsely occupied for a Friday evening, though Laura knew it was still early. She had intended to slide into a booth, but recognizing the young woman she'd seen before tending bar— one who had worked with Angie—she slid onto a barstool instead. The woman, a stout redhead who wore a little more makeup than could be considered flattering, beamed a bright smile in her direction and headed down the bar toward her.

"Hey there. What can I get ya?" she chirped, flipping a coaster down.

"Um, hey. I'd like to see a menu, and . . .how about a diet Coke?" she asked.

The redhead slid a plastic-coated menu toward her and smiled wryly. "Mighty warm one out there today. The beer's nice and cold." She winked, and Laura couldn't help but smile back.

"Yes, it is. Been a long week too." She sighed. "And I *am* celebrating. Got my first paycheck today. You know what? I'll take a beer. Whatever you have on draft that's light."

The redhead winked again and turned to draw the tap while Laura chewed on a thumbnail, trying desperately to remember the woman's name. Angie had mentioned it to her more than once, she was certain. Fannie? Flora? Damn, why didn't this place make their staff wear name tags?

When she plunked the ice-coated mug down in front of Laura, the redhead met her gaze with narrowed eyes. "You been in here before, right? With that Stanford guy." Her tone was almost interrogational. Laura drew back, hesitant.

"I have. I'm his roommate now. Didn't you used to work with his ex? Angie?" Laura asked, sounding more bold and brazen than she felt.

The redhead threw back her head and laughed so loud, the hairs on the back of Laura's neck prickled. Would this woman blame her for Angie's sudden exodus? Judge her for cozying up to Miller so quickly? She was grateful there were only two, maybe three other patrons in the bar. She curled her fingers around the icy mug and waited.

The redhead crossed her arms and leaned on the bar, studying Laura with a quizzical expression. "So you're Laura. How the hell did you ever get mixed up with the likes of airhead Angie?"

Laura whooshed out a breath and relaxed, lifting her mug to sip. "Yep. I'm the good friend she up and ran out on. Without notice, by the way."

"We heard. She ran out on us too, the bitch. We were all pulling doubles for almost two weeks. And poor Miller." The barmaid shook her head and began wiping clean glasses dry with a rag. "How's he doing? I hear his sister passed." Her bawdy tone had softened to a hoarse whisper.

Laura met her gaze. "Not well. He's a mess, to be honest. I wish I knew him better so I could be more supportive." She paused to sip her beer. "How well do you know Miller, Miss . . .?"

"Faye. I'm Faye. My sister, Trena owns this place." She motioned around her with one, long red fingernail. "Has for a long time. We've known Miller ever since he took the job up there at the Center."

Just then the door to the bar swung open and another patron shuffled in. Yes, Laura thought, *shuffled*. The guy was old and painfully thin, wearing clothes five sizes too big for him. He pulled nervously on his long, grey beard as his eyes scanned the room. He made his way down to the far end of the bar, and Laura was surprised when Faye smiled and tipped her head at him before leaning across the counter toward Laura.

"Now there's a guy who's been around these parts forever." Faye shook her head and flattened her lips. "Poor old Chaffee. He was one of MSC's casualties. When that place shut down, they kicked a bunch of 'em to the curb. Left a lot of them homeless. Most—of those still alive, anyway—still are." Faye flipped the rag she'd been using to dry glasses over her shoulder and headed down to take the old man's order.

Laura held her mug beneath her chin and watched as Faye rested her elbows on the bar to converse quietly with the old man, who still looked visibly uncomfortable. Although she couldn't hear Faye's words, she saw her slide the single dollar bill the man had produced out of his shirt pocket back across the bar toward him. Then she turned to draw a mug of beer from the tap.

Not even enough to buy himself a beer, Laura thought sadly. But she instantly liked Faye, seeing she intended to serve the man his drink anyway. As soon as Faye had delivered the beer, Laura tipped up her chin to get her attention.

"Listen. That guy's drinks are on me. And whatever he wants to eat. Just two beers, though," she added through a twisted grin. "I am the addiction counselor. Wouldn't look too cool if I got caught buying drinks for a stranger."

Faye beamed a genuine smile. "You're right about that. Chaffee's not really even supposed to be in here at all. They took him in at the homeless shelter again up on the hill just last week. He's been kicked out a time or two for spending what few dollars he has on a beer or three." She sighed and reached for Laura's menu. "Did you decide what you want to eat?"

"Uh, yeah. Just a chicken Caesar salad. Those pretty good in here?"

"The best. Trena makes the dressing herself." She patted the bar between them. "I'll be back."

After Faye had disappeared into the kitchen, Laura studied the old man down the bar. A pang of pity pinched in her chest. Bad enough to be homeless, but old too? And from what Faye indicated, he'd also been an inpatient at the Psych Center. She couldn't help but wonder what his problem had been. Or still was. Had she been wrong to offer to buy the man a few beers? Suppose he had been admitted to the Psych Center for alcoholism?

Sighing, Laura shook her head. Not likely he could get himself into too much trouble now, not without any money and living in a shelter. At least she'd have bought him a hot meal.

It being Friday, the evening crowd started filing in fast. Before Laura's salad even came out, she glanced around and noticed the only empty seat left at the bar, other than right next to hers, was beside the old man. She pursed her lips.

By the way he looks, he probably smells pretty ripe. But that isn't his fault, dammit.

And maybe—just maybe—this Chaffee guy could tell Laura something more about the people he'd known while living in the facility. She grabbed her purse from under the bar and rose, grabbing her half-empty beer in the other hand. Faye appeared through the swinging kitchen door carrying Laura's salad. Catching her eye, Laura tipped her head toward the end of the bar.

"I'll take it down here, Faye," she said, a warmth spreading through her when Faye smiled, nodded, and winked.

Twenty-Four

To Laura's dismay, Chaffee lurched when she slid onto the bar stool next to him. He stared at her wild-eyed, his watery blue eyes wary. Another pang of pity shot through her. Like a scared, feral animal, she thought. How sad, to have lived your whole life, only to end up like this.

"Hey there," she said, keeping her tone light. "Seems a couple came in and really wanted to sit together, and the only other empty seat was next to mine." She motioned toward the lone empty stool. "Do you mind?"

Chaffee's face remained expressionless as he studied her. Then he slowly shook his head, turning quickly back to stare into his beer mug.

"I'm new here," she began nervously. "At least, new again. I've been away at college forever, and I can't believe how much has changed in Middletown since I left." Laura plucked a napkin from the steel canister on the bar and tucked it into her lap.

The silence that followed went on so long, Laura figured she wouldn't get a word out of the man. She couldn't blame him. So many homeless got shunned, or taken advantage of. They learned quickly, she knew, to trust no one.

Hmm. Maybe me and this Chaffee guy have some things in common after all.

Laura had already lifted a forkful of her salad to her lips when the man spoke, though his gaze remained straight ahead.

"This here's a way different town now than when I wuz younger. 'Course, life wasn't exactly normal where I lived anyways." He sounded distant, and sad.

Not wanting to scare him off by telling him she already *knew* where he'd lived, Laura tried a different approach. "Listen, I've got a friend back in North Carolina who's doing a term paper on the history of mental healthcare," she lied. "You know, the place up here on the hill? Do you know much about the Psych Center? I mean, I grew up here, but being a kid, I really didn't pay much attention to it back then."

His watery eyes drifted back to meet hers again, and he nodded. "Sure do. Was my home for about ten years. When I got back from the war. They decided I had that disorder thing. You know, the one they used to call shell-shock?" He paused to take a long draft of his beer, and the foam clung to his straggly mustache. He swiped it away with the back of his hand and continued. "The Vet'rans, they took care of me real good. Until the State came along and decided they were tired of supportin' me." He met her eyes again, his gaze intense. "Me and a lot of other folks who fought for this country. Some never came back. Lots of 'em who did . . .well, they lost way more than me."

Laura chewed slowly, her appetite gone now as sadness, as well as curiosity, took hold. And much as she tried to ignore it, her assumption had been correct. The seat next to his had been empty for a reason. The man needed a bath, badly.

She cleared her throat. "What exactly did the war take from you, Mr. . . ."

"Chaffee. Lawrence Chaffee. Took the missus from me, for one. She's probably not worth cryin' over. But I couldn't work no more when I got back. 'Course, nothin' showed on the outside, so it was hard for folks to understand what the problem was. Unlike my buddy, Tom. He came home with half an arm." Chaffee chuckled wryly and shook his head. "Which screwed up way more'n his body, that's for sure."

Laura laid her fork down on the edge of her plate and blotted her mouth. She looked up as Faye appeared in front of them with a plate bearing a burger and fries. Setting it down in front of Chaffee, he blinked up at her in surprise. Ignoring him, she glanced at Laura's untouched bowl.

"Salad alright?"

"It's great, Faye. I've just been talking to Mr. Chaffee here. I will take another beer, though."

Faye nodded and returned momentarily carrying not one, but two mugs, plunking one down in front of both Laura and Chaffee. The old man regarded the barmaid through narrowed eyes.

"Your sister ain't gonna be too happy if you put her outta business giving away food and drink," he warned.

Faye leaned an elbow on the bar. "I'm not doing anything of the kind. This nice lady here's picking up your tab." She nodded toward Laura, then turned and whisked back down the bar.

Chaffee sighed. "Thank you, Ma'am. Much obliged." He lifted the burger and took a bite, closing his eyes and groaning. "This here's quite a treat."

Laura sipped her fresh beer, then nibbled on a piece of the grilled chicken topping her salad. After a moment, she asked, "Mr. Chaffee, this friend of yours—the amputee—what happened to him?"

Chaffee picked up a French fry with two fingers and popped it into his mouth. "Died. 'Bout a month or two before they kicked us all outta Talcott. Lucky bastard. Least he didn't have to learn how to sleep in a cardboard box at night."

Laura winced. The realities of how the homeless lived were something she, like most of the rest of the population, tried not to think about. But that didn't make the truth any less real. Or less horrifying.

She lifted her mug, sipped and swallowed before pressing on, tentatively. "Did they at least give him a decent burial?"

Laura jumped when Chaffee barked out a laugh. He faced her then, his grin revealing an incomplete row of decaying teeth. The pang of pity that filled her overrode her body's instinct to recoil in disgust.

"Tom got a decent burial, alright. Problem is, nobody knows where. The graveyard was already filled up by then, ya know. The one next door here." He motioned with one thumb toward the graveyard separating them from Miller's house. "They tucked him into a pine box—they had plenty of those all lined up in the sittin' room, just waitin' for the next one of us to croak. Then they tossed it up on the back of a truck and drove off with him." Chaffee shook his head. "Shame for his little girl, though. Leastways she got to visit him before he passed." He took another bite of his burger and Laura watched the grease trickle down into his grizzled beard.

She cringed. Surely the homeless shelter has shower facilities?

Swallowing around the bile that rose into her throat, she pushed her plate away from her. She cleared her throat and asked, "This friend of yours . . .Tom? What was his last name?"

Chaffee had suddenly seemed to pop back into the present from where he'd been drifting, inside his own mind and tangled up in unpleasant memories. He glanced at Laura's barely touched plate, then up at her, scowling.

"You kidding? I'm lucky I can remember my own name these days." He paused, pointing down at her plate. "You ain't gonna eat that? You're barely skin and bones, girl."

Laura shook her head. "Just not very hungry tonight." She was so close, right on the brink of getting some real information from this old man. If she could just push him a little more . . .

"Mr. Chaffee, Tom's daughter. Do you remember her name?" she pressed.

He blinked and stared at her, and she could see he was struggling to search back through the years. A softness came over his features then, and he suddenly looked ten years younger. A small smile curled his lips. Then he blurted out, "Gretel. Or Greta, something like that. She was the cutest damn thing. Loved her daddy, by God."

He paused, lifting his mug to drain it by half, again swiping at the foam from his hairy face with the back of his hand. Pointing a gnarled finger at Laura, he continued, "You know, they say she died not long after her daddy did. Of some bad sickness. We all figure she was the one who brought it in to him, when she came to visit that last time."

Laura's heart began pounding so hard she could barely hear as Chaffee raised a hand to catch Faye's attention and called, "Hey darlin', if this lady doesn't mind, I'd like to take the rest of hers with me. Could you bring me a box?"

Laura sat up on the couch waiting for Miller to come home from work that night. She knew he'd probably be in just minutes after eleven, since he didn't stop at the bar on his way home anymore. To her knowledge, he hadn't had a drop of alcohol since the day Mollie had died. He'd been not much more than a ghost himself lately, one lost and alone in his own house. Although he did still peek in to check on her on his way up the stairs, he usually came home, rummaged in the kitchen for a few minutes, then headed upstairs. She hoped he was carrying a sandwich up with him.

If he was eating at all. His face, Laura had noticed, had taken on a grey, sunken appearance. And the blankness behind his steely eyes told her he was broken. If she only knew how to help heal him. If only he'd let her get close enough to try.

But tonight, she'd insist he interact with her. She was excited with the information she'd gotten from Chaffee tonight. This "Tom" must surely be the Thomas Sanderson Jenna spoke of. The man—the father—whose grave the little girl searched for. Greta.

Greta's *ghost.* Laura pulled her grandmother's quilt up closer around her and shuddered.

She had drifted into a fitful doze when the click of Miller's key in the lock woke her. She watched as he shuffled in, hung up his hat and untied his boots, kicking them into the corner with more annoyance than she was used to seeing from him.

He'd become distant, moody, and irritable since Mollie's death. And from what Laura could see, had completely abandoned his online class. His laptop had lived in the middle of kitchen table, seemingly untouched, for at least three weeks.

Miller turned, apparently noticing the light coming from the living room. Pausing, he stared at her silently for a long moment. Then he barked, "What are you doing up? You sick or something?"

The coldness in his voice soured Laura's stomach. This was a man who now hated everyone, and everything. It was hard not to take his gruffness personally. But she stood, wrapping the quilt around her and taking a step toward him.

"Miller, I found out some information today. About the little girl. About the . . .the ghost."

He chuffed and shook his head, pinching the bridge of his nose between two fingers. "There's no fucking ghost, Laura. There's no such thing as ghosts. People are alive, and then they're dead. We put them in a box in the ground, where they rot. Like old garbage."

His words smacked Laura in the chest and she sucked in a breath. But she wasn't giving up so easily. She began shaking her head adamantly and stepped forward, reaching out one hand toward him. "No Miller. You're wrong."

He raised red-rimmed eyes to meet hers and narrowed them. "Life ends, Laura. Poof. Done." He snapped his fingers in the air. "Whatever you saw—whatever *we* saw—was brought on by stress. Too many beers. Overactive imagination. Something like that." He turned to walk down the hall.

Laura hurried to catch him, gently laying a hand on his arm. "No, Miller. You and I both know that's not true. There's more to this life than . . .than *this life*. Our souls go on."

She half-expected him to snatch his arm away, and was surprised when he didn't. Instead, he froze, and she saw his shoulders rise and fall emphatically.

"What do you want, Laura? I'd love to sit down and discuss our theories on life after death, but honestly, I don't have anything left to say. I don't have anything . . .left."

His forlorn tone, the way his words grew thick, wrenched her heart into a twisted knot.

And in truth, she didn't know *what* to say. Yes, she wanted to tell him about what she'd learned today, but he was in no frame of mind to hear it. The counselor part of her brain was screaming, *He's in no condition to do anything but shatter into a million tiny pieces.* But she wasn't his counselor, nor would he accept her as one. At least, not in this moment.

So, she did the only thing she could think of. She followed her instincts, knowing she was risking yet another harsh rejection. Dropping the quilt to the floor, she stepped around in front of him, and rose up on tiptoes. She gripped the back of his head firmly, and drew his face down to her shoulder.

It took a while. A full minute, she figured, if she'd been counting the seconds. But she was just so relieved that he wasn't pushing her away, barking at her or shrinking away from her touch. When she felt his shoulders begin to shake, her heart squeezed, sharing his anguish. His arms came around her then and he held her tightly, nearly lifting her off the floor as he buried his face in the crook of her neck.

And there, in his hallway in the middle of the night, the floodgates of Miller's grief finally opened, spilling out until Laura's hair, and neck, and shoulder were soaked with his tears.

When he woke the next morning, Miller was confused. He was laying on top of the comforter on his bed, fully clothed. And snugged up close beside him was a small, warm body, wrapped tightly in a worn, patchwork quilt. Laura's hand lay spread on his chest, and her mouth was slightly open, her breathing even. Her hair, always a riotous mess of curls in the morning, was flattened and matted to one side of her head.

He remembered then. Remembered falling apart in her arms last night, sobbing like a child on her shoulder until he'd finally scooped her up and carried her up to his bed. Where he'd cried some more, lying on his back and letting the tears stream down his face to soak his pillow. All the while, Laura hadn't said a word. Just combed her fingers through his hair and stroked up and down his chest until, at some point, he'd dropped off to sleep.

This morning, as the brilliant sunlight streamed in through his window, sparkling on her riot of golden curls, he could feel something had changed. Not between them, but inside him. His chest felt lighter, no longer full of the grief he'd kept bottled up for so long. Weeks, since Mollie's death. No, longer than that. Years, since the day in the parking lot of a high school gymnasium when his life had changed forever.

He'd finally let it go.

Miller heard a tiny squeak from beside him and looked over to see Laura struggling to free her arms from the multi-colored wrapping she'd twirled herself into sometime during the night. She stretched them over her head and yawned so big, he heard her jaw click. Then her eyes fluttered open and, after flitting about the room in momentary confusion, landed on his.

Her smile made the blinding sunlight pale in comparison.

Twenty-Five

"Good morning," Miller said, unable to contain his smile. She looked so right lying there beside him, on his bed, bathed in morning sunshine. But why the hell was she always bundled up in that tattered old blanket as though she were Linus on Peanuts?

"Good morning. How are you feeling?" she asked, almost shyly. "Better?"

He nodded and twirled one strand of her hair around his finger. "Yes, better. Much better. Thanks to you."

She closed her eyes and sighed, reaching out to wrap her hands around the back of his neck. "I'm glad," she squeaked around another yawn. "Sleep well?"

"I did. But I gotta ask you something, Laura. This quilt. I hardly ever see you without the thing." He fingered one frayed edge of the binding. "Looks like it's been around awhile, too."

"It has," she said, freeing one hand to pick up the hand-stitched pattern and examine it. "My grandmother made it for me. When my parents split up. I know it's kind of childish, but it's my comfort blankie. Makes me feel . . ." she shrugged, "I dunno. Safe? Plus, it's pretty warm, believe it or not." She paused, sighing wistfully. "Grammy sewed me a bunch of them. One for every *milestone of my life*, she called them. There's a few I'll probably never get to use."

Miller watched her face as an array of emotions skittered across it. Embarrassment, followed by a little sadness. Finally, she met his eyes, hers sharp with indignance.

"You think it's silly, I know. Too bad." She sniffed, jutting her chin.

He chuckled, charmed to his core by this adorable woman. "No, I don't think it's silly. Your grandma . . .the one with the trunk downstairs? The one that almost cost me a toe when you first got here?"

Her giant blue eyes flashed to his again, and he could tell she was struggling to stifle a giggle. "Yes. And you're such a drama king. It was a tiny little cut, not a near-amputation."

In a flash, she'd sat up and grabbed one of the small, square pillows Angie had insisted were *needed* to decorate his bed. Before Miller could raise his arms, Laura thwacked him on top of his head. Then she started giggling convulsively. She raised the pillow for a second onslaught, a mischievous twinkle lighting up her entire face.

Filled with a freeness, a joy he hadn't felt in years—hell, maybe never—he reached out and wrapped both his big hands around her waist, stilling her. Time froze as their gazes locked. He looked into her clear, blue eyes and swore he could see straight through to her soul. And what he saw amazed, and surprised him. How could he not have noticed the pureness, the goodness of her essence before now?

"Thank you," he murmured, never taking his eyes off hers. "Thank you for standing by me through all this, Laura. You had no reason to. No obligation at all. Yet you were there by my side, the whole time. Even when I pushed you away." He swallowed, struggling to contain the ball of emotion rising in his throat. "Thank you, Laura."

He watched as her eyes filled. Dropping the pillow, she stroked his cheek and gave a small, sad smile. "I'm not sure why, exactly, Miller. But the two of us were brought together for a reason. I believe everything happens for a reason. And I have to admit, standing there on your stoop that first day, I came very close to turning tail and running. I'm so glad I didn't."

He drew her to him, combing his fingers into her hair and drawing her face close to his. Resting his forehead against hers, he said, "I'm so glad you didn't either."

Together, they cooked breakfast. It was as though they'd done it a hundred times, Laura thought, as she reached around Miller to grab plates out of the cabinet. Fetch the orange juice out of the fridge. Pull two forks out of the silverware drawer.

As she went to set the table, she noticed his laptop sitting there in the middle, and glanced back over her shoulder. "I should move this, Miller."

He grunted, concentrating on flipping pancakes on one end of the griddle as the bacon sizzled on the other end. "Just set it on the counter over there. I haven't even booted it up in weeks," he said.

"I know. Did you drop your class, then?" She asked quietly, not wanting to open up any controversial topic that might spoil the perfection of this morning.

He nodded, keeping his back to her. "No point in continuing. I won't be getting that promotion anyway. Roger's already talking about how it's going to help him pay for his kids' college educations." Turning toward her with a platter heaped with steaming bacon, he met her gaze. "To be honest, even if I got Sarge's job now, I'd feel kind of guilty. It's not like anybody will suffer if I don't have the extra money. Not anymore."

A pang of sadness tightened Laura's throat. "You know, Miller, just because you don't have to take care of Mollie anymore, it doesn't mean you should stop pursuing your own life goals. Wasn't that one of them? To take over Sarge's job?"

Miller lips flattened and he tilted his head, considering. "I don't know. It was before, but that was purely because of the money. Now, I'm not so sure I'd be happy sitting behind a desk every day." He set the platters of bacon and pancakes on the table. "I guess I've got a lot of soul searching to do over the next few months." As they sat, he reached for Laura's hand. "Maybe you could help me figure that out?"

She smiled into his eyes. "Of course I will."

After they ate, Miller grabbed Laura's hand as she rose to clear the table. "We can get this later," he said. He flipped the one, matted side of her hair. "I think we both could use a shower. Don't you?"

She saw the glint of mischief in his eyes now, and it warmed her heart. "Sure."

The fifties-vintage tub was small, but that only made the experience sweeter. There was no way they could suds up their own bodies without jabbing an elbow into the other's ribs or back. So, they had to compromise. Work as a team. A symbiotic shower.

Miller began by shampooing her hair. Standing under the spray, Laura dropped her head back and let the hot water stream down, then moaned as his strong fingers worked in the lather. The bubbles tickled as they ran in rivulets down her body, rinsing away the tears of the night before—Miller's tears.

She couldn't help thinking how symbolic this moment was, for both of them. She had helped free him of his pent-up suffering, and now together, they would wash the pain away.

Next, Miller grabbed the green bar of soap and lathered his hands, running his fingers around her neck to stroke and massage her shoulders. His touch set her blood on fire. He worked his way down her chest, sliding his hands around her ribcage to run up and down her back. As he did, she fell forward, allowing their bodies to press close together. Heaven, she thought, couldn't possibly feel this good.

He continued his lathering of her body, down over her hips, then around to massage her buttocks. There was nothing sensual about his movements, though, which surprised and confused her. He was careful not to touch her breasts, avoiding her nipples, which were already taut and ready for attention.

Laura sighed. Perhaps Miller wasn't ready for anything more physical yet. After what he'd been through, she could easily understand.

When his hands stroked across her belly and down the front of her thighs, though, her body wasn't doing a very good job of being understanding. She felt the pressure building low inside, the need throbbing between her legs.

This isn't about me, she kept reminding herself. This was about being a friend, helping Miller get over his grief and heal.

When he handed the soap to her, she drew in a deep breath and avoided his gaze. How was she to bathe this man, stroke his broad, hard body without getting even more turned on than she already was? But she could do it. She *would* do it.

She began as he did, sudsing his hair, then running her soapy hands around his thick neck and over his bulky shoulders, having to stand on tiptoe to reach. He saw her struggling and turned his back to her, carefully so as not to bump into her and knock her off balance. With his massive, sculpted back and hard buttocks facing her, Laura gulped and tamped down her desire. What she wanted to do was to wrap her arms around his waist and press herself up against him. Let her fingers follow the happy trail of his golden hair down to his manhood.

But she couldn't do that. A tiny part of her feared she would find he wasn't aroused. And she knew she wouldn't be able to keep from taking that personally.

When his hands gripped her wrists to still them on his belly, she froze.

"I'm sorry, Miller. It's okay. You don't have to—"

"Don't be sorry," he growled, guiding her hands lower until she felt his arousal, thick and hard. She gasped.

He turned to face her and cupped her face in his hands, bringing his mouth down to cover hers ever so slowly. His lips were warm and soft, and he tasted sweet, like the maple syrup he'd poured on his pancakes just minutes before.

With a gentleness that buckled her knees, he parted her lips with his tongue and began his exploration of her mouth. She moaned and pressed her wet body against him, reveling in the throbbing of his hard cock against her belly.

With the spray of the warm water running over them, their tongues engaged in a sensuous dance, their slick, naked bodies pressed close, Laura could swear she'd died and gone to heaven.

That's when the warm water suddenly ran to cold.

It hit Laura's naked back first, as she was closest to the spray. She stiffened and pulled back, gasping, and for a brief moment,

Miller stared at her in complete confusion. When she scooted around behind him and the icy water hit his body, he was no longer confused.

"Fuck!" he barked, scrambling to turn off the water. He snatched open the curtain and grabbed a towel, bundling Laura into it first. "Are you okay, babe? Oh, damn it all to hell. I'm so sorry." Wrenching off the tap, he stepped out of the tub and grabbed the other towel off the bar on the opposite wall.

When Miller turned to face her, she had the giant towel wrapped up to her chin, covering her mouth. But he could see the glint of amusement crinkling the corners of her eyes. He realized her shaking wasn't because of a chill, but from laughter. He pulled a mock scowl and held his towel open wide, pointing.

"That's one sure way to extinguish a really great hard-on," he grumbled.

She snorted and stepped into him, burying her face against his chest. "I think, if we both get upstairs and dry off, I can help you with that," she murmured seductively.

As his arms came around her and he held her close, Miller felt like the Grinch in the Christmas cartoon he remembered from his childhood. Threatening to burst out of his chest, his heart swelled three sizes bigger. And he knew, as long as Laura remained in his life, it would never return to its former, hollow state.

He made love to Laura slowly on his giant bed, their only blanket a wash of warm sunshine from the windows high on his wall. And all she kept thinking was—*it's all so different this time.* There was no awkwardness, no nervousness, no fear. She didn't worry whether or not she was good enough, or beautiful enough, or giving enough. All her kisses, her caresses, came as naturally as breathing.

Rather hard breathing, as time went on.

Like a delicate dance, they took turns. After he'd kissed her stupid, to the point where she was panting and her core was throbbing with need, she pushed him over on his back and proceeded to worship his body. He was a giant of a man, his broad chest sculpted and hard, lightly furred with golden hair. She twirled her fingers in it as she swung one leg over him and watched the passion flare in his eyes. Then she bent to kiss him sweetly before beginning a journey with her mouth along his jaw and down his neck.

She felt his cock throbbing behind her as she slid down his body, planting kisses over his hard pecs. He stilled her, his hands nearly encircling her waist, and she met his gaze.

"Protection. I need protect—"

"Not yet. I have other plans for you first," she murmured, swinging her leg over, and settling beside him. He groaned and tangled his fingers in her hair.

Trailing kisses down his torso, Laura did experience a brief moment of uncertainty. Would she do this right? This wouldn't be her first time taking a man into her mouth—in the past, she'd been judged at being "not very good at it." But until this moment, she'd actually found the notion distasteful. Now, it seemed as natural and inviting as a kiss.

Which is how she began. Soft kisses, teasing strokes of her tongue, all the while keeping her hand wrapped firmly around the base of his now throbbing cock. Miller's moans and thrusts urged her on, building her confidence. Fueling her own need. When she finally could no longer contain her desire, she took him, licking and sucking and lathing him until he raked his fingers into her hair and stilled her.

"I'm almost there, babe. No more. Now it's my turn." His deep voice was gruff, struggling for control.

In one smooth, gentle movement she was on her back, and he was nudging her legs apart with his knee. He attacked her mouth first, his kisses more urgent and demanding now. Thrusting his tongue deeper, taking her breath away with the feel of him ravaging her mouth. The tension in her lower belly coiled and burned hot, and her hips began writhing against him of their own will. Breaking her mouth free with a gasp, she grabbed his hand and drew it to her breast.

"Here, Miller. I need more."

He suckled her taut nipple, swirling his tongue gently over the stiff peak, sending shock waves of desire to her core. She combed her fingers into his hair and arched into him, and he began on the other breast, his fingers picking up where his tongue left the first. His cock throbbed hot on her belly and she lifted both legs to wrap his waist, pulling him closer.

"I need you inside me, Miller. Please."

"Not yet," he breathed against her nipple, his tongue flicking one last time before beginning a trail down her belly. His hands were everywhere, stroking, teasing, kneading. Laura squeezed her eyes shut as she felt his hot breath on her inner thigh, and she began trembling. He stilled.

"Are you okay?" he asked softly.

"Yes," she moaned, panting and quivering all over. "But I'm almost there. And no one's ever . . ."

When she opened her eyes, he was grinning at her, his wolf-eyes devilish. "Never?"

She blinked fast, embarrassed. After a moment's hesitation, she shook her head. "Never."

"Then it won't take long," he growled, "unless I do this right."

Laura didn't realize how sweet torture could be. He licked and nipped and kissed her everywhere between her legs but *there*. Every time he came near enough for his hot breath to tickle her sex, he'd stop, blow gently, and trail kisses back down her thigh. Twice, when her panting spiraled out of control and her body trembled violently, she felt Miller's huge, warm hand on her lower belly.

"Slow down. Just breathe. I want this to be the best thing that's ever happened to you."

He waited a long moment, then began again, planting kisses on her belly, drawing circles with his tongue on her hip, then trailing it along the crease of her thigh toward her center. But when he stopped short of her spot this time, Laura was done waiting.

"Now," she growled, raking her fingers into his hair and pulling him in.

In the next thirty seconds, Laura felt quite sure her soul left her body. In the same instant as Miller's warm tongue lathed her clit, he slid a finger inside her. First one, then two. Sensations flooded her—hot, wet, sliding, stroking.

She hooked her ankles around the back of his neck and arched up, climbing so hard and so fast she couldn't catch her breath. Screaming his name, she crested, and wave after wave of mind-melting pleasure crashed through her consciousness.

Twenty-Six

Honestly? Miller had a hard time believing Laura had never been the recipient of oral sex. The way she'd worked him, so sweetly, yet with such confidence and finesse, he knew she'd had at least some practice on the giving end. But one thing he knew for sure by the time her orgasm nearly blew him off his own bed—no man had ever brought her to climax with his mouth before.

He was breathless and throbbing by the time she came down, and although he knew he should give her a few minutes to recover, his need had reached critical status. He was almost afraid to move fearing the friction of the comforter against his cock would cause him to explode.

But when he looked up, Laura eyes were fixed on him, her chest heaving, and tears were streaming down her cheeks.

Wait. Tears?

"Baby . . .what's wrong? Did I hurt you?" he asked gently, crawling up her body to stroke her cheek with the back of his hand.

She choked on a sob, then squeezed her eyes shut and shook her head. When she opened them, something in the depths of those clear, blue eyes shot straight through to his soul. And he wasn't sure if what he saw there made him the happiest man in the world, or scared him half to death.

He didn't have time to work it out, though. Laura cupped his face with her hands and pulled his mouth to hers. Her kiss was sweet, languid and slow. So sweet.

"Take me, Miller," she murmured into his mouth.

Okay, I'm confused. I just gave her a cataclysmic orgasm. Then she starts balling her eyes out. Now she wants me to take her. Miller shrugged inwardly. Women were such a conundrum. But as always, he'd do his best to be accommodating.

After retrieving a condom from the bedside table and sheathing himself, Miller balanced himself over her, again nudging her legs apart. She gazed up into his eyes the whole time, biting on her knuckle, tears still glistening in her eyes.

"Did I please you?" he whispered.

"Like never before in my life."

"Are you ready to please me?"

Her answer was to wrap her arms around his neck and her legs around his waist, lifting her hips up to meet him.

"Fuck," he groaned as he slid inside her, and her little gasp spiked his need even closer to the breaking point. "You're so fucking hot. So wet. So tight. I won't last long, Laura."

She silenced him with her mouth, her kiss rough and probing, urgent. When he started to move in and out of her, he realized he hadn't been exaggerating. He really wasn't going to last long.

"Can't wait, baby. Gotta let it—"

But he felt her body go rigid beneath him as her inner muscles tightened around him. When she squeaked his name against his ear and her fingers dug into his back, he thought, *Fuck. She's coming again.*

And that was his last thought before the world exploded into a million, flaming balls of fire.

When Miller awoke, he was momentarily confused. It was broad daylight, but he was sprawled nude across the top of his comforter on his bed. And from downstairs, he heard movement in the kitchen. Water running. Dishes clinking.

He folded his arms behind his head and sighed. When they'd dozed off—how long ago had it been? His bedside clock said it was now after noon. Anyway, the last he remembered he'd been spooned around Laura's back as she slept. They'd had the most amazing morning of sex he could ever have imagined. And now, she was downstairs cleaning up their breakfast mess.

Had she dropped out of a cloud, or a wet dream? He wasn't really sure, but he certainly didn't want this waking fantasy to end. Quickly, he pulled on a pair of gym shorts and grabbed a tee shirt as he headed downstairs to help her.

The smell of coffee—wonderful, non-chrome-cleaner-quality coffee—wafted to him down the hallway as he reached the bottom step. And before he made it to the kitchen door, she appeared, a mug in each hand, stopping short and blinking in surprise.

"I was just bringing you some coffee," she said, holding out a cup.

She looked like a woodland faerie. Wearing his Yankees jersey, which on her served as a dress, she stood there barefoot and pink-cheeked and smiling. Her hair was crazy wild, swirling every which way around her head and clinging softly to her neck. Miller took the mug, then reached out to brush a curl off her forehead.

"I was coming to help you," he said.

"All done. Come on. Sit by me on the couch. I want to tell you something."

Miller sat beside her as Laura shared the news about her meeting the old homeless guy, Chaffee, in After Shocks the night before. The information she'd discovered about Greta.

"He *knew* her, Miller. He knew that little girl. Well, at least he knew her dad. But he saw her, visiting him. Even mentioned how cute she was." She sipped her coffee and studied him, her eyes dancing across his face as she nearly vibrated with excitement. "Before she died, I mean. That's why I was waiting up for you last night. I wanted to tell you."

Miller dragged in a deep breath and whooshed it out. "Chaffee. That's the old guy we found half-dead in Talcott. I guess her father was his friend." He shook his head. "This is crazy, Laura. Are we actually going on a ghost hunt? To do . . .what, exactly?"

Laura's shoulders drooped and she frowned. "We have to try to help her, Miller. She doesn't know where her father is buried. She won't find closure, and be able to move on, until she does."

Setting his mug down on the coffee table with a little more force than necessary, Miller leaned forward, resting his elbows on his knees. "Help a ghost, Laura? Do you know how crazy that sounds?"

Laura dropped her gaze to her mug and remained silent for a long moment. Finally, in a tone barely above a whisper, she said, "I hate to imagine a spirit—especially a child's spirit—who's lost her way. Somewhere between this world and the next. I know it sounds insane, Miller, but this is something I have to do. I have to find out what happened to her father's—Thomas Sanderson's—body."

"Laura, the man has been dead for over twenty years. Where would we even start?" But even as the words left his lips, Miller had a feeling he knew exactly what Laura was about to say. About to ask of him.

"In the basement of Talcott Hall. I need to get in there, Miller. And I need the key to the bomb shelter that's hidden down there. That's where the records are."

Miller swiped a hand down his face and lurched to his feet, pacing. "Laura, I told you before. What you're asking me to do could cost me my job. Sarge made it perfectly clear—"

"Yes. He made it perfectly clear that no one is to open the old patient records of Talcott Hall. Doesn't that make you just a little suspicious, Miller? I mean, most of those people are long dead. What's the big secret? What is the State trying to hide?"

Miller stopped pacing, his back to Laura, his gaze drifting out the window. The graveyard looked almost pretty today, with long beams of sunlight streaming through the pine branches to pattern the ground in dapples. Pretty, if it wasn't a place of such emptiness. Such loneliness.

His mind flashed back to another graveyard, just a few weeks ago, where he'd stood and said goodbye to his only sibling. Forever. Another wave of grief hit him then, hard and fast. He covered his face with his hands.

Laura was there beside him in an instant, wrapping one small arm around his waist and resting her head against his shoulder. "I'm sorry, Miller. I shouldn't have brought this up now. Maybe it doesn't matter anymore anyway. I mean, neither of us have seen her—

Greta—for a while now, right? Since that night . . .out there." She pointed.

Slowly, Miller began shaking his head. "Yeah, but I saw her earlier that same day. She was with Mollie. The last day I saw my sister alive. I think now maybe Greta was . . .was coming for her. Though I have no earthly idea why." He chuckled darkly. "I guess there's nothing earthly about it, is there?"

He felt the shudder run through her, and turned to fold her against him. She wrapped her arms around his waist and sighed. With her ear pressed to his chest, his deep voice rumbled like an earthquake inside.

"I've been having dreams, Laura. I know it's probably just post-traumatic stress. Since Mollie's death, but—" He broke off, his voice suddenly thick with emotion. After dragging in a breath, he continued. "I don't think they're gone. Either of them. I know I won't be able to rest until this mystery . . .whatever is holding this ghost-child here, is solved." He pushed back and sought her eyes. "I know it probably sounds crazy. God knows, I've got plenty of reason to have gone completely over the edge by now. But in my heart, I know I have to try. For Mollie."

Almost unable to believe what she was hearing, Laura studied Miller's face. "Are you sure? Your job—"

"Yeah, my job. What's the worst that can happen? If we're caught in there together, I can always blame it on you." He grinned and chucked her under the chin. "You wouldn't mind being the bad guy, would you? I was simply doing my job. Apprehending an unauthorized trespasser."

Laura paused, her eyes flitting nervously about. "But the key. How will you get the key? And if they know you got the key to the bunker, then they'll know you went in with intent. Right?"

Miller cupped her face in both hands. "Not if we get in and out without getting caught. We'll go in under cover of darkness. In the middle of the night. Sarge is on vacation this week. The timing is perfect." He lowered his mouth to hers and kissed her, gently at first, then with more urgency. "Help me do this, Laura. Together, maybe we can put at least one little girl's spirit to rest. Maybe two. And hopefully, my tortured dreams will go away."

They spent the rest of the weekend taking care of the mundane. Together, they made a grocery list. Laura scoured the bathroom while Miller hauled out his godforsaken vacuum cleaner. She started the laundry while Miller booted up his laptop and paid bills.

Paying bills. She'd almost forgotten about getting her first paycheck yesterday. Anxious to bring him her rent money, she trotted down the hall into her room and snatched out the check she'd proudly written out before leaving work yesterday. The State had deposited her salary directly into her account.

But when she held it out to him, he glanced from the check to her face, then frowned.

"Why don't you just hang onto it this month, Laura. Keep it in the bank in case something unexpected comes up. You can start paying next month."

"No. Take this, Miller. I don't expect you to take care of me."

Without his eyes ever leaving the computer screen, he began slowly shaking his head. "It's not a big deal, Laura. Not anymore."

She felt her stomach turn over on itself, not quite sure what he was saying. Why was it no longer a "big deal"? Because their relationship had changed? Because he no longer considered her only a roommate?

Laura's mind raced. They'd only known each other weeks, barely over a month. Surely, he couldn't be suggesting he wanted to support her.

His financial situation, though, had changed. She knew Miller no longer had the responsibility of the big nursing home payment. Yet what she saw in his face was light-years away from relief at the disappearance of the financial strain. His shoulders slumped, and he looked . . .resigned.

But that didn't mean she would take advantage of him. Hell, she'd done that enough over the past six weeks. No, she was done being *taken care of*. She'd depended on her father all her life, financially, until now. It was time for her to pull on her big girl panties and support herself.

She stepped forward and waved the check in front of the laptop screen. "You don't have to take care of me, Miller. I've got a good job, and I can pay my own way while I stay here. I'm not Angie."

Laura stumbled back when his chair clattered to the floor. In two steps, he was around the table and pulling her into his arms. The check fluttered from her fingers.

"While you stay here? You make it sound so transient," he choked out, this voice thick. "And don't ever compare yourself with Angie, Laura. I guess I should thank the bitch for bringing you into my life, but just hearing her name makes me nauseous. What's going on here is . . .different."

She could hear his heart pounding under her ear as it pressed up against his warm, hard chest. Oh, how enticing it was, this feeling of being cared for. Part of her wanted to stay right here, wrapped in his strong arms forever.

Another part was screaming, *Stay strong. You're finally asserting your independence. Don't cave now.*

Closing her eyes, she swallowed, then murmured against his chest, "I appreciate your wanting to take care of me, Miller. But it's time I learned how to take care of myself. You don't owe me anything just because we sleep together."

He pulled back as if she'd slapped him, gripping her shoulders and looking deep into her eyes. "Is that all you think we are? Fuck buddies? Is that really how you see . . .*us*?"

Perplexed, she pressed her hands on his chest and pushed him away, far enough to where she could see his face. Keeping her eyes fixed on his, she tilted her head. "Us? Is there an *us*, Miller? Aren't we just accidental roommates?"

With one finger, he lifted her chin and pinned her with those steel-grey eyes. "It's true, our . . .our situation came about by accident. But I know damn well it's the best one that ever hit my life," he growled. "Finally, a *good* accident."

Laura swallowed the growing ball of emotion in her own throat. She knew how vulnerable he was right now. But she couldn't let herself fall into another situation where she depended on someone, financially or emotionally.

Before she could say anything more, though, he continued, still pinning her with his eyes, searching her face. "Don't you feel it?" he whispered. "Don't you feel what's happening between us?"

A crazy, confusing cocktail of joy and fear gripped Laura's chest, and twisted. It made her heart pound so hard she swore it would vibrate right out of her chest. What the hell *was* that?

Realization came slowly, and she nodded. Instinctively, she knew what it was, though she'd never experienced *this* kind before. But before she could say another word, Miller went on.

"I know we've only known each other a short time. But I think I'm falling in love you, Laura. Either that or I'm having the happiest heart attack anybody could imagine."

Her heart clutched. Laura had always believed love—true love—sunk its roots down into two people who already had their feet firmly planted on the ground. Had their heads on straight. Their shit together. That description certainly didn't apply to either of them at the moment.

Was this love? Or just co-dependency, for both of them? He'd just suffered a traumatic loss. She'd just begun to spread still-damp wings of independence, but still wasn't sure whether or not she could fly. Whether or not these wings of confidence really fit her.

Yet, in some odd twist of fate, they'd become a team. Like two parts of a puzzle that somehow fit together, perfectly. One's strengths cancelling out the other weaknesses. Much more powerful, much happier together than they'd ever been apart. Was that not the definition of love?

What could it hurt to ride it out and see, even if just for a little while?

When his mouth covered hers, she let the tension in her body slip away and melted into his arms. His kiss was gentle and sweet, and although she already knew he owned her body, she felt her emotional armor slipping too. Tiny, clanging alarm bells sounded in her head, but she chose, for the moment, to ignore them.

Was it possible for a woman to give her heart to a man without losing everything?

Laura had a feeling she had just embarked on the journey to find out.

Three days later, Miller was waiting in the hallway for Laura when she stepped out, dressed and ready for work. She'd left him softly snoring in his bed an hour ago when her phone buzzed, waking her as unobtrusively as possible.

Startled, she blinked up at him in confusion. "What are you doing up? Everything okay?" she asked.

Without saying a word, he gazed down into her eyes and stroked a finger down her cheek. Laura wasn't sure she understood the expression in those silvery eyes. But it almost looked like resolution.

"Tonight." His voice was still gruff from sleep, yet he sounded sure, determined. "Are you sure you're ready to do this? If you've had second thoughts, Laura, I completely understand. As creepy as it's going to be, we have to go in at night."

A chill slithered up Laura's spine. The thought of poking around in the big, old building was scary enough in daylight. But in the dark? Yikes. She was a different person now than she'd been a few months back, though. Braver. Bolder. And she was more than ready to take this chance. For Greta. For Mollie. For Miller.

"I'm in," she said. "Tonight?"

Miller nodded. "Sarge is in Belize. Not expected back for another ten days. I've already spoken to Patricia about getting the key. She won't rat me out—she's Kip's wife, and he's my best friend. It's just Roger I have to worry about. But I'm sure I won't have to work very hard convincing him I can handle keeping an eye on Talcott Hall alone. He's terrified of the place."

Laura swallowed and studied Miller's face. The worry and uncertainty of the past few days had him looking older than his thirty years, and it saddened her. She lifted one hand to cup his cheek. "But you are down with this, right? You're not just doing this for me?"

He shook his head and turned away to stare out toward the graveyard. "No. I'm not doing this just for you." His shoulders lifted and dropped with a heavy sigh. "I think of Mollie . . .like you said the other day. What if she's out there floating around, not knowing where to go? Trapped. Unable to move on, like Greta. The thought makes me feel like I have ice-water running through my veins." He crossed his arms over his chest. "We have to do this. And if it costs me my job, well, then I just start over." Turning, he pulled her against him, stroking the back of her head. "Together, we'll start over."

Twenty-Seven

The perfect storm, Miller thought. That afternoon, Miller arrived at the security office a few minutes early. Patricia, who always flirted with him as he signed out his weapon, added a knowing wink as she passed him his pistol. He felt the key she had taped to the barrel as she pressed it into his palm. Roger, she informed him, had called in sick. Miller would be working the campus alone tonight.

How fucking perfect was that? Miller couldn't have hoped for a better night to plan this excursion.

"Hey Stanford?" Pat spoke quietly as he turned to leave, a knowing look of concern creasing her brow. "Be careful, 'kay?"

He nodded, then headed out. As he approached his cruiser, Mike, one of the daytime guards, called to him as he was climbing into his personal vehicle to head home.

"Hey, Stanford! You might want to spend a little more time circling Talcott tonight. The weekend guys told me the past two nights they'd had to chase a pack of creepy looking kids away from the fence. Both nights, right around midnight. Stupid bastards. Not sure what they were up to, but I'm pretty sure it was no good."

Miller touched the brim of his cap in acknowledgment. "Will do, Mike. Thanks for the heads up."

Holy shit. Yup, the perfect storm. Almost as if this crazy mission he and Laura were about to embark on was meant to be.

The plan was that Miller would swing by his house around midnight and pick Laura up, then head back to Talcott. He still wasn't sure what they would find—what they were even looking for—

276

but somehow he knew they had to do this. Had to at least try to dig up the records on Greta's father.

If they didn't, Miller was pretty sure the tortured child's soul—as well as that of his sister—would haunt him for the rest of his life.

Laura felt like a co-star in a detective flick. Miller told her to wear all black. Hell, she wasn't even sure if she owned an all-black outfit, particularly one she could move easily in. Then she remembered the yoga outfit her mother had given her for Christmas last year. Long sleeves, stretchy leggings, and jet black—except for the little multi-colored rainbow embroidered on the cuffs of the long sleeve top.

Laura pulled her hair back and secured it with a twisty tie. A glance at her watch told her it was nearly midnight. Miller should be driving by any minute.

The minute she slid into the cruiser, Laura felt Miller's eyes raking up and down her body.

"What?" she asked. "You said wear black. It's *almost* all black." She held out her arms to show him the rainbows.

But Miller wasn't looking at her wrists. "Wow. I didn't think you'd look so damned hot. Talk about providing a distraction . . ." His voice was tight, though, and his teasing didn't quite ring true. Laura knew how nervous he'd been about pulling off this caper.

She reached over and laid her hand over his. "You okay with this?"

He nodded, but kept his gaze straight ahead as they drove up Dorothy Dix Drive toward their destination.

"You have the key?"

He nodded again, still avoiding looking at her. Was he as scared as she was? Of course, he had more to lose, technically, than she did if this excursion didn't go well. But just the thought of creeping down the stairs into the bowels of that building had her stomach doing flip-flops. She fingered the tiny, high-powered flashlight Miller had given her that afternoon to take down into the shelter with her.

Geez. I hope, if we even manage to get in there and find the records, I don't puke all over the paperwork.

Miller circled the building twice, checking for those kids Mike warned him about. Thankfully, no sign of them. Apparently, they'd taken their mischief somewhere else tonight.

He parked the cruiser right in front of the double gates in the chain link surrounding Talcott Hall. The headlights shone through the fence, spraying an odd pattern of light over the brick walls.

Should he leave the headlights on? No use trying to hide the fact he was going in. He had the right to check out any suspicious activity, anywhere on campus, at any time. It was his job.

But this time, *he* was the one headed in to perform some suspicious activity. And taking an unauthorized accomplice with him. No, he thought as he doused the lights, better keep everything under the cover of darkness as much as possible.

He swallowed the bile rising into the back of his throat. Hell, he hoped he wasn't making a mistake. Who knew what they'd find down in that godforsaken hole, or what they'd bump into, step on, or climb over to get to it.

The last time Miller had been inside Talcott Hall was the day he'd discovered Chaffee doing his best to die. And it hadn't escaped his notice then, just as the old man had told Laura, there were pine boxes—crude, plywood coffins—lining the back wall of the great room.

. . .just waiting for the next one of us to croak . . .

Laura had repeated Chaffee's words with a grimace. Miller shuddered. If they kept coffins in the main room upstairs, what worse horrors might they find in the basement?

Miller turned off the engine and looked over at Laura. "You ready for this?"

Her eyes glistened in the light from the streetlamp. "I am. I think."

He reached over and squeezed her hand. "Let's get it over with, then."

Miller fumbled with the padlocked chain in the dark, avoiding using his flashlight until they were inside the building. The heavy links made a loud zinging noise as they clattered free, and the gate swung open. Checking his belt to be sure his gun and baton were secure, he extracted the flashlight, then reached back to clasp Laura's hand.

"Here goes," he muttered, almost not believing how damned nervous he was. Hell, he'd been inside this building at least a half-dozen times over the past few years. Sure, most of the time it had been in the daylight. But more than once he'd seen a light glimmering through the broken-out windows, and had gone inside to investigate. One time it had been three kids, hunkered down over a bong in the very same basement where they were headed right now.

The other times, he hadn't been able to find anything to explain the lights at all.

Miller extracted the second key on his ring, the one that opened the lock on the double front doors. As cliché as an old Gothic horror film, they whined and squealed as he pushed them open. He felt Laura step closer into his side.

"Yikes. This place is like an old Alfred Hitchcock set," she whispered, echoing his thoughts.

He reached down and squeezed her hand. "You stay right beside me, you hear?" He pulled the doors shut behind them, then clicked on his flashlight.

They entered the same room where Miller had found Chaffee that night. The light snagged on the row of coffins, and he felt Laura shiver against his side. He whistled softly as he swept the beam across the big front room.

"The old guy wasn't exaggerating," she mumbled. "How sad. How incredibly, freaking sad."

"Yeah. Man," he replied, then turned his flashlight toward a doorway on the side wall. It gaped open, its thick door hanging drunkenly from its hinges. The blackness filling the space beyond swallowed his light beam, revealing nothing.

"That's the stairwell to the basement," he murmured. Resting his hand on the small of Laura's back, he urged her forward.

They crept down the stairs slowly, Miller sweeping the steps with light before they descended each riser. No telling what they might find, from litter, to a hunk of broken plaster, to a dead rat. But there was nothing, and when they turned the corner at the stairs' base, he could feel, more than see, a huge space open up around them.

The smell of dampness, dust, and mildew engulfed his senses. It was also at least ten degrees cooler down here, even though the three narrow, rectangular windows along the front had long ago lost their panes. But the overgrown grass and vines twisting around their rusted frames failed to block all of the light from the streetlamp outside.

Thank you, God.

Beside him, Laura sneezed, then asked in a hoarse whisper, "Have you been down here before? Do you know where the bomb shelter is?"

"Yeah, I do. It's over that way." He turned and pointed his light toward the back of the space, the one farthest away from the windows. "Of course. They wanted it as far from possible outside contamination as possible."

As he spoke, Miller scanned the floor before them. Crumpled fast food bags and crushed cigarette packages littered the concrete atop a layer of dust and dirt blown in through the broken windows. In one spot, the concrete was blackened with what looked like the remnants of a small campfire. Over in one corner was a pile of old clothes and tattered blankets, mounded into a makeshift bed.

"I guess kids and vagabonds get in here more than I realized," he muttered, kicking at an empty beer can. The sound it made as it skittered away startled a rat hiding in the corner. It screeched as it darted into a crevice in the stone wall, making Miller jump. Laura gasped beside him.

"Come on," he growled. "Let's get this over with."

When they reached the rear wall, Miller kicked a cardboard French-fry carton away from a hasp sticking up from the floor. The heavy, ancient looking padlock was nearly buried under years of grime. He handed his heavy flashlight to Laura.

"Hold this, will you?" he asked. "God knows if the thing will even still open after all these years."

He snapped on a pair of the neoprene gloves he always kept tucked into a pocket on his belt. Stooping, he extracted the key Pat had retrieved for him from the evidence closet. While Laura shone the light on the lock, Miller set to work.

"Good thing Pat knew where this key was. And that she likes me," he said, adding, "as well as being Kip's wife." He fumbled for several seconds just trying to fit the end of the damn thing in the lock, swearing at how his hands were trembling. "Fuck," he muttered.

Finally, the key slid home. It took a moment or two of wiggling to work the tumblers free from the ancient mechanism. But with a final, firm twist, he heard a loud click. "We're in," he said, and heard Laura whoosh out a breath above him.

The door sealing the shelter was bigger than Miller expected, as well as being blasted heavy. Made of steel and at least a couple inches thick, he was glad the door was split, the two halves joined at the center. Grabbing the hasp which doubled as a handle, he heaved one side open.

The screeching of the timeworn hinges echoed loudly in the space around them, sending a cold chill down Miller's spine, and causing Laura to drop the flashlight as she stumbled backwards. Fortunately, the sturdy device kept burning, but sent a crazy light show skittering across the floor as it rolled away.

"Damn it. Damn it. Sorry," Laura stuttered as she chased to retrieve it. When she returned to Miller's side, he took it from her in silence, then pointed it down into the hole beneath them. A concrete staircase led down to another door, about ten steps below. This one stood partially open with only blackness beyond.

Laura swallowed hard, the reality of what she'd signed up for hitting her. She was going to have to go down there and dig through god knew how many boxes of files, looking for one man's name.

Thomas Sanderson. She wasn't even sure of the exact dates he'd been a patient here. She felt her heart rate skyrocket, and blood was pounding so hard in her ears she almost didn't hear Miller's next words.

"I'll go down and make sure it's safe, but then you're on your own, Laura. It's just not wise for both of us to be down there at the same time. I'll have to stay up here while you search. Once you think you've found the right box, pull it to the door and I'll come down and carry it up."

They never got that far. Miller's foot had barely landed on the first step when all hell broke loose.

Though the air had been eerily calm moments before, a great wind kicked up around them, its force so strong it nearly knocked Laura off her feet. The sound it made was terrible, a tortured moan as it swept them both back, stumbling away from the bunker's open doorway. She grabbed Miller's arm and shrieked "What's happening?"

The last thing Laura heard before his voice was drowned out completely was Miller's panicked bark—"What the fuck?"

Dirt and dust blew up around them, engulfing them in a virtual sandstorm. Laura coughed and lifted a hand to shield her eyes as her face was pelted with flying grit. She buried her face against Miller's chest, panic threatening to melt her legs out from under her. For several long moments that seemed like eternity, the world around them disappeared, obliterated by a roaring, violent vortex of wind and sand.

A tornado, Laura thought in terror. This is a tornado, or a cyclone. But that's impossible. The night had been clear and calm. And this wind wasn't coming in from the outside.

It's coming up out of a hole in the ground.

Twenty-Eight

Paralyzed by shock and terror as the wind howled around them, Miller acted on instinct, wrapping his arms around Laura and dragging her back, away from the bunker. He was unable to keep his eyes open for the pelting grit swirling around them. He staggered drunkenly, completely disoriented. Every impulse compelled him to get her—hell, both of them—out of there. He felt shudders racking Laura's body as she huddled against him.

When she screamed into his chest, the blood-chilling sound sliced through his brain.

But seconds later, as suddenly as it had begun, the wind stilled. Dirt and grit made a sound like rain as it pattered on the concrete floor all around them. Hesitantly, Miller opened his eyes, and gasped when he realized they were no longer alone in the basement.

Orbs of light, the ones he'd watched dance outside the building night after night, were streaming out of the half-open bunker door. Like air bubbles from under water, they rose up through the opening to float free, gathering in a cluster over the bomb shelter. Their luminescence cast an eerie glow in the darkened space. A wave of terror washed over him.

Although he'd seen the strange balls of light many times hovering outside Talcott Hall, he'd never been this close to them before. He'd always been able to convince himself they were odd reflections from the headlights of passing cars, or the streetlamp playing tricks on his eyes. But now, with a dozen or more orbs hovering not more than ten feet away, there was no denying their existence.

He cupped the back of Laura's trembling head, whose face was still buried against him. Ducking down, he whispered against her ear, "Look."

She gasped when she turned and saw them, and for a moment Miller was afraid she'd start screaming again. He shushed her as he stroked his hand down her hair.

"Shh. The orbs I told you about," he murmured. "The ones I've seen so many times floating around outside . . .outside this place. Do you see them? Do you see them too?"

Silently, he felt her nod against his chest.

At least now I know I'm not crazy.

That's when he noticed that, just as he'd witnessed before, two of the orbs glowed brighter than the rest. Gradually, the pair floated off, a little way from the group. Yet they remained so close together they almost seemed to touch. He blinked, and in an instant, they pulsed brighter, the light growing so intense he was momentarily blinded.

When he opened his eyes again, there were two people standing before them. A man with his right arm ending in a stump just below the elbow, with a little, blonde-haired girl clinging to his side.

"Greta," Laura gasped.

The child wasn't crying, but her small, dirty face was still twisted with emotion. Miller's heart clutched. She held tightly onto the complete, left arm of the man as she stared at them with tormented eyes.

"Greta," Laura repeated, "is this your father? Have you finally found him?"

The child answered with a small nod, her mouth turning downward as she began to cry. "For a little while. But he can't leave here. He can't go with me."

Miller swallowed, feeling as though his heart might vibrate up into his throat and choke him. Sucking in a breath, he found his voice.

"Mr. Sanderson. What happened here? Why are you . . .you and all these others," he paused and motioned toward the group of orbs still hovering over the bunker. "Why are you still here?"

The man stared at them for a long moment, and Miller wondered if the man's image was just a shadow, a phantom—not a spirit who could, like Greta, hear and communicate with them. But then he opened his mouth to speak. His voice was a howling, otherworldly whine that sent icy knives of terror through Miller's body.

"De-se-cra-tion," he said, the word drawn out and too loud, echoing eerily. It seemed to come from another, faraway place. "Our bodies were desecrated. Tossed into the incinerator with the trash. Burned to ash."

He felt Laura stiffen and gasp again. "Oh my God," she whispered. "Oh my God."

Sanderson spoke again, the words not quite syncing with his lips, his voice reverberating in the space around them. "It's all in the records . . .down there." He pointed a finger of his one hand toward the open bunker door. "Not buried. Not cremated. Our records are stamped *disposed*. Along with the dates we were added to the trash hopper. All of us—the last dozen patients who died the year I was here—were disposed of. Like garbage. *With* the garbage."

"Oh my God," Laura whimpered. "But . . .why?"

Sanderson turned his icy blue gaze on her. "No money for proper burials. No room left in the graveyard. Waiting on State funding. New fiscal year."

Laura shuddered violently against his chest, and Miller clutched her tighter against him.

"Jesus," he muttered, squeezing his eyes shut briefly. Then he asked, "Where . . ." Miller's voice was quaking so badly he almost couldn't make his words understandable, "where did they take you . . .your remains? Your ashes?"

"A field. Not far from here," the man said, his voice echoing even louder, now sounding as though he were standing in a culvert. "We were spread on an open, unmarked field. Like fertilizer. On unhallowed ground."

Laura coughed and gagged, and for a moment Miller feared he might throw up too. Sickening. Shameful. Sacrilege.

Sanderson's image began to flicker and grow translucent, then transparent. The orbs hovering nearby began to fade as well, as if the energy feeding their glow was growing weaker. Greta, who had not loosened her hold on her father's arm the entire time, began to squeal, jumping up and down in panic.

"No, daddy. No! Don't go away and leave me again. Please!" Her words came out on a sob that shattered Miller's heart into a thousand splintered shards.

But in the next instant, her father's apparition was gone. And, like the night when Miller had encountered them both outside Talcott Hall, Greta flopped down and ground her knuckles into her eyes. Wailing miserably, she slowly faded out of sight. Her sobbing echoed in the room around them for long moments after she had disappeared.

Still holding Laura and welded to the spot in shock, Miller jolted when a sudden noise above them broke the silence. Impact, something bumping on the floor over their heads. Glass shattering. And almost simultaneously, a horrific whooshing, followed by a crackling sound. Terror took Miller's breath away.

This did not sound good.

Gripping Laura's waist, he turned to bolt for the stairwell. He froze in shocked horror when he saw it was bright with flickering, orange-red light. His already piqued terror escalated to yet another, horrifying level when realization hit him.

He and Laura's only means of escape from this godforsaken dungeon was engulfed in flames.

For a heart-stopping moment, Laura was confused, uncertain why Miller had screeched to a halt in their progress toward the stairwell. Toward their escape from this damned pit of hell, with all its horrifying secrets. Within seconds, though, reality pierced through the fog of her panic and shock. The flames licking around the edge of the wooden doorframe delivered their message, loud and clear.

Just as did as Miller's strangled curse. "Fuck. We're fucked."

He left her side and sprinted across to the doorway, shielding his eyes as he peered up the stairs.

"This place will go up like dry kindling," he muttered, and Laura began to tremble uncontrollably.

Already, the planks above her head were glowing with the flames eating them up from above, and the crackling roar of burning timber filled her with dread. The smoke, fortunately, was still headed skyward. But she knew it wouldn't be long before it stole every breath of oxygen from their lungs.

She ran to Miller and grabbed his arm. "The windows. Come on. We can climb up out of the windows," she screamed.

But when Miller turned and studied the long, narrow, barely foot-tall basement windows, the trepidation in his eyes was palpable, and terrifying. "Let's get you out of here," he said solemnly.

As they stood beneath the iron-framed openings, Laura could hear the wailing of the Fire Department's whistle in the distance. Help would be here soon, she thought. Help, for both of us. Then everything will be alright.

She shrieked when she felt Miller scoop her up, one arm around her waist, the other beneath her butt, lifting her towards the opening. "Grab a hold," he demanded. "Pull yourself up."

Instinct forced her to thrust both elbows through the narrow opening and into the soft earth outside. She felt Miller's hands on her bottom, pushing. In the next breath, she was outside, in the cool night air. And as she flopped onto her back in the grass and looked up, the sight before her turned her blood to ice.

Talcott Hall was lit from within, like a Christmas village church with a candle inside. Except the candle was burning out of control. Flames licked out of the arched openings in the brick edifice. The entire first floor was already completely engulfed.

Crawling frantically back toward the window, Laura screamed and reached for him. "Miller! Come on. I'll help you. Hold on."

His big hands gripped her upper arms as she knelt before the narrow opening. But not only wasn't she strong enough to heft his bulky body, but stark logistics quickly plunged her heart into panic.

Miller's head barely fit through the space. There was no way his thick, broad body could pass through the opening. Although it was old and rusted, the window frames were made of iron. Solid, formidable, and inflexible.

After a brief struggle, she felt him go limp and slide away from her. The truth hit her like a heart attack.

The next few moments blurred into a hysterical frenzy as Laura repeatedly dove through the window, screaming, frantically reaching for Miller. But he had disappeared into the choking haze now billowing from the basement. It wasn't until strong hands gripped her from behind and dragged her away, sliding on the grass on her belly, that she realized help had finally arrived.

Gasping, sputtering, her eyes and throat burning from the acrid smoke, she fought her rescuers blindly, screaming, "Miller! He's still inside. You have to save him!"

But powerful arms held her down, flipping her to her back. Then a cooling mask covered her mouth and nose. She struggled for only a moment longer until she realized she could suddenly breathe easily again. Oxygen. They were giving her oxygen.

Her eyes fluttered open, and though they were stinging so she could barely see, she recognized the dark face hovering over her. The fireman wore a yellow helmet and jacket, and was studying her face in panic. It was Kip.

"Did you say . . .Miller? What the hell is he doing . . .?" he choked out frantically.

She nodded, her entire body quaking as tears streamed down into her hair. With one hand, she knocked the oxygen mask free and sobbed, "You've got to save him, Kip. Get him out of there."

By the time Miller had succeeded in pushing Laura out of the narrow opening, he was gasping for breath. The air was thick and heavy, and flames were greedily consuming every ounce of available oxygen. If not for the inferno sucking fresh air in a steady stream through the windows, Miller was certain he would have lost consciousness already.

Gripping his flashlight with trembling hands, he swept the beam around the nearly empty space. The hazy fog of smoke prevented his light from reaching too far into the gloom. But this small room, he realized, wasn't large enough to match the footprint of the building above. Apparently, the basement had been constructed in divided chambers, with separate stairwells leading into them. Hugging the wall, where the fresh air still flowed in, Miller began searching for another way out.

When he reached the back wall, where there were no windows, his hands groped desperately, finding nothing but a solid, concrete wall. There was no other exterior access to this chamber. And back here, where there was no circulation, every breath seared his lungs. Miller's throat closed against the searing heat, and he lifted his collar to cover his nose and mouth.

He'd heard the sirens as Laura had struggled out. He knew help would be here soon. But unless the firemen could breach the wall of flames in the big front room where the blaze had started, there was no way for them to reach him.

With a mighty crack that sent a wave of terror through him, one of the overhead beams let go, raining splinters of flaming wood to the floor only feet away from him.

This is it, Miller thought. The beginning of the end.

Well, I'd rather suffocate than burn to death.

Coughing and choking into the cloth of his shirt, his eyes stinging and leaking all over his face, Miller headed for the bunker. If it had been designed to protect lives from a nuclear bomb, surely it would keep the flames from cremating him.

Too bad the air supply, he knew, wouldn't last long.

He climbed down into the small underground space and pulled the bunker door closed behind him. A high-pitched whistling told him that the fire was feeding on the air within this chamber too, through the filtered outlet pipe in the basement floor. Already struggling to suck in enough air to satisfy his screaming lungs, Miller sunk down onto the cold floor.

He doused his flashlight and closed his eyes, preparing to die. Every breath took more and more effort, yet delivered less precious oxygen.

At least we solved the mystery, he thought. Laura could now take steps to set free the trapped spirits of Thomas Sanderson, as well as all the others. And Greta, an innocent yet tenacious child-spirit, could finally rest in peace.

Maybe too, he prayed, the spirit of my sweet sister. And mine.

His last conscious thought, he tried to say aloud to the emptiness around him. But there wasn't enough air left to form the words. So, they resonated in his head as he drifted down into a dark place of eternal sleep.

I'll miss you, Laura Horton. I hope you find another good man to go on with you in your life. One who will love you as much as I do.

Kip's stomach did a nauseating roll at Laura's words, at the realization that his friend was trapped below a blaze that was developing rapidly into a five-alarm fire. He didn't know much about the blueprint of this particular unit—it had closed down before he'd even graduated high school. But there wasn't time now to research for the info on escape routes, even if there was someone left to ask.

Leaving Laura sitting on the grass, sobbing uncontrollably, he sought his chief, Tim, who was near the truck radioing in another alarm. Kip grabbed his arm and shouted, "There's a man still inside. In the basement, where the girl came out."

The look of shock, then despair on his chief's face hit him like a sucker punch in the gut. Tim's eyes wandered toward the blaze. With air feeding the fire from below through the broken-out basement windows, and solid brick walls containing and intensifying the heat, the monstrous structure had rapidly transformed into a huge, blazing hearth.

Tim shook his head sadly before looking back toward Kip. "Unless he can get out the way the girl did, I don't see how we can get to him, Kip. I can't justify risking my men's lives—"

Kip tightened his grip on Tim's arm and shook him. "You don't understand, man. That's my friend in there. He's too fucking big to crawl through those openings."

Yet even as he spoke, Kip knew his chief was right.

Tim continued to shake his head. "So are our men, Kip."

The men had already been forced to back the ladder trucks further away because of the intensity of the inferno. Flames had now engulfed the second floor as well, and were licking angrily around the iron frames of the arched windows. There was no way of stopping it, of even slowing it down.

And for the life of one man, it didn't make sense to risk a half-dozen. Kip released Tim's arm and covered his face with his hand, turning away. He hadn't seen any sign of Miller since he'd pushed Laura out twenty minutes ago. For all Kip knew, he might already be gone.

Engrossed in his pain, it took a moment before he became aware of a tugging on the hem of his jacket. He started and wheeled. Gasping in surprise, he found himself looking into the glowing eyes of a blonde, little girl.

Twenty-Nine

After Kip left her, Laura struggled to her feet and headed back toward the building, toward the window where Miller had put her out. Saved her life.

Dread choked her, lodging a painful ball in her throat. She had to find a way to get him out too, somehow. Guilt and grief consumed her. It was her fault they were in the building in the first place.

Please, God. No. I can't lose him. Not now. Not like this.

The way her heart felt shredded in that moment, Laura knew she could never bear the thought of losing Miller. Not ever.

But before she'd gotten within twenty feet of the building, the heat was so intense she could barely breathe. Then a shout from behind and a strong arm around her waist prevented her from taking another step.

"Other side of the fence," the fireman shouted. "Get back." He pushed her in that direction, and none too gently. Broken and sobbing, she stumbled away.

The fire had lit up the night sky like a carnival, and flames were now shooting out of nearly every window in the building. The world had been consumed by chaos—chaos of the most terrifying, uncontrollable kind. Fire.

Yet, as she stumbled away from the inferno, her heart melting inside her with more pain than she'd ever imagined, something caught Laura's eye.

Turning, she spotted Kip standing beside the ladder truck. Beside him stood the form of a child, glowing, like a holiday lawn ornament. Illuminated from within.

Laura took off at a dead run toward them.

"Greta. Greta! Miller . . ."

The little girl was tugging frantically, trying to lead Kip away. But Kip was frozen to the spot. In a voice that somehow echoed over all the crackling and roaring and shouting around them, Greta was repeating, "This way. This way." Yet Laura knew she was hearing the child's words from inside her own head.

Kip looked up at her as she approached, his mouth open, and white rimming his dark irises. He could see the child, obviously. She wondered if he could hear her, too.

"This way," Greta urged, then released Kip's jacket and took off, running laterally across the frontage of Talcott Hall. Without a moment's hesitation, Laura followed, hoping yet unsure if Kip was behind her or not. There must be another way in, and if Greta knew of it, maybe, just maybe . . .

When Greta reached the end of the building, she turned the corner and led Laura through the tall grasses and around behind. The flames had not yet consumed this back side. Greta, seeming now to float rather than run through the grasses, headed straight for a small, brick structure about thirty feet behind Talcott Hall. Laura struggled with each step, her knees lifting like pistons to plow through the thick, waist-high weeds.

Laura stopped. "No, Greta," she shouted. "Miller. He's trapped. In there." Her finger stabbed the air frantically in the direction of Talcott Hall. "We have to help him!"

The ghostly echo sounded again in her head with a calm certainty. "This way."

The brick shed didn't look large enough to house even a moderate amount of maintenance equipment. Perhaps eight feet square, its entrance stood open—a heavy, wooden door hanging uselessly off to one side. Running on blind faith, Laura followed the glowing form of the child inside.

On the floor of the shed, embedded in the center of a concrete pad, was a steel door much like the one enclosing the bunker in the basement of Talcott Hall. But the hasp of this door held no padlock, and it stood open. One side of the heavy hatch had been lifted.

Before she could retrieve her flashlight from her pocket, she watched as Greta floated down into the stairwell, illuminating an underground passage. One that led in the direction of Talcott Hall.

Laura trotted down the steps behind her, ducking under the overhead beam at their base. The tunnel was narrow and low, and up ahead, curved slightly out of sight. But there was light coming from around that bend.

She found Greta waiting for her where the tunnel dead-ended against a door-sized plate of rusted metal. Searching its surface in desperation, Laura's heart sank as she realized there was no doorknob. No handle, no hasp or lock. Nothing. Just the sheer face of an ancient barrier set into a wall of solid concrete. Hysterical, Laura slammed her body against the door and beat it with her fists.

"Miller! Miller, can you hear me?" she screamed, her voice echoing in the close, underground space. She turned toward Greta, who was standing close beside her now, lighting up the entire end of the tunnel like a fluorescent fixture. "How, Greta? How do we get in?" she shrieked.

Greta pointed, and Laura gasped when the child's arm disappeared, sliding effortlessly through the solid metal. "This way," she repeated. Laura blinked in disbelief as Greta stepped forward and vanished through the door.

The tunnel was plunged into complete blackness, and that's when Laura's tenuous grip on sanity fell apart. All of the horror of the last tumultuous hour gathered like soda in a shaken bottle, bubbling up to break free. She belted out a nightmarish scream.

The sound bounced off the walls and reverberated down the length of the tunnel. Laura threw herself once more against the impenetrable door, then slid down into a limp puddle on the floor. Completely blind in the absolute pitch darkness, disoriented, and frenzied with despair, she fisted her hands into her hair and screamed again.

As the echoes of her wail faded away, a sudden squeak made her yip and scramble clumsily back to her feet. She blinked as a sliver of light glowed along one edge of the solid barrier, followed by the scraping of metal against stone. Laura covered her mouth with her hand.

Greta was pushing the door open from the other side.

Like the breaking of a vacuum seal on a giant freezer, the movement of the door made a sucking sound, with air whooshing into the space behind it. With apparent ease, the ghost-child pushed the barrier aside, revealing a small room beyond. In the light from her glowing form, Laura could see boxes stacked against the stone walls of the subterranean space. Beyond, on the other end of the bunker, she saw the set of steps rising up to the door inside the basement of Talcott Hall.

And in the center, on the floor, sprawled the body of Miller Stanford.

Unsure of what he had just seen or heard, Kip hesitated, frozen with shock. He watched as a glowing, ghostly effigy of a child disappeared around the far end of Talcott Hall with Laura close behind. Raising his fists, he rubbed his stinging eyes. Tears streamed from them. He knew they were not only from the acrid smoke. Nor was that the cause of the heaviness in his chest making it hard to breathe.

My best friend is in there. Dying, possibly already dead. And there isn't a damn thing I can do about it.

Perhaps, he thought, I'm having a breakdown. The thought of losing Miller, like this, in a situation where I'm trained to rescue lives. Training I pride myself on. Yet here and now, I'm powerless. The helplessness, and the grief, it's costing me my stability. I'm hallucinating.

So, I'm hallucinating. Still, I can't discount this feeling in my gut.

Ignoring the fray going on around him, with the hoses and the ladders and the shouts of his colleagues, Kip followed an impulse he couldn't seem to dismiss. An inexplicable instinct. A desperate hope. Snapping on his helmet lamp, he took off after them, jogging clumsily in his heavy gear and boots. If there was any chance they were being shown another way in—no matter how bizarre it might seem—he had to follow through.

He'd rounded the rear corner when he heard Laura's hideous scream, and stopped short. Where had it come from? Not from his left, toward the building. It seemed to have come from the small shed a dozen yards to his right. Seconds later, another scream confirmed his suspicion.

Kip's light splashed on the stairway leading down into the ground. There was nothing else in the tiny room. She must have tried to find access to the basement through this tunnel.

"Laura!" he called. Her screams still echoed in his brain. God knows what she encountered in this godforsaken dungeon.

When the big man reached the bottom step, he smacked his head on the low beam and was knocked backward, landing hard on his butt on the concrete step. Swearing, he silently thanked God for his helmet, and then again that his clumsiness hadn't knocked out its lamp. He scrambled to his feet and ducked into the tunnel, then shuffled down its cramped length awkwardly.

"Laura!" he called again, his voice echoing back to him. He paused, listening, but heard nothing. Panting now, he trudged on, skidding to a halt when he rounded the passageway's slight bend. He swallowed hard and gulped in a breath.

The scene before him was otherworldly, impossible, and both glorious and terrifying. The luminous outline of the child stood within a small chamber, illuminating the space to near-daylight with nothing more than the glow emanating from within her tiny form. Beside her was Laura, on her knees, crouching over Miller's prone body.

"Come back to me, damn you," Laura sobbed as she heaved every ounce of her upper body against Miller's chest. She'd been administering CPR, complete with mouth-to-mouth, for several minutes, without success. And with every second that passed, she knew the chances of his survival dwindled.

When she'd found him, he wasn't breathing. There probably had been no air left *to* breathe. But for how long? Had it been seconds? Minutes?

She paused, watching his ashen face. "Please, don't give up on me, Stanford." But he didn't stir. Her tears ran freely as she cupped Miller's face in her hands, then brushed a gentle kiss across his lips. Pressing her cheek to his, she whimpered, "Please, Mills. Don't leave me."

"Laura!"

Kip's voice reverberated from down the other end of the tunnel, and Laura raised her head to see light splashing against the concrete walls. But he was too late. They had both been too late. She burrowed her face against Miller's neck and wailed. The pain in her heart was so great, she wished it would stop beating.

I've waited all my life for you, and because of me, you're gone. What have I done?

Breaking through her anguish, Greta's soft words sounded inside her head. "Not yet. It's not his time."

Laura stilled and sucked in a hopeful breath.

In the next second, Miller's hoarse gasp rocked Laura back on her heels, and she watched in disbelief as his chest heaved. His face contorted as he fought to fill his lungs with air, like a man who'd been saved—and barely—from drowning. Then his eyes fluttered open, and he struggled up on his elbows. He blinked, studying her in confusion.

"How . . .?" he asked.

Kip must have rounded the corner then, as the light from his helmet flashed across the walls of the space. But Laura couldn't take her eyes off of Miller, who had locked gazes with her. To her horror, he seemed as though he didn't recognize her.

Was he really back? All of him? Or would he go on living in body only? Like his sister?

Laura turned to look for Greta, but the spirit-child was gone.

Thirty

Searing pain ripped through Miller's lungs as he dragged in air. His throat was raw, and for a few moments, he found opening his eyes impossible. He'd been so peaceful, dreaming. Why hadn't they just left him alone?

He'd been dreaming of Mollie.

Mollie, as she'd been before the accident. Ten years old, spritely and smiling, she'd appeared through the haze of smoke in the basement of Talcott Hall. Had she been one of those orbs he'd seen?

But the dream ended too soon, and sadly. When he'd reached out to hold her, Mollie drew back, sobering and shaking her head.

"Not yet," she'd whispered to him. "It's not your time."

And then he'd been thrust back into the hell that was his aching body. Every breath was pure torture, yet seemed imperative. So, he pushed through the pain, fighting his way upward to the surface of consciousness. When he finally found the strength to open his eyes, a faerie angel was looking back at him. Huge, blue eyes riveted his. Golden curls framed her face.

No, wait. Maybe I did die after all. But I know this angel from somewhere. I've seen her before . . .

And then it all came flooding back. Laura. His very own, personal angel.

Two weeks later, Laura watched, giggling, as Miller attempted to fold himself into the passenger seat of her tiny car.

"I don't understand why the hell I can't drive us," he barked, then swore again when he cracked his knee on the dashboard. "Or why you couldn't drive my truck," he muttered through gritted teeth, rubbing his knee.

Laura ran her fingers down his arm, smiling. "I have enough trouble maneuvering *this* big vehicle around," she said, teasing. "I don't think I could handle your truck, too." She started the engine and put the car in gear. "You can drive us home. After the doctor clears you."

Miller had spent three days in the hospital undergoing every test they could think of to explain how, after what had to have been at least ten minutes of oxygen deprivation, he'd fully recovered. They finally declared him a medical miracle and discharged him. But his doctor had placed limitations on his activities for another ten days. No driving. Until today.

And today, after the checkup, they were scheduled to attend a funeral.

Miller stood in uniform beside Laura, just inside the pasture gate of an open field on Mount Hope Road. It was just a mile or so away from the entrance to the old Psych Center's grounds. Priests from three different Christian religious affiliations, along with a rabbi, had gathered to bless the ground on which the remains of twelve deceased patients from Talcott Hall had been spread. Only a half-dozen of the patients' families had been located, but every one of them had made the trek for the ceremony. A few had come from clear across the country.

Lawrence Chaffee had only to bum a ride from the daytime security guards of the Center to attend. Miller's daytime counterpart, Mike, was happy to oblige.

Squeezing Laura's hand as they stood solemnly in the warm summer sunshine, Miller clutched his cap to his chest in his other hand. Finally, he thought, twelve souls could rest peacefully. Move on to whatever lay on the other side.

No, thirteen. A lost spirit-child was now free too, no longer tethered to this world in search of her father.

All because of a wonderful woman Miller was still convinced had fallen through a hole in the floor of heaven. She'd swooped in and landed on his front porch just in time, saving more than just his sorry ass. This woman wore a suit of armor, cleverly hidden under that angelic exterior. She'd crusaded, despite her fears, to uncover an ugly secret. A horrific truth. To set all these trapped souls free.

Laura also succeeded in bringing this big, strong man to his knees. She saw him to the gates of hell, then picked him back up and breathed life into him again—both his body, and his heart. His special angel.

As the men of religion recited their rituals, Miller couldn't help but wonder if his beloved sister had somehow escaped the imprisonment these souls had endured. They hadn't seen Greta since the night of the fire. He wouldn't even be able to ask.

He'd never know for sure.

Three Months Later

They arrived at the cemetery at dusk, and Laura scrambled out before Miller could come around to open her door. She cradled the bunch of gorgeous, lavender gladiolus against her chest and stepped up close beside him as he exited the car and stood. The shuddering breath he dragged in made her heart wrench, so she hooked her arm through his and squeezed.

"You can do this, babe," she murmured. "We'll do this, together."

Today was Mollie's birthday. She would have been twenty-three this year. Laura had watched Miller "X" out each day on the calendar until September 23rd. She had insisted they go together to his sister's grave.

Neither spoke as they made their way across the neatly mowed grass toward the southwest end of the cemetery. Their path wound around the giant, old maples dotting the serene acreage. She'd only been here once before—the day they'd laid Mollie in the ground.

They say that time heals all, but three months isn't nearly long enough to mend a heart ripped open like Miller's had been. His mourning had begun even longer. He had been grieving Mollie's loss since he was eighteen. Since that day at his high school playoff game, when his mother had broken the news to him through her sobs, in the back of a police cruiser.

"Your dad's gone. Your sister, she's hurt . . . real bad."

As they drew closer to the site, Miller paused, dragging in another ragged breath and pinching his fingers to the bridge of his nose.

"I should be over this by now," he growled, angry with himself. "She's been gone, I mean, *really* gone, for over twelve years now."

Laura's heart ached as she clenched his arm and rested her head against his shoulder. "She's at peace now, Mills. She's no longer suffering, or in any pain. Or in some kind of limbo."

She knew the minute she'd spoken those last words, they had been the wrong ones.

He wheeled, pulling away and glaring at her. "How do we know that?" he shouted. "Especially now. After we know what Greta went through trying to reunite with her father's spirit? How can we be sure Mollie isn't going to just float around . . .trapped between worlds? Hell, at least Greta knew what she was looking for. Do you think Mollie will be searching for *my* father? Fat chance. Fat fucking chance."

He barked out a laugh, but with his next words, his voice cracked. "This is a waste of time. She's not here. We both know that. We don't know where the hell her spirit is."

Laura rocked back, but wasn't surprised. She'd seen this side of Miller now enough times to know his aggressive armor was just a facade. A protective shield to obscure his floundering, softer side. Like a knight suddenly stripped of his chain mail. Fighting a losing battle to protect the vulnerable, sentimental side of the man.

Not so long ago, Laura had been intimidated. Afraid to challenge the big, bad Miller Stanford. Not any longer.

Throwing back her shoulders, she stepped into him, causing the cellophane-wrapped flowers to crackle between them. She tipped up her chin and locked on his piercing gaze. A muscle in his jaw tensed and worked.

"You're absolutely right. We don't know," she began, never breaking eye contact with him as she spoke decisively, forcefully. "But we do know this, Miller. There are ways for spirits to find their way home. We've both proven that. Helped it to happen. From what you've told me, Mollie was a smart girl. With spunk, and spirit. She will find her way home. Just like Greta did."

Dusk had started settling in earnest around them, and Laura heard the almost deafening call of crickets pulsating from the woods surrounding the cemetery. An early fall chill made the air feel clammy, damp. Funny, not so long ago, just being in a place like this in the near-dark would have frightened her to death. Now, she was braver. Wiser.

"Come on," she snapped. "I want to put these flowers on Mollie's grave *on* her birthday, not the day after."

Her nails bit into his bulky forearm as she surged forward, and for a brief moment, she wondered if she'd have to literally drag him. Or make a feeble effort toward that aim. But he didn't resist. After only a brief hesitation, he followed silently along beside her.

The grass had already grown in, lush and light green, on the rectangle defining the place where they'd lowered the coffin just a few months ago. You almost couldn't tell where those cruelly cut edges had been.

Funny, Laura thought, how quickly and efficiently nature endeavors to close over the wound, bury the past. If only the human heart could heal with such expedience.

When they reached the grave, Miller dropped to his knees, resting one arm along the stone's upper edge and laying his forehead against it. It killed her to see his grief, a pain she knew she could do little to ease for him. And she also knew, all too well, that closure wouldn't occur for a long, long time. If ever. Maybe not until he joined his sister in the next dimension.

She shuddered at the very thought.

After busying herself unwrapping the dozen, delicate flowers, she arranged them in the spiked holder they'd picked up on their way in. Gladiolus—signifying strength, in memory of the Roman gladiators. She'd chosen this flower specifically, to help fortify Miller on his journey to heal.

Laura skewered the vase into the soft earth, and then dropped to her knees beside Miller, laying her arm at his waist. This was all she could do. Be here for him. Hold him. And love him.

A sound in the distance caused them both to raise their heads. Two or three rows down toward the north end of the graveyard, Laura heard voices.

Laughing. Children.

They both stared in that direction, but Laura saw no one. There had been no other cars parked besides theirs when they'd arrived. Did the neighborhood kids screw around in this graveyard after dark for kicks? How sick and twisted was that?

"Come on!" one voice called. "This way!"

Miller's sharp intake of breath caused Laura to turn toward him. He was staring intently in the direction of the north woods. She turned and followed his gaze.

In the gathering gloom of twilight, the shadowy figures of two young girls flickered into view, not very far from where she and Miller knelt huddled against Mollie's marker. Laura blinked and squinted in an effort to make them out. But there was too little light left to see them clearly.

Both slight and young, the girls were maybe ten or twelve years old. They were weaving between the headstones, waving playful arms like carefree yearlings, chattering with words Laura couldn't decipher. Yet the laughter came through loud and clear. They were both giggling, holding their hands over their mouths to muffle the sound. Like two pre-teens trying not to wake up their parents on a sleepover weekend.

In the dim light, Laura couldn't make out details, other than one had long dark hair. The other's hair was short and pale. The blonde was leading them away, pausing every few steps to reach out her hand to the brunette.

"Come on. It's this way," she chanted. Over and over again.

Miller stumbled to his feet and clutched the gravestone with such sudden force, Laura nearly fell backward on her heels.

"Mollie!" he shouted.

A stab of pain seared Laura's heart like a hot knife. This was too much of a coincidence, and the very last thing Miller needed on a night like tonight. Damn these kids, fooling around in a sacred place on a Saturday night. Damn their arrogant nerve, she thought bitterly. She clamored to her feet, and was just about to call out to them, scold them, chase them away.

Until the dark-haired girl stopped and turned.

As if they'd been viewing the figures through the lens of a camera, the girls' images came into focus. Sharp and clear, and suddenly illuminated from within. Laura blinked, and in the next moment, their images faded, then reappeared. As if they'd been drawn closer by a zoom lens.

The brunette stood only feet away from Miller.

It was Mollie.

Although she'd never seen the child before her disfiguring accident, and before that only in photographs, Laura recognized her instantly. She looked so much like her older brother. The same silver-flecked, grey-blue eyes, the same aquiline nose. The same rueful, child-like, impish smile.

Mollie didn't say a word, only reached out her hand toward her brother. Miller's breath came in short rasps, and instinctively, Laura laid a hand on his shoulder. But he was already stepping away, around the marker to get a few steps closer to his sister.

Her face wasn't ruined, as Miller had described it. A perfect cherub's face, with bright, expressive eyes, she appeared untouched and perfect and gorgeous. And she was smiling. Beaming, in fact.

Their hands never did touch. Within millimeters of contact, both Miller's and Mollie's fingers glowed bright in the gathering darkness, as though they'd been playing with goo stolen from the tails of sacrificed fireflies. A flash of lightning sparked in the sky overhead, even though there weren't any clouds.

Heat lightning? Laura wondered. No. She knew this was more than just a meteorological phenomenon.

"Come on," the blonde girl coaxed, her tone tinged with urgency. "It's time to go now."

It was then Laura recognized the little blonde's face. Her squared jaw, and blunt-cut, flaxen bob. Her impish, knowing smile.

Greta.

Mollie stopped, seemingly torn between worlds. She glanced back at Greta before turning again to cast a sad smile at her brother. Then her words echoed inside Laura's head. And too, she knew, inside Miller's.

"I'm okay. I'll see you again. I'll be waiting for you. I love you, Mills."

Another flash of lightning lit up the sky. And then, they were gone.

Epilogue

November, One Year Later

"Mills, how do you connect the upholstery attachments for this thing?"

Miller looked up from the recorded wrestling match he was watching, and blinked in shock. The vision before him was adorably amusing. Standing in the doorway of his living room. with his gargantuan and super-efficient vacuum cleaner, was Laura. Right next to Big Bertha.

Hell, the damn thing probably weighs more than she does.

"Wh-what?" he replied, chuckling. "What the hell are you doing? It's seven o'clock on a Friday night. You know I always vacuum Saturday mornings—"

Laura's face screwed into an aggravated pout and she slammed one fist onto her hip.

"I know," she retorted. "But tomorrow won't work. Abby and Jack will be here in the morning—with the baby. I want this place as slick as a whistle when they get here." She grabbed the huge, wheeled machine with both hands and began dragging it toward him. "And this sofa has got to be vacuumed," she growled through gritted teeth. "You're going to have to move your lazy ass off while I . . ."

She froze when Miller could no longer subdue the laughter that wasn't merely quaking his shoulders now. It had burst free into an all-out guffaw.

"What's so damned funny?" she quipped, her eyes narrowing. "Is it so wrong of me to want this place clean and spiffy for my best friend and her brand-new baby boy? The tyke isn't even two months old yet."

Miller knew Laura had been looking forward to this visit from her old college roommate ever since Abby and Jack's baby boy made his grand entrance. He'd met the couple at the wedding, back in June. Abby had waddled dutifully down the aisle as Laura's Maid of Honor, baby bump and all. Miller had been impressed the couple made the nine-hour trek from North Carolina for their wedding, even with Abby so obviously far along in her pregnancy.

Now it was November, and Miller calculated in his head. Laura and he had been living together over a year and a half. Married for almost five months.

Did she really not know how to work his vacuum cleaner?

Shrugging, and struggling to tamp down his amusement as best he could, he clicked off the wrestling match and stood to engage in one of his own.

The next morning dawned sunny and decidedly nippy—a classic fall day in New York. Some trees were already bare, the trees' remaining leaves falling in earnest. The world was blanketed in a crisp, spicy mantle of brown.

Laura was as anxious as a neurotic cat, up before dawn, doing her best to spit and polish the tiny, puke-green bungalow she and Miller shared.

After all, this was her good friend coming to call. Along with her husband, Jack, who, although Laura had only met him once—at the wedding—seemed like a true gem of a man. A bit older than Laura expected. But older men, she remembered, had always been Abby's weakness.

They were due at ten, and Laura already beat Miller into the kitchen to make the coffee—her decent, drinkable brew. She'd spread the kitchen table with a continental breakfast of sorts: fresh fruit, some Danish from the bakery, a pitcher of orange juice—fresh, un-expired orange juice. Unlike what she'd found congealing in Miller's refrigerator the first day she'd arrived.

Had it really been over eighteen months since then, when she stood trembling on Miller's front porch?

She sighed wistfully just as the doorbell chimed.

"Miller," she shrieked down the hallway. "They're here."

Miller, who had finally finished the renovation on the upstairs bathroom, was probably still in their brand-new shower. Damn him, she thought. But his workout with Rip had run over, and she knew well when he'd tumbled in the front door a half-hour earlier, rumpled and sweaty, he'd never be ready on time.

That bathroom renovation? Now *that* had been a fiasco. Thank God, Rip had a friend, an electrician who also did some handyman work. Daniel Rudd was looking to pick up some side work, having landed an out-of-state job, and treading water until his move.

Laura had liked the tall, handsome, tawny-haired Daniel right off. He and Miller had remodeled the bathroom, together, in a little over a week, the two of them exercising their jaw muscles as much as those in all other body parts. She enjoyed listening to their easy banter, and was almost sorry when she found that Daniel was leaving town. He was headed, he told them, for a promising new position with an electrical team somewhere in central Massachusetts.

Too bad. Daniel and Miller, she thought, could probably have become good friends.

The doorbell dinged again just before Laura opened the front door and sucked in an awed breath.

"Abby," she crooned, opening her arms wide. She buried her face in Abby's thick mane of chestnut hair and swallowed the huge ball in her throat. "I've missed you," she managed thickly.

"Me too," Abby said, then quickly pulled away and turned to her husband. "Get the baby inside, Jack. It's freezing up here."

An hour later they all sat in the Stanford's modest living room, holding paper plates filled with sweet treats in their laps. The house was definitely not big enough for a crowd this size, Laura thought. When Kip and Patricia heard Abby and Jack were coming—with their new baby—there was no way they could be kept away. They had met at the wedding last spring and become, to Laura's pleasant surprise, fast friends.

Jane and her friend, Carla, had made the trek from Connecticut. Neither Miller nor Laura had seen much of his mom since Mollie's death. Shortly after the funeral, Jane had sold the family home in Chester and moved in with a widowed friend of hers. One who lived conveniently close to the Foxwoods Casino.

At least, Laura thought, Jane had stopped depending on Miller to fund her gambling habit. She'd gotten counseling as well, and was controlling her spending, keeping it within her budget.

The last to arrive were Laura's dad and stepmom. As she passed through the hallway with a full coffeepot in hand, Laura spotted Deirdre's cheerleader-style wave through the glassed front door.

"Hey!" she said through a grin. "I wondered if you guys would make it. Abby and Jack can't stay too long. They're on their way to Boston." As she ushered them in, she held up the pot. "Coffee? There's fruit, and Danish too—"

"Just black coffee. For us both, Laura. You know your father's got to watch his sugar intake these days."

Manny folded Laura into an awkward hug, avoiding collision with the hot carafe she was toting.

"Dee's always looking out for me, sweetie," her dad whispered in her ear. "Just like Miller looks out for you."

When all the extra kitchen chairs had been dragged in, along with a few folding chairs Kip snagged from the fire department, everyone finally had a seat in the small living room. Laura turned on some soft, instrumental background music. With everyone settled, Laura plopped down on the sofa next to Abby and breathed, "Can I hold him now?"

With a smile that made Abby's nose wrinkle, causing light to flash off the diamond chip in her left nostril, she nodded. She bent to pick up baby Jackson from the rocker carrier, and handed the swathed bundle to Laura.

As she cradled the sleeping baby to her chest, Laura looked down and watched as the child's cherubic, pink-cheeked face blurred and swam in her vision. She hadn't expected quite this reaction. Laura loved children, always had. But she was an only child herself. Had never been around babies much.

As her arms molded protectively around little Jackson Wood, her heart swelled to three times its size, then cracked. A longing she'd not been brave enough to acknowledge before now rose to the surface and burst free, like a geyser. She swallowed hard, hoping the tears stinging her eyes wouldn't actually spill over.

She and Miller had never discussed having children. She knew he'd spent most of his life, up until recently, taking care of Mollie, and his mother, Jane. He'd expressed the sentiment on more than one occasion that he didn't need any more helpless souls to take care of.

He often told Laura that one of the things he loved about her was how she was strong enough to take care of herself.

So Laura *had* been surprised when Kip talked Miller into signing on to coach Middletown's Pop Warner Football team last summer. Though Miller had been certain by then that a desk job wasn't his thing anyway, he'd still been a little down when Duvall landed Sarge's position. That's when Kip stepped up to convince his friend he needed help with his team of tiny Pee Wees.

Laura cried the first time she saw Miller out there, doing what he swore he'd never do again—pick up a football. He did great with the kids. *Other people's* kids. Ones, he said, he was glad he only had to deal with for a few hours a week.

Children of their own, she figured, would be out of the question.

Three hours later, their company was gone. Laura was collecting the last of the paper plates from the living room while Miller went down the hall to retrieve Big Bertha.

But as Laura stepped out into the hallway with a pile of paper plates in one hand, a tower of empty juice cups in the other, she almost plowed right into Miller.

"Geez, Mills. I thought you went after Big Bertha," she whined, aiming to scoot around him.

But his big hand closed around her arm, causing her to stop and gaze up into those feral, flinty eyes.

"I'll take these to the kitchen. Meet me on the sofa. We need to talk," he said. His voice was deadly serious.

Shocked, and more than a little unnerved by his tone, Laura handed the trash to Miller and turned back into the living room, her mind whirring. Had she done or said something to piss Miller off during their visit today? Had the clogging of their house with so many people put him off?

What the hell? Laura plopped down on the sofa and folded her legs up under her. Then she wrapped her arms around herself and waited.

Miller had a fiery temper, she knew. Not that it had much power over her—not anymore. Whatever had torched his ire, she would deal with it. She always did. She'd long ago figured out his anger was a defense mechanism. His warrior's shield. She wasn't intimidated by it any longer.

That was when she heard the creak—the unmistakable, characteristic squeak of the lid of her grandmother's trunk. The heavy steamer chest still lived in the corner of the hallway, partially obstructing the foot of the stairwell. But she just couldn't bear to banish Grandma to the basement.

One day, after Laura had repeated Miller's long-ago episode of smashing his big toe on the crate, she had begrudgingly suggested moving Grandma downstairs. Miller's reaction had shocked as well as touched her. He'd been adamant.

"No. Grandma stays right there. Where she's been since the day you both moved in."

Laura sighed. Every, single time Miller struggled to maneuver his massive cleaning machine around the old steamer, she thought, *it's time*. Time to retire the family heirloom to the basement.

After all, there was only one quilt left in the old cedar chest anyway. Over the past year, Laura had found good homes for all the rest—quilts her grandmother had lovingly stitched to mark all of her future life's milestones. Leaving Laura with a legacy she could hold onto and wrap around herself—literally.

Her high-school graduation quilt dressed her bed in her old room downstairs. The one Grammy said was for when she graduated college, fashioned with a tasseled, black cap in the center, she'd had suspended from dowels. It now adorned the hallway wall—directly across from Miller's high school football photo, which Laura had reproduced onto a large canvas.

The wedding ring quilt, from the day she and Miller had said their vows, had adorned their bed upstairs.

Her oldest, most well-worn, times-are-tough, Mom-and-Dad's-divorce quilt still lived on the back of the sofa. Tattered edges and all. She reached over now and fingered the soft cloth, aching to drag it down over her again. The morning had been exciting, exhausting, and more than a little emotional for her. And now Miller had his briefs all twisted up over something.

What now?

He came around the corner without saying a word. In three long strides, he was before her. She scooted aside, making room for him to sit beside her. But to her surprise, he dropped to one knee.

It was then Laura noticed what he was carrying. Clutched to his chest was a mini-sized, hand-stitched quilt. One fashioned in shades of pink, and blue, and yellow. The edges were finished in a delicate, pale green fringe. A baby quilt. The one Grandma said she hoped and prayed Laura would use someday.

"It's time," Miller said, locking gazes with her. His voice was thick, and his eyes, to her amazement, were misty. He held the quilt out toward her, his hands trembling. Clearing his throat, he said, "It's about time . . .we gave Grandma's last quilt a job."

THE END

Spirits of the Heart

A Note from the Author

Thank you for joining Laura and Miller on their journey. I hoped you enjoyed reading their story as much as I enjoyed writing it.

Please, take a few moments to leave an honest review on Amazon and Goodreads. Reviews are incredibly important to authors—it's how our stories reach more readers like you.

If you loved this ghostly tale, check out my first Haunted Voices novel, **HEARTS UNLOCHED**, which was named a winner in the 2016 New York Book Festival. It's available for Kindle, in paperback, and in audiobook on Amazon.

A psychic interior designer reluctantly agrees to renovate a sexy investor's abandoned hotel on Loch Sheldrake, a lake rumored to have once been the mob's body dumping ground.

Interior designer Kate Bardach loves her single girl's lifestyle, living in Manhattan and spending weekends at her lake house. She's passionate about her career, too—reinventing old buildings. But there are some projects she can't take on because of the spirits trapped inside. Kate is psychic—she sees dead people.

Marco Lareci is one of Wall Street's most successful investment brokers who's achieved all of his life's goals—except for finding his soulmate. His latest project, an abandoned resort on Loch Sheldrake, needs a savvy designer to transform the crumbling complex into a boutique hotel. When Marco meets Kate, he can't believe his luck. She's the perfect match for his business and his heart.

Marco's body excites Kate even more than does his renovation project. But he wants more than a casual relationship, and she's not willing to give up her freedom. Plus, the haunting at Marco's resort, a bonafide poltergeist, affects her on an intensely personal level. Kate's aunt disappeared from the place fifty years ago.

Will the spirit doom Kate and Marco's love, or drive them closer together?

~~~

My newsletter subscribers are the first to know when the next Haunted Voices novel comes out, so please consider signing up at my website, www.clairegem.com. Also, visit me on Goodreads, Facebook, and Twitter. I always love connecting with my readers.

Remember—when you're in the mood for an intensely emotional romantic journey, think—

CLAIRE GEM

40207619R00192

Made in the USA
Middletown, DE
06 February 2017